IN PRAISE of *The Bermuda Privateer* by William Westbrook—

"WELL DONE. An exciting tale." —James L. Nelson, author of the Norsemen Saga, the Revolution at Sea Saga, & more

"WILLIAM WESTBROOK is not afraid of action . . . blood, history, or politics. This is only the first book of a series about Bermuda-born Nico Fallon, who becomes embroil d with a ruthless pirate, a Spanish bullion *flota*, and a . . . hurricane and mass shipwreck. [Westbrook demonstrates] . . . a truly impressive expertise. A great maiden voyage!" —Jan Needle, author of the Sea Officer William Bentley novels

"AN ACTION-PACKED insight into one of the most fascinating, deadly, and captivating predators of the seas—the privateer." —PAUL BRYERS (Seth Hunter), award-winning director and author of the Nathan Peake novels

". . . treachery on land and blazing cannons at sea." —Michael Aye, author of *The Pyrate* and the Fighting Anthonys

". . . leaves readers gripping the edge of their seats . . . Nicholas Fallon and his crew of misfits battle a maniacal pirate and traitorous allies, while forging friendships in unlikely places." —Cindy Vallar, Editor of *Pirates and Privateers*

"AN AGE OF NELSON adventure, told from an unusual perspective, with authenticity." —Joan Druett, author of the Wiki Coffin mysteries and *Island of the Lost*

THE BERMUDA PRIVATEER

A NICHOLAS FALLON SEA NOVEL

William Westbrook

McBooks Press, Inc.
www.mcbooks.com
Ithaca, New York

Published by McBooks Press 2017

Copyright © 2017 by William Westbrook

Cover painting of *Sea Dog* © 2017 by Paul Garnett.
Book design by Panda Musgrove.

Library of Congress Cataloging-in-Publication Data

Names: Westbrook, William, 1945- author.
Title: The Bermuda privateer / William Westbrook.
Description: Ithaca, New York : McBooks Press, 2017. | Series: The Nicholas Fallon sea novels
Identifiers: LCCN 2017028217 (print) | LCCN 2017015414 (ebook) | ISBN 9781590137444 (hardback) | ISBN 9781590137451 (Kindle) | ISBN 9781590137468 (ePub) | ISBN 9781590137475 (pdf)
Subjects: LCSH: Privateering--Fiction. | Merchant ships--Fiction. | Treasure troves--Caribbean Area--Fiction. | Pirates--Fiction. | Naval battles--Fiction. | Bermuda Islands--Fiction. | West Indies--Fiction. | BISAC: FICTION / Sea Stories. | FICTION / War & Military. | GSAFD: Sea stories. | Adventure fiction.
Classification: LCC PS3623.E84753 B47 2017 (ebook) | LCC PS3623.E84753 (print) | DDC 813/.6--dc23
LC record available at https://lccn.loc.gov/2017028217

Visit the McBooks Press website at www.mcbooks.com.

Printed in the United States of America
9 8 7 6 5 4 3 2 1

With Gratitude—

I'd like to give special thanks to Tripp Westbrook, Cabell Westbrook, Bob Westbrook, and Kerry Feuerman for their invaluable support and critical advice; and to my beautiful wife, Susan, for her love and steady encouragement. I couldn't have done this alone.

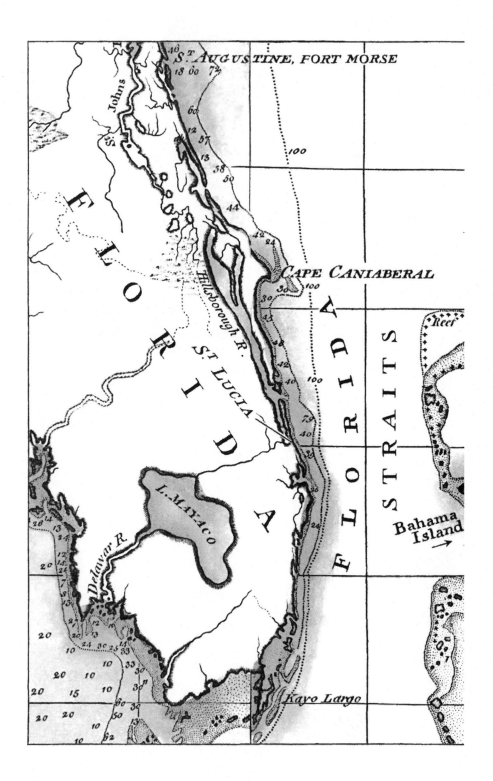

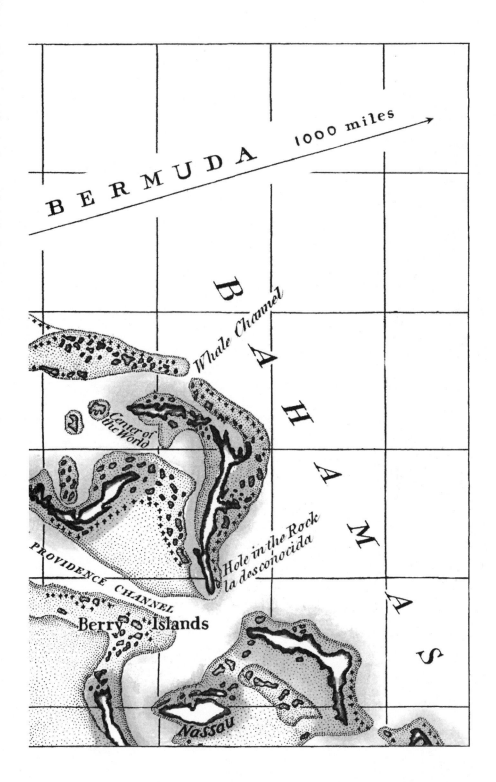

To my good and great friend Pat Fallon—
I could not let you leave this world, not entirely.

ONE

*V*IGO, S*PAIN:* dawn expected.

    A dark, warm wind found the narrow alleys, blowing the dry leaves into swirls. They blew along the walkways and scratched in the doorways. Otherwise, there was no sound.

    A lone figure moved through the shadows, silent as a secret. Beneath the cloak a man, or perhaps a woman, with a light yet purposeful step. Thirty paces to a courtyard, turn right. Sally the edges of the alley, hesitate, and breathe. Now a small cut to the left, along cobblestones placed by the Romans or even the Saracens and then, at last a pause, at a door with the faintest light showing under.

    The figure withdrew a packet from the cloak, held it an instant to kiss its seal, and slipped it under the door.

    A dog barked somewhere. A light shone from a courtyard window in response. But the figure had disappeared.

TWO

THE SENTRY at his door shifted weight, and instantly Nicholas Fallon's eyes opened. He lay in his cot, listening. The ship's low noises were nothing out of the ordinary, he decided. He also knew instinctively it was deep in the middle watch, two hours before first light. The small cabin was surprisingly cold, and he squirmed like a child down into the covers of his swinging cot. So, he wondered, *where the hell is summer?*

He closed his eyes, but sleep had quit him. His mind turned to the ship. She was close hauled on larboard, some one hundred miles off the coast of Portugal, moving northeast to slowly close the coast. He judged her speed by the gurgle of water rushing past the stern: twelve knots.

His ship was fast, as fast as anything on the water for her length. The Somers Salt Company had built the pretty schooner at St. George's shipyard on the eastern end of Bermuda. For some time, pirates and French privateers had overwhelmed the trade in salt to America, and Ezra Somers, owner of the company and Fallon's employer, decided to build a ship to fight back. *Sea Dog* was 100 feet on deck and more than 200 tons, deep-hulled and stiff, with scantlings to handle twelve 9-pounders, plus two 18-pound carronades in the bows of the ship. She was fore-and-aft rigged, with two raked masts—an idea that originated with the Dutch *bezaan jachts* and was incorporated on fast Bermuda sloops. She was built with the most-available wood on the island: Bermuda cedar. It made her virtually rot-proof, not to mention aromatic below decks.

Sea Dog was far from home. Fallon had chased a mysterious sail for five days to the northeast before losing the ship in fog. He had pushed the men hard, spreading every inch of sail day and night, but the mysterious ship was close to *Sea Dog's* equal for speed in light airs. He had figured she would head for France, yet he had continued to follow in the hopes of sighting her again. But, nothing. Perhaps it was a folly to chase a prize so far away from home. Some would say his pride had gotten the best of him. He had sailed far, too far, and had been found wanting. As Ezra Somers often said: *Some days you're a rooster, some days a feather duster.*

Somers was feisty and profane and gout-ridden. And wealthy from salt. His salt was much in demand to preserve food, and his ships ran regularly between the *salinas*, or salt pans, of the Turks Islands, and the eastern ports of the United States. The ships dropped their cargo of salt, picked up foodstuffs and cotton, timber or tools, and returned to Bermuda, thence down to Grand Turk. Or they had. Three Somers cargo ships had been taken in the past year; the last had fought bravely with the few guns in the ship but was captured off the Exumas. The captain, as well as the crew who were still alive, were put ashore on Watling Island, an arid rock without food or water. They were rescued finally, weak and dehydrated and starving, but alive.

Ezra Somers had connived a letter of marque from the British Admiralty for *Sea Dog* to *"raid, plunder, and otherwise disrupt and destroy Great Britain's enemies from Ushant to the Caribbean."* Well, Britain's enemies were always in question, being prone to change and change again over the past fifty years. Only France had been relatively constant. The French Navy wasn't so much a problem; they were effectively bottled up by blockade for much of the time. The problem was pirates and French privateers and their damnably cunning captains who were too good at their jobs. They attacked unguarded Indiamen or British sloops—or even brigs—with insolence.

They were Fallon's quarry now. He was determined to be good at his job, as well.

He rose, involuntarily shivering, and pulled the blanket up around his shoulders as he walked to the small stern windows. Beneath him the sea, yards away, breathing slowly. He balanced easily by now against the roll of the ship, eleven months into this new commission. His eyes strained to see out the windows toward— what? A white wake stretched to the stars.

He decided he would shave. The mirror saw a deeply tanned face, with unruly black hair hanging over green eyes. In a certain light he could perhaps be called handsome. He was lean, with a chest and shoulders bigger than his body deserved.

His father had given him a wry smile, but his mother had added a penchant for melancholy to his eyes. He thought of her briefly, dark and lovely and troubled by demons. She had spent her whole life waiting for bad news. One day it came, and when the doctor said she would die, she did.

It was unexplainable to an eight-year-old boy. One moment he had a mother, alive and vibrant, and the next he stared at her body, cold and grim. He would remember the ticking of the hall clock outside her bedroom door the rest of his life.

His father went to work that day, still. Well, it had seemed like the only thing to do. The White Horse was the oldest pub still leaning in St. George, as his father liked to say, and had never closed a day through two generations of Fallon ownership. Townspeople came by to pay their respects. She was so young, they said.

Young Nicholas had lain on his bed at night and written her poems and letters. He agonized over each word. Finished, they accumulated in a drawer by her bed. His days were spent in listless wandering; in the mornings he walked the island and scared up shorebirds, pausing at certain times to look out to the horizon. Nothing out there looked changed; behind him, everything was different.

In time, he retreated to the White Horse, standing on a stool behind the bar serving out drinks and eavesdropping on conversations. Bermuda was a stop for merchantmen and Royal Navy alike, for traders and immigrants, for castaways of the world—lost souls like he was, running away or hiding—or for adventurers, explorers, and inventors of stories. You could learn a lot about the world from behind the bar. In consequence, he could talk to anybody about anything and learned to speak and read a bit of several languages in the bargain.

Shaking off the past, Fallon finished shaving, called for coffee, and dressed in a warm coat before ascending the companionway steps.

"Beauty! Here you are! Wherever in the ship have you been?" Fallon called, appearing suddenly in the gloom, bringing his particular penchant for wryness to the morning and looking at his first mate with mock-curious eyes.

Beauty McFarland was used to curious eyes. She was a she, first. A short, roundish she with callused hands and strong arms. A woman who possessed intelligence and wit and, owing to a foot infection that had turned gangrenous when she was eighteen, a peg leg. A woman not to be trifled with. Men had tried and had suffered in consequence. Women didn't bother.

"I've been doing my job, Nico," she said. "And you should be doing yours, which is tending to the cut on your chin. What's on your mind today, Your Majesty?"

Ah, Beauty.

"Jesus, if this was a man-o-war you'd be flogged," Fallon said, feigning offense at her insolence and enjoying the informality that he permitted and even encouraged aboard.

"True enough," Beauty replied, "but if this was a man-o-war, I wouldn't be second-in-command and you wouldn't be first, and this bunch of misfits and buggers wouldn't be a crew."

Well, she had a point. It *was* a ship of misfits. Though *Sea Dog* had a letter of marque as a British privateer, she carried the crew of her captain's choice and loosely followed the relaxed practices of British merchantmen at sea. There were pirates and farmers on board, and carpenters and shopkeepers and a few convicts thrown into the mix. Beauty was the only woman, and she was the most capable of all the hands. The ship's normal complement was 55 crew but, being a privateer, she carried more than that so she could man her prizes.

Fallon had known Beauty—Beatrice McFarland—since they were children racing skiffs on St. George's Harbor. She had usually beaten him; actually, she had beaten everyone. She had the instincts of a born sailor. Beneath her wind-beaten face was a keen mind that knew when to tack. For someone whose Scottish ancestors had fought Cromwell, courage went without saying. Beauty as second-in-command had been an easy choice for Fallon, if unorthodox. As for the rest of the crew, he knew them all from the island. Knew them to be excellent sailors, no matter their profession. Over a third of Bermuda's men were always afloat, somewhere. Some of his crew sought a second chance on *Sea Dog* to put their lives right. Some a third. All needed prize money.

The Somers Company was generous in the matter of prizes. Because the company controlled most of the salt trade from the Turks Islands, it was in its best interests to shut down enemy raids. Every privateer or pirate that was captured was a double win. First, the ships and cargoes were sold at auction or to the Royal Navy, with the proceeds divided half to the company, half to the captain and crew. Second, the taking of a pirate meant one less fox to prey on the chickens.

"I'd like the men drilled at the guns today, Beauty. Put the watch on them, please," said Fallon.

"The watch it is!" replied Beauty, as her captain and best friend turned for his morning exercise along the windward side of the ship.

The sea's rollers were lying down after a show of force in yesterday's storm. The wind had sent small messenger waves ahead to warn them, and when the rain and truly fierce wind had set upon them they had been ready. Nothing had been carried away and there were no injuries, and now the morning watch had already been called and was busy with the scraping and holystoning of the deck. *Sea Dog* was coming alive in all respects with the breeze filling in from the southwest, the ropes growing taut, and the prospect of the sun's warmth turning to reality.

Another day when anything was possible. *Money could come sailing by*, Fallon thought. A prize would make the crew happy and make Fallon feel like less of a fool. It would make Ezra Somers very happy. It might even make Somers's rebellious daughter, Elinore, happy. Or not.

Nathaniel Becker, the nominal sailing master and an old friend, approached Fallon with the morning's observations once the captain was through with his exercise. Becker had a deeply lined face, with white hair and perpetually worried eyes.

"I believe I see the loom of Spain, Nico," he said. "And I believe—only believe mind—that the wind should moderate by noon."

"Thank you, Nat," replied Fallon, having received confirmation of his own calculations, though he would not have dared for all the world to point it out to the sailing master. "And how are the youngsters coming with their sightings? Is Tom Pleasant having more success?"

Tom Pleasant was a particularly bright spot among the young boys, being generally liked for his personality and wicked humor, but bedeviled by mathematics. Fallon worried he would never understand geometry, and a sailing ship required geometry.

"Well enough, Nico," said Becker. "Although the mysteries of the heavens have yet to reveal themselves completely. Tom Pleasant, in particular, seems mystified by the mysteries."

Fallon grinned. It was never "Tom." Or "Mr. Pleasant." But "Tom Pleasant" in its entirety. There must be something oddly secure in having your whole name to present you, leaving nothing out, Fallon thought. *Here I am and kiss my hand.*

He mused on that as he headed below decks for breakfast, light of step, and unusually happy. Indeed, it was a day when anything was possible.

THREE

*T*HE ABBEY *burned candles relentlessly, in every passageway, day and evening. The monks dutifully made the candles from the beeswax they collected from the hives in the fields; tallow was more ordinary for candles, of course, but the beeswax was readily available and the candles burned longer.*

A hooded monk walked deliberately up the steps to the tower, following the dim pools of light round and round until, breathless, he emerged into a circular room, unfurnished except for a writing desk and chair. He sat noiselessly at the desk and pulled the sealed envelope from his sleeve. It was lighter than usual, though that bore little on its importance.

A shaft of sunlight found the center of the room but provided scant warmth, certainly not enough to warm the stone floor. The monk hesitated with the weight of his duty. Nothing easy under God, he said to himself. But surely this was not God's business. And then he ripped open the envelope.

When he had read the instructions through, he read them again. They were simple enough, but to follow them would implicate him in the grand schemes of the war that seemed to engulf most of the known world. He would be a minor figure, but a figure just the same.

The room had eight windows, each with a candle; half looked to the sea and half to the village of Vigo to the east. Tonight he would blow out three of the candles in the windows, leaving only one visible from the sea. He placed the envelope and its contents to the flame of one and watched it burn, Spain's golden seal the last to crackle and disappear.

FOUR

HE'D GROWN up in rooms with mice.

The Fallon family lived over the pub and, before they got the cat, mice were a plentiful diversion for a curious mind. Young Nicholas became quite good at catching them and examining them with a penknife. He soon learned a good deal about organs and muscles, and he enjoyed showing off his success in dissection to the screams of little Elinore Somers, who lived nearby and often walked past his house, singing. She seemed unappreciative and not much interested in science.

When he was older, Fallon spent his idle time on the sea. He would patch and caulk his small skiff in a standoff with rotting wood and time, and sail close inshore in case he sank. Fallon and Beauty would often sail together, taking turns at the tiller and sail handling.

Once, caught on a lee shore in an overtaking storm, they'd foundered and nearly drowned. Beauty had urged him to leave her and swim in, but he would not. They had swum until they were too exhausted to raise their arms, then held hands and floated with their faces turned to the jagged sky. Fallon made Beauty talk to him, told her stories, and even had her sing with him until the thunder stopped. Sometime just after dark, the wind and waves pushed them into land. Their bottoms bumped the bottom, and they yelled for joy together. Still holding onto each other, they stumbled ashore and picked their way along the small hills and shrubs toward home.

They were laughing uncontrollably when they saw the loom of St. George Town. They'd been walking so long they were dry.

"DECK THERE!" roared the lookout. "Two points to starboard! A sloop, and she's French!"

Fallon turned his face to the right as he reached for the telescope from Becker. It took him but a moment to find the ship, definitely French. Definitely the enemy of Great Britain. She had seen *Sea Dog*, as well, and was just raising more sail.

"Beauty! Call all hands, all hands!" Fallon ordered. He quickly considered wind and tide and asked Becker to lay down a course to intercept the sloop. He was calm, for there was no reason to think the French ship could escape. *Sea Dog* had the weather gauge.

Sea Dog made her gradual turn to starboard as her big sails popped out in the wind and began to draw. "Trapped against a lee shore, by God," observed Beauty. "Damned bad spot to be."

"No question," responded Fallon. "Bad luck for her. Wonder why so far inshore?"

"Something's odd," replied Beauty, never taking her eyes off the Frenchman. "But we'll know soon enough."

Sea Dog sprang to life like a hound after a fox. These were sailors who knew their work, and the schooner jumped to the scent. The French sloop was no match for the speed of a Bermuda schooner, though the sloop carried 12 guns, two of which were long guns. One fired a ranging shot when *Sea Dog* was still over a mile away.

Fallon was unperturbed by the shot and could trust the men to be patient, even though it was not easy to be fired upon and not return fire. Beauty stood by his side as they studied the developing scene together, talking strategy. In particular, Fallon relied on Beauty's tactical thoughts, though the situation was fluid, of course, and required a certain elasticity in thinking because anything could happen at sea.

Sea Dog closed the angle of the triangle made by the ships within thirty minutes, and Beauty ordered the helmsman to come up closer into the wind, just for a moment, to give the ship's guns a firing angle. *"Fire!"* yelled Fallon, and *Sea Dog's* 9-pounders sent their deadly balls flying across the water into the French sloop. Instantly the air was rent with French cries of shock and anguish. Quickly, Beauty ordered the helmsman back onto his old course, and as the smoke cleared, there was the Frenchman's deck in shambles with an upturned gun, her larboard railing blown apart in places and several bodies hanging over the side. But here were Frenchmen gamely massing at the guns to return their own broadside, and it came with a fury that seemed to pause the moment in time as Sea Dogs were blown about the decks, several bleeding and others too concussed to speak. The forestay was parted and the jib shot through, and there were deep furrows in the deck into which blood was now running. Fallon rallied the men, called to them by name, and urged them to drag the wounded away from the starboard railing.

"Boarders ready!" yelled Fallon hoarsely. "Standby the carronade!" The ships edged closer together, and for a moment it was oddly silent, as if time held its breath. *Fire!* The carronade belched the grapeshot that Fallon had ordered loaded for this moment, and he could see the Frenchmen's faces through the haze, grimy and terrified in the second before the iron balls tore through them.

Sea Dog's crew massed at the railing, cutlasses and pistols to hand as the French fired again, a ragged broadside that blew holes in *Sea Dog's* mainsail in two places and ripped Number Four gun from its breeches. There had been men standing there an instant ago.

Beauty laid *Sea Dog* alongside the sloop in a deft maneuver, luffing up into the wind just so at the last moment. "Boarders away!" Fallon yelled as he led fifty screaming men onto the French sloop's deck. The Frenchmen recoiled in horror, reclaimed their wits, and fought gamely. Pistols fired and jammed. Cutlasses clanged and blood ribboned into the scuppers. Fallon hacked at anyone in front of him, stabbed and slashed at Frenchmen without thought.

He fought his way toward the *capitaine*, who looked too old to be fighting as fiercely as he was; but now he was tiring and edging backward as Fallon was coming forward, the question of surrender or death written on his sagging face, his last decision. With the tip of Fallon's sword to his neck, the *capitaine* surrendered.

It had been a nasty business. The French sloop's deck hosted a massacre, with wounded and dying in heaps and survivors in shock and disbelief. Fallon himself was near swooning, for although he was unhurt in the fighting aboard the sloop, he was bleeding from a splinter wound to his scalp. It had been a near thing.

Now the French flag was on the deck and the *capitaine*'s sword was handed over. Beauty took charge of organizing the prisoners and setting the ships to rights, detailing men to specific tasks, assessing the damage and sending Fallon back to *Sea Dog* to the surgeon.

Sea Dog's surgeon, Pence, took his time with Fallon's stitches, making sure first to get every piece of the splinter out, for splinter wounds were notoriously prone to infection. He whistled absent-mindedly as he probed and stitched. Unlike most surgeons in the Royal Navy, he knew his medicine. And was sober.

"You'll live, Nico," Pence said. "But an inch lower and you'd be as blind as Millie Oakford's cow." That was blind, indeed, for Millie Oakford's cow had been dead for years. The surgeon smiled at his own humor.

Fallon was in no mood for jokes, however. "How bad was it for the crew?" he said gravely. "We took some shot here and there."

"None dead, thank God. But some who will be. Poor Mason and Trembly were together at Number Four when it blew up, and they're not entirely in one piece. They won't see morning. Several stab wounds and lacerations, one critical. I've got seven in for splinters of some sort, but they should heal. And Betty copped it, you heard?"

"The goat?" said Fallon. Betty had been their best milker. "Well, the cook will know what to do."

A knock and Beauty opened the door. "How are you, Nico? We're all worried. Not too much, mind you, but a little. How's the head?"

"Well, I'm much better than others, including poor Mason and Trembly, I'm afraid. Pence, do what you can for the men and don't spare the laudanum. I'll be in to see them after I've interviewed the French *capitaine*."

"Aye, Captain," said Pence, scurrying off to tend the other wounded.

The French sloop was the *Fleur*, and the *capitaine* was stone-faced and uncommunicative when brought to Fallon's cabin. Tom Pleasant followed quickly with the ship's papers and logbook and, best of all, the signal book, which miraculously had not been thrown overboard. The French *capitaine* had rather dramatically underestimated the speed and character of his attacker.

"*Capitaine*," Fallon said in his best French, "it is the worst of luck for you and no fault of your own that your ship has just been taken. Had we not been blown far off course in yesterday's storm, we might have easily never had the opportunity to meet. I am Captain Nicholas Fallon of His Majesty's privateer *Sea Dog*. And you, sir?"

The French *capitaine* stared blankly past Fallon's shoulder. He was clearly unhappy. He was a frail, deeply wizened man of an age too old for a larger command, and Fallon knew the ignominy that attached to the captain of a captured ship.

"I see," said Fallon. His head hurt terribly. He moved to the logbook. The *capitaine*'s name was Viceux. He had called at Lisbon for wood and water three weeks ago. Three weeks ago? That meant *Fleur* had been idling off the coast of Spain for days.

Fallon considered the documents. There were the usual lists of ship's stores, powder, and shot. Nothing out of the ordinary. *And yet.*

"Capitaine Viceux, the ship's papers seem to be here, except for your orders. I am wondering, sir, where they might be?"

Viceux flinched and made to touch his breast before catching himself. Fallon smiled. "Come, Capitaine Viceux, I can have your coat taken off or you can hand them to me."

"This is very dishonorable of you, Captain," said Viceux, having suddenly found his voice. "I demand to be treated with honor." He was clearly agitated and barely under control.

"*Capitaine*, there is no dishonor intended. But a French sloop whiling away her time off the Spanish coast for days makes one curious. Was she waiting for something? Perhaps a passenger. Or a cargo. Or a message of some sort? I will be interviewing each of your crew and searching your ship. Whatever I find, even if I find nothing, will not change your fate. You are my prisoner, sir. And I will have your coat."

Fallon watched Viceux consider and decide. Well, he was in no position to decide anything else. Slowly he pulled an envelope from a pocket hidden inside of his coat. He held it for the briefest moment, out of feigned honor, and dropped it on the desk.

Sea Dog plunged ahead to weather. Out of sight of land, only dull sky and gray ocean visible. Men went about their tasks while the ship worked through the miles, her wake a daily diary of routine. The ship's noises became song in the men's ears: the thrum and whine of rigging. The surrender of wood bending against its fibers, accepting its destiny with grudge and moan. For most sailors routine was a godsend. Simple minds embraced it. Complex minds were made to accept it.

As was his own routine, Fallon paced the deck deep in thought. He wanted to call for Beauty, but she was commanding the prize crew in *Fleur*, trailing *Sea Dog* astern. Fallon was still recovering from his head wound, and more, from the shock upon reading Viceux's orders. It seemed that *Fleur* had been ordered to wait off Vigo for a signal from shore. When the signal came, it meant that, after years of fighting Revolutionary France, Godoy of Spain had about-faced—*to ally with France against Great Britain!* Viceux was to carry the news immediately to a French squadron, patrolling to the northeast, lest they continue to attack Spanish ships along with British.

The news was bad, indeed. Damn Godoy for a turncoat! And here was Great Britain now facing Spain as well as France. How in God's name could Great Britain survive the both of them? Well, there was nothing to be done about the alliance; in fact, the news was likely already in Paris and Madrid. But the news was not at sea, by God! The French squadron would be awaiting their sloop's arrival with open arms. There might be a plan in there, somewhere.

FIVE

IS FATHER had hoped young Nicholas would decide for the pub after his mother died, but the boy did not want his father's life. They had grown closer though and were often seen walking along the shoreline together, the Irish in them sharing a laugh.

With his father's blessing, and without influence, young Fallon signed as a ship's boy in the Royal Navy. A fifth-rate ship, the frigate *Bon Vivant*, 36, had called at St. George looking for volunteers and the boy offered them a good sailor with a head for numbers and angles. Leaving St. George had been difficult. His father had treated it like a wake, alternatively drinking and laughing and crying.

Beauty hugged him so hard it almost broke his back. She made him swear he wouldn't die before he came home. He feigned to consider, and agreed. It would be years before they sailed together again.

On board his first ship, he was subjected to all the joys and horrors of the lower deck. Men were cruel and violent, kind and protective. Well, they were seamen.

As a lad he kept his own counsel, never ratted out a bully, and fought his fights till he could not stand. He grew stronger and began winning at age sixteen. Then things got interesting.

The boy became a man when he passed for lieutenant. His skills in mathematics and cleverness in general made him a natural navigator and much respected by the crew. He saw his first action as a second lieutenant off Ushant in 1771. It was a victory against a French ship-of-the-line, but with horrendous loss of life. Blood painted the decks. He vomited fear for a week.

There were few occasions when women entered his life. He would have liked for more, but he lived on the sea. He grew tall and capable and had eyes that women found . . . well, they enjoyed looking into them. It was as well he was mostly at sea, aboard ship and away from temptation. Still, there was the occasional small romance, brief and to the point.

At age twenty-three he was given command of a bomb ketch and ordered to the Baltic. It was a relatively uneventful mission, his ship being no more than a support vessel for inshore operations. Unfortunately, the commodore of the squadron to which he was attached was new to the Baltic and ordered Fallon to stay too deep into the winter before heading for home. The ketch was nearly iced in during the freeze of '74 and, as a consequence, Fallon was horribly wounded by a storm of splinters caused by a cannonball skipping into the ship from a Danish fort across the frozen Kattegat. For weeks the surgeon thought he would die from infection.

Dodging ice, the ketch sailed for England and Fallon was transferred to a hospital in Ipswich to convalesce. He lived, weakened and frail, his back scarred like a cutting board. In the spring, he mustered out, returning to Bermuda with the clothes on his back and a deep hatred of the French in his soul.

FALLON'S JAW was tight as the ships bore on toward the Bay of Biscay. *Sea Dog* and *Fleur* were thrashing to windward under shortened sails. The Bay was being what it always was—notorious. *Sea Dog* was carrying barely more than handkerchiefs aloft, as much to keep the schooner under control as to stay in sight of *Fleur* which, with Beauty in command, was sailing as well as could be expected. The French prisoners had been transferred to *Sea Dog*, it being the larger ship, and were safely under guard below decks, no doubt feeling the unique hopelessness and anxiety only prisoners of war can feel, locked in the black, fetid air of the holds.

Fallon and Beauty had contrived a plan to use the information gleaned from Viceux's orders to advantage, though everything depended on finding the squadron. And timing. And a thousand things they couldn't control. So, not much of a plan.

On board *Sea Dog* the men on watch were wet most of the time, the crew below decks not much drier. The schooner worked at the seams and was tossed about by gray walls of water that blocked out the sky day and night. It was thoroughly unpleasant sailing, and only Fallon's remaining on deck most of the time gave the men any heart for it. Still, watches turned out on command, spirits were piped up on time, and meals were somehow hot, mostly. It was tedium, but the crew knew something was afoot and bore their unique misery with equanimity. At one point, at the *worst point* it seemed, several of the hands lashed themselves to the mainmast and attempted to play a tune and dance—to the great amusement of the watch on deck. The fife tweeted and the whistles whistled until a great slab of green water broke over the whole affair and water spurted from the whistles and everyone laughed themselves silly at the ludicrousness of their effort.

They were after the proverbial needle in a haystack, and Biscay was an enormous haystack: more than 85,000 square miles of water, often violently angry. Blockading British ships paid a price in winter, wherever they were, but nowhere more than the Bay of Biscay.

Fallon moved about on deck, checking rigging for wear and having a word with his crew. It was the first dogwatch, about 4:00 PM, and the men who turned up found the weather had moderated in the forenoon and was actually tolerable. The sea had lain down with the lessening breeze, and there was a chance of late sunshine.

"Deck there!" the lookout called. "Sail two points to starboard. Can't make her out yet, though!"

Instinctively, all eyes turned to see—*nothing*. The sail was miles away and the light still uncertain.

"Tom Pleasant," Fallon roared from the foredeck, "bend on our French flag and signal to *Fleur* that a sail is in sight to the northeast." Quickly the signal and flag went up, and moments later *Fleur* answered with a French flag of her own. Being a privateer, *Sea Dog* carried every nation's flag and flew whatever served, at least until battle. Then the home colors went up.

On they sailed, French to all accounts, in the afternoon's dying light, toward an unidentified ship. Fallon paced the deck, chin tucked into his chest. Minutes passed, then the best part of an hour. The sun suddenly broke free under the low clouds to the west.

"Deck there!" the lookout called again, "A brig! North nor-east and French! No other sails in sight!"

Fallon considered. A lone brig could perhaps mean anything, but odds were it was the eyes of a squadron, as yet unseen. It was what he had hoped for. He could feel a chill on his arms as the hair stood on end. Now he was doubly grateful to have retrieved *Fleur*'s signal book.

"Tom Pleasant, make the French private signal."

The French brig responded with the appropriate answering signal, and Fallon ordered Tom Pleasant to send up the next one.

Have prize and important dispatches.

Moments passed, and then the signals flew from the French brig: *Heave-to and report aboard.* Fallon muttered under his breath. *Now we shall see.*

He could see *Fleur* and Beauty making more sail to bring the sloop up to *Sea Dog.* He could also see *Fleur*'s guns being loaded but not run out. *Part of the plan.* Fallon called a ship's boy to bring him Vieux's hat and coat from his cabin. The fit was close enough, and Beauty would think he looked jaunty.

The Sea Dogs were in place behind closed gun ports, many wearing the French prisoners' clothing and scarves, nonchalant. As the three ships drew closer, Fallon could pick out the details of the French brig. She was beautiful in the setting sun's light, a low wave creaming at her bow. He could see French sailors standing at their stations, alert with anticipation, but seeming unthreatened. The brig's sails were reddening in the lowering sun, and the whole scene had a painterly aspect. *Fleur* had inched ahead now, perhaps a quarter of a mile, and was just rounding up into the wind to heave-to and set the trap. The French brig sailed closer and, perhaps two cable lengths away from *Fleur*, hove-to, as well. It was a ponderous process for a square-rigged brig, much easier for a fore-and-aft-rigged ship. But finally the brig settled down, her sails set against one another so the ship fought against herself and would go neither here nor there.

On *Sea Dog* came, full speed up from the rear. Even in this wind she was a racer. As he passed Beauty, Fallon doffed his French *capitaine*'s hat to her, and *Sea Dog*'s gun ports flew open as the schooner bore down on the French brig, now sitting defenseless with gun ports closed and confusion creeping into her timbers. Down came the French flag from *Sea Dog*'s gaff and up went the British ensign. And out came Britain's guns.

"*Fire!*" yelled Fallon, and the starboard broadside thundered out the full weight of its metal. French sailors scattered like pins in a game, and the brig desperately tried to both get underway and man her guns.

"Round up, lads!" Fallon cried. "Give it to her again!"

Sea Dog rounded and sent another broadside into the brig's fragile stern, all but obliterating her hopeful name, *Triomphant*. The starboard carronade first, then gun after gun. Glass and wood were blown to bits as the 9-pounders did their deadly work. But *Sea Dog* would have to sail off and tack to press the battle. *Triomphant* countered with an uneven broadside aimed high for *Sea Dog*'s rigging. Shot holes appeared in the massive foresail, the fore-top was blown apart, and the windward preventer snapped like a shot.

By now *Fleur* had gotten underway and was coming up on *Triomphant*'s starboard side. Still preoccupied with *Sea Dog*, the French were late running out their starboard battery and Beauty got a roaring broadside off before she tacked away, briefly exposing her own stern to the French brig. *Triomphant's* fore-topmast cracked, and then fell over the side, taking the fore-topgallant with it and virtually stopping the ship in its tracks. Yet she fired several guns into *Fleur's* stern, blowing out the windows and demolishing the taffrail. Beauty was standing by *Fleur's* helmsman as a splinter shot through his buttocks, and he fell screaming. Quickly she took the helm and wore ship, ordering the crew to prepare for boarding.

Fallon ordered *Sea Dog* to the crippled brig's larboard side. The two ships clashed together as Fallon led the Sea Dogs onto *Triomphant's* deck, the men screaming with the ferocity only prize money can stimulate as they fell on the startled Frenchmen. Fallon drove his sword into the belly of an onrushing French sailor in an officer's uniform whose eyes opened wide in surprise, never to close again. The Sea Dogs hacked and speared, but the French fought back just as violently. Now there were fresh screams from the starboard side as Beauty's boarders rushed over the railing. More shots were fired and swords sliced into soft flesh, and everywhere men were fighting and bleeding and dying.

It was too much. Fallon called for surrender, and slowly the French sailors laid down their weapons, many collapsing as they did. Their *capitaine* lay decapitated by a round shot, their officers were either dead or dying, and the fight had gone out of the men.

"Captain, more sail to the east!" called an alert lookout from *Fleur.* It had to be the French squadron.

Fallon wheeled around. There was not a moment to lose. "Beauty," he called, "get underway quickly! We'll meet tomorrow!" They had agreed to rendezvous at a pinprick on the chart a day's sail away if things went as planned. So far, they had.

Jumping back to his own ship, Fallon yelled, "Tom Pleasant! Clear the wreckage aft quickly. Tom . . . " But Tom Pleasant did not answer, and would not again. Fallon turned around as fear gripped him. His eyes settled on the boy's body lying against the starboard bulwark, his small legs distorted and folded almost backward. A jagged splinter had pierced his chest straight through. Momentarily forgetting his command, Fallon collapsed at the boy's side, but there was nothing for it. The youngster's eyes were open, looking at his captain expectantly a last time, waiting for orders.

Fallon staggered to his feet, his mind still assaulted by the din and grasping for direction.

"Nico! The prize, what are your orders?" It was a voice he knew, someone close to him, calling in the fog. Turning his head, he saw Becker, a kind face with wild white hair.

"Nat," he mumbled, his mind coming back to the situation at hand. "Take command of the prize, and get the prisoners into the brig's boats as quickly as possible."

He looked quickly at the squadron, now noticeably closer. "And bring up Viceux and the other prisoners and get them in the boats, as well. Give the boats lanterns. You men, get the ship to rights and prepare to make sail. Hurry lads! And for God's sake, get Tom Pleasant below. Easy with him!"

Fallon forced himself to take charge again and put the youngster's death in a compartment to be dealt with later. *My God, Tom Pleasant.*

The French squadron had set all sail to the topgallants and were sailing as fast as possible down toward *Sea Dog*, but the wind was holding light and the sun was all but gone and they were too many miles away. When Fallon's little armada at last sheeted all sails home and began to slip away, it was virtually dark. The prisoner's boats had all lanterns lit, and as the lights bobbed and danced and slowly disappeared, Fallon hoped the French *capitaines* would do the proper thing and pick up their countrymen. Both *Sea Dog* and the captured brig were darkened and in very little time they simply disappeared into the night.

SIX

THE THREE ships, tiny on the grand expanse of blue ocean, sailed for home. They were battered and shot through and leaky, and the crews worked watch on watch to patch and caulk and mend them with what they had aboard. They were sober crews, glad to be alive. Eleven of their friends and shipmates were dead, and twice that many were under Pence's care for wounds ranging from slight to grievous. These men, *hors de combat*, might never fight again.

The devastation, physical and human, had been much worse on *Triomphant*. *Sea Dog*'s eighteen-pound carronade had sent its deadly ball crashing into the brig's stern, into and through the *capitaine*'s cabin. At short distance, the shot had traveled halfway through the ship, stern to bow, exploding splinters through the deck.

Fallon's business now was to get home with three ships more or less intact. His own *Sea Dog* was lightly damaged compared with the others, owing to French tactics of shooting for mast and rigging on the up roll to destroy maneuverability. British tactics favored broadsides into the hull on the down roll, causing catastrophic destruction that killed and maimed the enemy's crews. As a consequence, French casualties were usually higher in any sea action.

"Signal from *Fleur*, sir!" shouted the lookout. Fallon knew Beauty was short on water, as they all were, and the signal meant she was cutting to half rations.

"Signal affirmative," said Fallon—almost expecting Tom Pleasant to answer. Instead, another ship's boy bent on the signal and sent it aloft. *Sea Dog* had been on short rations for the past two days, which meant a half gallon of small beer per man instead of the usual gallon. From a medical standpoint, besides the effects of half rations, Pence would be worried about disease, as he should be. Disease was the greatest killer of men at sea, by far. Well, men kept in cramped and damp conditions, with poor nutrition, stressed by fear of imminent death or wounding were going to get sick. Or go insane, which was a greater problem at sea than on land.

Pence was one of the more progressive surgeons Fallon had known, though some of his theories about eating greens and root vegetables to ward off illness seemed far-fetched. He could afford wild theories since he wasn't actually in the Royal Navy, mused Fallon. And limes, by God! Pence squirted lime juice into every cup of water, even the men's grog. The men complained bitterly at first but learned to tolerate the taste. And to give the devil his due, there had been no scurvy on Fallon's ship. So perhaps Pence knew something, after all.

On they sailed, still more than three thousand miles from home and cottage, with the mauls ringing out over the sea as the repair work continued. *Triomphant* was jury rigged and put reasonably to rights, although her stern was poxed. *Fleur* looked sound, with fresh patches on her mainsail and foresail. Beauty had found paint below decks and had the crew painting the newly scarfed railings.

Tom Pleasant, the boy who struggled with geometry, was buried with a gunner's mate and a helmsman, their bodies sewn into canvas weighted with shot and slid down a plank on a 45-degree angle into the sea. It had put Fallon in a low mood, and as a consequence he left his cabin irregularly and ate alone instead of keeping table for his officers. This was the trouble with handpicking your friends and neighbors for privateering. He would go to Tom Pleasant's family—to all the dead crewmen's families—and explain, but there was no real explanation except they were dead, buried at sea, with wives and children and even parents left without a grave to tend.

Fallon would divide his share of prize money among the families, but that would not put a father or son in the house again.

They sighted no other ships in the final weeks of sailing. Although it grew warmer, most days were gray, while the wind blew reliably from the east and they sailed on a broad reach day and night. Fallon consulted the charts and predicted landfall in St. George in time for his twenty-eighth birthday. It would be good to see his father, to be at the White Horse and get news and gossip and not be responsible for anything or anyone for a while. That thought was the only thing that brought him on deck anymore.

SEVEN

ELINORE SOMERS watched the ships glide into the harbor
and drop anchor. In the glare of the noonday sun it was
difficult to tell who was aboard and who was not. She could
see Nico Fallon standing at the railing of *Sea Dog*, however, and
that was whom she was looking for.

Elinore was twenty-four years old and had never seen the world.
Never been away from Bermuda, in fact. In her mind she was
caged as surely as the parakeet in her bedroom. She thought of
Fallon breaking free from the island's grasp, as men could do, and
it filled her with both envy and anger. Both emotions worked on
her face now. Hers was a lovely and complex face, and her blonde
hair blew about it in the wind, uncontrolled and unmanageable.
Her radiant blue eyes missed nothing, and there was an intelligence behind them that demanded and expected respect from
everyone she met—or the relationship would not go well. With
most of the young men on the island, it did not go well.

Fallon had been her tormentor when they were young, and she
had hated him. When he left as a boy to go to sea, she hated him
more. He was leaving, she was staying, simple.

But now, not so simple.

She was a woman now and had begun to feel the stirrings of
something she had never felt before. For a year she had watched
Sea Dog being built, Fallon working with the men in all weather.
When it was hot, he sometimes took off his shirt to work, and she

could see his scarred back, which was when things began stirring in her body. *What is going on?* she thought. But she knew.

When, finally, Fallon took up his command in *Sea Dog* and made to leave, she had been unprepared. Well, she had memorized a bit of something flirtatious to say and had also thought about throwing herself into his arms and begging him to stay. All that. But when he had come to say good-bye, she had shut the door on him, literally. She did not even say good-bye. It was inexplicable, even to her.

Now he was home with two prizes, a hero. She felt confused and off balance when she thought of him. *What had he left thinking?*

EZRA SOMERS saw his daughter walking down to Somers Wharf, where he stood waiting in anticipation of his captain's report. He was exuberant at the prizes he saw, though of course the prize court would need to determine their value. The Admiralty agent would have been alerted to the arrival of prizes, no doubt, and could be expected to parse over spar and shot before arriving at the value of the ships. Meanwhile, repairs would be made to *Sea Dog* to put her to rights.

Somers smiled at the name of his little fighting ship, named for Sir Francis Drake's band of privateers—called *Sea Dogs* in the Elizabethan era. He knew their history because history was important to him. His library was probably the largest on the island, and he was well read on a variety of subjects.

Literature and wisdom were his gifts to Elinore, but to date they remained unopened.

Somers's wife had died at childbirth, and a light had dimmed in his heart. It had been a late pregnancy, difficult and ultimately tragic. He had, at least, hoped for a boy, but it was not to be. Nothing was as it should have been. He was left to raise a young girl by himself, a subject that none of his books could explain, for once, and about which he knew nothing. For twenty years he had tried to understand Elinore, and sometimes he felt he had gotten close. But as she grew older, she fought his opinions, dismissed his good intentions, and kept to herself more and more. Somers knew she felt confined and misunderstood and no doubt resentful that her mother had died and left her to him to raise, but this was their life. It was disappointing that she could not make the best of it.

He turned to Elinore now as she walked down the dock toward him, tall and beautiful as her mother had been. He observed the lightness in her step and took it for happiness in their good fortune with the prizes. It did not occur to him that he could be mistaken.

FALLON CLIMBED from his gig to the dock and was greeted by Somers and Elinore; the old man was congratulatory while Elinore gave Fallon a light hug, awkward and shy. He was not at his best, for though he was certainly glad to be home, his task for the afternoon weighed on his mind. After some perfunctory acknowledgment of his welcome, he took his leave.

Indeed, the day would be spent making the rounds of the families of the dead crewmen. Fallon went up and down the streets and alleys, for he knew where they all lived. Each house greeted him the same, for a wife or daughter knew the news the moment they saw his face. Tom Pleasant's family was left to last. He had said what he could to them, a man trying to make sense of the death of a child to parents who stared at him silently. Words like "hero" and "gallant" and "ship's favorite" left his lips and floated softly to the parlor carpet. The task had left him drained and soulless. It was a wretched business, but he had not wanted to leave it to gossip. They deserved to know from him.

It was late when he turned down the lane to the White Horse. Many of his crew would be there celebrating their good fortune, or drinking away their fear. His father saw him come through the low door and rushed to embrace him.

"Nico, my God!" his father exclaimed. "'Tis good to see you in one piece. You're all the talk, son. I've heard about the prizes and your wound. Let me take a look."

"Almost healed," said Fallon, feeling like a boy again with a scrape to show his father. "Others got it much worse, I'm afraid. You probably heard that, too."

"Yes, the price of this damned war. How did the families take it?"

"How would you take it if I had not come back to walk through your door?" said Fallon in a sudden flush of anger. His father did not flinch.

"I'm sorry. You didn't deserve that," said Fallon, ashamed. But the father knew his son, knew who he was and knew that today had utterly destroyed him.

"Come, have a glass and join your mates," his father said kindly. "I think you could use something wet. It will mean a lot to them to see you, Nico. We can catch up later."

Indeed, Fallon got quite drunk. Good and Irish drunk, as his father would say. When he at last stumbled up the stairs to his old bedroom it was early morning—the old Irish saying that you never walk into a pub and leave on the same day applying. He did not notice his father pulling off his sea boots or placing a blanket across him. He was not conscious of the kiss on his forehead or the soft touch on his wound.

This night the water was calm and the winds light, and the nearest storm was far away.

EIGHT

FALLON ARRIVED on time at the Somers's house and was shown into the library by the servant. The card inviting him to dinner with the date and time was in his pocket, and he fingered it nervously as he stood surrounded by more books than he thought one person could read in a lifetime. By the look of their worn backs and pages, however, it appeared they *had* been read.

"There you are. Hello, Nico," Elinore said lightly as she crossed the room to offer a cheek.

"Hello, Elinore," croaked Fallon, feeling badly that he hadn't really paid attention to her on the dock, such was his low mood. But now he most *definitely* was paying attention, for now she was radiant and warm and—there was no other word for it—*stunning*.

Elinore blushed at the movement of his eyes over her body. She wore a blue gown, cut low to reveal her décolletage, which was further shown off by a dazzling sapphire necklace.

She looked down, not knowing quite what to say next, but finally, "I'm sorry about the men, Nico. And especially about the boy, Tom Pleasant. I know it was hard."

"Yes. Well, I mean, yes. Thank you." Words had quite left him. Even the melancholy in his eyes had stepped aside, at least momentarily. Fighting to recover, he asked how she had been, how were things on the island, all the small things he could think to ask. Elinore answered simply and politely, not going into much detail because there was not really much detail to go into.

Fallon was on the verge of running out of questions when Elinore ventured one of her own. "Tell me, Nico," she said seriously, "are you anxious to get to sea again?"

Fallon looked at her curiously, but he could see it was not an idle question. She wanted to *know*. Why, he had no idea.

He turned to look out the library window. Night had fallen quickly, and he could see his own reflection in the dark glass. "Yes, I guess I am. Since I was a boy it's all I've done." He laughed self-consciously. "I think it's all I know how to do."

Elinore smiled at his answer. "I doubt that, Nico."

Fallon turned from the window to face her, beautiful by candle-light, her eyes widening just a bit. He suddenly felt pressure in his chest. *Oh*, he thought: *I've been holding my breath.*

Ezra Somers entered the room just as Fallon inhaled rather deeply. Somers heartily shook his hand and congratulated him once again on a profitable voyage. He made to pour wine, and Elinore slipped away to the kitchen, offering a last look toward Fallon that said—*something*.

What just happened? Fallon wondered as he watched her close the double doors behind her.

Somers limped from gout, but he could still move quickly, at least toward wine. They settled with their glasses before the fire, for a late spring cold front was passing over the island, and for a long moment neither spoke. It was not awkward, just a quiet moment between men before business began.

The fire blazed and crackled and spit sparks up the chimney. The wind brought the sound of the sea to the porches of every home; it had been so since Bermuda was first settled in 1609 when *Sea Venture*, a British ship sailing for Jamestown, had wrecked on Bermuda's reef and inadvertently started a colony of survivors.

"Nico, you've done damn well," began Somers. "Considering your last prize and these, you're on your way to becoming a wealthy young man. But you looked buggered coming off the ship; I watched you."

Fallon squirmed and stared harder into the fire.

"My guess is that you feel rotten and responsible for the loss of some of your crew. So, hear me: Your crew chose to sail with you as much as you chose them. Each had his own reasons: Debt, running away from hell, running toward heaven, we don't know. But it was their choice, and they knew the risks."

"Yes," Fallon said softly.

"So you made them heroes to their families and did your duty by them. Well done. Now, you've got to fight the damn French and pirates and privateers again. They're all over the Caribbean. Hell, I've got a ship a week late calling at the Turks; I don't know why. Repair your ship and recruit more crew and get to sea again. It's the best medicine. And listen to me, I'll pass out your share to the families, like you asked. Hell, I'll give part of my share to Tom Pleasant's family, too."

"I don't know what to say, sir. I didn't expect . . . " That was a *lot* of money.

"I'm getting old, Nico, call it that."

Fallon stared at the fire. Between Elinore's attention and Somers's concern for him he suddenly felt caught out, almost embarrassed.

"One more thing, Nico," continued Somers, "and this is the reason I asked you here tonight. I'm getting on for this game, and Elinore has no use for it. The business is fine if we can keep our enemies out of our pockets, but I'm just too damn old for it. I want to offer you a partnership. We can work out the details later, but look, you're the best damn captain I could find on the island. You've got a good head and heart and one day the war is going to be over and you'll want a living. The world will still want salt, I think. Plus you're the closest thing there is to somebody I'd want for a son. I want this company *to live* after I die. I can't say Elinore is the one to carry it on, but you could be."

Fallon made to protest, but Somers waved it away.

"Don't answer now. I just needed to say it and give you something to think about. I'm not going to change my mind. The offer will still be here when you come home again."

Here Somers rose to stoke the fire; the logs glowed and sparks drifted up the chimney. The smell of roasted ducks came through the room, and suddenly Fallon was very hungry.

"This next cruise will take you down to Grand Turk," Somers said quietly as he sat back down to face Fallon. "I want you to learn the salt business, see how it works, and find out what's happening to our ships. If we can protect our salt at sea, then we have to figure out how to keep it out of the hands of the Bahamian government. Do you know they've declared ownership of the Turks Islands, by God? Hell, we're all English but they act like pirates, sitting in their offices in Nassau. They want to tax our damn salt!"

Fallon knew a little of the story. Although the Turks Islands belonged to the British Empire, they were not actually a colony; rather, the islands were for the "common good" of British colonies. The Bahamas were to govern them, but the Bermudians had other designs, as usual, having been on the islands raking salt since the late 1600s. For Bermudians like Ezra Somers, paying a tax to the Bahamian government was out of the question.

There was a light cough behind the closed doors and, when they opened, it was Elinore to announce dinner. Fallon wondered how long she had been behind those doors and how much she had heard, but perhaps he was imagining too much.

One thing he wasn't imagining. The look in Elinore's eyes told him something had changed between them. Again he wondered, *what just happened?*

NINE

AFTER DINNER with Somers and Elinore, Fallon detoured away from the path home to walk down to the harbor. He wanted to clear his head from a surprisingly confusing evening. Between Elinore's unspoken interest and Somers's offer of a partnership, there was a lot to sort out. His walk took him naturally to Somers Wharf, where *Sea Dog* was snug at her lines, her repair work well underway but some time before completion. Fallon felt small and insignificant looking at his ship, a ship that had fought for him, killed for him, and brought him home safely from so far away.

The moon was on the water now and the harbor was silvery and alive. It was here, barely a hundred years ago, that rough Puritan justice was carried out against women accused of witchcraft. As a test of guilt, a suspected witch was thrown into St. George's Harbor. If she didn't sink, she was pronounced guilty. Of course, if she sank she died anyway. There was really no win. Many of the accused women floated because of their skirts and petticoats. These unfortunate souls were pulled from the water and burned at the stake.

Fallon shuddered, and looked away westward, toward Beauty's house, and wondered briefly what the Puritans would have made of her independent spirit. God help the Puritans if they came for her, he decided. He smiled at the thought and then decided to cut off to see if she was home. He had not seen much of her since they'd returned, which he blamed on himself. It was a long walk to her house, but it would do him good to talk to her about Elinore and get a woman's perspective.

The moon was well up now, gibbous and half illuminated. It matched his mood. The evening was still and the walk was energizing as he made his way along the path that encircled St. George's Harbor and then bore off to Suffering Lane.

The path curved away from the water up through a few scattered cottages. He turned down an alleyway out of habit, remembering afternoons fetching Beauty for a sail and her running out the back door carrying her jacket and hat. Her parents were dead now, but she stayed in the house she grew up in. Though it was against British law for a woman to inherit a house, no one really wanted to argue the point with Beauty McFarland. He went to the back door as always, and he could see through the glass into the kitchen and, beyond, into the parlor. He raised his hand to knock, and then stopped. Beauty was inside, but she was not alone. She was sitting with another woman, holding her, stroking her hair, and kissing her hands. He could not see the woman's face, nor did he want to. He had seen too much already.

Quickly he turned away, ashamed of lurking in the dark and peeping. He stepped noiselessly off the porch, retraced his steps to the path, and turned for home. Maybe he had always suspected, but he had never *known*. It didn't change anything, he told himself. And he was sure that was true.

This was true, as well: Life ashore was complicated, uncertain, and confusing. A path you had walked a thousand times could still lead you to a surprising place.

TEN

HMS *Harp*, a small frigate of 32 guns and 130 feet, crept into the harbor late in the afternoon just as Fallon was finishing the day's inspection of *Sea Dog*'s painting. It had been several weeks since Fallon had sailed into the harbor with prizes. Tomorrow victualling would begin, with Beauty supervising the loading of powder and shot to get the ship's trim right, and the water casks the last to be loaded. The ship would sail in two days.

Harp rounded up and dropped anchor less than a cable's length away, her captain's gig immediately lowered and manned. Even without a telescope Fallon could see the gold epaulets of the captain's full dress uniform in the gig's stern. His gig's crew were turned out in their best frocks. A little show coming to shore.

Suddenly the gig veered, having seen *Sea Dog*'s transom, and at the command of "*Oars*" ceased rowing and glided to the schooner's starboard side.

"Ahoy, *Sea Dog!*" yelled the captain's coxswain, standing up, cupping his hands like a trumpet. "Is the captain aboard?"

"He is!" called Fallon. "Nicholas Fallon, at your service, sir. Your captain is very welcome to come aboard."

The contrast in captains could not have been more pronounced—Fallon in his working slops, the frigate's captain puffed out in gold trim. A bewhiskered, red face came into view over the side railing, followed by a corpulent body, followed by a wheeze.

"Captain Fallon, I am Hammersmith Bishop, captain of His

Majesty's frigate *Harp*, lately of Falmouth," he said self-importantly. He pulled himself up to his full, still rather short height as he spoke. "Might we step below for a word, sir?" Getting right to business, but missing nothing of the work of the ship, eyes darting around the compass.

Fallon led him into his small cabin, which is to say there was enough room for a cot and a table and not much else. The stern windows dominated the rear of the cabin, with a small bench seat and cushions below. Two wooden chairs would have to suffice for this meeting, however. After a few pleasantries and apologies over the accommodations, including the fact that the wine was not yet aboard, the business began.

"Are you aware, sir, of the privateer-turned-pirate Jak Clayton?" Bishop asked. "Also called Wicked Jak within his trade. No? Then allow me to acquaint you, Captain. He is the devil. At one time, Clayton operated out of the Leeward Station in the Caribbean and always with a letter of marque as a credential. He did well for the Crown, mostly plundering the odd Frenchie or American. But last year, sir, he turned rogue and attacked an Indiaman out of Tobago carrying spice and cotton. He approached her under British colors and took her by boarding. There were supernumeraries aboard, some women. You can well imagine a pirate with no honor and those . . . temptations. He took every farthing in the ship—I believe there was some specie—all the jewelry and even pewter. Took off twenty prime seamen in the bargain . . . they *volunteered*. And then he sailed away back to his hole in the wall."

"Jesus, we've had no word!" Fallon said, astounded.

"I'm afraid it gets worse. Much worse. You are aware, sir, of the Treaty of San Ildefonso? Spain has gone over to France—they are both enemies of Great Britain now. Had you heard?"

Fallon nodded, remembering Viceux's secret orders.

"Last winter this bugger Wicked Jak took a Spanish frigate!" Bishop went on, flushing scarlet with anger. "Near Martinique. He approached under Spanish colors for a parley between countrymen and seized the captain and first lieutenant and slit their damn throats in front of the men. *Cold-blooded bugger!* You know Spaniards, the crew collapsed in fear and Clayton had the ship. By God, sir, I wish you had wine."

"I regret I cannot offer you any," Fallon said. And he meant it, for it was a lot of story to tell without wine to wash down the bitterness. Also a lot to hear. A privateer turned pirate had history, of course; William Kidd and Thomas Tew came to mind, but that was in the 1600s. Fallon knew of no other in recent memory. He watched Bishop; clearly he was agitated. A pirate in command of a frigate would mean no ship was safe. Wicked Jak had the Royal Navy's attention.

"I am under orders to bring Clayton to justice or hang him," Bishop said. "The Admiralty will not have Englishmen attacking British ships. It looks terrible in the *Gazette.*"

Bishop shifted weight and tried to assume a posture of authority. It would seem very like him to worry about what the London *Gazette* printed, particularly about *him.* "Which brings me to you, Captain Fallon. I am under orders to secure what help I may need, and as I understand you know the Caribbean and have a fast ship, I must place you under my command. I will send written orders to you as yet today."

"No," Fallon said emphatically.

Bishop sat bolt upright, his face forming something like an offended scowl. *What did you say?* was bursting from his pores.

"I am employed by the Somers Salt Company with a letter of marque, as you must know," Fallon said coolly. "I am already employed, Captain. I sail in a few days for the Turks Islands to investigate the loss of a ship."

Hammersmith Bishop, friendly up until now, was not used to being disobeyed. "Sir, you are a subject of the Crown. My orders are clear—"

"Then I will see your orders, Captain."

With that, the conversation moved to the next level of

confrontation. Bishop was startled and livid, his face turning a deeper, more violent red, his eyes wide and exploding in anger. Fallon knew it was outrageous to ask to see Bishop's orders, and no British captain would stoop to show them. But Fallon didn't believe Bishop had specific orders to commandeer ships, private ships at that, to fight his battles.

Fallon was Bermudian through and through, and his natural inclination to resist British pressure or dictates or orders was on full display. Bermudians were an island people, proud and opportunistic and *independent,* who had learned to look out for themselves first and the Crown second. They had a history of generally getting the better of the British, and during the American War for Independence many Bermudians temporarily set aside their loyalty to Great Britain and profitably supplied the Americans with guns and ammunition and ships—literally building America's privateer fleet for them.

Still, a frigate preying on Somers's ships was no trifling matter. Fallon offered Bishop an olive branch. "Captain, perhaps if the opportunity presents itself we might work together to bring Clayton to heel. After all, if he sails in the Caribbean he threatens our business. And therefore he is my enemy, as well. But hear me: I will not risk my ship under a frigate's guns. Especially against a pirate who faces hanging and will fight to the death to prevent it, giving no quarter."

Bishop took the olive branch, and Fallon saw his face relax. Here was a chance to salvage honor. Fallon watched the man shift his considerable weight, his breath sighing in and out.

"Captain Fallon, a partnership is exactly what I intend," Bishop said with relief. "Let us cruise together to the Caribbean and, if Jak Clayton is about, we will coordinate our efforts to bring him to heel. Your ship need not dare face Clayton's fire. Independent action will not do, sir."

Here Bishop was stating the obvious and here, more or less, the meeting with the Royal Navy ended. Bishop was off to pay his respects to the Governor, his crew navigating the gig smartly through the harbor to the government dock. Fallon watched from *Sea Dog's* bow as he considered Jak Clayton, a pirate with a frigate and God knew what else at his disposal. Bishop was right; a co-ordinated effort was the only way to defeat an enemy of superior size and weight of metal. But *Sea Dog* was made for open water where speed and windward ability offered advantage. Close fighting was for ships built with the stoutest timbers and framing to take the punishment of relentless broadsides. Fallon looked back toward *Harp.* She certainly looked well-found and smart. Time would tell how well she was handled. One other thing entered into it: Bishop did not seem like a fighting captain.

The meeting with Bishop was troublesome, but it gradually left Fallon's mind as he dealt with the myriad tasks necessary to get a ship ready for sea. The damn lists were endless; they were part of the minutiae that filled in the odd spaces of his day, like dust in the cracks of a wooden floor. Soon enough he was tired, and the last moments of the afternoon suddenly became the first of evening.

As Fallon walked up Somers Wharf at twilight, a figure stepped around the corner of the loading shed. He knew instantly it was Elinore, and his instincts told him what she wanted.

He walked toward her, his heart pumped like a luffing mainsail and, he thought, just as obviously visible.

"Hello, Nico," Elinore said confidently. She stepped up to him and smiled, a beautiful *well here we are* conspiratorial smile. A smile that said everything without saying a word.

"Hello, Elinore," he said. And then *"you look beautiful"* slipped out before he could stop it. Well, he meant it. Her blonde hair cascaded onto her shoulders and she wore a loose jacket over her dress, a sailor's pea coat, really, unbuttoned, her hands in the pockets and just opening the coat now. *An invitation.* Very unladylike, very daring and provocative, and it set him on fire.

They stood looking at each other for a few moments, Fallon wanting to be sure before taking the next step. Then Elinore took it for him, looping her arm through his and leading him up the dock and through the marsh to a place she had chosen, a place warm and dark and hidden in childhood memory.

They giggled as they walked along the path to the small fishing shack with a candle in the window and a coal fire in the small stove. This had been her uncle's retreat, and now it was hers. Elinore produced a padlock key from under a loose porch board. As the door swung open, within seconds they were inside, stumbling toward the bed, wrapped around each other and quite forgetting or not caring that the door was still open.

ELEVEN

B EAUTY TURNED from supervising two men splicing one of the braces and watched Fallon come down the wharf. They had decided to sail with the tide early the next morning and all stores and shot were aboard. In all respects, they were ready for sea. All respects except the captain looked love-struck and might be dragging his feet a bit.

She had not seen much of Fallon outside the ship, first owing to where she lived at the far end of Suffering Lane and, second, because she hadn't wanted to be seen. Privacy was a virtue to Beauty McFarland, like an eleventh commandment: *Thou shalt respect another's privacy.* Here on a tiny island in the middle of the Atlantic Ocean, one's sexuality could not stay hidden long, she knew that. But she wanted any revelation to be on her terms, and she wasn't sure what they were yet.

"Beauty, we'll get underway at first light with the tide tomorrow," Fallon said to her for the umpteenth time since he had moved his things back aboard *Sea Dog.* Really, the boy was heeling badly.

"Aye, your Majesty," she replied with exaggerated patience. "What about your frigate, there?" She nodded toward *Harp,* just swinging to her anchor in the shifting breeze. "What's the plan going to be?"

With this they moved together to his cabin to pore over charts of the Caribbean with Becker, the master. Their course would take them almost due south on mostly a beam reach for almost fifteen hundred miles.

The frigate, with Captain Hammersmith Bishop in command, would leave this afternoon. They had agreed to rendezvous with *Harp* in Cockburn Harbor on Grand Turk at the Somers office and get news. Had anyone heard of Wicked Jak Clayton? Beauty wondered. It seemed like a fantastic rumor.

After Becker left with a chart of Cockburn Harbor to study more closely, Beauty and Fallon paused a moment in companionable silence. They'd always been like this, not needing to talk to be friends. But something clearly needed saying, she thought. Something was working on Fallon's face.

"I suppose I should tell you something personal," he finally said, smiling. *A good start.* "I've become . . . that is, I've been . . . I mean to say, I'm quite taken with Elinore Somers. Lately. I mean, now."

Beauty laughed. "Lord, Nico, I thought you were going to tell me a secret!"

Fallon looked startled.

"Nico, Nico, the whole island knows you two are sweethearts," she said laughing again. "Just look at your silly face! Have you looked in the mirror lately? A blind hog could find that acorn!"

Fallon blushed and put his head in his hands.

"I, for one, think she's the luckiest girl on the island," Beauty said. "And you're the luckiest boy. She's got her own head, and there's something in it besides cotton balls. Plus, she's got spit."

Fallon grinned, and Beauty grinned with him, the secret between them not a secret at all. Beauty stared at him a moment, relaxed and relieved, and briefly considered telling him about her own, well, *friend.* No, she decided, it could wait for a better time.

They worked through the last-minute details of crew allocation, typically Beauty's job, but Fallon knew a few of the new hands that she did not. The watches were reviewed, along with the gun crews and who had the lightest touch on the helm. The ship was ready for sea, ready to quit the land and sail over the horizon. Fallon gave Beauty a quick hug as she left his cabin. It felt good.

Fallon had ordered the crew to sleep in the ship that night. *Sea*

Dog had been warped away from the dock and rode at anchor, her captain's gig bobbing and bumping alongside in the gathering dusk. Beauty expected Fallon would use it tonight to row to the wharf and meet Elinore, and she was glad of it. They were a good match, and besides, it was good to see her normally unflappable friend with his compass spinning.

TWELVE

SEA DOG caught up with *Harp* inside three days and passed her, the frigate under reefed topgallants and apparently in no real hurry—a bad sign. But Fallon would not sail under her coattails all the way to the Turks Islands, that was for sure. He wanted his independence to be seen, early and clearly. Bishop had fired a cannon as he went by, either a salute or something else.

Beauty set the watches to their tasks; the gun crews practiced loading and running out till they were exhausted and begged for a tot. The ship was coming together, and Fallon was elated. As usual, *Sea Dog* carried more crew than was actually needed to work the ship, but that was a privateer. The extra men found someplace to sleep on deck, propped against gun carriages or snugged against the sides of the ship, and rotated in and out of gun crews and watches. For the most part everyone accepted the overcrowding as a small price to pay for the possibility of greater riches.

They had glimpsed a few distant sails but had not altered course to learn more. The missing Somers ship was a concern, and the faster they got to the Turks, the faster answers could be found. Hopefully. At least that was the theory right up to the time they found the French squadron.

Or rather, the French squadron found them.

The crew spotted the squadron to the southeast, perhaps fifteen miles away. Fallon had a fast ship, but the French were spread out over several miles like a fan, and the squadron was sailing more or less downwind, on a broad reach, which was a good point of sail for square-rigged ships. *Sea Dog*'s windward virtues would not help now. And her speed would not help her if she held course, so spread out were the French that she would be intercepted. Of course much could happen to change the circumstances. A sudden squall. A waterspout. A unicorn could appear in the sky and take everyone's breath away. Short of that, Fallon knew a certain moment was at hand.

He clamped his jaw tight. The French were never anxious for a sea battle unless strong odds presented themselves. Which they had, in the form of *Sea Dog*, sailing alone, deserted by luck. Fallon considered bearing off and running downwind. Not the schooner's best point of sail by a long shot. Even if *Sea Dog* succeeded in out-running the squadron in a long chase, it could take Fallon weeks to make up ground to windward.

And, too, there was *Harp* to consider. She was perhaps half a day behind *Sea Dog*. As things stood, she, a lone frigate with a question-able captain in gold lace, might well sail right into the jaws of the squadron.

Fallon needed a plan that he didn't have, but he had to prepare the ship for action. "Beauty, call all hands," he said firmly. "But leave the gun ports closed."

All hands ran to stations pre-ordained by drills and instructions. Men who were old hands showed the newer ship's boys where to go, what to do. Shot, powder, and tubs of sand to safely hold the smol-dering slow match were brought up; gun crews assembled by their charges.

The lookout counted six ships. The French, of course, counted but one. In all respects, Fallon was at a disadvantage. He ran through the options once more in his mind. Logic said turn and fly. Play the game out in a long chase. He thought of Hammersmith Bishop looking through his telescope at six French ships converging upon him, wondering why that coward Fallon hadn't warned him. He shuddered; no, that wouldn't do.

All faces looked to him. He knew each one, every name. Wiggins and Charles and Henry Matson and Cline and Burger and the Swedes and on and on. Asking them to go into battle for glory or prize money was one thing—sending them to their probable deaths another.

There was no win in it. If he sailed onward, his ship would face terrible destruction. A twelve-pound cannonball crashing into a frail wooden structure wreaked unbelievable devastation on vessel and crew. Each ship, even a French ship, could fire half her guns every two to three minutes. Assuming the squadron of six ships totaled three hundred guns that would be over one hundred cannon shot at close range tearing into *Sea Dog* for as long as it took her to sink. Likely, not many minutes. The loss of life would be catastrophic.

Time to decide on a course of action. Fallon was focused energy now, his mind alert and running lines and calculations. Options were few.

Beauty appeared at his side, her telescope on the enemy, judging wind speed and course. "Not long, Nico. How're the funeral plans coming?"

Fallon smiled at her dark humor, but he desperately needed time to think. On the French came, the line a bit more formal, anticipating action. A signal flag: *What ship?*

"Beauty, up with the French tricolor," Fallon ordered, ignoring the request to identify his ship. "And send for the signal book we took off *Fleur*. Pick out a man with good eyes and send him aloft with it." Fallon was desperately trying to stall for time. But, of course, the reality was that time was running out. With each passing minute it seemed the French squadron could be seen more clearly, and the crew shifted foot to foot at their stations.

Then, an idea at last, the smallest worm of an idea began wriggling in Fallon's mind. In a flash *it was the only thing to do.* Of course, it was insane—and yet he was mad with it.

"Beauty," Fallon said quickly, "we've got to make the French believe we're afraid over here. Which we are . . . but not because of *them!*"

Now Beauty nodded, a big smile beginning. "Aye, aye, Captain," she said with relish . . . and not a little relief on her face. "What's next?"

Fallon sorted through the French signal flags laid out on the deck and picked out the message he wanted hoisted.

Enemy in sight.

"Now, Beauty, let's hope the French buy our little ruse!"

Immediately, *Enemy in sight* went up. And now there were squadron signals flying. And the French, who loved to talk, began chattering. The Sea Dogs stood by, clearly mystified and growing increasingly worried.

"Lookout there, what are they saying?" yelled Fallon.

"I think they're confused, sir. They think we're French!" This without a trace of irony, considering they were flying French colors. Well, Fallon hadn't said the lookout had to be brilliant, only have good eyes.

"Deck there," called the lookout. "They're repeating *What ship?* again!"

The French could be counted upon to be worried about an enemy in the offing, but first they wanted to be sure with whom they were dealing. Fallon had to give the French Commodore something else to worry about, something at the next level of concern, to distract his mind from *Sea Dog's* identity.

He sorted through the French signal flags again and finally spelled out *British squadron.*

"Ha!" laughed Beauty. "That ought to tighten up their French asses over there!" The flags were sent up, and Fallon and Beauty waited expectantly for the reaction.

"Deck there, signals are flying so fast I can't make them out."

Fallon considered it a brief reprieve. He imagined the French were worried, confused, but they were probably not convinced. He looked around at the men's faces, all looking back at him, all counting on him to work some magic and save the ship. But he was out of magic tricks. Fallon feared the French hadn't bought the idea and were even now laughing at his feeble attempt to escape.

He looked around the ship, looked at the sea rushing by, and finally up to the sky—hoping for divine intervention—but saw only the sails and the French tricolor at the gaff. Yet . . . there it was, *by God*, right in front of his eyes, the coup de grâce. It would be risky, terribly risky, and lives hung in the balance, but the thing had to be seen through. The cake was out of the oven, as his mother used to say. Time for the icing.

"Beauty," said Fallon as calmly as he could. "Let's send up a last signal. We'll have to spell it out perfectly."

"And then what happens?" Beauty asked.

"And then we'll surrender—to the British!" Fallon exclaimed.

Beauty grinned at the audacity of the idea, the pure fantasy of the idea, really, but its utter genius—well, *if it worked*. Fallon worked the signal out on deck, letter for letter, *V-i-v-e l-a F-r-a-n-c-e*. The French ships were noticeably closer now and becoming clearer without a telescope. But Fallon was wonderfully calm, it seemed to the men, which both confused and reassured them, equally.

At last, *Vive la France* flew. One last cheer for the republic.

"Now," Fallon ordered, "have the helmsman put the helm over and make to come hard on the wind, *toward the French squadron*." Beauty's eyebrows went up, and her mouth came open. "I know," Fallon answered the invisible question, "but we're French, remember? Running for the squadron's skirts."

The order was given and ropes were pulled tight as the ship came up toward the eye of the wind. Fallon's mind was committed now, his throat dry and tight. If he should fail . . . well, to put the ship in this danger, voluntarily, was virtual suicide.

"Now, Beauty," Fallon said, "for the hard part . . . but trust me, it's our only chance. On my word, come dead into the wind and stall the ship. That's right. On my word, now, and then *haul down the French flag!*"

Beauty swallowed hard and nodded. *Sea Dog* sailed on toward the French, yard by yard getting closer. There was no turning back now, of course.

"Now!" Fallon ordered, "Come up, come up! That's right, luff there! And strike the colors!"

Beauty obeyed without a moment's hesitation, knowing it was all or nothing. Slowly, *Sea Dog* came to the eye of the wind and lost way, two hundred tons of movement suddenly all but dead in the water. The sails flapped, lines slapped, and men looked around with their mouths agape. The French tricolor came down—the universal sign of surrender—and every Jack Tar held his breath.

"Lookout there! What signals?" yelled Fallon, no longer the calm captain now, for *Sea Dog* was helpless. The French were signaling furiously, and the schooner was a sitting target.

Fallon's confidence was waning by the second. The pressure in his chest was unbearable, and he was on the verge of surrendering *for real*.

"Signals!" called the lookout. "From the flagship: *Wear in succession*. By God! They're wearing, sir. The French are breaking off and turning around!"

Fallon raised his telescope and saw the lead ship, by now a distinct image in his glass, ponderously turn her stern toward him. The rest followed suit. A new course, then, to the northeast, away from a trick. So close to certain death, and now a reprieve.

The wind was lying down, but Fallon would need to keep up the game until the French ships were settled on their course and virtually out of sight. It had been a dangerous ruse, to position *Sea Dog* so nakedly. Yet she was virtually helpless anyway at 6-to-1. Even the French could handle those odds. He had counted on them abandoning him to the invisible enemy to save their precious ships. This time, he had been right.

The men were standing around grinning in disbelief at their good fortune. The schooner was almost becalmed in the fading afternoon light when Fallon decided all was finally well.

"Send the hands to dinner," he said to Beauty, who had just gotten the ship squared away and back on course. "Up spirits for each man, and send for me if the breeze freshens or the enemy reappears."

Suddenly, Fallon was numb from exhaustion. All his energy drained, he made his way along the ship to his cabin. It had been a near thing, with death or worse in the balance. But *Sea Dog* had lived to fight again. There would be another time for heroics. For now he needed his cot and a moment to close his eyes. Just a moment, he thought, but it would be hours before he awoke.

THE SHIP glided over blue, silky water, alive with confidence and a sense of preordination. The men skylarked and went about their daily duties uncomplaining and even joyful. Older hands helped younger hands, the youngsters took to their navigational studies with more earnestness, and a general sense of optimism grew in the ship as the warm trade winds blew them along. The escape from the French squadron made *Sea Dog* a lucky ship and, as all sailors were deeply superstitious, luck was much prized aboard. Prized even above rum.

Meanwhile, Fallon sat on the stern seat in his cabin, staring at dust swirling in a bar of sunlight. He was trying to organize his thoughts about Ezra Somers's offer, writing them down as short sentences both for and against. The biggest question mark was whether his relationship with Elinore complicated things, *which of course it did*. She was Ezra's daughter. She was also Fallon's lover. It wouldn't do to deceive Somers on the point. If Fallon accepted a partnership without disclosing his relationship with Elinore, Somers would be outraged. He closed his journal. It was too much emotional calculus to figure out.

He wore a frown up the companionway steps into the bright air, in sharp contrast to the expression of the ship. But his spirits were lifted by what he saw: From bow to stern the hands were relishing the sailing qualities of the ship, her plunging speed, the fully engaged sails fore and aft drawing every ounce of power from the wind. It was glorious, and only a fool of a captain would pout in front of the men and against such a display of joy. He got over himself and gasped in wonder. *My God, such a sailor!*

Becker had them less than two hundred miles from Cockburn Harbor on Grand Turk. Cockburn Town was home to Somers Salt and most of the enterprise was managed from there. The daily accounting of salt and ships coalesced into a monthly report that was routed through the Bahamas and north to Bermuda and then onto Ezra Somers's desk. John Nilson was Somers's manager on Grand Turk and, though Fallon had never met the man, he had heard Nilson knew his business, though he was insufferable personally. Fallon had never seen salt raked or harvested, was ignorant as to the procedure, and was anxious to understand it. He hoped Nilson would show him the operation.

Then there was the matter of the lost ship. Perhaps it had turned up, safe and sound, sailing into Cockburn Harbor with stories to tell. Or perhaps it was lost, sunk, or taken. Or perhaps they would never know. Well, he had to know *something*.

Elinore sailed with him in his imagination. Her hair blew in the wind, totally untamed, and in his mind they walked together along the windward side of the ship every evening, huddled closely together, nuzzling private words. He would imagine that she touched him, and the fire would light up his body like a torch.

Tonight he would imagine her walking with him again and, with the freshening breeze, he would hold her even closer.

THIRTEEN

IT WAS a mystery even to seasoned sailors, at least those who'd ever thought about cosmic things, how in the great expanse of ocean two ships could chance to find themselves in exactly the same longitude and latitude, having started their separate journeys from God-knows-which parts of the globe. Against all odds, wind and current and tide, storm and calm, they were brought by fate to the exact same spot, as if there were a giant X on the water, to meet.

This happened on the morning of June 23, 1796.

It began as a normal, if cloudy, day with no portent of evil or omen to concern the captain. Just after breakfast the call came down from the lookout.

"Deck there! Ship dead ahead!"

All eyes looked southward, and Fallon and Beauty grabbed their telescopes and went forward to the bow. What they could see was a ship; at least it looked like a ship, but without sails. It was difficult to see in the morning haze, but it certainly looked ominous. They kept their telescopes trained on the mystery for a full five minutes without speaking.

Finally, "What do you think, Beauty?"

Beauty rubbed her right eye and raised her telescope again, studying carefully. "It's a ship, all right, but a ship that's been knocked about horribly." Indeed, the sails were shredded, the foremast was over the side, the rigging a tangle. It looked very much like the ship had simply died. Brutally.

"Call all hands, Beauty," ordered Fallon. "Shorten down and go slow. Let's see what we see."

Sea Dog took way off and slowly sailed down to a ghost ship. Her larboard side was shot through, with jagged holes and up-turned guns and what looked like dried blood in her scuppers. It was eerily quiet, and the Sea Dogs were mute with suspicion and curiosity.

Fallon studied the ship from perhaps a cable length away, a big ship for hauling cargo of some sort. "Beauty, heave-to and lower my gig. I'll want six men to go with me. If this is a trap, open fire immediately. Don't worry for our safety. Open fire. That's an order."

Beauty nodded, but frowned, and then muttered under her breath, "Damned if I will."

Fallon and the gig's crew rowed across to the ship, the scene becoming more macabre by the stroke. A ghost ship, indeed, settled low in the water. They clapped onto the hull and climbed up the side and over the railing to a scene from hell itself. She was a slaver; her cargo had been human, her ballast below decks once living and breathing. It looked as though the hatches had been opened, the slaves had tried to escape or been ordered up, and the slaughter of crew and cargo was recorded in the blood and frozen, pleading faces of the dead. Bodies lay scattered about, hacked and sometimes unrecognizable as a man or a woman; someone had taken delight in mutilation.

Fallon rushed to the railing and threw up, the bile burning his throat. He tried to get his breath, gasping for air, only to vomit again. He was not alone at the rail as most all the crew found someplace to be sick. Dead sailors were nothing new to these men, but this was beyond anything that any of them had ever seen. Finally, weak and nauseous, Fallon turned to measure the destruction.

The deck was scarred by cannon shot, the helm smashed, and the few guns upended and pointing skyward. The bodies looked days old, perhaps a week, and the stench was putrid and overwhelming. Most of the slaves wore little clothing, some had manacles or chains. God knows where they had come from or where they thought they were going. Fallon could only imagine what waited below decks, and it took every ounce of resolve he possessed to send him down there.

They began the search for survivors, which they were certain they would not find. Dead slaves were everywhere, twisted between barrels and in piles of lost humanity, staring like owls in the darkness, deck after deck. While Fallon made his way below to the captain's cabin, his crew began moving the length of the ship, looking in hiding places. No one caught in the open had lived.

Fallon found nothing that told the story in the stern cabin; typically, slavers kept a record of their cargo, but the ship's papers had apparently been taken or thrown overboard, for the stern windows hung open. He had just turned to go back on deck when he heard one of his men cry out.

"Come here, you bugger! I'll not hurt ye, my word!" rang out in the stillness and Fallon froze, half in terror at what he was about to see. Cully, *Sea Dog*'s ablest gun captain, was dragging a squirming but clearly weak boy out from behind a water cask. The boy's eyes were terrified, and his clothes, what there were, were soiled and ragged. He was horribly thin, his ribs showing clearly against the taut, dark skin of his chest.

Cully half carried him up the companionway steps with Fallon close behind. The boy collapsed on deck, whimpering and moaning and recoiling into a writhing, wretched ball as Fallon approached.

"My God, my God," Fallon muttered. He knelt and tried to talk softly to the boy but got no response, just fear. The boy covered his face with his hands as if fearing the sword's blade coming.

"Cully, you and Hammond get him into the gig," said Fallon. "You men, one last pass through the ship to look for any more survivors. Look hard, men. Where there was one hiding, there may be more."

They looked carefully, calling out into every dark spot, but there were no more survivors. Just the one boy. They bundled him in their own clothing and rowed back to *Sea Dog*, the boy cowering in the bottom of the gig. It was a somber, concerned crew that handed him up the side to waiting hands. Pence was summoned to take the boy below to be examined, and Fallon ordered the cook to take him some pork and pudding.

It was early afternoon now, and Fallon pondered what to do about the battered ship. Somehow it couldn't be left to just drift away, carrying all those rotting bodies. No, that lacked the dignity of a funeral. Plus, it was a hazard as it was and an indecent testimony to the brutish nature of man.

"I think we should burn the ship," Beauty offered, as if to read Fallon's mind working through the problem. They both stared across the short space of water to the drifting hulk. Fallon agreed that firing the ship seemed like the best option, and by the first dogwatch smoke was curling through the hatches of the ghost ship, the end coming in a fiery inferno no man could ever forget. It was a rotten business until the last burning timber hissed in the sea.

Finally, the boy. Fallon wondered whether the boy perhaps had a mother or father in the ship, as well, and whether they were taken or killed. Whoever attacked the ship had been after slaves and had no doubt taken off the ablest ones, killing those they didn't need or those who fought back. Maybe the boy's father was even now on his way to a market to be sold, perhaps a market in Bermuda, for there was one there. Fallon grimaced. Slavery was grotesque and inhuman but perfectly legal in Bermuda, if not in most of the world. Legal perhaps, but it repulsed him.

He went below just as Pence, the surgeon, was stepping from around the cockpit screen. Raising a finger to his lips, Pence motioned Fallon to the captain's cabin to talk.

"He's sleeping now, Nico; I gave him a draught after he ate his supper and he's resting," said Pence in a whisper.

"Did he speak at all?" asked Fallon softly. "Tell you anything of what happened on his ship?"

"Nothing," replied Pence. "He hasn't spoken a word. I don't even know if he understands English. He may not, you know. Maybe they came straight from Africa. Looking at his rags, maybe."

"How is his condition?"

Pence considered. "Well, he's been without food for days, maybe longer, so he's thin and weak as a kitten but should be fine. He's a strong boy. He ate his supper like a wolf."

"Good for him!" said Fallon. A boy with an appetite was a boy on the mend, he thought. Now he left the cabin and went on deck to find Beauty. She was at the binnacle, just finishing a check of their position on the slate as he approached.

"Pence says the boy is going to be all right," said Fallon. "But he hasn't spoken. Doesn't know if he even speaks English. I'm thinking we should take him on as a ship's boy because if we let him loose in the Turks he either won't survive or he'll be picked up as a runaway and put back into slavery. What do you think?"

She smiled. "I've already entered him in the books." *Once again, Beauty was ahead of him.*

Now Fallon smiled. "How did you enter him?"

"Mr. Boy," she said. "I guessed he was twelve. Listed him as a volunteer. I'll take him under my wing, Nico; let's put him with the other youngsters."

"Excellent," said Fallon approvingly. "Let's hope Mr. Boy takes to the ship, and the ship to him."

That night, Fallon sat at his small desk and wrote:

> *Tell me something now, my love*
> *Is your heart lost and alone?*
> *For I'll set my ship*
> *a-sailing and ask the wind to*
> *bring me home.*

Well, he was melancholy and lonely and at sea in more ways than one, and he was thinking sappy thoughts. *So, love.*

FOURTEEN

S UNDAY.

They sailed through the Turks Island Passage before noon and, because the wind grew light between the islands, it was not until almost sunset that they rounded up and let go in Cockburn Harbor. A pretty harbor, with a few buildings, some trees, and two cargo ships at anchor off a main dock to the northwest where Fallon ordered his gig landed in the yellowing light. He made his way to Cockburn Town, past a few shops along a main thoroughfare, and found the Somers office closed for the day.

A warm evening and a soft breeze made him want to linger, and then he heard the chanting and singing of evensong. "Rock of Ages" drifted over the little town.

> *Rock of Ages, cleft for me,*
> *Let me hide myself in Thee;*
> *Let the water and the blood,*
> *From Thy riven side which flowed,*
> *Be of sin the double cure,*
> *Cleanse me from its guilt and power.*

Fallon followed the sound past a blacksmith's barn to a small, shingled church set against a dune. Candles were flickering in the open windows, and the large front doors were standing open. He eased up to the church and peered in to see the small congregation standing with their backs to him, singing solemnly. He knew the song from childhood, though he'd not sung it for years. Then he stepped away and retraced his steps back through the settlement to the dock, oddly hopeful. His men were still sitting in the gig and pushed off as soon as he was aboard. They rowed slowly away from the land, in no particular hurry, the church's music drifting to them.

But now Fallon heard more singing, not from the church, but from *his ship!* More than fifty voices joining the island congregation:

> *While I draw this fleeting breath,*
> *When mine eyes shall close in death,*
> *When I soar to worlds unknown,*
> *See Thee on Thy judgment throne,*
> *Rock of Ages, cleft for me,*
> *Let me hide myself in Thee.*

The crew lined the starboard rail of *Sea Dog*, many holding candles and lanterns. Oars stopped as the men in the gig stared in amazement, a few joining in.

It was a spectacle, really, men who gave no quarter in battle, rough and often violent men, who now paused from life's circumstances to sing to an island of strangers. It was a solemn moment, wonderful in its way.

Fallon thought of Elinore again, perhaps in church herself, and wondered if she had a thought for him today. Normally confident, Fallon felt oddly insecure as his feelings for her became deeper. Perhaps she was just a fickle girl, not a woman at all, for whom loyalty was a stage in life she hadn't yet reached. The thought sank his heart.

The gig tied off handsomely and Fallon went up the side, staring at the men. The crew finished with "Heart of Oak," for the Mother Country, and dispersed in twos and threes, at ease in a safe harbor. Beauty smiled broadly at Fallon from the binnacle. Mr. Boy stood next to her, dressed in ship's slops, his eyes wide.

"What a wonderful thing, Beauty! The crew sounded like St. Alban's choir!"

"Their idea, Nico. They wanted to do it," said Beauty proudly.

Fallon looked down at the boy.

"And how are you doing, young man?" Then, kneeling: "I like your new clothes!"

But the boy said nothing, rather stepped backward, eyes wider still.

"It will take a while, Nico," said Beauty soothingly. "With what he's seen—being kidnapped and the slaughter—it would take me forever."

"I know. It's beyond imagining. Well, there's certainly no rush. But if we get into it, I will want him safely below decks. He will be scared to death, I'm sure. But I want him safe." Then, as an afterthought, "Has he spoken any words yet, of any kind, any language?"

"None that I know about," said Beauty. "Whatever he's thinking is staying inside his head."

Quitting the deck, Fallon made his way down the companionway to his cabin. He saw it almost immediately, the moment he entered, something out of place, something where it shouldn't be. A small package on his desk in the lighted circle of a flickering candle. He tossed his hat to the stern seat and sat down, staring at it. His fingers untied the blue ribbon and the paper fell away.

A small key, tarnished and gray, which he had seen only in Elinore's hand in the moonlight. There was no note, for she knew he would know why she'd given it to him.

She would go there with no one else.

FIFTEEN

AFTER BREAKFAST the next morning, Fallon and Beauty
went ashore to meet Nilson at the Somers office. It was a
lovely Caribbean day, warm and bright; they passed pastel
buildings and women in broad straw hats with curious eyes. There
were carts selling baskets and scarves, and children playing with
sticks in the sandy street.

Fallon was in lifted spirits, although he had not worked out exactly how Elinore had gotten the key to Beauty. Or whether Beauty
knew what the gift had been. He smiled at his own naïveté: *Women
had their ways.*

Nilson was just as Fallon had imagined him: proper, haughty,
white mustache, ruddy face. He had little blue veins in his nose and
a very high opinion of himself. His office was a simple affair with
cedar walls and ceiling courtesy of Bermuda, a few desks and chairs,
and a writing secretary. Brown and plain.

Nilson introduced his clerk at the secretary as Mr. Hewes, in
charge of schedules and numbers on papers; he had a plain face,
someone you met and instantly forgot. *Did he have black hair or
brown? A scar?* At any rate, he was busy adding figures and couldn't
be bothered with anything else.

After introductions, Nilson opened fire. "Before you ask,
Captain Fallon, we've had no word of *Calypso,* our missing ship. We
are presuming she's lost to privateers or pirates. We don't know, for
sure. *But* it has cost us a pretty penny, I can tell you." He looked

squarely at Fallon, as if putting the blame there. "At this rate there will be no salt business in a year! The Royal Navy has been no help; what do they care? And now I have a single ship when I need ten for protection. And I am sent a captain new to these waters who doesn't know salt from shit! By God, I hope you have a plan, sir."

Beauty turned on him immediately. "Our plan is to protect *Mr. Somers's* ships and find those French buggers or whoever they are and put a boarding pike up their asses, Mr. Nilson," she said with all appropriate indignation before Fallon could open his mouth. "That's our fucking plan."

Ah, Beauty.

Fallon beamed. Nilson rocked back at Beauty's broadside, his mustache twitching nervously. It was quite possible he'd never met a woman with Beauty's particular vocabulary. Fallon concealed his emerging laughter with a cough.

"Tell me, Mr. Nilson," he said, "what's your estimate of the number of pirates and privateers in this part of the Caribbean?"

Nilson composed himself, looking away from Beauty, preferring to do business with Fallon. "They've always been thick, Captain. Pirates work out of the Bahamas, which does nothing to stop them. The Bahamian government wants control of the Turks because they want the salt. So helping Bermuda stop our pirates ain't in it." Here his voice became conspiratorial. "But now we have this rascal named Clayton, who commands a frigate he took by cunning. He renamed her *Renegade*, an apt name, sir. He's taken several prizes and turned them into his own private squadron, even attacking other pirates and privateers and driving them off. He has a virtual monopoly between here and the United States. I tell you, sir, it will take the Royal Navy to stop him. And even then—"

"Just such a ship is coming to join the hunt for Wicked Jak Clayton, as I hear he is called," said Fallon soothingly. "HMS *Harp*, 32 guns, will call here in a day or two if I am not mistaken. Captain Bishop's orders are to stop at nothing to deal with Clayton."

Surprise made Nilson's mustache twitch. "Then I hope you

will place yourself under his wing, Captain," he said in a low voice. These last words more of a command than a suggestion. Beauty made to rise to it but Fallon cut her off.

"Perhaps while we endeavor to see the salt operation you can tell us more, Mr. Nilson," he said. "I'm sure you have much more to share."

They left Hewes in the office and walked to a waiting buggy that would take them to the *salinas*, or salt pans. Nilson was quite cautious with his words now, keeping a sly eye on Beauty. After they discussed the loss of shipping and Calypso in particular, Nilson turned the conversation to the business of salt—*white gold* he called it. He was a fount of information on the subject. By his reckoning, it was the only real preservative for food that the world had; salt's properties prevented slaughtered animals and fish from rotting into inedibility. And salt was particularly important aboard ships, of course, where sailors were fed a steady diet of salt pork, salt beef, and salt fish. As Somers had discovered, the major market was to be found in the United States, which had no salt production to speak of.

"Imagine what Grand Turk would be without salt!" Nilson exclaimed as they arrived at the salt pans. "There would be nothing here. Salt is the total economy of this wretched place. Columbus may have discovered Grand Turk, but salt made it famous."

Nilson explained that Bermudians had worked the salt flats for generations, flooding the pans at will by building dams, allowing the seawater to evaporate, and raking the leftover salt into huge mounds that dominated the island's scenery. "Do you have any idea how much salt Grand Turk produces annually?" Nilson asked, but he did not wait for an answer. "I bet not, for it is astounding. Over thirty million pounds!"

Fallon and Beauty were impressed, truth be told. Somers had a big business, indeed. As they toured the salt pans it occurred to Fallon that he was glad he had the job he did, for the sun was already growing warm, on its way to very warm, and the thought of working in the *salinas* all day made his mouth suddenly dry.

"Tell me about the rakers," he said. "It must be brutal work."

Nilson was nonchalant. "Oh, the temperatures get over 100 degrees in the summer, and the rakers sometimes get boils on their feet from being in the brine all day. And then one or two go blind because of the glare off the salt. Most men wouldn't want to do it I daresay, which is why we have slaves to do it for us."

Here Fallon swallowed hard, feeling the same sick feeling he always felt whenever the subject of slavery came up. He thought of Mr. Boy back in the ship; perhaps he'd been on his way to this very island to be sold into a life of boils and blindness raking salt. The thought made him shudder. And it made him angry. It also presented him with a conflict: Becoming a partner in the Somers Salt Company would make him a partner in slavery. He was not naïve; he knew slavery was part of many businesses, seen or unseen. It was a fact of life in much of the world, but to *employ* slaves would somehow make him complicit in their exploitation, and the thought deeply troubled him.

Nilson seemed to sense it was time to move the conversation along. "Now, what do we do with all this salt, eh?" he asked, again not waiting for an answer. "Our ships sail north to call at southern U.S. ports, like Charleston, where we unload our salt. Then they return to Bermuda and Grand Turk with grain, sugar, rum, lumber, cotton, and the supplies we need to live. Lovely, isn't it?" Indeed, it was a tidy enterprise, Fallon thought, managed through the skill and ingenuity of John Nilson, your humble servant.

The tour over, Fallon and Beauty returned to the ship more enlightened about the salt business than they ever expected to be. Fallon still turned Somers's offer of a partnership and the slavery issue over in his mind; well, it could wait for a later time to wrestle to the ground.

Beauty had given the hands permission to go ashore, in groups, and the men who were still aboard were at menial tasks. Mr. Boy stood watching Cully teach a group of young gentlemen the art of loading and ramming home. He *seemed* interested. He was already beginning to fill out his clothes and looked less hollow and worn. He wasn't doing much in the ship yet, just watching. Beauty was right: He would go at his own pace.

Fallon motioned for Becker and Beauty to join him in his cabin. Nilson had asked about a plan: *Well, what was it?* To the north lay almost one thousand islands of the Bahamas, with shallow water and coral reefs well-known to locals, but not to him. Hiding places beyond counting. This was where most of the raids on shipping occurred. The Somers Salt Company sent their ships north toward the United States where the demand for salt was high. They were plundered by pirates who then sold the salt and ships to France via one of the French islands in the Caribbean, killing or abandoning the captured crew along the way. The pirates then scampered back to their Bahamian redoubt.

Well, you had to admire their head for business, Fallon thought.

As Becker talked about wind and tide and shallow water, Beauty studied the islands for likely places to hide pirates and captured ships. She noted small bays and coves, and she and Becker discussed entrances and exits, keeping in mind wind direction along the shipping route. They were familiarizing themselves with the challenge ahead, but the meeting ended where it began—without a plan. Fallon was strangely quiet throughout, for something nagged at him. A question was forming in his mind, *what was it?* Something Nilson had said, or something he saw? No, he had it. *It was something he forgot to ask Hewes.*

THE NEXT day Beauty was supervising the loading of water barrels while Pence was tut-tutting as vegetables and fruits came aboard. Apparently, Pence had found and purchased every leafy green edible thing on the island, plus root vegetables that would keep on a long voyage. A pair of goats also came aboard, along with chickens in small coops and even a heifer. It was going to be close below decks.

The harbor was busy with fishing craft coming in from the sea. There were lateen rigged boats, log canoes, and all manner of rowing skiffs moving about their business. HMS *Harp* lay anchored two cables from the town dock, having arrived the previous night, still looking smart. Fallon had seen Bishop being rowed to shore in his gig earlier, perhaps looking for an official to announce himself to. He would be disappointed when he learned there was none.

Fallon had been idly watching the work of the ship when his gaze shifted to the two Somers ships taking on salt. They were bulky cargo ships of 4 guns each, which had probably never been fired. The closest to shore was *Desmond*, obviously English built, with Captain Smithers in command. Farther off was *Castille*, with Captain Wallace in command. His ship was Spanish built, no doubt taken by a privateer at some point in its history before finding its way into the salt trade. Fallon had met the captains, both of whom seemed capable enough for their commands, though neither was practiced in small talk.

Lighters brought the salt out in forty-pound bags, which had been packed and stored ashore for months. In a week the two ships would be fully loaded with the stuff.

Fallon had himself rowed to shore and walked the now familiar path to the Somers office. "Good morning, Hewes," announced Fallon as he stepped inside the office. "Is Mr. Nilson about?"

Hewes started at the interruption. "No," he replied, not deigning to look up. "Mr. Nilson left for Salt Cay to check on some matter or other. He'll be a half day, I'm guessing."

Fallon pretended not to notice the sullen tone. "I understand, of course. Tell me, when will *Desmond* and *Castille* sail?" he asked.

"I've scheduled them to leave in ten days, sir," said Hewes, imperially officious, in charge now in the office, still not looking up. "That should give them ample time to fit out and be loaded. American ports are clamoring for salt, and assuming—"

Fallon caught the inference: *assuming they get there*, Hewes meant. He turned to leave the office when an afterthought appeared to strike him. "Could they leave sooner? Say, three days if we could get the salt loaded?"

This time Hewes looked up, incredulous. "I have a schedule, Captain." As in: *You be the captain, I'll be the scheduler of ships.*

Fallon paused. "Very well. What route do they usually take?"

Hewes reacted with surprise. "The windward passage, of course," he said, barely hiding exasperation. "It's days longer to go to the leeward side of the Bahamas and up through the Straights past Spanish Florida."

"Right you are," replied Fallon, feigning embarrassment to have asked so obvious a question.

By NOON Fallon had sent a note asking Bishop, Smithers, and Wallace to meet after dinner on *Sea Dog*. He should have invited them to dinner, but accommodations on the schooner were wanting. He had hoped Bishop would take the lead but when no invitation came from *Harp*, Fallon had issued his own. As the captains came aboard, he introduced them to Beauty and Becker and then directed them below to his cramped cabin. A screen had been removed to give them more room, but that was barely enough to make much difference. Fallon had at least laid in a good stock of wine for the occasion, and he dutifully filled their glasses during the small talk.

Bishop nodded to Fallon over the wine. "By God, sir, you have a fast ship," he said with admiration. "Fairly blew by us easy as kiss my hand." He chuckled to both of the other captains, who seemed neither surprised nor much interested. "A good ship in a good wind, Captain Bishop, sometimes she gets a bone in her teeth," replied Fallon, accepting the compliment on behalf of the ship.

Smithers shifted his weight. The pleasantries of small talk over several glasses of wine were not for him. It went on like that for a few more minutes more until, finally, with a nod to Wallace, Smithers cut to the chase. "Captain Bishop, what are you going to do about the pirates, the bloody buggers?" he demanded.

Wallace blurted out: "We want your protection, Captain." He glared at Bishop with squinty eyes, as if trying to read fine print.

Bishop's face hardened momentarily, hearing it like an order. Then he recovered himself and smiled. "Our plan, exactly, Wallace. We'll get you past the Bahamas safe as houses, mark my word." Here he looked at Fallon for confirmation, clearly having no other thoughts of his own. Fallon was running through an idea in his mind, the hair on his arms beginning to stand up. It would be risky; if it should fail he would face humiliation or worse, and the captains had to buy it.

"Yes, I believe we can get you to Charleston safely," he said softly, the cabin collectively exhaling, and Bishop looking relieved. "But not as you may think."

SIXTEEN

FALLON FOUND Nilson and Hewes in the office the next day. It was an unusually warm morning, even for July, and both men were working in shirtsleeves. They looked up with surprise when he stepped across the threshold; surprise turned to annoyance when he closed the door and shut out the breeze.

"Gentlemen, good morning to you both," Fallon began. "As we will be leaving soon I wanted to let you know our sailing plan."

"Excellent, Captain," said Nilson. "You'll be escorting our ships, I presume?"

Here was the moment.

"We are sending the salt ships along the leeward passage and up through the Florida Straights," Fallon said. He could see the instant dislike of the plan on their faces, but he continued. "It will take a bit longer, but it is the safer route, I believe. I will escort them in *Sea Dog*. Captain Bishop has his orders to deal with Clayton and will sail the windward passage hoping to discover his hiding place and ferret him out. I'll join him after we're past Spanish Florida and the ships are on their way to Charleston."

"But that will throw the schedule off, Captain!" protested Hewes indignantly. "We're already late, drastically late, due to *Calypso's* loss. And surely with a British frigate as escort—"

"I think, Hewes, the captain has a very good plan," interrupted Nilson. "Clayton has always attacked our ships on the windward passage. This is quite clever."

"Why not send the ships on the windward passage under the protection of the frigate?" countered Hewes. "Clayton wouldn't dare attack a frigate!"

"He attacked and took a Spanish frigate, sir," countered Fallon. "Have no doubt of his abilities. And remember, he is probably not sailing alone."

Silence hung in the air like a bad smell. Hewes absorbing the delay in schedule, no doubt running numbers in his head, not liking the change of route. Nilson looking at Fallon curiously. Finally, Nilson raised his hands in surrender. "Whatever you think best, Captain. I am sure you and Captain Bishop know your business. I suppose a small delay is nothing as long as the ships get there, eh, Hewes?" He paused to look at Fallon. "But Captain, these ships *must* get to Charleston."

There was more than a plea in his voice. There was a threat.

BACK ABOARD *Sea Dog*, Fallon called Beauty into his cabin to describe the meeting with Nilson and Hewes and the trap he hoped he had set. Now it remained for Beauty to organize a party to go ashore and *discreetly* watch and wait for further developments. Beauty suggested Cully lead the group, and Fallon agreed. They were to leave immediately and report back at dawn the next day.

Then Fallon called for his gig and crew to row him to *Harp*. As he approached the side he reviewed the events of last night in his mind. Smithers and Wallace had initial objections to the leeward passage, it being less familiar, often shallow, and taking longer, but the promise of escorts persuaded them. In return, Fallon insisted they keep the plan to themselves.

ONCE FALLON was on board *Harp*, the first lieutenant—Ramsbottom was his name—showed him below to the captain's cabin. Bishop had just refilled his wine glass, and as he brought it to his lips he gave Fallon a particularly ugly look. Clearly he was still perturbed at having had no part in the creation of Fallon's plan.

"Captain Fallon. I assume you informed Mr. Nilson of your thinking and he agreed?" Bishop asked with something very like a sneer.

"Yes, I did earlier today," replied Fallon, ignoring Bishop's rude manner. "Except for one detail. I told him you were sailing the windward passage alone while I escorted the ships through the leeward passage. He and Hewes balked at first, but I told them you had your orders to capture or kill Clayton. Not avoid him."

Bishop fairly spit out his wine. "You told them what? How dare you bandy with my orders!"

Fallon had anticipated an explosion, and he reacted coolly. "Captain Wallace told me that he'd personally rescued the crew of one of the last salt ships taken, and the men said it seemed like the pirates sailed out from behind an island at the exact moment they approached. Suppose, sir, that Clayton has an ally on Grand Turk, an accomplice, someone who reports to him when the ships are about to leave. It would only take a few days to sail up the Bahamas to deliver the news. A few coins would exchange hands and the business would be done."

Bishop looked flustered. "Good God! Are you saying Clayton is lying in wait like a snake in the grass?" The conversation was clearly getting away from him.

"I wonder enough about it to be on guard. These ships are easy prey for him, not much fight in them, and profitable. For all we know he's picking off our ships and selling our salt and ships to the United States!"

"But why lie about the windward route?" Bishop objected. "Why not just *take* the windward route?"

"In spite of what I said to Nilson, I doubt if even Wicked Jak Clayton would attack a prize with a British frigate and heavily armed schooner as escorts," Fallon replied. "We might well see our salt ships safely to Charleston if we took that route, but we would be no closer to putting an end to this menace. Your orders are to find Clayton, and you've convinced me to help you execute them."

Bishop's eyebrows shot up. *He had?* Perhaps this young captain had listened to him, after all. *Really?* Well, that put a different odor on things, yes it did. Bishop's bearings began to come back through an alcoholic haze. This was more like it; he felt back in charge, *somehow.*

"So, if my suspicions are correct," Fallon continued, "word will get out to Clayton's earpiece that two ships laden with salt and only lightly defended by a schooner will sail the leeward passage. He would have time to shift his position and be ready for us. And we shall be ready for him!"

Fallon paused, *hope for the best, plan for the worst.* "I will have men posted around the harbor tonight and tomorrow watching small craft leave. These locals know the waters like the back of their hands. It would be nothing to sail off at night, pretending to be fishing. So we shall see."

Bishop's mouth was a snarl. "Really, sir, you have taken very independent action, I must say. All this is so much speculation without any proof. I must protest, Captain Fallon. You presume too much. Too much by far!"

"Captain Bishop," said Fallon, losing patience, "you asked that we sail together to stop Clayton. And we shall. If I am wrong about a conspiracy, we will have a comfortable passage through the Florida Straights and on to Charleston. That would be an excellent outcome, don't you agree?"

Cold logic shot through the warm cabin air like a weather front. Bishop glared at Fallon with a mixture of astonishment and envy but was deeply, secretly relieved to have the burden of decisive action off his shoulders, and more relieved still to be sailing in company.

"Captain, this will not work without your support. I hope you know that," Fallon said, coming with flattery, the coup de grâce.

"I will consider it, sir," said Bishop, almost back to full color. "The plan may have some merit, I believe."

And with that, the meeting was over.

+ ✦ +

THE SLIVER of moon rose over the island before midnight, casting faint shadows on the salt pans. It was cooler now, a steady breeze pushing small waves against the shore. A noiseless evening, and Cully sat quietly against a palm tree, invisible in the darkness.

He had been careful to place his men thoughtfully around the harbor, near moored sailing craft or boats pulled up on the beach. They had idled there all afternoon, lazily passing time, and then melted into the shadows at dusk.

On his own initiative, Cully had visited the Somers office earlier in the day and talked to Nilson and Hewes, ostensibly looking for his captain, but actually getting the lay of the land and the full picture in his mind. Land was always so complicated to navigate for a sailorman. Normally, Cully was a jovial sort, white hair in a long pigtail, a grin across his broad face. Tonight, though, he was a different sort, serious and intent, and he carried a marlinspike for small comfort. He had no idea what to expect, but his orders were clear: observe but don't interfere.

During the long night, the arc of moon was occasionally covered by cloud, at which point things got really dark. A brief shower, barely enough to soak his shirt, then brought clearing. Cully began to nod, then shook himself and pinched the skin on his hands to ward off sleep.

Suddenly he was fully awake, though. Silently, two men had stepped around the makeshift windmill used to pump water into the pans. They were talking quietly, one gesturing with his hands emphatically, the other listening. Cully figured they were perhaps one hundred feet away, still unrecognizable in the faint moonlight. They stopped at the water's edge, a final few low words, then one went into the water and began wading out to a small fishing boat tugging at her mooring. The other, the emphatic one, lingered a moment and then turned behind a large salt mound and disappeared into the shrub on the far side of the pans.

Cully froze, not knowing what to do, sworn not to interfere, but

knowing he had seen something important. The first man was raising sail already. Cully decided to follow the second.

He loped across the salt flat and entered the shrub, some of it
quite tall, at the spot where the second man had entered. He was on
a path, showing slightly lighter in color because of the sand, and he
could follow it with no difficulty. It wound in a lazy S for one hundred yards and opened onto a clearing on the edge of the settlement.
Obviously, it was the back door to the salt flats, no doubt used by
overseers and Nilson to get to the beach.

As Cully reached the clearing he saw the second man just disappear behind a building, and he sprinted to the spot. The man
continued walking maybe thirty yards along the main thoroughfare,
then cut off down a path to a cluster of low buildings. Past those
was a modest-sized cottage with a view of nothing much, a dark
silhouette against a darker sky. The man went inside. Cully moved
like a hunting cat along the side of the building. A candle was lit
inside, or a lantern, and a bit of light shown out the window not
ten feet away. He inched along the outside wall and peeked around
the corner window trim. He saw a plain enough room with simple
furnishings, a bookcase crammed with paper and books, and a few
chairs around a table where Hewes sat, just pouring himself a glass
of wine.

SEVENTEEN

THE FOUR ships left before dawn three days later.

Behind them a dark village, not yet awake, under a pin-pricked sky. Ahead lay uncertainty and risk and not inconsiderable danger.

They sailed north into open water, roughly in a straight line, but bearing off downwind before Maguana Island, fully committed to the leeward passage. Their course would take them through the Caicos Passage, and then past Crooked Island and Heneago Key's dangerous shoals before they would turn roughly northwest again toward the Great Bahamas Bank.

At the captain's meeting on *Harp* the evening before sailing, Bishop had been brief and direct, unsuccessfully trying to hide the fact that he was merely restating Fallon's idea. *Sea Dog* would take the lead with a sharp lookout, a local man borrowed from Smithers, who knew the inside route well, day or night. The Great Bahamas Bank was shallow and could get treacherous in a strong breeze, kicking up steep waves and pushing the unwary onto uncharted reefs. Consequently, they would shorten sail at dusk in the evening, if it came to that, moving cautiously, burning blue lights off their sterns to keep track of one another: *Sea Dog*, then *Desmond* and *Castille*, followed a mile astern by *Harp*.

They had reviewed the signals carefully, with Fallon explicit on the point of staying together if attacked. In that event, the plan called for *Desmond* and *Castille* to sail ahead, in effect to run for it, while *Sea Dog* entertained Clayton until Bishop could sail up to them and open fire. The plan put Fallon at great risk, but he had the faster, more maneuverable ship; Bishop had the firepower. Bishop had tried to appear clever during the meeting; in fact, he intended to lie back even farther than a mile, he had said, so that Clayton would be sure to take the bait before he engaged.

THE FIRST few days had been uneventful, with *Sea Dog* sailing under reduced sail to keep the packets close. Thankfully, there were no sightings of any strange ships. Each night Fallon ordered the sails reefed even further, and the other ships followed suit, each burning blue lights to keep one another in sight. Mornings found them all together, to Fallon's great relief.

The middle of the third day, the little fleet was on the leeward side of the Bahamas' chain of islands; once around Acklins Key they were on the Bank, the shallow water growing lighter in color. They could see large turtles swimming under them and the occasional barracuda. They were on a beam reach now, Cuba on their larboard side with its many shoals and coral heads, and up ahead Verde Island, which they would need to cut inside to leave to larboard. Fallon gave the order to harden up early so that the less weatherly square-rigged ships could pass the island safely.

"Mast there," he yelled to the lookout. "Keep a weather eye on those islands!" Fallon could feel his body on high alert, on edge, every mile seeming to prove that his suspicions about a spy on the island were absurd. But Cully's report had convinced him he was right. Hewes was their man, a little man with a mean life toiling at the end of the world who saw an opportunity to make his fortune. Perhaps to escape. Who knew? Well, there would be time enough to deal with him when he returned to Grand Turk. *If he returned.*

On the chance that he might not, Fallon had left a letter for Ezra Somers with a dock boy to be placed on the next Bermuda packet. He had outlined his impressions of the Grand Turk operation, the brusque and self-important Nilson, the ferret Hewes. He had included Cully's observations of three nights ago, knowing that Somers would know what to do in the event Fallon was not successful against Clayton. Either way, Hewes was not long for Grand Turk.

The little string of ships wound their way up the Bahama Bank on the leeward route. Past Mucares Island, Ragged Island, and Lobos Key. Other than a few small fishing boats, nothing. The tension on the ship was palpable, with Beauty thumping along with her peg leg to check tackles and stays more than once, the crew silent and tense. Up ahead was Exuma off their starboard side; it called for a decision whether to leave the three islands of Andros off to their larboard or starboard. The wind was veering more northerly here, and Fallon made the decision to leave Andros to starboard so as to comfortably weather it without forcing his charges to tack in order to pass it. He wondered what was going through Bishop's mind. Was he hoping for battle with Clayton, or not?

Fallon trained his telescope on the gaps between the three islands, searching for signs of a mast. The wind was coming back more easterly now as they cleared the lee of Exuma, and he began to doubt himself again for his conspiracy theories. *Well, damn it,* he thought, *what was Hewes doing at the salt pans then?*

On they sailed toward a cluster of small islands, which they would leave to starboard, and then ahead was fairly open water after they rounded Great Bahama Island. The day was warm and beautiful, the air bright and warming.

A cluster of birds rose squawking from the islands ahead. Fallon was about to remark to Beauty that he wondered why they were disturbed when he found out.

"Deck there!" called the lookout. "Two sail coming out from Cat Key. One's a ship!"

Fallon and Beauty whipped their telescopes forward. In the small, upside-down image, Fallon could see a large frigate's bowsprit just appearing from behind the island, the other pirate ship not yet visible from the deck. Apparently, Clayton had a lookout on shore who'd seen the salt convoy approaching.

"Beauty," Fallon called, "call all hands and signal to the ships: *Enemy in sight*. God help us they follow orders."

The picture was quickly becoming clear. *Renegade* moved slowly out from the island, sailing as close as possible on the wind, looking dark and menacing. Close behind her came a sloop, nimble and handy and no doubt loaded with extra hands to handle prizes. Fallon studied them carefully, wondering how they would work it. He hoped Bishop could see Clayton and even then was setting more sail to close the gap, but he couldn't take his attention off the pirate ship and her sloop; what they did would determine what he did. He had run through this in his mind, of course, and had considered his options. At all costs he had to protect the salt packets until Bishop could close; then the battle would be even. Until then, *Sea Dog*'s crew had to be ready for any order.

He looked at Beauty. Her face seemed strained and pale. Well, a ship coming toward you with maybe a 5-1 size and gunnery advantage would do that to you. The pirate's sloop was a yellowish color, that was plain now. She had inched ahead, leading the way, closing at perhaps sixteen knots with the combined speeds of the two vessels. Time was running out for a decision. Fallon quickly looked back to the packets. Thank God they had followed *Sea Dog*'s example and had shaken out their reefs, and they were sticking together. Beyond them he could see *Harp* through his telescope, more than a mile away. Why was Bishop taking longer to catch up than he ought?

Fallon's plan was to divert attention away from *Desmond* and *Castille*, harassing Clayton without being overwhelmed by boarding or losing a spar or being shot to pieces. But first, the yellow sloop.

"Beauty, hold course for the sloop's bows, and have all guns loaded with grape. Then run out on the larboard side," he ordered. "We'll head up at the last moment and rake him. Elevate to sweep the decks. An extra tot for all hands if the captain falls."

"But Nico," Beauty objected, "do you want to signal your plan so soon?"

"Yes, I want the yellow sloop to know," Fallon said emphatically. "But more important, I want Clayton to believe he's up against a nincompoop captain. Which he probably is, you know." This with a smile, though tense. Beauty returned the smile, with a wink, getting the plan now and wondering for a moment how she ever beat this man around the buoys in St. George's Harbor.

On they came, separated by only a quarter mile now. Time enough to contemplate your mortality, your lover, or whatever men thought about during the moments before imminent death. Beauty had put Cully in charge of the guns, while she took the helm, trusting no one more than herself to the coming maneuver. Fallon looked over his shoulder briefly, *where was* Harp?

One hundred yards. Fifty. Twenty-five. *Now, Beauty, now!*

Beauty headed up just as the two bowsprits all but touched, blowing by the yellow sloop to windward. *"Fire!"* Fallon ordered, and *Sea Dog's* larboard guns fired independently as they bore, raking the yellow sloop's decks with grapeshot, clusters of small iron balls flying at almost seventeen hundred feet per second. Smoke engulfed *Sea Dog's* larboard side and blew across the yellow sloop as she fired her guns in response. Every shot seemed to tell, as Sea Dogs flew across the deck in the concussion of cannon fire. An arm cartwheeled over the starboard railing, its owner stunned into insensibility. Cedar splinters flew into soft flesh and blood splashed across the decks. The shock was stupendous in such close action, and Fallon fought to take in the destruction while readying for the next onslaught from the frigate ahead. Ship's boys were helping the crew drag the wounded below, pulling the dead or near-dead to the center of the deck.

Fallon checked Beauty with a nod. The ship was battered but intact, and Clayton was almost upon them. *Sea Dog's* larboard guns were reloaded and run out, but the starboard crews were at the ready, as well, their guns loaded with grape. *Renegade* seemed enormous, like a wooden battering ram bearing down on them, deadly and all-powerful, showing her larboard side guns. Beauty sailed *Sea Dog* straight toward her bows, as before, timing the move, holding her nerve until the last moment. Now! *Sea Dog* ducked low, her starboard guns running out with effort against the heel of the ship.

"*Fire!*" yelled Fallon, hoarse from excitement and rage against the odds. The iron balls flew across *Renegade's* decks, through the soft flesh of human bodies and canvas sails and the wooden ship's boats, sending splinters flying through the smoke like knives. Clayton was caught off guard by the maneuver; Fallon spotted him on the quarterdeck as the smoke blew past, wide-eyed in anger and disbelief at having been fooled, screaming at his stunned men to run out the starboard guns, but it was too late. In a flash *Sea Dog* was past without suffering a shot, already rounding up on Clayton's stern, and with one carronade saved for this moment, firing into her name board and blowing the name *Renegade* apart.

"Hurry, you men, clear the deck of that wreckage! Reload both sides again!" yelled Fallon, mad with fighting. "Beauty, back to the ships quickly!"

Sea Dog came about on larboard as Beauty quickly tacked through the eye of the wind and behind *Renegade*. Fallon could see the pirate ship's shattered stern and her men fighting to cut loose the wreckage of a lost mizzenmast. It had been a lucky shot, but they would need luck today. Up ahead the yellow sloop had swooped in amongst the packets, loosing a ragged broadside that appeared to have mostly missed the rigging, while the packets fired off their popguns to little effect, though their bravery buoyed Fallon. *Sea Dog's* broadside had put holes in the sloop's sails and dead men were being thrown overboard so, that was something.

Where was Harp? *Goddamn it!*

Sea Dog was on a fast beam reach now, gaining almost two feet of distance for every one of *Renegade's*. Fallon did not want to overtake her, though, did not want under her guns. He looked down the deck and saw Mr. Boy by the companionway, against his orders to stay below. He was staring at Clayton's ship, trembling, shaking his fists in the air. Fallon wanted to get him below but there was no time.

The packets would take their punishment, no doubt; even now *Renegade* was running out her larboard guns. But Fallon was counting on Clayton trying to dismast the packets and to shoot away rigging, crippling them for boarding later. Here was where Bishop would come into action according to the plan: a pincer attack with *Renegade* and the yellow sloop caught between *Harp* and *Sea Dog*.

So much war in one piece of air. The horizon was virtually blotted out by smoke between the salt ships and *Renegade*. The yellow sloop had rounded and was coming up the windward side of the packets, preparing to unleash another volley. Beauty eased *Sea Dog's* sails out to pick up speed and made to pass between the yellow sloop and the ships, all pretense and ruse gone now, *Sea Dog* running out her larboard guns.

"*Fire!*" Fallon ordered, and the entire broadside went home. Smoke blew back over *Sea Dog*, blinding the gun crews as they bent to reloading, filling the air with an acrid smell. They were close enough to the yellow sloop to hear screams of agony from across the water. Then came the answer from the sloop and the world seemed to stop. *Sea Dog* shook from the blast of a point-blank broadside. Guns were upended, cannonballs cut down men and material, and the ship seemed a wounded thing. The smoke blew over the ship briefly before the devastation was revealed: men blown open with their bowels laying on deck, their blood splattered on the faces of the living, a seaman at Number Four gun staring stupidly at the place where his leg used to be. Boys hauled the wounded below as best they could, for no man could be spared. Pence would have his hands full down there, thought Fallon.

Fallon turned to Beauty and saw her dazed but steady, her hands like iron on the wheel. He quickly surveyed the rigging—*Sea Dog* still sailed! A shot hole in the mainsail but all standing rigging still stood. A weak cheer went up from the men, and Fallon looked over his shoulder at the yellow sloop—her mainmast had fallen over and she'd sluiced around, helpless, with the big spar dragging rigging overboard to act like an enormous sea anchor. Now was the time to finish her off, thought Fallon ruefully, but even now *Renegade* was approaching *Desmond*. Smithers had sensibly ordered all the crew except gunners to lie down on the deck to avoid slaughter.

Fallon scanned the horizon for *Harp*, who should just now be approaching the battle, running out her guns and preparing to engage. Smoke was hanging in the air and it was difficult to see ahead. But here came Smithers, bravely firing *Desmond*'s few guns into *Renegade* and in turn receiving a hail of metal into her stout sides and delicate rigging. Next came *Castille*, having to absorb only a partial broadside as Captain Wallace had sailed close astern *Desmond*, as Fallon had ordered, giving *Renegade* little time to reload.

The salt packets sailed past *Sea Dog* and on toward the yellow sloop, which was in no position to stop them. Both *Castille* and *Desmond* opened fire on her still, more in anger now than self-defense, and it cheered Fallon to see it.

Suddenly the air was rent by two broadsides screaming at once as *Harp* finally arrived and *Renegade* stood to meet her. *Thwump! Thwump! Thwump!* The cannon roared and echoed as the two ships fired at less than two cables' length. Fallon had to tear his eyes from the action because his own ship badly needed his attention. Men were dying on deck and those who lived were horribly concussed and must be roused to action. Here was Cully sprawled near the mainmast, one leg useless and Mr. Boy attempting to drag him away. Becker lay near his station at the helm, his once-worried eyes staring at the blue sky, unworried at the last, his body torn in half, guts pooled like jelly. Fallon's bile caught in his throat but his mind fought it down. *Sea Dog* was in a dangerous position still, well within range of *Renegade*'s cannon if she should break off from *Harp*. *He had to take command.*

"Beauty," he yelled, "come about and—"

But out came *Renegade*'s guns on the larboard side as *Sea Dog* turned, exposing her starboard side to the full weight of the frigate's metal. Eighteen guns belched fire and iron across a sliver of water, hell erupting all around the schooner as the shots told and the ship shuddered. *Sea Dog*'s bowsprit was blasted to kindling and fell over the side with sail and rigging, and the ship was slowed to a crawl. Fallon wheeled around, astonished that *Renegade* had broken off the fight with *Harp*—but no! *Harp* had broken off, by God, broken off and was sailing away! *Bishop was leaving them, Goddamn his eyes!*

Beauty had given over the helm and left to take charge of cutting the fallen rigging away when Fallon saw *Renegade*'s guns run out again. *Oh God, please not again* was the last coherent thought in Fallon's mind before the next broadside sent the world to total blackness.

EIGHTEEN

MOTHER, AM I going to die?
When young Nicholas Fallon fell out of the tree, he hit his head so hard he saw stars, or at least little pricks of light, which fascinated him momentarily and kept the news of his broken ankle from reaching his brain. He was seven years old and adventurous and the tree had begged him to climb up and take a look at the world from up there, so one afternoon he did.

His father had carried him to the pub and upstairs to his room, unconscious. The doctor was sent for, and Nico's mother pulled off his clothes, which is when his swollen ankle was discovered and the story of his fall from grace began to reveal itself. He was still unconscious when the doctor arrived and began his examination, and he did not regain consciousness until an hour later.

His mother never left his side, stroking his hair and singing softly to him, reaching into his mind with her voice. In some way he could hear her voice still, hear the soft song calling to him to wake up, as he had done years ago, to ask the question again.

Am I going to die?

NINETEEN

IT WAS unbearably hot in the little huts where the prisoners were kept. The three huts were strung out on a low rise with a rock wall behind them, blocking the wind, their fronts looking out on the harbor where three ships tugged gently on their anchor rodes, pumps working on the sloop and the schooner every three hours to keep them floating. Two pirate guards, one at either end of the line of huts, sat under lean-tos with muskets, a bucket of water at their sides. They were dirty and bored and partially drunk; well, it had been over a week since the battle. The only entertainment had been the two wounded prisoners who went raving mad before they died, hallucinating and calling for angels to take them to heaven. That may have happened, but they left without their bodies, which the pirates dragged to the beach and tossed in the surf so the barracuda could eat them.

One long hut held *Sea Dog's* healthiest crewmen, that is to say the least grievously wounded; one held Fallon and several seriously wounded; and one held slaves taken from a slaver some weeks before—males only, for female slaves were never kept because they could not handle severe manual labor and would only cause fighting among the men to claim them. Every morning the slaves and the seamen who were healthy enough to work were marched to the beach and rowed out to the ships to pump in shifts, patch the hulls, and replace rigging. The pirates themselves did nothing but drink and lie under the trees. Except for Wicked Jak Clayton, who had a pirate woman with him and rarely came out of his hut. When he did appear, he was usually the worse for drink and in foul humor, having himself rowed out to the ships to inspect the work and, if he found fault, shooting someone for it.

He was a large man, with long black hair tied in a queue held by a scarlet ribbon. His face showed a sparse, ragged beard, with pockmarked skin and a bulbous nose that somehow was off center. Oddly, his voice was of a higher register, quite high when he screamed, which was often, and when he laughed, which was less often.

Several times Clayton had personally inspected the huts with the guards, commanding them to watch this prisoner or that one carefully. He was particularly interested in Fallon and whether he would live, for he particularly wanted him to. He had a plan for him if he did.

It was not clear if Fallon would accommodate him. He had been unconscious since the main boom had fallen on him like a tree, striking a glancing blow off his head before he could jerk completely away. If he didn't awaken soon he would die of starvation or dehydration, or just plain die.

Beauty was in the hut with him. Though she was not hurt seriously—a lacerated arm from a sword—Clayton allowed her to tend Fallon in the hopes that she would have a positive effect on his progress. Cully was in the hut as well, his fractured leg having been set by Pence before the doctor died clutching his heart and was then fed to the barracuda. Two other seamen—the Swedes—were also in Fallon's hut and slowly recovering from puncture wounds and splinters; they would live if infection didn't do for them.

Beauty bathed all their wounds in seawater each day, the salt helping to heal them. She demanded a fresh bucket every morning; the guards refused at first but a swift kick to the groin of the biggest guard—causing a rare high laugh from Clayton—had the desired effect and a bucket of seawater was at the hut's doorway every morning thereafter.

Mr. Boy had been shoved into the slave hut, still uncommunicative except for his obvious concern for Cully and Fallon. At night he would pry open a board in his hut and crawl between buildings on all fours. Then, at Fallon's hut, he would push aside another board and crawl inside, saying nothing, just sitting on his haunches and staring wide-eyed in the darkness from the corner. Beauty would nod, letting him know things were unchanged, and the boy would leave as silently as he came.

The days passed like this, repetitive and punishing, with the healthy men going to work and the wounded struggling to live, fighting infection and flies and malnutrition.

And then one afternoon Fallon opened his eyes.

"Mother, am I going to die?" he asked softly.

Beauty's hand froze on Fallon's forehead, the wet rag sending rivulets down his temples and into his ears.

"I hope the hell not, you fucker," she gushed in shock. "Or I've wasted my best years taking care of you." She smiled, tears shooting from her eyes in spite of her usual stoicism. "God, you gave me a scare, Nico. Oh, my God, you're back from the dead."

Fallon managed the smallest smile himself, too weak to say more. Beauty tilted his head to take fresh water, while Cully and the Swedes crawled over to him smiling with joy.

"You're going to be all right, Nico," soothed Beauty. "Goddamn it you are."

"Where are we? What happened? How long . . . ?"

Beauty shushed him. "Not now. We're prisoners somewhere is what I know. Some island where Clayton hides out. I think it's Rum Cay. You need to drink some water now." And with that she ladled a little more fresh water into his mouth, and after he swallowed he closed his eyes and went back to sleep.

Beauty studied his face. His beard was growing and covered much of the bruising from the boom, and he had withered. His broad shoulders and chest had shed muscle, which was most of the weight he'd lost. She thought about how much she should tell him, how to spoon-feed him the scale of their disaster and their predicament.

Sea Dog had lost more than forty seamen to outright killing or mortal wounds, which left them with nearly thirty in some sort of condition. When Fallon had gone down, they had fought gamely, with Beauty directing the battle until Clayton had moved to board the schooner and the hand-to-hand fighting had begun. Pirates swarmed over the side, screaming wildly, and Beauty had been wounded by a particularly fierce and ugly brute before pushing a pike through his chest. Seeing her men butchered and falling around her, with no hope of retreat, she had sunk to the deck in exhaustion and surrendered the ship.

Sea Dog had suffered horribly. Her bowsprit was gone, and with it the foresail and rigging. The main boom was on the deck, having detached from the mainmast to fall onto Fallon. Five guns had been totally upended, the deck gouged with deep furrows from cannon shot, and the helm all but shot away. Men and human parts were strewn on the deck like branches after a windstorm.

When Clayton had leapt aboard he had demanded to see the captain, and Beauty's eyes had inadvertently glanced toward Fallon's inert body, his legs protruding from under the mainsail, which the boom had pulled down. It had taken ten men to lift the boom off Fallon, it being the size of a tree, and Clayton had stared for a moment at his body, sizing up the man who had cost him two prizes, which were now over the horizon, not to mention a dismasted sloop and lost men.

The least wounded seamen were forced below decks, the dead were thrown overboard, the badly wounded left where they lay, and *Renegade* took *Sea Dog* under tow. The yellow sloop was left to fend for itself. All that afternoon and night they progressed slowly, *Sea Dog* trailing astern, a pirate prize crew aboard and in command. Below decks Beauty could sense they were sailing southeast, the way they had come through the Caicos Passage, and then the next day they had turned north, the wind now on starboard. Some days later they arrived at a small, rocky island with a tiny cove on the leeward side where Jak Clayton could anchor unknown and undetected. It was a perfect spot to hide, near the traditional route of salt packets and other prizes coming from the south.

If it was indeed Rum Cay, which Beauty had guessed, it was about ten square miles, with coral outcroppings and a few trees ringing the cove. The cove itself was a pristine Caribbean scene, with three ships at anchor, swaying palms on shore, marred only by the ramshackle huts and lean-tos. At the far end of the cove, a larger hut, almost a bungalow, and a number of smaller huts. At the near or eastern end, a string of smaller huts perched higher on a hill. It was to these huts the prisoners were escorted, with guards posted, their own ship's food and water served to them. Fallon had been carried on a makeshift stretcher by his own men, as gently as they could carry him, though he never moved or groaned.

By midnight the cove was quiet. The torches were all but extinguished. The mood among the pirates was subdued and defeated. They had lost two fat prizes to a single schooner, a mystery to them. And a source of deep anger and humiliation to Wicked Jak Clayton.

TWENTY

IN TIME, the small packet carrying mail and supplies reached
Bermuda, having sailed from Trinidad and called at Grand
Turk Island for passengers and mail before sailing north again.
Ezra Somers was at work at his desk, and Elinore had just brought
lunch for the two of them. Somers could not help noticing the
change in his daughter's demeanor, her attentiveness to him, her *respect*. Why this had suddenly happened he hadn't a clue, but a bond
was growing between them, he knew that. He was worried lest he
say or do anything to break it.

The dock boy brought the mail from Grand Turk, the usual reports from Nilson along with the news that there was no news of
the lost ship. A letter of a different sort, addressed in a different
hand, was the last item to leave the mailbag. Somers took a bite of
lunch and opened it.

Elinore took notice when he stopped chewing. She saw a dark
shadow cross her father's face and worry creep into his eyes. She
had seen her father in times of stress, had seen him hunker down to
battle, and knew this was one of those times.

Slowly he passed the first page to her. Though she had never
seen Fallon's handwriting, she knew immediately it was from him.
The letter outlined his feelings about Nilson and followed with his
initial suspicion about Hewes. It described his plan to flush the
rabbit, and Cully's observations at the salt pans and later through
the window at Hewes's cottage. The second page, now passed to

Elinore, described Fallon's plan to winkle Clayton into battle with Bishop, his meeting with the Captains Smithers and Wallace, and his hope to return home to Grand Turk within a month.

The last page presupposed that might not happen. Fallon asked that he be remembered to Elinore, whom he had grown to love, not wanting to die without Ezra Somers knowing it, not wanting to betray the trust between the two men. Somers dropped the third page on the table and closed his eyes. Elinore picked up the page, read it with fear and courage in equal parts gathering inside her, and waited for her father's probable explosion.

Instead, wisdom made an appearance. Unannounced as such, but dressed for the occasion.

"Elinore," he said as he opened his eyes, "it's been almost three weeks since he wrote this letter. We need to know what's going on. And I need to deal with this bastard Hewes. Maybe Nilson, too. But most important, let's find out about your young man. Would you like to come with me to Grand Turk?"

THEY LEFT on a Bermuda sloop after hurriedly arranging and provisioning for the brief trip south. The fresh breeze was invigorating and the trades carried the sloop quickly toward southern waters. Somers and Elinore spent most of their days below as the wind blew spume and spray across the decks; the sloop heeling dramatically, carrying perhaps more sail than was prudent, but Somers demanded speed. Below decks, a reunion of two people who basically had lived together their whole lives without noticing the color of the other's eyes.

For Somers, the discovery of a daughter's love that he thought he had lost, if he ever had it at all, was overwhelming—joyous, astonishing—name the word. All his life he had longed for the closeness that he found below decks as the sloop thrashed along to God-knew-what future. And for Elinore, sharing the secret of her love for Fallon, *saying it out loud*, freed her from her father's judgment and made him her friend, finally.

When the sloop dropped anchor at last in Cockburn Harbor, two very different people disembarked. Nilson, who had come down at word of a strange ship coming into the harbor, saw with surprise that it was the owner and his daughter aboard, and he noticed they were holding hands as they stepped ashore.

CAPTAIN HAMMERSMITH Bishop watched the Bermuda sloop sail into Cockburn Harbor and drop anchor as well, and had an uneasy feeling. Since returning to Grand Turk for repairs to his ship and recuperation from his wound, he had been engaged in enlarging his role in getting the salt packets through to safety and decrying his inability to save *Sea Dog*. Well, it had been smoky and hot work that day and, what with his wound, it *was* difficult to remember events clearly. The pain he felt when Number Two gun had recoiled over his smallest toe, however, was real and clear. Even if it had been something of a lubber's mistake, the toe had to be amputated and his foot still hurt like hell and he limped when he went ashore.

That was not often. Shame and cowardice have a way of working on a man's soul, even a man skilled at pretense, and Bishop left his ship, indeed his cabin, less and less. Thank God he had a large store of wine aboard, for he had a bottle open continuously. His men hung their heads as they went about their duties, for you could not fool a seaman with pomp and gold lace, and they knew their captain's cowardice had brought shame upon the ship. Even the bosun's starter snapped with less pop on the men's backsides, such was the black mood aboard.

Bishop had kept the truth of the battle with *Renegade* from Nilson, who had been congratulatory and appeared relieved that the biggest shipment they had for some time had made it through to Charleston. Nilson gave full credit to Bishop, who accepted it gratefully. Of course, Nilson had asked about Captain Fallon, though in truth he'd said he found him personally disagreeable. And, he noted, he had questioned the plan to sail the leeward passage but Fallon was insistent, even arrogant as he recalled. Still,

Clayton seemed to have supernatural powers, somehow finding his prey no matter what the route, and he would be a constant menace until brought to heel. Bishop offered that he would be back in action soon after the repairs to *Harp* were completed. Perhaps next week she could resume her mission.

Now Bishop wondered about the older man and younger woman disembarking from the Bermuda sloop and being rowed to the dock. Who were they and why were they here? It was curious, odd, in fact. In his present state of mind he didn't like surprises. His uneasiness only grew as he watched the old man stride quickly up the dock, limping a bit, but with purpose and passion in his step, like one-half a collision searching for the other.

TWENTY-ONE

SOMETIME IN the middle of the night Fallon awoke. He had been dreaming again, this time of Elinore, and his mind fought gamely to relive each detail. When he found he could not, he opened his eyes. Beauty was asleep close by, the Swedes asleep in the back of the hut, Cully asleep near the door, bathed in moonlight, and Mr. Boy was squatting in the corner with those wide eyes. Fallon tried to smile, and the boy smiled back, and then silently left on all fours, crawling under the loose board in the back of the hut.

Now the events of the battle with Clayton, and the betrayal and cowardice of Bishop came back to Fallon, albeit through a splitting headache. He could see it all unfold slowly: his decisions and orders, the acrid smell of powder, the concussive blast of *Sea Dog*'s first broadside, the thunderous crash as *Renegade* loosed her own broadside into his frail ship. His last memory was watching in disbelief as *Harp* sailed away, and then the world went dark. Beauty had said they were prisoners now, confined by Clayton on a small island in the Bahamas. He had to know more: Where were the other prisoners? What of his ship? Questions that had no answers in the middle of the night.

Morning came, and with it Jak Clayton, a bit blurry to Fallon's eyes, but impressively big and, truth be told, wicked-looking all the same. Beauty was feeding Fallon a little gruel when the pirate stood over them both, hands on hips, an amused smile on his face.

"So, Captain, we meet on my little island," said Clayton in his falsetto voice. "You seem to be recovering, which is good because I do not like to hang a wounded man. The men take it badly, thinking it's bad luck or some other rot. On the other hand, I may not hang you at all. You could be useful to me in other ways, perhaps as a captain, eh?"

"I would rather hang than help you, Clayton," answered Fallon through clenched teeth. "So get your rope ready."

"Ah, a brave captain," said Clayton. "Well, perhaps when you are fully aware of your predicament you will be more willing to talk about . . . options. For now, Captain, grow stronger. No matter your fate, I need you to at least be able to walk." With that, Clayton issued a high-pitched laugh that had the effect of freezing everyone, a cruelly feminine laugh that was as frightening as it was otherworldly. And then he was gone.

Beauty resumed feeding Fallon. "Now, that was scary," she said calmly, and Fallon thought he could see her spoon hand shaking. "Have you ever been hung before, Nico?"

"No," he croaked, "it will be something new."

Between mouthfuls, he listened to the full rundown on their situation on the island. Beauty had been careful in observing the changing of the guards, the distribution of prisoners, and the layout of the pirates' sleeping huts. Two guards were left on *Renegade* each night, no guards on *Sea Dog* or the yellow sloop, inexplicably named *Emerald*, which had limped in two days previously under jury rig. To Beauty's eye, it looked like repairs were very nearly complete on *Renegade*, while a new bowsprit had been fashioned for *Sea Dog* and the rigging was about to be run up. Her sides were still shot through, guns ahoo, but she still flew the British ensign.

"How are the men, Beauty?" Fallon asked.

"Well enough, I guess," she answered. "They know you're alive and that's picked up their morale. Every day they work on the ships with the slaves, but with no real effort. Clayton shot two of them— Bridges and Sloane—for insolence in the first week. Now everyone keeps their eyes down. Clayton's a brutal man, Nico, unpredictable and ruthless. His men are terrified of him—for good reason."

The little hut was growing warmer now, lighter, and Fallon could get a sense of it. Slabs of driftwood and planking made up the walls, with a sail fothered over the top as a roof. The floor was dirt; there was no door as such, just an opening that looked down to the beach and the ships, a languid and peaceful scene if you weren't a prisoner soon to be hanged.

"Beauty, how do we get out of here?" Fallon asked.

Beauty looked out the doorway to the beach, pensive. "I've been thinking on that, actually. Going through the options while waiting for you to join the living. Hard to coordinate anything with the men in the other hut, and then we've got the slaves who don't exactly speak the King's English. So, damned if I know. And Clayton may be crazy but he's not dumb. He's got guards on *Renegade* and a couple walking the beach at night. Some of them might be drunk, but they're still there, stumbling around with guns."

"So we're fucked, is what you're saying."

"Pretty much, Nico. Fucked."

TWENTY-TWO

ENGLISH HARBOR, Antigua, was full of ships coming and going; indeed, it was the liveliest harbor in the Caribbean. Also the most developed, with shops and government offices packed together above the beach, while pastel homes dotted the landscape like bright flowers in a forest of green hills.

Rear Admiral Sir Harry Davies was the senior naval officer in the Caribbean, based in Antigua, and his flag flew at the mast of *Avenger*, 74. Much of his time was spent with reports, the bane of senior officers on station, and the constant requests and negotiations with the Admiralty for more ships, more men, and less interference.

Davies had found the Caribbean simple and pleasant upon first arriving six months ago from his last commission in the Baltic. At first, he'd appreciated the contrast, the warm sun and languid pace. But in a short time the Caribbean had grown complicated and somewhat less pleasant as it revealed itself. First, there was the problem of pirates and French privateers—the same thing to his mind—all bastards. They were like damned mosquitoes, everywhere biting and sucking the blood out of the British Empire, everywhere until you tried to kill one and then off they flew. Second, the problem with slavers, or to be more precise, with his own conscience. There was a growing feeling in Parliament to take a stand against slavery, a movement that he personally subscribed to, but in the Caribbean it was business as usual and he was order bound to protect British slavers with the same zeal as attacking French or Spanish warships. Third, the French, and their constant taking and re-taking of Caribbean islands. The political map seemed to change monthly, or even weekly, as allies became enemies and friendly ports became dangerous.

The entire fleet under Davies numbered three sloops, two brigs, and two frigates—one of which was at the dockyard waiting for its copper to be refastened and the other supposedly patrolling for pirates, though there had been no news of success. In its way the Caribbean station was more frustrating and vexing than the Baltic, where at least his orders were clear and his mission understandable. Here, he was Lord Governor of a mess.

Davies was ashore often, in part to relieve the tedium of his duties aboard, and in part to find release in the company of his brown-skinned mistress, part French, part island mix, she of the dark eyes and light, quick hands. He was a handsome man of thirty-five years, lean and reasonably fit, and women had never been hard for him to find. He wore his blond hair in a club, for he had a reverence for the traditions of the Royal Navy with its prescribed order and regimen and *look*.

Today one of his sloops had brought mail from the north, including a report from Captain Hammersmith Bishop on his activities aboard HMS *Harp* trying to root out pirates in the Caribbean. Davies sat at his desk to read the report, the ship's work going on over his head and around him as he did so, but such was his focus on the document that he was oblivious to the sounds, which, at any rate, he had heard on a thousand mornings such as this.

He knew Bishop, of course, had in fact written the orders that sent him to Bermuda to put an end to a certain pirate in command of a captured Spanish frigate. Bishop had patronage in Parliament, having been put forward by his cousin Lord Delemere, who stood for East Londonderry. When Bishop had reported to him in Antigua, Davies had taken an instant dislike to the man. He was offensive in every way that mattered to Davies: a toady who had gotten his ship through influence, not qualifications; a captain more concerned with appearances than seamanship; a soft man in a hard business.

So, it was with unusual interest that Davies began to read Bishop's report. The more he read, the more he felt uneasy. It wasn't what was written—that was simple enough, in its way, placing a Bermuda privateer under his command, devising a plan to flush Clayton from his hiding place and force battle, the battle itself, casualties and his own wounding, though suspiciously vague. Then the pirate Jak Clayton escaping under the skirts of the salt packets, the smoke and confusion, such that *Harp* was unable to continue firing lest innocent people be killed and private shipping destroyed.

That was all easy enough to understand. But Davies didn't believe a word of it. Unable, or *unwilling* to continue battle? *That was the damned question,* and Davies thought he knew the answer.

That afternoon, he made his usual visit ashore to his always-willing mistress, forgetting Bishop and the war while her light hands moved over his body, first this, that, and the other thing. Her brown skin glistened from the heat and acrobatics as she finally arched over him, a groan in her throat, *le petit mort* she called it—the little death—exhausting her finally, *finally,* as she collapsed onto him, sweaty and spent, falling asleep almost instantly.

He lay awake, however, his mind slowly leaving her pleasures behind and returning to problems at hand, calling him back to his duty. *And that damned question.*

TWENTY-THREE

E ZRA SOMERS had hired Nilson because he was efficient and competent, and because few people wanted to take a job on a desolate, remote island in the business of shipping salt. Somers thought he had been fortunate; now he was not so sure.

He and Elinore followed Nilson from the dock toward the company's office, past the settlement's few shops, the noonday heat having driven most people to indoor shade. When they arrived they found Hewes was there, hunched over his books like a rodent feeding on cheese, and Elinore fixed him with a dark gaze.

There were no preliminaries to the conversation.

"Nilson, what news of Captain Fallon?" asked Somers. "We have heard nothing for weeks."

Nilson was clearly taken aback. "We know nothing more than what Captain Bishop of HMS *Harp* reported, Mr. Somers," he said defensively. "Captain Fallon led the packets through the leeward passage, where they were set upon by the pirate Clayton. Captain Bishop drove Clayton off, at great risk to his ship—he himself was wounded—and the packets got through, which is the main thing. Of Captain Fallon we have no word, and I presume he was either killed or captured or perhaps continued on with the packets to Charleston. Captain Bishop reports it was heavy going, and he lost track of *Sea Dog* in the intensity of the battle."

"You say they took the leeward passage," probed Somers. "Is that customary?" *Putting out the bait now.*

Nilson took it. "It was Fallon's plan, sir, to avoid Clayton. It seems it didn't work. If it weren't for Bishop deciding at the last to follow behind—locking the barn door, so to speak—it would likely have been a total loss all around, I'm sure."

Somers noticed Hewes out of the corner of his eye, pretending to add columns, trying to be invisible. Elinore had not taken her eyes off him and the man was sweating, drops dripping off his nose onto his precious numbers.

"Is Bishop aboard his ship?" asked Somers.

"I presume so, sir," answered Nilson. "I believe his recovery goes slowly, for I have not seen him for some time."

Somers was clearly inflamed, but under control. Nilson's report all sounded logical, that is if he hadn't had Fallon's letter in his breast pocket. "Come with me, Nilson. Let's take a walk to the salt pans. Afterward I shall call upon Captain Bishop. Elinore, would you please wait for me on the ship? I won't be long."

Elinore made for the door, hesitated with her hand on the knob and then turned around. "Mr. Nilson, you do not seem overly concerned with Captain Fallon's fate or the lives of his crew, all of whom are employed by the Somers Salt Company, *as you are at present*. All of whom are known to us, if not to you, while you, sir, are barely known to us at all."

With that, she was out the door.

The flame inside Ezra Somers was stoked higher, if possible. What a daughter he had! What a shot over the bow, just close enough to throw up spray in anticipation of real damage to come. Jesus, that was magnificent!

He followed Nilson out the door and down the path to the salt pans, without conversation, Nilson like a child heading to the woodshed. As they came to a clearing near the beach, Somers turned on him with a fury.

"Nilson, you are either a fool, or a liar, or perhaps both. There is treachery afoot, sir, and if you do not see it I can only conclude you may be part of it!"

Nilson made to answer but no words came forth. His face seemed to suddenly sag, taking all expression with it. He stared blankly at Somers, mouth open, his mind sounding retreat.

"You are fired, Nilson, gone like you never existed. You and that rat-faced clerk of yours. And I promise you this, sir: If Nicholas Fallon is not found safe, you will not be safe. Ever in this life. Mark me, for these are the last words you'll hear from me until Judgment Day. Pray for his safety, Nilson. Pray hard."

With that Somers turned and walked back up the path. Nilson sat down where he stood, put his head in his hands, and tried to breathe. But the air was hot, like fire, and he could not get his breath.

CAPTAIN BISHOP was alone in his cabin, dozing in an alcoholic stupor when he was awakened by Somers's hail asking permission to come aboard. After a few moments spent fumbling into his best uniform jacket, he received the two strangers into his quarters.

It was quickly apparent they were father and daughter and had specific questions regarding the loss of *Sea Dog*, a topic that put Bishop on guard and filled the crevices between his fat neck rolls with perspiration. He poured a glass to settle his nerves and offered the same to his guests, who declined.

"Captain Bishop," began Somers with an opaque look, "my daughter, Elinore, and I own the Somers Salt Company and Captain Fallon is an employee of ours. We are naturally trying to learn the details of the battle with Jak Clayton the day he was lost. Pray enlighten us."

Bishop considered. They seemed harmless, asking about an employee, but there was an edge in the old man's voice. An edge Bishop didn't care for at all. Proceed with caution, he told himself, and bear off slightly.

"Certainly, Mr. Somers, certainly," began Bishop, shifting his mass to be more comfortable for what he thought might be a long interview. "Captain Fallon and I agreed that the leeward passage would be safer to see the salt packets through to Charleston. We further agreed he should lead the van. He seemed capable enough in conversation, although not Royal Navy, to be sure." Here, he paused to let the shot go home; instead, he received a withering look from Elinore that told him perhaps he should stick to the story without editorial. He sipped his wine and continued cautiously. "At any rate, Captain Fallon let it be known on the island that I would take *Harp* on the windward route, as a ruse, for he had a rather far-fetched idea that there was an informant abroad."

"So you were never really to take the windward route, is that correct?" Somers leaned forward in his chair, not antagonistically, but *physically interested.*

"Er, just so," Bishop said, trying to remember exactly what he had told Nilson. "But really, who knew where Clayton would strike next? The point is that I insisted we work together to get the packets through, do you see? We were just approaching Andros when the pirates came out: two of them, a sloop and Clayton's ship. We engaged them, of course, and gave as good as we got, I promise you. The pirate sloop was mortally wounded and, as I was heavily engaged with Clayton—it was hot work, let me assure you—I did not see what became of Fallon. But as I held off Clayton, your salt packets were able to slip away. Which should make you very happy, indeed. When Clayton finally broke off and ran for it, evening was closing on us, and we were crippled, which made searching for Fallon impossible."

"Hmmm, your story is very interesting, Captain Bishop. And I understand you were wounded?" Somers seeming genuinely concerned, seeming to be tracking along. Bishop finished off his glass, relieved.

"Yes, a trifle. One expects worse in battle, sir, from my experience." Bishop feeling good now, sure-footed, *in command.*

Elinore had been silent until now. Silent and intent as a fox staring at a chicken dinner. "Tell us, Captain, how badly was your ship hurt?" Intentionally asking the question like a woman who didn't know a boom from a belaying pin. "It was a very hot battle, you said. Yet your ship looks remarkably well-found."

Bishop smelled the faint odor of a trap, but ignored it. Not from this beautiful young woman, he thought. "Thank you, Miss Somers. We have been working night and day to get *Harp* ship-shape as quickly as possible. My orders are to find and destroy Clayton, and by God I shall do that."

"What keeps you in port, then, Captain?" asked Somers. "Clayton is still free as a bird, presumably preying on shipping, and our Captain Fallon is still missing. When do you plan to sail?"

There was the edge again, thought Bishop. Questioning his orders? His intentions? *Really, this was too much.* English civility only went so far, and Bishop exploded. "I will leave when I leave, Mr. Somers, which is up to the British Navy and not to you. If your Captain Fallon hadn't been so headstrong and poppycock sure of himself and his big ideas he might be alive today. Perhaps if he had come to my aid we might have finished Clayton, *working together,* as I had urged. Perhaps he just had no heart for the fight!"

"Captain Bishop," Somers said coldly, rising out of his chair, "I believe we have learned all there is to learn here. But let me say that you go too far with your mythmaking and storytelling, and you will soon face the cold, hard steel of truth. You are a liar, sir. And a slanderer. And when I have gotten a clearer picture of what happened on the leeward passage, an *honest picture,* I will come back to call you out. On my word, sir, I hope you are good with a pistol. Because I have never missed, particularly a fat target."

Bishop was enraged, trembling with emotion, the pale folds of his skin quivering. He opened his mouth to order them out, but they were leaving already. Goddamn their eyes! *How dare they challenge his word! He was a British captain!*

ELINORE AND her father dined alone in the sloop in the late afternoon. They spoke little, full of emotion and determination, but Elinore knew her father would not rest easy until he learned more.

By dusk, Somers had rowed himself to the town dock, two pistols in his waistband, his jaw set. The early evening was cooling down, and the moon was just making its appearance over the island. A beautiful night, really, if you weren't chasing intrigue.

He made his way to the salt pans, pushing through the pain of his gout and into the shadows, remembering Cully's report now, hiding like he had hidden, looking for a traitor. The hours crept by but Somers stayed alert, focused on his anger, wondering how it would play out if his suspicions held.

They held.

Just before midnight two figures crept along the settlement path, both carrying duffel bags and portmanteaus, whispering and stumbling over roots until they reached the clearing by the salt pans, and dropped their belongings on the sand. A lantern was produced, lit by a flint, and held aloft for a moment. From the darkness beyond the breakers another light, briefly, and then darkness. Slowly, a sail appeared in the gloom and a small fishing boat glided toward the beach on the soft rollers. As it crunched on the small pebbles at the water's edge, Ezra Somers stepped out from the shadows.

"Taking a trip, I see," he said coldly. "Where would you be going this time of night, I wonder?" His voice steady, hard, not really interested in answers.

Nilson and Hewes stood stock-still. Behind them the dark figure in the little sloop leaped ashore to control the boat in the surf.

"Let me tell you where you are going. You are going to your friend Clayton's side, to hide under his skirts, because your work here is finished, eh? But he has no more use for your information, so what use are you to him?"

Nilson appeared frozen, his face contorted with anger. "Look here, Somers," he feigned explanation as he quickly made to draw a pistol from his waistband. But Somers was ready, as ready as he'd been for anything in his life. He drew quickly, and two shots rang out simultaneously. Somers had told Bishop the truth, he *was* good with a pistol, his ball going through Nilson's throat and sending him backward over his bags. But Nilson's shot had been close, grazing Somers's head and sending him down to one knee, a bloody gouge across his scalp, and making him drop his pistol in the sand.

Somers was stunned. Hewes gasped, dropped his bags and made a dash for it, plodding in the heavy sand and salt, an easy target in the moonlight for a dead shot, even one with blood in his eyes. Somers drew his other pistol and brought him down within ten strides.

The figure at the little sloop hurriedly pushed the boat off the beach and jumped in. Somers knelt on the sand, blood covering his eyes, as the figure sheeted the mainsail home and sailed away. The old man rose unsteadily, stepped over Nilson and walked to where Hewes lay. He threw down the pistol next to the body, thinking of the story the bodies told, two guns and two dead. Well, somebody would make up something. Perhaps a lover's quarrel, he thought ruefully.

He knelt down in the surf, washed the blood from his face and held a handkerchief to his wound. The walk back to the dock was a little shaky, a lone figure looking the worse for drink if anybody noticed, which at that time on that night they did not. *Two down*, he thought, *but not done.*

TWENTY-FOUR

A NEW DAY in the Caribbean was inevitably warm, usually golden, and often found Rear Admiral Davies at *Avenger's* windows, coffee in hand, contemplating his fate in life. He had to visit Government House that afternoon, always a trying affair, and then arrange for water hoys and beef cattle to be brought to his ship. The officials would want some small favor, a *bestikke*, as the Swedes would say. He'd had his fill of that in the Baltic.

Last night dusk had come to Antigua softly, like a whisper carrying a secret. Indeed, last night Rear Admiral Davies had received an Admiralty dispatch marked *Urgent*, with the latest intelligence on Spanish movements in the Caribbean. Since signing the treaty with France against Great Britain, Spain had felt the French Revolutionary government's pressure for silver and gold to fund its armies and navy. Spain had given, but France wanted more. British intelligence believed a large fleet of Spanish ships had left Cadiz laden with mercantile goods, arms, and manufactured items as ballast and sailed for South America some months ago, passing through the Lesser Antilles, though not undetected. They were to off-load their goods in Cartagena, Colombia. Then several ships— a treasure *flota*—were to split off and sail for Portobelo, in Panama, to load silver and gold brought from the mines of Bolivia. This flotilla of heavily laden treasure ships was expected to sail across the Gulf of Mexico to reunite with the main body of the Spanish fleet in Havana. Thence the re-combined fleet would sail northward, up

the coast of Spanish Florida to catch the northerly winds back to
Spain. The treasure fleet would be heavily armed, for it carried
the fortune France would need to continue to press the war with
Great Britain.

Now Davies faced a critical decision; indeed, it would not be
coming at it too high to say the fate of Great Britain might rest
on his shoulders. Stop the flotilla and it might strangle France, or
at least slow her advancing armies for want of food and supplies.
Britain could perhaps catch her breath and regroup.

But he had no ships with which to patrol the Caribbean! One
frigate was in for repairs, its captain gone back to England. A
fraud commanded the other frigate. *Jesus, Mary, and Joseph!*

Of more immediate concern to Davies was the knot in his
stomach. It was the knot in his stomach last night, remembered.
What to do about Bishop at Grand Turk, or wherever the hell he
was right now? It was no small thing to distrust a captain's reports,
more serious still to confront him, and more serious still by a hundred to recall him, especially a captain with *influence*. It had ended
many a career, and Davies was under no illusion about his own
stature in the Royal Navy. He was a minor player in the British
Empire and easily replaced, transferred on an Admiralty whim to
blockade duty, his position in the Caribbean eagerly coveted by a
hundred senior captains on the list. Shit, this was a damnable position to be in on a fine morning.

As always when big decisions loomed, Davies asked himself
what his father would do. His father had always been right, all
his damned life; he was a man of little education but strong in the
department of judgment. What would his father do? Chase an in-
tuition or stay home under the covers?

The sounds overhead told him the ship was fully active now,
fulfilling the destiny of every crew of every King's ship the world
over, tending to a thousand small tasks aboard. Davies listened intently, hearing the quiet talk of the men, the running bare feet, the
snap of the bosun's starter on a laggard's behind; he listened until

he heard what he needed to hear.

His father's voice.

ONE HOUR into the first dog, the flagship was coming alive, with anchor pawls clicking as the huge two-ton anchor was pulled out of the seabed dripping mud and weeds. The tide was making, and it was no trouble navigating the maze of boats in English Harbor until at last *Avenger* sailed into the open arms of the sea. Soon enough they caught the trade winds and turned north for the one-thousand-mile run to Grand Turk.

Rear Admiral Davies stood on the quarterdeck, feeling alive after the stifling time at anchor, sailing into what he didn't know, and somehow thrilled by it. At the least he would teach Captain Hammersmith Bishop how to write a fair report; at the most he would face something darker.

"Captain Kinis," Davies called to his flag captain, "it is a beautiful morning, is it not?" Kinis turned away from the binnacle, a stoic expression on his face. "It is, sir. A capital morning, as you say."

Kinis was tall and dark, with coal black hair and a grim set to his mouth. These two men had a somewhat formal relationship owing more to the strict hierarchy of command in the British Navy than to their personalities, although Davies felt Kinis would be hard to get to know even in different circumstances. The morning greeting done, Davies took a stroll around the ship to reacquaint himself with the movement of a ship at sea and the sights of the crew at work. As rear admiral, and a thoughtful rear admiral at that, Davies would not deign to interfere with the running of the ship. That was Captain Kinis's responsibility, but he noticed what he noticed and could have a word with his captain in private if necessary. He knew Kinis took his rare criticism in stride and would take care to set things right in his own time. Satisfied that all was well and in extraordinarily good hands, Davies went below for his breakfast and coffee. Enjoy this sail, he told himself, for in a few days he had to go to work.

TWENTY-FIVE

A WEEK PASSED on the small pirate stronghold and Fallon's strength began to return, the headaches less frequent. He wasn't strong yet, but he felt that he would be strong at some point, and that was strength in itself. He could feed himself, sit up by himself, and lately stand by himself. Walking was a concern, still.

In fact, he was standing at the entrance to the hut when he saw Clayton emerge from his own bungalow down by the beach, walk along the shoreline, and begin the climb uphill toward the prisoners. It was the purposeful stride of a mind made up, and Fallon could not help feeling that today was the day he would be hung.

Fallon looked past Clayton to the harbor, the three ships almost repaired now, rigging and yards set up, a small evil fleet. He gazed longingly at *Sea Dog*, almost set to rights, and despaired of ever sailing her again. Already, he was beginning to let her go in his memory.

"Ah, Captain," said Clayton as he stepped up to the doorway, "I see you are up and about. Excellent. We must arrange to dine together one night when you are able."

Fallon recoiled involuntarily, as much from Clayton's breath as the idea of dinner with him. *Really, what had he eaten last night?* "I would like to check on my men," he said, ignoring the dinner invitation, "but your guards will not allow it. Surely that is not too much to ask."

Clayton rested his hand on his sword hilt, fingering the gold knob, and decided to be magnanimous. "You may check on your men, yes. But only once, and a guard will be with you. And, Captain, you should check soon. Your ship is almost out of food and water, and unfortunately that means your men will soon begin dying."

Fallon refused the taunt. "Death is preferable to living without honor," he said evenly, looking directly into Clayton's eyes.

Fallon saw Clayton's eyes flare as the insult hit home, but the pirate shrugged it off.

"Captain, there is a way to save your men," Clayton said evenly, "but it will take your help to do it. Are you willing to save your men, Captain? And yourself?"

Fallon looked past Clayton toward Cully and the Swedes. "What do I have to do?" he asked, suddenly tired from standing, going a little wobbly in the knees. He literally had not much of a leg to stand on in this negotiation, with no leverage and no strength.

"I think you are a very important man to the Somers Salt Company," Clayton said. "I'm sure they would want you returned unharmed. I would propose a ransom, Captain, or rather *you* will propose a ransom in a signed note which I will have delivered to your employer. If he agrees, you and your men will be exchanged. So, Captain, it had better be a good note, eh?" Clayton laughed in his high voice now, amusing himself.

"I won't do it, Clayton," spat Fallon. "So don't waste your time. I won't beg for my life."

"Wait, Captain, you haven't heard my terms yet," said Clayton with a smile. "I think you will sign the note, because I will kill one of your men every day that you don't." With that, he drew his sword, lunged to the back of the hut, and plunged it into the chest of one of the wounded Swedes. Fallon gasped and stumbled as he lurched for Clayton, but fell to the ground, supported by Beauty's arms. "Bastard," he said through clenched teeth. "Bastard."

"Yes, I admit it, Captain," Clayton said. "I was an illegitimate child." Again came the high falsetto laugh of a madman, filling the hut and no doubt ringing across the harbor. "He was for today," snarled Clayton, motioning to the bleeding Swede, lifeless in the dirt. "Who will be tomorrow?"

Clayton wiped his sword on his pants leg and sheathed it, looked around the hut a last time, and left. Fallon could hear him order the guard to allow him a visit with the other prisoners. Then, silence.

My God, thought Fallon, what have I done? The Swede's blood was on his hands because of his stubbornness and arrogance. He closed his eyes and punished himself with his thoughts, ruthlessly. *God, what a fool.* Friends who trusted me are dead. Over and over again.

Fallon looked into Beauty's eyes and saw her defiance, and he knew he'd given Clayton the right answer, but that would not bring the Swede's life back. He followed her gaze to the back of the hut and the Swede's body, the other Swede crying over his friend and countryman, and then Fallon looked to the corner and there sat Mr. Boy, eyes wide open as always. Had he seen Clayton through the boards? Jesus, what this boy had seen in his short life, Fallon thought. *What does he think of the world?*

Then, something remarkable. Mr. Boy crawled to Fallon, leaned over to where he lay, and *spoke.*

"Captain, sir. We must leave here, yes?"

Fallon's eyes opened wide in astonishment. The boy could speak! Which meant he could always speak, could always understand. For a moment it was all he could think: The boy could speak! It was just for a moment, and then he thought about what he had *said.*

Fallon sat up, out of his stupor now, free of his pain and guilt and his self-punishment, and focused his mind on the task at hand: *Leave this fucking damned island.*

The thought hit him like a fist, energized him and seemed to simultaneously leap like lightning to everyone else in the hut, Beauty and Cully and the lone Swede, who now looked up from his crying. They had to leave, but how?

"Beauty, what time do they change our guards?" Fallon asked.

"Every four hours," said Beauty. "But the guards who come at midnight are usually drunk and late."

"Cully, can you walk?" he asked his gun captain.

"Aye, Captain, I could run out of here!" said Cully, and made to rise as if he were ready to leave then and there.

"Captain, sir," said Mr. Boy hesitantly, "there is a big fire tonight. The pirates have piled wood high on the beach. I think they killed a cow to eat."

Fallon looked at the boy in wonder. Really, had this young boy been spying on the pirates this whole time? Crawling among the rocks, watching and listening without being caught or even noticed? It seemed impossible. No one knew? *Good God!* thought Fallon.

"How do you know this?" Fallon asked incredulously.

"I squeeze through the boards at night and sneak around," the boy answered humbly. "The pirates are usually drunk and asleep so they don't notice. Plus, it is dark and so am I."

Here the boy smiled weakly, and it seemed to break the tension in the hut a little. Fallon looked at him with new appreciation. Then his mind returned to the news of the fire on the beach tonight. A big fire meant a celebration of some sort. Drinking and who knows what debauchery. *Maybe there was a way.*

Fallon asked, "Tell me, can you communicate with the slaves?"

"Yes, Captain, sir," said the boy. "They came from my ship and are mostly from my old village so we understand each other."

So it was Clayton who had attacked the slave ship! Fallon remembered the boy shaking his fist at *Renegade* from the companionway during the battle off Andros Island. Now it made sense. The slaves would be anxious to help, and perhaps exact revenge.

"It will be dangerous," Fallon said, "and some may die tonight, but promise them this for me: Every man who escapes will be set free. Tell them that. Then sneak back here just before the guards are to change tonight. We'll go over the plan then. *I just have to come up with it*, he thought ruefully.

Then, an afterthought, Fallon added, "And pay no attention to the fighting and screaming you hear in here later. We won't really mean it. Now, off with you."

The boy scampered out the back, and Fallon and Beauty put their heads together. His own head was throbbing, but he had the beginning of an idea. Beauty must play her role. *Then luck must play its role.*

It was to be all or nothing tonight.

TWENTY-SIX

THE FIGHT started like fights do.

Beauty screaming, Fallon yelling back. Then, more serious, Beauty throwing herself on Fallon, her hands at his throat, yelling obscenities and bent on murder. The guards rushed in and quickly pulled them apart, Beauty kicking with her wooden leg and catching Fallon smartly on the shins, sending him rolling in the dirt in pain.

"Get the bitch out of here," he yelled. "I'll kill her." And he looked like he meant it.

"You fucker, after everything I've done for you it's come to this!" Beauty shouted. "Goddamn your eyes for a whoreson!" And she lunged at him again, only to be restrained by one of the guards.

"Here, throw her in with the other prisoners and be done with this shit," said the other guard. "We don't need this!"

With that they dragged Beauty kicking and cursing and threw her into the other hut with the healthiest prisoners. She landed on her behind in the middle of the men. She lay there cursing some more, until the guard had left and returned to his post, and then she motioned for the men to gather close.

DUSK CREPT onto Rum Cay on a dying breeze, and then suddenly it was dark. The moon would not rise until well after midnight, and by then the plan would have either worked or failed with disastrous results. Or something in-between.

The fire was lit on the beach, a great roaring thing, and the yelling and drinking began. Fallon wondered what the pirates were celebrating, thinking it could be the anticipated ransom money. Or it could be a morale booster on Clayton's part. The scene was eerie in the light of the fire, pirates coming in and out of darkness, whooping and laughing like madmen. It went on for several hours, getting louder and drunker, more laughing and fighting, higher flames.

Midnight. Just before the guards were supposed to change. Mr. Boy crept through the loose boards in the back of the hut and moved to where Fallon was. For some time, Fallon had been sitting stock-still, anxiously reviewing the plan in his mind, trying to ignore the obvious holes in his thinking. By now Beauty had briefed the crew, so Fallon explained it all to the boy, who nodded his understanding and left to communicate it to the slaves. Two of the bravest and strongest had to execute the first phase.

Now it was down to waiting. Fallon had given up the success of the plan to the gods; it was himself he was worried about. He was still very weak and would need help just to get to the beach. Fighting, if it came to that, was out of the question.

Up the hill stumbled the two replacement guards; one fell on a loose rock and cursed, and the other laughed. Finally, they settled into their posts, and the guards they replaced left immediately to join the revelry on the beach. The two pirates sat on crude chairs at each end of the string of huts, maybe 75 feet apart, in view of each other and the openings of the huts. Within an hour they were nodding, and within another half hour one was snoring.

Two black shapes moved silently along the rear of the huts, one large, one small. They took their time: A step and then listen, a step and wait. The larger figure crept behind the sleeping guard outside the slave hut, slipped his own rope belt around the guard's neck and tightened it. After a few kicks, it was over. The far guard was up, and the warning yell was in his throat when Mr. Boy plunged a fork into his neck from behind with remarkable strength and passion and, when the guard had fallen, into his heart. It was not supposed to be this way; the boy was to ask two of the men to do the killing. But he'd elected himself, for his own reasons, and now the boy was *blooded*.

Quickly, several prisoners pulled the dead guards into the larger hut and stripped off their clothing. Then two seamen put on the dead guards' shirts, pants, scarves, and hats and attached the guards' powder bags to their own belts. A paste of dirt and water was put on their faces to both partially disguise them and also to match the filthy look of the pirates.

Fallon sat outside the large hut with Beauty and Mr. Boy, who had ascended to a leadership role in rather dramatic fashion. They could see the celebration still going on the beach, perhaps 75 yards away. They could also see that several pirates had collapsed or simply passed out where they were standing. Close to two hundred pirates were still at it, many holding torches and dancing around. Fallon could see Clayton sitting on a wooden throne-like contraption with his woman, a sword in one hand and a bottle in the other, watching, roaring with laughter, hopefully blinded by the firelight.

Fallon looked at the sky. The moon would be ascendant in less than an hour. The thing had to be timed right: Get to *Sea Dog* under cover of darkness, then sail with the moon coming up to show the way out. This was assuming they could even get to the ship. They could barely *see* the ship at this point, but Fallon knew that the yellow sloop was closest to them, with *Sea Dog* anchored in the middle and *Renegade* on the far side of the harbor, closest to the pirate huts and Clayton's bungalow. Four small boats, which were used to ferry men to the ships and back, were pulled up onto the beach, not far from the fire. The closest boat was the largest, for it was used to take the men to work on the ships each morning and return them each afternoon.

The two seamen dressed like pirates began to ascend the hill behind the huts. Quickly they were invisible, beginning their loop around the island to reach a point near the fire undetected. Theirs was the most dangerous role, and Beauty had chosen them especially for their courage, cleverness, and ability to swim. Since most seamen couldn't swim, and many weren't particularly imaginative, the pool of candidates had been necessarily small.

All of the prisoners and slaves now crept low to the ground to avoid being seen against the sky. Beauty's strong arms helped Fallon down the hill toward the beach, the rocky hillside providing footing for her peg leg, and when they were as close as they dared, they lay flat where the sand met the rocks at the base of the hill.

Fallon studied the scene on the beach intently. Any moment now two brave seamen would emerge from different parts of the darkness, staggering and closing up their pants as if having gone to the heads, to merge with the other pirates around the fire. And then Fallon saw them step out of the darkness, from his vantage point indistinguishable from the other pirates. One picked up a musket where its owner had dropped it before falling unconscious, the other grabbed a fallen torch. The seaman with the musket seemed to stumble, laughing, and fell down. He almost rolled into the fire, still laughing, and as he rose he kicked his musket discreetly into the coals. Fallon tensed as the two sailors began dancing around in a controlled stagger, staying on the edge of firelight, gradually stumbling past other dancing figures, moving ever so slightly away from the fire in the direction of the far huts.

Fallon looked at Clayton to see if he noticed anything. It was then that the law of fire and gunpowder took hold and the musket seemed to explode on the far side of the fire. For a moment the blast drew everyone's attention, including Clayton's, and then the pirates erupted in laughter and the two seamen drifted off into the night, toward the far side of the cove, arm-in-arm, singing.

Fallon breathed, unaware of how long he had been holding his breath. From that or from his injury he was light-headed. Minutes took forever, and all the prisoners' eyes were focused on the far side of the harbor, still very black and quiet. Until . . . until in the distance a tiny prick of light! Then a bigger light that could only be a flame, then an eruption of flame as Clayton's bungalow caught like a giant torch. Then one by one the flames sped along a trail of gunpowder laid down by the seamen, moving from hut to hut, each shack exploding in fire. One half-drunk pirate gave a yell and began running toward the burning huts. Now they all followed, like a game of Follow the Leader, with Clayton clambering down off his scaffold, throwing his woman aside, and bringing up the rear of the pack.

That was the sign Fallon had waited for. The prisoners broke into a dead run now, some carrying the weak or wounded, Fallon carried along by a sailor and a slave, Cully and Beauty helped by others, hopping together as they made for the waiting boats on the beach. They needed all the boats to be off that beach. Quickly they climbed aboard, Fallon the last to leap, catching his breath, still watching the pirates.

On instinct, Clayton turned around. His high-pitched scream could have awakened the dead, and it certainly got the pirates' attention, even drunk as they were. His men reversed course and charged back toward the beach, real venom in their screams now, swords out. The Sea Dogs and slaves pushed off in the boats just before the first of the pirates ran into the surf, the seamen pulling like their lives depended on it, which was more than true. In fact, they rowed like the seasoned sailors they were, orderly, in harmony with one another, if with more determination than usual.

Out to *Sea Dog*, and up the side came the crew, back suddenly to familiar stations, loosening sails, hacking at the anchor rode, Beauty at the helm. *By God they were alive!* The slaves, who knew nothing about sailing, had the good sense to stay still, with Mr. Boy speaking to them softly and urging them to remain quiet. The sails were raised, the anchor rode was finally parted, and *Sea Dog* began to make way. She sailed as sweetly as she always did, gliding to the far side of the harbor, where two very tired seamen were treading water as the ship momentarily hove-to in the light air to pick them up.

The moon was just showing over the island as they crept out of the cove and, as foreseen, the moonlight showed the way, revealing the small boats they'd taken from the beach trailing astern, soon to be cast off at sea, the final, glorious indignity.

TWENTY-SEVEN

BEAUTY CONNED the schooner around the island and *Sea Dog* met the full force of the trade winds and consequent rollers on the nose but she tacked expertly, a man in the chains casting the lead and constantly calling out the depth. Fallon lay on deck, too exhausted to go below. He slept occasionally—Mr. Boy having provided a rolled-up blanket for a pillow. It was a beautiful night for a sail, especially an escape sort of sail.

Beauty stood at the helm all night, sailing south past Long Island before bearing off to the southeast. The ship felt right, made almost as good as new with the materials at hand on Clayton's island, and Beauty reveled in her new freedom. She had wanted to sail for home, to Bermuda, but Fallon had insisted on finishing some business in Grand Turk first, *tying up loose ends* he'd said. Well, she could guess what those loose ends were.

It was an exquisite night, such as you could only find at sea, the stars sitting in the sky like tiny punctures in a black curtain. The hands were quiet. Most slept, while those on watch huddled at their stations and dozed with little need for sail handling because of the constancy of the trades. Three days should see them in Grand Turk if outside events did not overtake them.

Beauty thought of the pirate Clayton and the utter hopelessness they'd felt only hours ago. The plan to escape had been simple, but so much could have gone wrong and, if it had, they would all be food for barracuda this very moment. She looked at Fallon sleeping, with Mr. Boy sitting on his haunches watching over him. Like the other Sea Dogs, she had seen the boy in a new light this night and would never look at him the same.

Her mind drifted to Bermuda, to home. She thought of that night at her cottage, when she'd seen Fallon out of the corner of her eye at the back door, about to knock. At first she was terrified that he *knew,* then she was oddly relieved. Her sexuality was literally the only secret she'd ever kept from him. After that night he'd never said a thing, never changed a thing between them, and she loved him all the more for it.

All night they plunged southward, the only sounds the familiar ones of ropes stretching tautly, water gurgling down the side of the ship and frothing at the stern, and the hiss and splash of the ship as the waves met the ship beam on. By morning they were well on their way to Grand Turk.

Fallon awoke at daybreak, savagely hungry, *alive.* The hands had tiptoed around him, letting him rest. But now that he was awake the ship could be normal, with the hands changing watches and food served out, of which there was plenty left—Clayton lied, to no one's surprise.

Before changing helmsmen and sending Beauty below to get some rest, Fallon asked her to call all hands. It was time to address the crew. They gathered in a loose circle and Mr. Boy helped Fallon to his feet.

"Men, I want to commend each of you for your bravery and courage in getting everyone off that damned island," Fallon said. "Somehow Clayton will pay for what he did to us, for what he's done to many others, as well. This isn't over. We're going back to Grand Turk now, to settle some business and then home to Bermuda. For some of you, well, you may have had enough of this privateering business. I won't blame a single man for wanting to go back home and stay there! As for the slaves, I promised you your freedom and you shall have it. You may join this ship, or stay in Grand Turk to find work as free men. But whatever you decide, you will never be slaves again."

At this Mr. Boy conferred with the other former slaves in their language and the men nodded soberly, heads bobbing and finally faces smiling broadly.

The speech exhausted Fallon, but the men cheered and huzzahed and clapped one another on the back, and a few clapped slaves on the back, as well. It was a good moment. Fallon waited for Mr. Boy to finish talking to the freedmen and then motioned him to the larboard railing, for he had questions for him now that he knew he could answer back.

"Young man," he began, "you are a most amazing fellow. Not only can you speak, but you can fight and . . . lead! What you did on that island was extraordinary, bravely done, really. Now, where the hell did you come from? How do you come to speak English? I am totally fascinated to hear your story."

The boy seemed embarrassed by the compliments and for being singled out by Fallon. He looked out to sea before speaking, gathering his thoughts, or perhaps getting his memories in order.

"I was born on a farm in West Africa," he began. "My family worked there as slaves and, when I was old enough, I was put to work in the house, mostly in the kitchen, helping clean for a white family from England and I began to understand the language. The English family was good to us with food, but my father and mother had to work very hard in the fields. Then one night there was a raid on the farm, and these men from a different village than ours captured us and tied us up. I don't know what happened to the white family but there were shots and I remember women screaming. We were taken on wagons to the coast, to ships there, and divided up. I don't know what happened to my family."

Here the boy paused, tired of crying old tears, determined to soldier on. "The pirate Clayton attacked my ship and . . . you saw what he did. They took these men"—the boy motioned to the freedmen huddling near the main mast—"and they . . . they killed the women. I found a place to hide, but I heard the killing and when it was quiet I crept on deck and saw *Renegade* sail away. I was the only one left alive."

The boy was crying now, lost in the memory of that afternoon slaughter, his body trembling. "I thought I was going to die on the boat until you found me," he said between sobs. "At first I thought you were going to kill me, Captain, sir, but you saved me."

Fallon listened, thunderstruck, and put his hands on the young man's shoulders. "Young man, *you* saved *me*. Without you we would still be on that island, or dead, and I would have been hanged by now, doubly dead."

The boy smiled hesitantly, and wiped his tears away with his hand, trying to put an awful memory behind him. Fallon still held his shoulders, giving him strength. "But tell me," Fallon asked softly, "what is your real name? I can call you by your real name now."

"My name is Ajani, Captain, sir."

Fallon considered a moment, putting the face with the name. "What does your name mean, Ajani?" he asked. "I have heard that all African names have a meaning."

"Yes, all babies are given names with meaning. Sometimes it is a big meaning, like a warrior name, but sometimes it might be simpler, like a name that meant you were born on Thursday. Different villages celebrate a birth in different ways."

"And your name?" asked Fallon.

"Ajani means *He who wins the struggle*. My father gave me a name he hoped would make me strong enough to survive in the world."

"Ajani is a wonderful name," said Fallon. "And it is the perfect name for such a brave young man. I believe you will always win a struggle!"

Ajani smiled broadly, for his tears were dry now, his story told. Shyly, barely above a whisper, he said to Fallon: "My father called me Aja." He looked at Fallon and smiled again.

"You can call me Aja," he said.

LATER THAT day, Aja helped Fallon make his way to his old cabin.

His clothes had been stolen, his private things were gone, all his books and papers and things apparently thrown overboard. Well, maybe not *everything*.

When Aja left, Fallon knelt slowly down by the stern window and pressed on the corner of a plank just so. It raised a bit—enough for him to pry it up. There, just where he'd hidden it, was the key to the fisherman's shack. Satisfied, he raised himself slowly and, as he turned to go back on deck, caught his reflection in the mirror. It was a haggard, much older Nicholas Fallon who looked back at him, almost unrecognizable, pale and thin. So much for appearances, he thought, and the smell of his own clothing drove him up the companionway to fresh air.

TWENTY-EIGHT

HMS *Avenger* hove-to off Grand Turk, not trusting the soundings on the charts for the entrance to Cockburn Harbor. Captain Kinis ordered the pinnace lowered and sent off to sound the channel through the reef that virtually encircled the island. It was late afternoon, still several hours of golden light left, and the sun would be behind them as they picked their way toward the harbor.

"Sail ho!" came the shout from the masthead, and all eyes scanned the horizon. "North nor-east. Looks like a schooner!"

Captain Kinis could just make out a smudge in the distance, and he certainly had no great concern for a schooner, even an enemy privateer. "Send up the colors, if you please," he said calmly to the signal boy.

The British ensign rose up the mast, followed by another shout from the masthead. "She's hoisted British colors, sir!"

Well, she might be British and she might not be, thought Davies, who had come on deck at the sound of the lookout's hail. He decided to ask Kinis to run out the guns on the larboard side just in case, knowing he could fall off in a moment to open fire if need be.

They had been hove-to for over an hour already, waiting for the pinnace to return. The pretty schooner—appearing smallish from the upper deck of a ship-of-the-line—came on boldly, with all the confidence of one British ship about to rendezvous with another.

She was certainly handled smartly enough, the helmsman a real sailor by the looks of it and the crew sharp as she rounded up into the wind and hove-to not fifty yards from *Avenger*.

"Ahoy," yelled Kinis across the water. "What ship?"

Fallon had arisen from his resting place near the railing and stared across at the massive wall of timber and armament and men. She was English all right, and hands from both ships were smiling and waving.

"His majesty's privateer *Sea Dog*," he yelled back. "Lately a prize."

Kinis looked quizzically at Davies. "Ask the captain to come aboard, if you please," said the rear admiral. "Send my gig. I think we may have found a ghost ship."

The gig was lowered and rowed across, and Fallon, who was still quite weak, was helped down into it by several hands. At the last Aja leapt into the gig as well, unbothered by the lack of an invitation. Fallon smiled in spite of himself—Aja, his protector, his young "coxswain." Well, it had been a good thing so far.

Fallon slowly but determinedly climbed up the side and stepped onto *Avenger*'s deck to stunned and curious looks from all hands, for he looked a fright in his shredded clothes and matted hair. Aja stood by his side self-consciously.

"I am Kinis, captain of HMS *Avenger*," said the flag captain as he approached his visitors. "Whom do I have the pleasure of welcoming aboard my ship?"

"Nicholas Fallon, captain of *Sea Dog*, late of Rum Cay, bound for Grand Turk. And this is my coxswain, Ajani." At this Fallon and Aja smiled at each other self-consciously.

Davies stepped forward now. "I am Rear Admiral Davies, senior on his Majesty's Caribbean station in English Harbor," he said. "I welcome you both. Captain, may I invite you below for some refreshment? We are awaiting our pinnace, sent to sound the channel into Cockburn Harbor. Come, please."

With that, Davies led the unsteady Fallon below to a spacious cabin, invited him to sit, and ordered some cold hock. They looked at each other for a moment until the steward had left with orders to show Aja around the ship. Then Davies raised a glass.

"To your escape from captivity, Captain, if indeed that is what happened. I am anxious to hear your story."

And so he did. For almost an hour Fallon spoke while Davies listened intently, clarifying a point here and there, probing for a deeper narrative. Fallon told the entire story beginning with his suspicions about a spy on Grand Turk to the battle with Clayton to the crew's escape from the island. He was careful not to impugn Bishop, fearing to cast one of the rear admiral's captains in a bad light, but Davies' curiosity was piqued.

"Captain Fallon, how many broadsides did *Harp* fire?" asked Davies.

It was a direct question that required a direct answer. "One," said Fallon.

"And then he broke off?" asked Davies, wanting to be sure.

"Yes," answered Fallon flatly.

"And the packets had sailed through, I understand? It was just you and Clayton?" asked Davies.

Fallon nodded.

"One last question on this point then, if I may," said Davies, "for I fear it is getting late to be getting underway, and I can hear the pinnace being hauled up."

"Oh, *Sea Dog* can lead you in, sir," said Fallon. "Have no worry on that count."

"Excellent, thank you. So *Sea Dog* and *Renegade* were exchanging fire. I am curious as to your relative position vis-à-vis *Harp*.

"*Harp* was about a cable's length away from *Renegade*, to the east, and I was in the lee of *Renegade*, to the west," said Fallon with certainty.

"So you were in no danger from *Harp*'s broadsides?" Davies wanted to be clear on the point.

"No," said Fallon with complete honesty.

So *Harp* could have fired, *should* have fired, but did not. Davies didn't like what he heard or the conclusion he was reaching: Bishop had *refused to engage the enemy.*

The interview was over. Davies took Fallon by the arm and led him up the companionway and asked him to yell across for *Sea Dog* to lead them through the channel. In moments Beauty bore away and made for the harbor, followed by a necessarily slower maneuver by *Avenger* just behind. The sun was sinking fast, and they would just get in with anchors down before it set.

Davies and Fallon stood in the bows of *Avenger*, both seamen occupied with the same thought. Both wondering, unknown to the other, whether *Harp* would be at anchor in the harbor. Both hoping she would be.

IN FACT, *Harp* had not moved for some time. Captain Hammersmith Bishop was rather the worse for drink at just that moment. He had been fortifying himself all day, trying to work up the courage to leave and go after Clayton, determined that tomorrow would be the day. Now, as he sprawled on the stern seat of his large and beautifully appointed cabin, looking out the stern windows, he saw a sight he could not comprehend, could not in a million years have imagined, a sight that would be the end of him. *Sea Dog* was leading Rear Admiral Davies' flag ship into the harbor!

How could that be? Bishop half lay, half sat in the stern seat and closed his eyes. Everything he had worked for all his life, his reputation, his place in London society, it was all *over.* He slowly began to cry, like he had cried in his mother's arms as a boy, ashamed of his childhood cowardice at the hands of schoolyard bullies. His life, indeed his whole career, had been a mask of bluff and bluster, and now he was exposed. His mother's arms had brought safety and comfort, but there were no arms to hold him now, and his body shook with great huge sobs of hurt and shame and helplessness.

On the ships came to their anchorages, sailing into the pretty harbor, the low buildings of Cockburn Town glowing like gold. They shortened sail, crawling past the dock and *Harp* at anchor and, as they rounded up to let go, a sound like a shot rang out, though from where the sailors could not tell.

For a moment, silly as it seemed, Fallon actually thought someone was glad to see him come back alive.

TWENTY-NINE

THE SUN was gone from Cockburn Harbor, but a golden light still lingered, if barely, and it certainly was enough for *Harp*'s lookout to see his ship's number hoisted to *Avenger*'s gaff, followed by a signal: *Captain repair on board.*

Rear Admiral Davies was anxious for the interview with Bishop, though he was fairly certain he had the facts in hand. Still, Bishop deserved to tell his story and would be given the chance. He watched impatiently as *Harp*'s gig dropped into the water.

Davies had quickly called away his own gig to take Captain Fallon and Aja back to their ship. This was not a time to have Fallon aboard. In the event, he offered one of *Avenger*'s boats to be made available to Fallon and, indeed, it trailed along behind the gig as the pair were rowed to their ship.

It was growing dark quickly and, as the moon was still some hours from making its appearance, Davies could not see the corpulent Bishop in the stern but soon enough heard the gig's hail.

But Bishop did not come aboard.

Instead *Harp*'s first lieutenant, Ramsbottom, came climbing up the side and, once on the deck, presented himself to Davies with a solemn, almost ashen face. He was tall and awkward, with a perfect uniform and real silk stockings. He didn't pay for those on a first lieutenant's pay so, *one of those officers.* Davies knew of Ramsbottom, knew he had been specifically requested by Bishop to serve as first lieutenant. Scuttlebutt had it that he was insecure in the extreme with regard to his abilities and experience and masked his weakness by constantly finding fault with his men.

The man looked like he could use a glass of wine, and Davies immediately invited him below, eager for an explanation for Bishop's absence. The door of the cabin had barely closed when Ramsbottom blurted it out.

"Captain Bishop is dead, sir. He killed himself with a pistol this evening. I don't know what to say, sir."

"Good God!" exclaimed Davies, genuinely shocked. "Shot himself? Jesus, are you sure? Well, of course you're sure. What was wrong, Ramsbottom? Was anything amiss in the ship?"

A clearly agitated Ramsbottom said, "I don't know, sir. He had been keeping to his cabin more of late. I believe his wound may have been troubling him greatly. But . . . "

Davies could understand Ramsbottom's predicament. He was obviously hiding something, but to reveal its nature would likely cast a bad light on a dead man, and possibly on himself, as well.

Davies sat down heavily. Well, Bishop was dead and there was nothing for it. Ramsbottom still stood at attention, and Davies let him stand there while he considered the situation. Bishop would need to be buried, and Davis preferred to do that at sea, not knowing Bishop's religious preference for a service on land. And the sooner it was done the better. Then there was the matter of petitioning the Admiralty for a new captain—or promoting Ramsbottom to command, which Davies was loathe to do. He could instead promote *Avenger*'s First into *Harp*, which Kinis would understand but not like and Ramsbottom would surely object to. No matter, he had a frigate without a captain, so a problem.

That presented a particular problem just now, with a Spanish flotilla due into the area within a month carrying enough bullion to win a war, if the intelligence was to be believed. And even if that weren't true, that damned Clayton was still about. Damn and hell, Davies thought. *I have no idea what to do.*

Ramsbottom cleared his throat, an effort to remind his Rear

Admiral that he was still at attention. Davies ignored him; in fact, disliked him all the more for his sense of entitlement. But reality prevailed. Captain Bishop couldn't be allowed to rot in his cabin; he must be given a decent naval burial, and Davies was recalled to his duty.

"Mr. Ramsbottom, Captain Bishop is to be buried at sea," he said. "Please prepare to weigh tomorrow and sail with the first tide. I will accompany you, of course. And Mr. Ramsbottom . . . " Here he hesitated, but thought better of what he was about to say. "You are dismissed."

THIRTY

Ezra Somers and Elinore had settled into the small rooms above their company's office on Grand Turk, nominally used for storage but perfectly suitable for them temporarily. Before Somers bought the building, in fact, the upstairs had been rooms to let.

Life on Grand Turk had pretty much returned to normal since the discovery of two bodies on the beach near the salt pans. A double murder, some said, or a falling out of some sort. Somers did not comment, nor did he feign to grieve. There was no real law or system of justice on the island; serious grievances were filed with the Bahamian authorities or, more likely, settled on the island. This was one of those times.

Of course, the Somers Salt Company still had a business to run, and Ezra searched about for replacements to staff the office. After a week of interviews—well, two interviews—a possibility presented itself in an unlikely form: a tax collector sent from the Bahamian government to attempt to collect taxes on salt exports. Of course, it was preposterous. Bermuda controlled Grand Turk's salt—not the Bahamas—but nonetheless Nassau used every opportunity to press its claim on the island. Somers was not about to be intimidated by the tax collector but, rather than shoot him—for there had been too much of that lately—he invited him to dinner.

He was an amiable tax collector, Mr. Carteret by name, and seemed to grasp both the absurdity and futility of his mission to

Grand Turk. In a previous life he had been a milliner in Nassau selling women's hats, the big straw ones the best sellers. He found he had a head for numbers, not for hats, and opted for a steady paycheck over the limited joys of the small merchant. That evening, after two bottles of claret, after the delicious chicken and vegetable dinner Elinore had prepared, Carteret was officially the new head of the Somers Salt Company's Grand Turk office.

That done, Somers turned his mind to Bishop, whom he knew was lying, but knowing that and proving it were two different things. What infuriated him more was Bishop's lack of interest in finding Fallon. Bishop had been in harbor for weeks, hadn't moved, hadn't made any effort to move, and for all Somers knew Fallon had been captured and cast ashore on an island without food or water and was very probably dead by now. He didn't share his thoughts with Elinore, of course, but she had her own thoughts and they were no doubt just as dark.

That is, they were dark thoughts until two days later when word swept the settlement that *Sea Dog* had sailed in.

Elinore and her father had been taking a walk after dinner, walking toward the harbor as they usually did, when the dock boy had run to them with the news. *Sea Dog* and the *biggest ship in the world* had sailed in and dropped their anchors just at dusk. *Could it be?*

Then there was a shot, from where they could not tell, but it seemed to confirm the news.

That sent Elinore running and Somers hobbling as fast as he could go and they burst onto the dock and, *"By God there she is!"* exclaimed Somers. A small skiff was at hand, tied up to the dock, and they leapt into it and hurriedly began rowing out to the ship. It was a zigzag course—they were not expert with boats—but soon enough they reached *Sea Dog*. They were hailed and welcomed aboard by Beauty, and stood in shock as Fallon emerged onto the deck wearing only his pants, his ribs sticking out of his chest, surprise on his face. Elinore held the gasp in her throat and ran to him, would have thrown herself at him but that would have sent him back down the companionway. Instead she stopped just short, mouthed *I love you* and put her arms around him gently so that he wouldn't break.

Somers and Beauty and Aja looked away. Well, Aja didn't *really* look away, this being all new to him. It was clear to him that, whoever this woman was, she was obviously very important to his captain. Finally, they could all gather around Fallon, Ezra pumping his hand, Elinore holding him, Aja in the dark until he was introduced and then smiling broadly, a little important himself.

The crew stayed in the shadows, giving the moment its due. It was overwhelming and wonderful and Fallon worried he would cry. And later, after all the questions were answered and the wine drunk, when Elinore and Somers been seen safely back ashore and he had finally tumbled into his cot, he did.

THIRTY-ONE

DAWN FOUND Fallon on deck looking across the harbor at *Harp*. She was a beautiful ship, one of the class of smaller frigates the Admiralty had ordered to be built at the beginning of the war. There were sixteen gun ports to the side, two acres of canvas aloft when she sailed, and enough timber to build several good-sized homes. In fact, England was building so many ships that the countryside was rapidly losing all its trees. War took strange things from a country.

Fallon clenched his jaw. There was business at hand with Bishop, and he intended to take care of it this morning. The tide would make within the hour, and he could see *Harp* making preparations to weigh. He would need to hurry. As he turned to go below to dress and get his sword he heard a hail from *Avenger's* gig, which had come up from astern totally unnoticed by Fallon, so absorbed was he with *Harp*.

Rear Admiral Davies rose from the stern sheets, and once the gig's crew had clapped on he climbed up the side and was aboard.

Fallon stood in his nightshirt, looking at Davies come over the side in his Rear Admiral splendor. He was puzzled at this early visit, and worried *Harp* would sail before he could get aboard.

Davies read the expression on Fallon's face. "Good morning, Captain," he said. "You are looking better this morning, I'm glad to see. I also see you are looking at *Harp*, perhaps wondering where she is going, perhaps wanting to have a word with Bishop. I don't blame you, but believe me, Captain, she will not sail without me."

Fallon stared at Davies, uncomprehending, his nightshirt flapping about his legs. Davies stepped closer, his voice lower. "Captain Bishop is dead, sir. A victim of . . . himself. I suspect he saw our arrival and looked into the future and did not like or could not endure what he surely knew would happen. He shot himself last night, Captain Fallon. And for the sake of the service I will bury him this morning at sea."

Fallon was stunned. His father had always said *life was just one damned thing after another,* and it was true. He took a moment to absorb the news. Well, he thought, he wouldn't be killing anyone this morning, which is exactly what he'd been contemplating ever since Bishop abandoned *Sea Dog* and ran from Clayton.

Davies looked at Fallon and thought carefully about how to phrase what he wanted to say next. Something about injustice and apology, but he had the sense to be silent while Fallon's mind worked it out. In the event, he took his leave with a long look into Fallon's face before he turned and climbed over the side.

Fallon watched him being rowed to *Harp.* He liked this man, respected him and the way he handled *situations.* Soon enough *Harp* would weigh anchor and let fall, sheeting home her sails to glide out the channel for sea. Fallon tried to figure out what he was feeling, but he was empty. Perhaps Bishop had done him a favor, but somehow he felt sorry for the man. His hatred was gone, which surprised him. And it made him wonder if it had ever truly been there at all.

Fallon wanted to shave and dress and have a massive breakfast. Today he would leave the ship and not return until he was too tired to stay ashore. He wanted to see Elinore, to walk with her on the beach and say all the things he wanted to say in private. And he wanted to talk to Somers, who had said last night that Nilson and Hewes were no longer *employed.* And he had said it without emotion. That was something to find out about.

✦ ✦ ✦

WHEN BEAUTY had seen Fallon safely over the side and handed down into *Avenger*'s boat, with the crew being extra careful with their captain, she set about inspecting *Sea Dog* from stem to stern. They would need wood and fresh water before leaving Cockburn Harbor, and two weeks' worth of rations, although the trip to Bermuda was only a week. It paid to err on the side of safety when going to sea.

When she had made a mental note of repairs and things to be set to rights, she divided up the hands for the tasks, being careful to place the former slaves into groups with the older hands. Every man would be expected to pull his weight, experienced or not, else morale would suffer.

The thought of going home pleased Beauty. She was comfortable around men, found she had much in common with them, but needed time away from the ship. She was ready to tend to her own private life.

It wasn't at all clear to her what *Sea Dog* could do about Clayton. Fallon's plan to winkle him out of his hiding place while under *Harp*'s guns had been a good one, but it wouldn't work twice. And, anyway, Bishop was dead and on his way to the bottom by now and a new captain would have to be appointed or sent for. Who knew what Davies' orders would be now? Certainly Fallon would not take *Sea Dog* against *Renegade*'s guns again, and no one could blame him. But meanwhile, Clayton.

The day was warming quickly, even with the sun mostly hidden behind enormous puffy clouds. Beauty had no desire to go ashore, but she did need clothes and a few things since the pirates had stolen everything in the ship that wasn't bolted to the deck. This afternoon would be make and mend on the ship and all hands would strip down and wash their clothes. Probably best to let Fallon come back for that. Then she could row herself to shore.

Her mind turned to Aja and the former slaves and what they might decide for their future. *Sea Dog* could use the hands, no doubt of that, but adapting to a life at sea from life on a farm would not be easy. And then there was the language issue, although most of the newly freed men were beginning to understand and speak English to some degree. None, however, like Aja.

He had certainly blossomed into a surprise in the weeks since he'd been rescued from the slaver. He was a natural leader if Beauty had ever seen one, and he was filling out nicely into his clothes, a young man now. Cully had done wonders with him, showing him knots and splices and the rudiments of gunnery, the thousand names of things aboard. He learned quickly and was clever, and Beauty believed he would stay aboard in Bermuda.

Bermuda. It couldn't come fast enough.

THIRTY-TWO

PORTOBELO, MIDNIGHT.

Capitán Alfonso Camaron walked the deck of his ship, the massive *Punta de la Concepción*, and looked across the bay into a darkness that stretched to Spain. He wished he were there now. For the hundredth time, no the thousandth time, he asked himself where the damned Silver Train was.

At sea nothing was predictable, only perhaps *probable* due to wind and weather. *But on land?* Surely a mule train could be loaded, even a mule train of one hundred mules, and sent on its way in a reasonable amount of time.

The Silver Train carried silver and gold by mule from the mines of Potosí, Peru, across the Isthmus of Panama to Portobelo. Camaron's orders were to load the bullion as soon as possible and rendezvous with the Spanish Combined Fleet, comprising seventy ships, in Havana before they all sailed for Spain.

Besides his own *Punta*, a 79-gun ship-of-the-line, Camaron had *Estrella*, 54, as his only frigate. *Río de Oro*, *Valiente*, *Corazón de España*, and *Nuevo Año* were cargo ships, so lightly armed. Camaron estimated it would take less than a week to load the treasure on his ships and be away. But first, the damn mules had to get there.

Capitán Camaron had never been a patient man. He was short and dark, with a body that had seen leaner years. His black mustache had lately shown flecks of gray, which he refused to see, even when he shaved each morning, concentrating his vision on his cheeks and chin.

The bullion, if it ever arrived, would need to be off-loaded from the mules and loaded onto the ship's boats and rowed out to the fleet's anchorage, for there was no deepwater dock in Portobelo. The silver was in bars weighing thirty to forty pounds each, the gold in coins. Once the boats were alongside the six ships, the treasure would be hoisted aboard using the ships' booms and block and tackle. Maybe a week was too conservative, but Camaron would order the *capitáns* to push their men to the point of exhaustion. They were already three weeks behind schedule and every day would be a black mark against him.

Tomorrow those damn mules had better show up.

IN THE event, the mules did come plodding along the next afternoon, up over a rise and down the hill into Portobelo, moving, as mules do, at their own pace. Each mule carried three hundred pounds of silver and gold, with the whole accompanied by a regiment of seventy guards on horseback and various wagons and carts to supply the entirety of the Silver Train. The treasure was unloaded by nightfall, guards posted and mules hobbled, and Camaron called a late night *capitán's* meeting to stress once again the need for haste in getting the ships loaded beginning the next morning. If anything, he was even more agitated than he'd been the last three weeks, the gold and silver being so close by. He was anxious to be away and felt the burden of his responsibility keenly, knowing nothing was certain at sea.

THIRTY-THREE

THE DAY was hot, and Fallon, Somers, and Elinore passed the afternoon under a canvas awning rigged on *Sea Dog*, drinking lemonade and talking about this and that, almost like a family. Cockburn Harbor was quiet, a few fishing boats sailing in on a light, indifferent breeze, *Harp* and *Avenger* at anchor, their men at small tasks. They could hear hammering ashore, Carteret remodeling Hewes's cottage to be his own, showing real commitment to his new job.

Somers watched the interplay between his daughter and his captain with interest and a growing sense of appreciation. He liked what he saw in Fallon, their relationship easy and open. Well, almost open. Somers had not broached the fates of Nilson and Hewes to his captain. There was not a single pinprick of conscience that bothered him; that was not it. But if Fallon was going to be part of the company or, hell, maybe part of the *family*, he deserved to know the rage inside Ezra Somers.

It had always been so. As a boy his parents had sent him away to boarding school in England. It was what wealthy Bermudians did. In school, young Somers had first experienced the extreme cruelty and arrogance endemic in the British class system, where entitlement was commonplace, cleverness was highly valued in boys, and hard work was looked down upon. And Somers had had to work hard. Being an outsider, a Bermuda boy, he had never fit in, never made real friends, and found books his solace.

He had returned home to Bermuda vowing never to return to England, and he never had. But working in the family business he met British *gentlemen* by the scores, and he could smell a phony around the corner. He had held his nose when he'd hired Nilson, going against his better judgment because finding someone who qualified and who was willing to work on a remote island seemed too good to be true. And it was.

Nilson was one of a type of Englishman who played cards at Blacks or a club like it, who lost more than he won, no disgrace except one had to keep up appearances, and who in the end simply had to have more income. The only option left was to get a job, *egads* and all that. But working for someone in an office was simply deplorable, especially because one should be *running* the company, not working for it.

No money actually exchanged hands in Nilson's office; that was all done on Bermuda. But Nilson had still seen it as a route to riches, far away from the eyes of the home office, for he was *clever*. No doubt he had made contact with the pirates as soon as possible, offering his *services* in exchange for money. And enlisting Hewes in the scheme lest he be found out and his crime be reported. Of course it was illegal, but the thing is, Somers found it *offensive*.

Nilson needed killing; and Hewes too, come to that. Not just because they were responsible for theft on a massive scale, and for the death and starvation of innocent men, but because they were finally getting what they deserved.

Fallon listened intently while Somers told him what had happened on the beach. He began with Fallon's letter, then his own suspicions aroused when Nilson blatantly lied about the route and Bishop's role. He shot both Nilson and Hewes when they tried to escape, simple as that, really.

Fallon nodded at the telling, not casting any judgment, and Somers could feel him wondering what he would have done in similar circumstances. Somers guessed he knew the answer.

✦ ✦ ✦

FALLON HAD listened to the story of the killings on the beach with admiration and growing respect for Somers. Here was a man who saw what needed to be done and took care of business. One thing: Anyone who crossed swords with Ezra Somers had better be ready. He looked at Elinore's face as her father ended his story and saw only love in her eyes, no judgment. They were all three of a mind, then, and the conversation under the awning moved on to lighter topics.

Fallon found himself staring across the water at *Harp*. A very pretty ship, black hull with buff trim and gun ports, a mermaid playing a golden harp at her bow. He didn't envy Rear Admiral Davies the problems he faced; in fact, he was surprised Davies had stayed on Grand Turk as long as he had. Bishop had been buried almost five days ago.

As Fallon thought about Davies he saw the admiral's gig lowered away, and Davies climb down into it. Rather than row toward *Harp*, however, or the town dock, the gig's bow was pointed squarely toward *Sea Dog*. Coming to say good-bye, no doubt, thought Fallon. Davies was decent that way.

Up the side Davies came, stepping under the awning to greet them all; he'd gotten to know Ezra and Elinore since returning from burying Bishop at sea and was warm to them, a shared history beginning to form. Fallon called for fresh lemonade and Aja, always at hand when he was needed, scampered off to attack the lemons.

"Captain, you are looking remarkably well," said Davies as he sat down. "Really, your ordeal is barely written on your face."

"Thank you, sir," replied Fallon. He saw Elinore blush and knew she was feeling at least partly responsible for his quick recovery. "My advice is to avoid falling booms at all costs, however. Bad for the constitution."

Laughs all around. Lemonade all around. Really, Fallon thought, if you could just squint your eyes and not see the worries of the world, life was delightful. Even Somers was relaxed, not his usual compact mass of barely contained energy.

"If I may, I would like to share some intelligence I received from the British Admiralty two weeks ago," said Davies, growing serious. "By now it may be more well-known in certain harbors than I would like, but as it could have a large role to play in the outcome of the war, and perhaps your own plans, I want you to know."

Davies had everyone's attention now, the little group drawing closer, listening intently, with Aja hanging just outside the awning, but listening. Fallon in particular paid attention, noticing the hair on his arms getting up, not sure why, the emotion taking its time getting to his brain.

Then Davies told them about the intelligence received at English Harbor, the twenty tons of treasure perhaps even then loading in Panama, and Spain's intent to give it all—every last bar and bag—to France to help prosecute the war with Great Britain.

Eyebrows shot up. The value of twenty tons of silver and gold could not be estimated in your head, but Fallon figured it would take five or six large ships to transport it all.

"I assume the treasure flotilla is escorted?" he asked.

"Usually the ships are heavily guarded and commanded by experienced captains. We have the French effectively blockaded, at least the Atlantic squadrons, and it is no doubt well-known that the Royal Navy is somewhat, shall we say, less powerful in the Caribbean." Davies smiled ruefully, and his expression told a story of endless pleas and demands for more ships and men, unheeded.

The group was silent as the news went down. Fallon thought of Britain, locked in an intractable war against a ravenous country, the outcome of which was by no means certain. Yes, twenty tons of bullion could tilt the table against the Mother Country and weaken the chance for victory, no question.

"What about pirates, sir?" Fallon asked intently. "If they hear about the flotilla they'll go after those ships with a vengeance."

"Pirates are always a concern for the *flotas*, of course," Davies answered. "But these Spanish ships sail in convoy and the pirates are usually more effective sailing in the shadows, swooping down to attack stragglers or single ships scattered by a storm. I believe that word of the *flota* is on the waterfront in Nassau, however. How could it not be? And pirates are thick as sand fleas there."

Somers and Elinore had remained silent, watching Davies speak mostly to Fallon. It was Elinore who spoke up for both of them now.

"Admiral," she said. "You mentioned that this information might affect our plans. I believe it must affect your plans, as well. I don't believe you will stand by and just let these ships pass. Not when it could be the ruination of Great Britain. But what can be done?"

Fallon looked at Elinore and saw the color rise in her cheeks, perhaps sensing as he had that the real purpose of Davies' visit was at hand.

"I think we have only one chance, Miss Somers," responded Davies. "I have only one frigate, and that without a captain. I have several small brigs and sloops, based in English Harbor, but they could be anywhere on patrol at this moment. And, at any rate, they could be useful but not decisive in battle."

A pause here, the slightest deeper breath. Even Aja crept closer.

"Captain Fallon, you have proven yourself resourceful and brave. I wish you were still in the Royal Navy! And that is what I am asking today. With your permission, and of course the blessing of your employers,"—here a nod to Somers and Elinore—"I would like to appoint you into *Harp* as acting commander, a temporary commission only, to join forces with me against the *flota*."

Fallon sat stunned. He had expected something, but not *this*. Of course he would not do it, could not be expected to do it. Command a frigate, for God's sake! Not knowing a soul aboard ship, and a tainted ship at that, with a crew likely ill trained and resentful at the humiliation Bishop brought aboard by his cowardice. No, it would not serve.

"I see you don't like the idea, Captain Fallon," said a perceptive Davies. "I wouldn't blame you for saying no. There are a host of reasons why this is a terrible idea, but one reason why this is a very good idea: It is the *only* idea I have to help England."

So that was it. Plain and direct. Somers and Elinore both looked at Fallon, giving him all the room to say yes or no, promising in the look their full support either way. Fallon's jaw showed a hard *no*.

Davies opened all the gun ports now, nothing to lose, hoping for a lucky shot. "One last thing to reassure you on several obvious points. Whether it will convince you, I doubt. But *Harp*'s crew is hungry for a leader and a chance to redeem the ship. I believe you would find them willing in all respects to follow you. The first lieutenant is a dolt, and I would take him aboard my own ship rather than saddle you with him. You could choose your own first, or I can provide one from *Avenger*. Likewise any of your crew you want to bring and, of course, who would want to serve would be welcome aboard. Finally, one last thing: If we are successful in capturing treasure, you will share in the spoils. I will personally see to that. Captain, I do not say this in any way to hold out a carrot, only to state what is fair. I don't think you are driven by profit, in any case."

The whole conversation sat on their table like a dinner that no one was hungry to eat. Davies, who was good at *situations*, made to leave.

He rose and bowed to Somers and Elinore, then extended his hand to Fallon. "Know this, please. I will not think any less of you if you decline the role of commander, Captain Fallon. This is my problem to solve, not yours."

"Then what would you do, sir, if I should refuse?" asked Fallon.

"I honestly don't know, Captain. But I would do *something*."

THIRTY-FOUR

THE NEXT day the three of them met again, Somers and Elinore and Fallon. They were sitting at a small café in the settlement, drinking coffee that was not very good but was very hot. They talked about Davies' proposal back and forth, this way and that, and by the second cup of coffee everyone knew it was Fallon's decision to make. Alone. Somers made it clear he would support whatever that decision was, and Elinore bit her lip and concurred.

Fallon left the café, fair to say, deep in thought. If he were honest with himself, he was not overcome with loyalty to Great Britain—the British had made a hash out of governing Bermuda, and general resentment persisted on the island as a result. France, however, was Great Britain's enemy, and the aggressor. Bermudians had been ambivalent about fighting the Americans in their War for Independence because they were sympathetic to anyone attempting to escape the yoke of Britain. He bore no such feeling for France. Oddly, however, he *was* sympathetic to Davies, who shouldered enormous responsibility and whom he had grown to like and respect. So, a conundrum.

That afternoon he asked Beauty to his cabin so he could lay it out for her, because sometimes she just *knew* him. He felt himself itching for action after so long away from it, but what were his options? He started with Clayton, whereabouts unknown, so still a menace but one they could not attack alone. Then the treasure flotilla, likely sailing soon for Spain, and heavily armed. Prizes rich beyond all imagination but, again, no chance for *Sea Dog* against ships-of-the-line. And finally, there was Davies' request for Fallon to become acting commander of *Harp* based on his fears for Great Britain should the bullion get through to France. For Fallon, this was the craziest option of all.

Beauty heard him out, nodded her understanding, and stared at Fallon for a full minute, saying nothing. The hands were at sail drills in harbor, and Fallon could hear the young boys skylarking, Aja's voice cutting through the noise. Then Beauty rose to look out the stern windows toward *Harp* riding peacefully at anchor. She stared another minute.

"You know, Nico," she said finally, without taking her eyes off *Harp*, "the thing you were always good at when we raced on St. George's was knowing when to sail off on a flyer, be damned what any other boats were doing. If you saw that you weren't going to win, given the way things were going with wind and tide, you said *fuck it* and tried a different tack. Many times I remember being in the lead thinking *that fucker doesn't stand a chance*, and then off you'd go. And then way off in the distance you'd tack, catch clean air and a fresh slant, and I'd think *shit!* And then here you'd come with a bone in your teeth, barreling toward the finish line. Sometimes I won anyway, but sometimes you won, against all odds. I always admired your instinct for making a hard call when you didn't have good options." She paused and turned around to face him now, bringing herself to her full, short height. "If it's action you want, if you want a chance to *win*, I think you don't really have a choice. I think you've got to take a flyer."

Fallon looked at her, heard the truth of what she was saying, her words matching the instincts he'd been trying hard to fight.

"One thing, Nico. This time I'm not keeping course while you sail away. I'm tacking off, too."

"I won't let you do that," Fallon said emphatically. "You're bound for Bermuda, and you and the hands need to go home. If it comes to that, I'll make that an order."

"Well, Mr. Acting Commander," said Beauty sarcastically, "you won't be giving orders to a private ship. I seem to remember that didn't work for Bishop, and it won't work any better for you now. We signed on together, all the hands, and once they hear about the treasure ships they'll be damned if they sail to Bermuda. Besides, you'll need eyes you can trust, and a friend you can count on. You know I'm right. *Sea Dog* helps the odds."

She walked to him, put her hands on his shoulders and said, "I'm going to get the ship ready for sea now. We'll need some help from Davies: a surgeon's mate or loblolly boy or two to help with wounded, maybe some powder. I'll give you the list. Now, Nico, you have work to do on your own. I'd start by explaining sailboat racing to Elinore. Believe me, she already knows what you're going to do. You just need to explain why."

EVENING.

Fallon found Somers in the office as usual, reviewing numbers. They talked business for a minute, both hoping that Smithers and Wallace were back in Bermuda now, unloading cargo, having brought payment from Charleston buyers for several tons of salt. Somers was in full support of Fallon's decision to take temporary command of *Harp* and Beauty's demand to sail in support under his wing. He himself would return to Bermuda with Elinore on the sloop they'd sailed in on a week ago. It was a brief conversation, as if Somers had been expecting it all along. Good luck. Good hunting. God speed.

That done, Fallon walked up the stairs to see Elinore, who, upon opening the door and seeing his face, threw stoicism aside and leaped into his arms. Beauty had been right; she had *known*.

They walked on the beach; the dark night had only the white lines of the surf to interrupt the blackness. They walked like lovers do, leaning into each other, heads barely apart, saying private things. In a soft sand valley between two dunes they lay down, and anxious fears were quickly pushed aside by need and desire. Fallon fumbled with her clothes in the dark until she glowed white above him; her hands found him and coaxed him gently, and then urgently, until she released a deep primal scream that held both agony and ecstasy and stunned them both senseless with its ferocity before they held each other, trembling, and cried.

THIRTY-FIVE

THE LOVELY sloop that Elinore and her father had sailed on from Bermuda carried them out of the harbor the next morning. Elinore was at the taffrail, a single, still hand in the air, her hair blowing wildly in the wind. Fallon stood in the bows of *Sea Dog*, his right hand placed over his heart. They remained like that until the sloop turned north, for home.

Taking control of his emotions, Fallon called for Aja to make a signal to *Avenger: Request permission to join.*

Moments later the reply came: *Welcome aboard, Commander. Repair onboard* Harp.

Fallon and Aja had their dunnage lowered into the waiting boat and, with a wave good-bye to Beauty, were rowed across to *Harp*. Aja would come aboard as Fallon's steward and nominal coxswain, with no real responsibilities except to look after his captain. It was a role he fell into naturally, and Fallon was sure he would have stolen aboard if he hadn't been asked.

Davies was already there to greet them when they came aboard, and he shook both their hands with enthusiasm. Ramsbottom had already transferred to *Avenger* as Davies had promised. When all the dunnage was finally aboard, Davies called *Harp*'s crew together to explain this very unusual situation. The crew gave knowing looks to one another as Fallon stood beside Davies; they knew who he was and the price he had paid off Andros, and all eyes were on the deck when he was read in as their acting commander with a captain's full powers over every detail of their lives. Davies saluted his new commander and stepped aside. Fallon stood blinking in the sunshine, not really knowing what to do.

But the moment called for a brief speech, something that Fallon should have anticipated. He looked out over the faces of several hundred men, *his* men now, and put himself in their shoes. What would *he* want to hear?

"This will not be a long voyage, and while you know who I am, I regret I will not get to know all of you," he began. "It is an unusual situation that's brought us together, but right tarpaulins handle everything the world throws at them, everything the French throw at them, and everything a rear admiral throws at them." That got a few smiles, maybe a laugh or two, so a start. "Hear me: This is a King's ship, and we all must do our duty. Whatever is in the past must be left in the past, and we will go forward together. *I know I can count on you.*"

Those last words had the power of a broadside, and every eye came off the deck and looked squarely into Fallon's eyes. It was forgiveness, and every man jack knew it. He dismissed the hands, but they did not dismiss, did not move in fact, and had no thought of moving. Instead, they stood quietly as the officers assembled for introductions and Fallon went down the line. First, he shook hands with the second lieutenant, Samuel Jones II, there being another Samuel Jones serving as an officer in the Royal Navy. Then Fallon went on down the line of officers to the other lieutenants; the master, Colston; then Crael, the surgeon—looking a bit worse for drink, almost a cliché for a surgeon; the purser; the major in charge of marines; and then the young gentlemen and the gun captains.

After, Fallon again dismissed the crew, and they finally shuffled off to their stations or below decks. Davies motioned for him to take a turn around the ship, and the two walked slowly down the starboard rail toward the bows.

Harp was 135 feet on deck, drew 13 feet below the keel, and had 16 long guns to each side, all located along one continuous deck, the upper deck. Below this was the berth deck where the men lived, slept, and ate their meals. She was full rigged and, though lighter in armament than *Avenger*, she was faster, lighter, and could stay at sea for up to six months. Total complement of men: 195.

"Captain, I want to thank you for joining me," Davies said with appreciation. "I know it is a great sacrifice, no doubt on many levels, but I believe we have a chance now, a fighting chance, to alter the course of the war against an enemy who will stop at nothing to destroy England. *We must not fail.* It will call for all our ingenuity and cooperation if we are to succeed."

"We will have *Sea Dog* with us, sir," said Fallon. "Beauty McFarland and the hands have all signed on, and Somers has agreed to lend his ship."

Davies stared at him a moment, then smiled broadly. "Damn, that is good of Somers!" he said with real enthusiasm. "And what a testament to you that the entire crew volunteered. Now I *know* we will not fail!"

They walked around the ship, then around the ship again, with Fallon stopping occasionally to have a word with a seaman at a task. Davies took note of the respect the crew showed. As Fallon was seeing Davies over the side, he asked for Jones to be promoted to first lieutenant, which both surprised and gratified Davies, appreciative that Jones would be given a chance to show his mettle out from under Ramsbottom.

They agreed to meet for dinner on *Avenger* that night, Beauty included, to begin laying out strategy for the weeks ahead. There was much for Fallon to learn, and maybe something he could contribute, as well. It would be a long dinner, lasting well into the evening and, when it was over they would all know each other immeasurably better. They would need that knowledge in the weeks to come.

Sea Dog led the way out of Cockburn Harbor, followed by *Avenger* and *Harp*. It was a perfect late summer's sailing day, blue sky like a glass dome over the world. Fallon watched intently as Samuel Jones

II gave the orders to up anchor and let fall, and then sheet home. He observed the sequence of actions on a frigate, the scale of the thing intimidating, although he remembered much from his time as Second on *Bon Vivant*.

Fallon stood at the binnacle as the ship cleared the channel and *Harp*'s full complement of sails billowed out like powerful white kites. The men seemed particularly intent on performing their duties properly, being under the eyes of both a rear admiral and an acting commander.

"Nicely done, Jones," Fallon said when they were under way. "Take station two cable lengths astern of *Avenger*. And when everything is squared away join me for breakfast, please. There are a few things I'd like to discuss."

With a final look around, Fallon went below deck to his cabin and called for Wilkins, his official steward, as opposed to Aja. *It was Wilkins, wasn't it?* Well, it would come in time. "Coffee and cheese toast and eggs for two, if you please," he said to the steward.

Fallon's new cabin was enormous, at least in comparison with his old one on *Sea Dog*. Bishop had spared no expense on furnishings, certainly, with velvet cushions on the stern window seat, a beautifully carved oak desk, and a wooden cabinet to match that held books by English writers and thinkers on everything from philosophy to economics to ancient civilizations. So Bishop was a reader, Fallon concluded, or perhaps the books were for show only. Likely that, Fallon mused, remembering Bishop's bluff and bluster and concern for appearances.

Samuel Jones II was shown in, drawing Fallon's attention away from his cabin appraisal. Jones was tall, with a fair, perpetually sunburned complexion, carrot-colored hair, and an appetite like a starving man. But he was extremely nervous, and Fallon hoped all that food would stay down where it belonged. Fallon went over the plans for the drills that he and Davies and Beauty had discussed, and then asked Jones for his assessment of the ship's readiness for battle.

Jones hedged. "Well, sir," he began and halted, then fumbled on. "The men are able enough, and willing to fight, no question. But they've had no real experience aside from, well, fighting . . . ahem, you know, sir."

Fallon guessed that the broadside against *Renegade* was quite literally the first time *Harp*'s great guns had been fired in battle. Clearly Jones was reluctant to bring up that shameful experience to Fallon. "Tell me, Mr. Jones," Fallon asked, "how is our supply of powder and shot? I assume we have plenty?"

"Aye, Captain," said Jones, looking at his feet. It was what Fallon had expected. Bishop had not trained the men at the guns to any extent, hoarding shot and powder like so many British captains did, but the consequence for the Harps was woeful inexperience at war. Well, Jones would not directly criticize his former captain, which was admirable. Fallon could see his obvious discomfort in reliving Bishop's command, so he decided to look forward and, turning serious, he explained in detail what he expected of the ship, putting it all on Jones's shoulders: the sail handling, gunnery, discipline, and execution of simple and complex maneuvers critical not only to success but to their survival.

"It will not be easy, Jones. We have but weeks before we expect to rendezvous with the flotilla. I want the men motivated to perform their duties, not punished into submission. But they must be driven, night and day, with practice and practice again. Nothing less will do, Jones. Nothing less."

"Aye, aye, sir. Nothing less." Jones sat with the gravity of Fallon's words and the urgency with which they were spoken. *Not Bishop's way at all.* "And may I say, sir, I am aware that you were offered a first lieutenant from *Avenger* and decided against it. You will never have reason to doubt that decision, sir."

Jones was dismissed, and Fallon turned to his breakfast with zeal. Jones would be given his chance to lead the men, and Fallon knew he would need his new first lieutenant to be a bridge between himself and the crew. Time would tell.

Meanwhile, Fallon lingered over a cup of coffee and thought of Elinore, who was almost home by now, and their last night on the beach. The memory brought back a rush of emotions, most of which needed to stay below the surface. Only the broad smile showed as he ascended the companionway into the warm Caribbean sunshine, alive and eager for the day.

A day when anything was possible.

THIRTY-SIX

MR. JONES," said Fallon, "you may begin the gunnery drill. We will fire first, then *Avenger*, and the lookout on *Sea Dog* will tally the shots."

They were off Miguana Island in the lower part of the Bahamas' chain of islands, having left Grand Turk far to the south. Barrels had been thrown overboard, and they now floated calmly almost half a mile away. Fallon had challenged Kinis in *Avenger* to a gunnery competition, and the flag captain had quickly accepted, welcoming the chance to exercise his gun crews. For Fallon, it was a chance to see *Harp*'s crew in action, *timed action*, where speed as well as accuracy counted. Each ship would fire two broadsides and the damage assessed. There was certainly no shortage of powder and shot aboard *Harp*; Bishop had used it only once.

The ships were hove-to in a gentle swell, visibility was excellent, and the eight barrels bobbed slightly, staying relatively nearby. *Harp*'s gun captains stood by, waiting.

"*Load and run out!*" came Jones's yell. The crews bent to their guns, rammers at the ready, and a little unevenly sixteen guns were loaded and slowly pierced the sides of the ship. "*Fire!*" Smoke and flame belched as the balls soared over the ocean. Fallon stood on the quarterdeck with his telescope to his eye watching the fall of the shot.

"*Reload!*" Jones called again as the men bent to their tasks. "*Gunners watch your aim!*"

Fallon saw no barrels explode, and no "hit" signals came from *Sea Dog*. He drummed his fingers on the railing; this was taking much too long. Finally, the order to *"Run out"* and then, *"Fire!"*

More than three minutes between broadsides. One barrel "killed." Fallon winced and watched to see what Jones would do. He stood holding his watch, wondering what to do himself. Meanwhile, *Avenger's* guns roared, only sixteen of them to be fair to *Harp*; *Sea Dog* signaled two hits, and Fallon timed her second broadside: two minutes, fifteen seconds. Two more hits. Not great shooting, but damn good by comparison.

With Jones standing meekly by, Fallon called to him curtly: "Assemble the gun crews." But suddenly the air was rent with another broadside, this from *Sea Dog*, unexpected, the schooner sending a message: *This small dog can bite!* Fallon whipped his telescope to his eye as the three remaining barrels flew to pieces.

Ah, Beauty.

Fallon stood in front of the gun crews, their faces seemed indifferent, certainly not embarrassed by their performance, not exactly pleased, but still . . .

"Men," Fallon began, "put your hands on the shoulder of the man next to you. Go on, everyone find your mate's shoulder."

The men shuffled closer to their mates and shyly did as they were ordered. "Good," said Fallon. "Now I'm going to explain some mathematics to you. Simple mathematics."

Every man looked at him like he was, well, *acting like a commander.*

"If we take three minutes to fire a broadside, and the enemy takes two minutes to fire a broadside, in six minutes they will have fired one more broadside than we have. In twelve minutes they will have fired two more broadsides than we have. And if we shoot with anything like the accuracy we just did, every man with a hand on his shoulder will be dead."

That effectively covered every gun crew, dead. The men looked at each other sheepishly, many jerked their hands away, as if that would save their mate. It was plain to see they'd never thought of gunnery in quite that way.

"We want to *live* for England, gentlemen," said Fallon soberly, "and keep living and fighting for her. Not die for her." He turned to Jones, but spoke loudly enough for the men to hear. "Mr. Jones, we are going to practice at the great guns every day until we take only two minutes between broadsides, and then we're going to learn to hit what we're shooting at!"

This said loud enough for the men to hear. "You may dismiss the hands from the guns and make sail. Signal to *Avenger* and *Sea Dog*: *thank you.*"

This was just the beginning of daily and even hourly exercises in sail handling and gunnery. The off-watch men would crawl into their hammocks, utterly spent, and often immediately hear *"All hands! All hands!"* and have to scamper up on deck to their stations. It was brutal and tedious work, and roaring hot under the summer Caribbean sun, but there was remarkably little complaining. The men now knew their lives depended on their skill, and their trust in their new captain grew each day. In one week they reached 2:30 between broadsides. It was time for more barrels.

Again the ships hove-to, and this time Fallon signaled for Cully to come aboard *Harp* to instruct the gun captains in laying their guns. *Harp*'s men could have been resentful, but they had seen with their own eyes Cully's handiwork. Davies in *Avenger* stood by silently, knowing it was costing valuable time but also knowing the success of their mission depended on *Harp*'s readiness.

Three barrels floated two cable lengths away. First, Cully had each gun crew fire a ranging shot, carefully sighting the fall of the shot and noting the gun's elevation. Sixteen shots, no barrels dead. Cully went gun by gun, suggesting adjustments to the crews and, when he was satisfied, the guns roared again. Two barrels blown to pieces, by God! Fallon couldn't keep himself from smiling and yelling encouragement. But now Cully went gun to gun again, and each gun crew sighted and fired individually. No hits from the first twelve guns, but reasonably close. Number 13 gun blew the last barrel apart, and Fallon called for an extra tot for the crew. *Avenger* made *"good shooting"* to *Harp*, and *Sea Dog* dipped her colors in respect. *Now we're getting somewhere*, thought Fallon. And they were.

But the practice didn't let up. They tacked and wore, tacked and wore, and day after day climbed aloft to furl, unfurl, and furl again. Jones seemed to manage the men well, with new confidence, sensing when to push and when to encourage and when to bribe with rum. In two weeks Fallon wanted HMS *Harp* to be a new ship, one that belonged in the Royal Navy.

"Come," Fallon responded to the knock at his cabin door. Crael, the ship's surgeon, entered and Fallon motioned for him to have a seat while he finished up some paperwork. Crael sat uneasily, bleary eyed from lack of sleep or drink, or both. There had been a steady stream of minor injuries these past days as men struggled with torn muscles, sprains, and contusions, the inevitable result of heavy drills and practices without end. So the surgeon had been busy.

Finally, Fallon put his papers aside and contemplated the man sitting in front of him. Crael was of rather indeterminate age; Fallon had known drink to age a man badly. And the surgeon's complexion was pale, the eyes reddish going to yellow.

"Crael, I will not mince words with you," began Fallon. "In a few weeks, or even days, we will hopefully engage the enemy. It will be hot work, and every man aboard ship will be expected to do his duty. You, sir, are not fit to do your duty."

Crael looked up from studying his lap, a tremble on his lower lip, and made to protest.

"No, Crael, it will do nothing to argue. You are a drunk and discredit the Service. I have no idea what your problems are, and I don't care. I only care that these men who are carrying the fight to Britain's enemies are well fed and well cared for. It is the least we can do and, as it stands now, more than you can do. Damn it, man, you are not fit to tend screaming, wounded men! Men who need limbs cut off and splinters pulled out if they are to have any chance to live. So I am going to make you a simple bargain, Crael, one I hope you will accept."

Crael stared at Fallon, waiting for something he would not like. God, he needed a drink just then, just a little something to buck him up. *Where was that bottle he'd hidden?*

"Here is the bargain, sir. If I ever see you in a drunken state again I will tie you to the grate and personally give you twenty lashes!" Crael involuntarily jumped. "Then I will clap you in irons for the remainder of this voyage. I am sure you have seen what twenty lashes do to a man's back, not to mention his spirit. Mark me, Crael, I keep my promises."

The surgeon rose up out of his chair. "You can't do that! I am an officer in the Royal Navy. You can be court-martialed for this!"

"If I were in the Royal Navy you would be very right, sir," said Fallon coolly. "But as I am an acting commander only, and this is to be my first and last voyage, I don't fear a court-martial." That was not exactly true, but he said it.

Crael slumped, the hopelessness of the situation settling onto his body like a dark, massive weight. He had feared this from the moment Fallon had come aboard, in fact had kept his distance, refusing to dine with Fallon when all the officers had been invited. Bishop had been different, they had even shared a bottle or two, but that time was gone, ended with a bullet in Bishop's temple and his brains on the bulkhead. Crael feared he would be suddenly sick. He looked up, a plea in his watery eyes.

"Dismissed," said Fallon curtly, and went back to his papers.

THIRTY-SEVEN

CAPITÁN ALFONSO Camaron, *comandante* of the Spanish treasure flotilla comprising six ships, including his own, was so frustrated and angry he could scream. Actually, he had been screaming quite a lot, but to little effect.

It had taken more than a week to load the bullion from the Silver Train, which put him further behind schedule, which pushed his departure deeper toward August and unpredictable weather crossing the Atlantic. From experience, he knew the rendezvous with the larger Spanish fleet in Havana was coming into question.

The heat was nearly unbearable and the men *seemed* to work hard, but the days dragged on. Matters weren't helped when a block on *Valiente* broke and three hundred pounds of silver bars fell through the bottom of one of the loading boats, sinking it and nearly drowning the men onboard. The bullion was retrieved in due course, as were the men, but that in itself took the better part of a day. *Madre de Dios!*

The crews of his small flotilla were capable, though certainly inexperienced—the Spanish having for years avoided conflict with the French as much as possible before becoming their allies. Camaron was the most experienced and most battle-hardened *capitán* the Spanish government could send on such an important mission. But the list was not long.

At last the treasure was loaded and the ships set off. The warm trade winds were hot so far south, and every man was exhausted to the point of collapse. Many suffered from dehydration, and the smarter *capitáns* doubled the water ration. The ships were heavily ballasted with bullion, of course, which made for ponderous going when the airs went light.

On the second day the flotilla was beset by heavy squalls, common that time of the year, and Camaron ordered the fleet to heave-to off and on rather than risk a spar or sail carrying away in the unusually strong winds that accompanied the rain. The line of squalls continued all day and into the night, and little headway could be made to Cuba. *At sea, you never knew.*

At last they arrived in Havana, more than two weeks late, and owing to nervousness on the part of the Combined Fleet *Comandante*, they missed their rendezvous. Camaron was not particularly worried, however, as the main body of the fleet was less than a week ahead of him and with good weather he could overtake them. He would need to re-supply water and food and wood first.

And then he would need to sail fast.

THIRTY-EIGHT

It was early on the morning of the twelfth day out of Grand Turk when Fallon saw *Avenger* heave-to and send up the signal *Captains repair on board.*

"Heave-to, Mr. Jones, and please call away my gig," ordered Fallon. He had been waiting for this meeting, had been studying the charts for the Florida Straights and gathering his thoughts. If Davies was right, the Spanish Combined Fleet was heavily guarded with ships-of-the-line and frigates, and while the British Admiralty had little respect for the rank-and-file Spanish *capitán*, Spain would have sent her best on such an important mission.

Fallon and Beauty were both piped over the side onto *Avenger's* deck—a shrill whistle's call with side boys in attendance and marines standing at attention, a practice normally used to welcome visiting captains or dignitaries aboard. The rear admiral was there with Captain Kinis to meet them. Kinis was warmer now, at ease with the new additions to the little fleet, confident in their abilities—the gunnery practices had certainly impressed him. They were all led below to the great cabin and settled in around the charts.

Fallon had always found charts fascinating. To those not in command they were perhaps interesting just because they were *maps*, telling you where you were on the ocean relative to land. To those in command, however, they were more, much more. Overlaying the captain's or master's knowledge of wind and tidal currents, the soundings and anticipated weather patterns rendered charts as critical tools for the advancement of war, critical and massively important for positioning and strategy.

Davies once again reviewed the intelligence he'd received at English Harbor concerning the movement of the Spanish Combined Fleet and the smaller treasure *flota*.

"The task for us will be to disrupt the Combined Fleet and cut out the treasure ships—if we can identify which ships they are," Davies said. "Certainly they will be heavily guarded, and that should give us a clue. But beyond that we will have to see how they *behave* when we attack. Which wolves guard which sheep. I welcome your thoughts, please."

Kinis spoke first. "Our position is approximately here"— pointing his finger to a spot on the chart just off Eleuthera, roughly a hundred miles west of Nassau. "Are we sure the Combined Fleet will head north through the Straights of Florida before turning east for Spain? Might they try to navigate eastwards through the Bahamas instead?"

"With all respect, I think not, Captain Kinis," replied Fallon. "It would be difficult for the fleet to work through those islands, straight into the teeth of the trades, and the water can be very thin indeed for heavily laden ships."

"Excellent points, Captain Fallon," said Davies. "So we must assume they will go with the route they usually take."

Now they fell silent, studying the charts and hypothetically positioning their respective ships in their minds for best advantage. It was Beauty who spoke up.

"Of course, we don't know for sure whether we're too late, too early, or just where we want to be with our arrival. We still have several hundred miles to go just to reach Great Bahama and begin ranging over the area between there and Spanish Florida. So I'm wondering—"

"Yes? What are you thinking, Beauty?" questioned Fallon. According to British naval protocol, Beauty was captain of *Sea*

Dog now, and should be addressed as such. But true to his nature, Fallon preferred informality with his best friend.

"Well, *Sea Dog* would have no trouble picking her way through the islands to Nassau," Beauty explained. "We could put someone ashore for a night of debauchery, someone clever enough to get information without attracting attention. Maybe there's scuttlebutt about the treasure *flota*. Admiral, you said you thought the news of the Combined Fleet would be on the waterfront. It might save us from a fool's errand or, even better, help us be in position in time to strike."

Four heads bent over the chart, and Davies' head was the first to raise. "That is an excellent suggestion, Captain. You could be there by nightfall, arrive undetected, set someone ashore and be off at first light and back here by the forenoon tomorrow. Gentlemen, what do you think?"

"Excellent, Beauty," said Fallon. "Not without its challenges, however. Tell me, whom do you have in mind to go ashore?" Fallon wondering himself who that might be.

"I have someone who might serve," interjected Kinis. "He's a Dago whose life we saved just before pirates were going to hang him. You know of him, sir, Cortez, a topman."

"I do know him, Captain Kinis," said Davies. "He's got a bit of a piratical look about him already, if that's the one."

"Yes, that's him. Debauchery would come naturally to him, but he's got a clever way about him. He misses nothing in this ship."

"Totally trustworthy not to run?" asked Fallon.

"I would stake my command on it, sir," said Kinis without a hint of indignation.

"I like the plan," said Davies. "And I like the man. Let's suspend our planning here until we gather more information from *Sea Dog's* visit to Nassau. God willing, I'm hopeful we will learn something valuable. Captain Kinis, will you please speak with Cortez and see if he is game?"

Kinis left immediately and Davies called his clerk to write the orders that would commit *Sea Dog* to the plan. Fallon took the opportunity to have a private word with Beauty topside.

"Be careful with this," he said quietly. "Lots of tricky bits around those islands with coral heads. And Nassau will be teeming with all manner of dangerous characters. If you find trouble, there's no helping you."

"Well I know," Beauty said, thankful for her friend's earnest concern for her safety. "My thought is to enter the harbor just past dark. Kendricks, the master's mate Davies lent me, is familiar with the entrance and says it's pretty straightforward. Let's hope this Cortez is as reliable as Kinis says."

"So you already checked with Kendricks about the approach?" Fallon asked, incredulous. "You had this idea before we all met, didn't you?"

"Oh, Nico," Beauty laughed. "You know I like to steer my own boat."

THIRTY-NINE

*T*HE AFTERNOON *that* Sea Dog *sailed for Nassau, several thousand miles away two young children played on the highlands of Ethiopia. The boy threw dirt into the air and laughed as the wind took it away, swirling it into a dust devil, upward into the sky. The boy and girl played on for a while and, finally tiring of their games, wandered off to their village to get something to eat.*

Meanwhile, the dust swirled up into the atmosphere. It caught upper altitude winds and, still swirling, moved toward the coast of Africa. As the small, revolving mass of air arrived over the ocean, it created something like a vacuum, sucking up warm air from the surface and creating an unequal pressure. Air from surrounding areas with higher pressure rushed into the low-pressure area and picked up more warmth and moisture, only to rise and continue the cycle upward in a swirling motion. The system was moving now, growing stronger, the water in the air forming clouds that began to spin and grow, fed by the ocean's heat and water evaporating from the surface.

This particular force of nature took on an ominous cast as the clouds formed circular bands, with the wind blowing counterclockwise. The speed of the winds grew to fifty knots; then as the mass began traveling over still warmer water, the wind picked up more. It went to seventy knots overnight. There was no forecasting its path or trajectory, but it generally moved northwest following the ancient route of such massive ocean storms in late summer.

Which is to say it was generally making for the Bahamas.

FORTY

ORTEZ CERTAINLY looked the part.

It hadn't taken much for Beauty to imagine him as a pirate, or worse if there was such; he wasn't too clean to begin with and all hands contributed to his clothes, for ship's slops wouldn't do. A pistol was produced, a ribbon for his hair, a little grease for his face and *voilà! Blackbeard.*

Beauty stood beside Kendricks, the master's mate loaned from *Avenger*, as he guided *Sea Dog* between Eleuthera and Cat Island without difficulty. Something about Kendricks made her suspect he had done some smuggling in these waters before, but she left it alone. The sun was on the way to low when they turned north toward Nassau.

Beauty took Cortez aside and made sure he understood his orders. She stressed he not put himself in physical danger, to take it slow and get back alive without arousing suspicion. After all, he was a new face on the waterfront. If pressed, his story was that he had sailed in on a trader—he would need to casually ascertain the last one to leave Nassau—and decided to stay and look for better opportunities. Sounded good enough.

Beauty watched Cortez listen as if he didn't need the instruction or advice. It irritated her, and she worried he was more interested in the fun ashore than the information he was supposed to obtain. But there was nothing for it—he was their man.

Kendricks made the channel entrance just after dark, good as his word. They shortened sail and glided in on a dying breeze, undetected to all accounts, though a number of boats were at anchor and music could be heard onshore. *Sea Dog* rounded up and let the anchor go several hundred yards from a deserted part of the beach. Cortez climbed down into the ship's boat, began rowing for shore and, in less than a minute, had disappeared into a very dark night. Their last glimpse was of him smiling.

Beauty set a good lookout, not wanting to be surprised by anything. Satisfied that all was well for the time being, she set the watches and went below to have dinner, asking to be called immediately if anything came amiss.

Cortez rowed to an unlit stretch of shoreline and pulled the boat up onto the sand. Down the beach a few hundred yards he could see lights and hear laughter and music, and he cautiously made his way toward the sounds. There were shacks along the shore, rough wooden and thatch houses, mostly leaning to one side, all dark.

He came upon a stretch of buildings, bars really, lit by torches and candles and populated by all manner of humanity, seemingly from all over the world, drinking and laughing and whoring to excess. Nassau was wide open, and everyone came. In what passed for a street the beggars asked for money or food. An old woman squatted on her haunches holding a nut in her shriveled hand, for sale. Cortez looked away and took a deep breath, pushed his pistol down lower into his waistband, and stepped inside the first bar.

THE NIGHT crept on, the stars came splashing across the clear sky, and *Sea Dog* floated silently as driftwood. The glass turned, watches changed, and the music began to die onshore. Lights still twinkled here and there, particularly around Government House, but at *Sea Dog*'s end of the harbor all was quiet.

Beauty tried to sleep, but got nowhere. She thought of Bermuda and her home, of the woman who might be missing her and worried for her safety. She thought of Cortez ashore, wondering what he saw and heard and, briefly, whether he would even come back. Well, Kinis had been certain about his loyalty so that was enough for her.

The ship was quiet, the men on watch talking in whispers because voices travelled so far over water. Beauty rose from her cot and stood at the stern windows. There was nothing to see as *Sea Dog's* stern faced away from shore, which only added to Beauty's frustration and impatience. Two hours before dawn was all she could manage to stay below, and she thumped up the companionway to a spectacular sky, a black vault full of diamonds, perhaps just lightening ever so little there to the east.

She had made it clear to Cortez that he had until one hour before dawn to return or they would leave. She didn't want him passed out somewhere while the ship stood waiting.

An hour and a half before dawn, the eastern sky now definitely lightening. All hands nervous, making small talk at their stations, looking toward shore, waiting for the order to up anchor.

Then, *laughter.*

Incongruous laughter, more like giggling and barely contained whooping, and it grew louder. Out of the darkness Cortez rowed, his back to *Sea Dog,* while in the stern sat the *Queen of the Night.*

The men looked at each other and grinned. Cortez had brought a doxie out from shore, *by God,* the scoundrel! The boat came alongside and clapped on, Cortez climbed up the ship's side and landed unsteadily on his feet, obviously in his cups, and performed a deep bow to Beauty, who was visibly furious.

Here came the doxie, giggling at this new adventure, *a big ship— how fun!*—tumbling over the side to land on her backside, her skirt over her head, white legs akimbo. The crew got their eyeful before Beauty took command of the situation, ordering Cortez below to the crew's quarters and the doxie to the captain's cabin. The ship's boat was hauled aboard, the anchor weighed, and the ship gotten underway immediately. Kendricks took them out of the harbor on a small land breeze, silently and invisibly; no eyes from shore could have seen them as they sailed, first away eastward and then northeast.

Sea Dog hove-to in the forenoon of the next day, as planned, just off Eleuthera. *Avenger* was hove-to, and *Harp*, as well, approximately where Beauty had left them the day before. The signal went up to *Avenger's* gaff: *Captains repair on board.*

Beauty had gotten very little sleep the night before. She had put the doxie on the floor in Fallon's old cabin, now hers, with a guard outside to keep the men at bay, while she herself had dozed off now and then on deck. No doubt the doxie was still sleeping, and likely would be for the better part of a year judging by how hard the men had worked to wake Cortez.

Sea Dog's boat was lowered just as Cortez was lifted up the companionway steps looking very much the worse for drink. Beauty gave him a look that would melt steel, and he straightened his back as best he could and, with a little help, managed to go over the side and into the waiting boat.

Once aboard *Avenger* Cortez tried to make a show of propriety but all hands knew the *look*. They'd both worn and seen the look of a night ashore many times. Beauty took Cortez firmly by the arm and marched him below to the great cabin where Fallon, Kinis, and Davies waited.

"Now, Cortez," began Captain Kinis, looking at the dog's breakfast before him, "what did you discover in Nassau besides rum?" Smiles all around, but not from Beauty, who knew what else he'd discovered and drilled little holes into him with her eyes.

"I went to many places, *Capitán*," Cortez began. "There was much talk about the Spanish treasure, but just that. Talk. I was getting nowhere when I decided to go more into the town, to a place I heard of that was even more dangerous than the places I had been. I was not brave, *capitánes*, I was very afraid to go but more afraid not to go."

Here Cortez looked at each of the senior officers and smiled a weak, knowing kind of smile. *I had my duty.* It was exactly what Kinis had staked his command on.

"At this place there were many bad men," Cortez continued, "pirates, I think, or smugglers or I don't know, but bad. I bought a drink for a woman and pretended not to be interested in anyone else, but I heard things. Men were talking about the fleet and someone said someone had heard it had left Havana for Spain already. That was the story I heard."

Beauty saw Fallon watching Cortez closely. He looked crestfallen but totally absorbed in what the sailor was saying. "Is that all, then?" Fallon asked.

"No," Cortez answered, and Fallon's breath caught. "I heard something different from the man behind the bar, who looked pretty bad himself and was very dirty. He said 'Sure it left, but not with the treasure, is what I heard. Them ships missed the *run-de-vouz* so they got left behind.' That's what he said exactly, I remember it like it was yesterday."

Well, it *was* yesterday thought Davies. "Be sure, Cortez," he said, leaning in toward the man. "Is that exactly what he said?"

"*Sí, sí,*" answered Cortez with certainty. "That's what I heard."

Fallon felt the excitement in the cabin rise. Now there was something to hold onto, by God! But hold onto how hard? It was one person, likely trying to impress his friends and probably as drunk as any of them. He looked at Cortez. "Anything else?" he asked.

Cortez shook his head no, and looked at Beauty, preparing himself to be exposed for the doxie. But Beauty betrayed nothing of the truth, to his infinite surprise, and he suppressed the urge to hug her. Wisely.

"Thank you, Cortez," said Kinis. "Well done. Now off with you to get some rest," adding, "and a bath."

When Cortez had left, Davies went all in. "I think we have to believe in what the barman said. I know it sounds far-fetched, but why spread a story like that among pirates and thieves? Was it mere gossip or something more? We don't know. But I'm inclined to believe it *could* be true. Mainly because I would hate to find out too late that it *was* true. Are we agreed? We proceed as planned?"

Fallon looked to Beauty who looked to Kinis. Everyone nodded, new life in the cabin.

"Very good," said Davies enthusiastically. "Now, let us devise a plan to stop this *flota* from ever reaching Spain. Sinking the ships should be a last resort. I want that treasure for England!"

FORTY-ONE

SEA DOG led the Royal Navy around Great Bahama Island, well off Matanilla Reef and into the Florida Straights. The distance to Florida was only fifty miles, so the Spanish ships would have to sail through something of a bottleneck, and Davies intended to put a stopper in the bottle. This assuming the treasure ships were out there.

On board Sea Dog, Beauty faced a problem with the doxie below, confined to the captain's guarded cabin for fear the men would find a way to her, as men would. Beauty had spoken to her once, found her afraid and embarrassed but not ignorant. In fact, something like intelligence glowed in her eyes and Beauty softened to the woman. Still, women in her profession were a nuisance to have aboard, providing too great a temptation to men housed for months on end in a ship, especially if the temptress were willing.

The doxie's name was Theodora, and perhaps she was not willing. She seemed to recognize her situation for the hopeless mess it was, knew that it was in large part her fault, and seemed capable enough to fend for herself against unwanted advances. Beauty made that the bargain. Theo, as she preferred to be called, could be let out of the cabin and on deck but if she once, even once, so much as batted an eye at any man aboard she would be clapped in irons for the duration of the cruise, if they survived the cruise, and set ashore God knew where. Meanwhile, she would have to earn her meals.

They shook on it. Theo was issued slops and assigned to duties in the cockpit, under the tutelage of Garrison, a surgeon's mate from *Avenger* lent by Davies. In the bright sunshine, without makeup and powder, Theo was a normal-looking young woman of moderate good looks and long blonde hair, which she cut short immediately to make it clear to Beauty that she would do the work of a man. Beauty took the point and was encouraged. It was arranged that Theo would berth in Pence's old cabin.

Sea Dog sailed on, leading the ships into the Straights, the first to cross the strong north-flowing current between Great Bahama and the coast of Spanish Florida. The schooner moved briskly along under mares' tails in the sky. Upon turning south, however, into the teeth of the current, all the ships slowed as they took the rollers on the nose. It was a bumpy ride, the wind being generally out of the east-northeast.

Sea Dog's best man was at the lookout, the morning was warming, and Beauty went below to have her breakfast. Now it was about waiting.

DAVIES PACED and fretted on *Avenger's* quarterdeck, aware that they were leaving Great Bahama in their wake but damned if he knew what was ahead. He walked with his chin jutted out, deep in thought about *outcomes*.

The best outcome he could envision, assuming they were not arriving too late on station, was to sink or disable beyond repair one or two ships so that not all the bullion would reach Spain and, eventually, the French treasury.

He saw it in his mind. The flotilla would sail with the current up the Straights, likely a ship-of-the-line or heavy frigate in the van, perhaps another outside the line of ships, and perhaps still another on the other side. *Like sheep dogs guarding the flock.* His plan was for *Harp* and *Avenger* to attack the dogs while *Sea Dog* sailed among the sheep, using her expert gunnery to cripple as many ships as possible. He didn't expect the treasure ships to pose a threat; but how many sheep dogs did they bring along?

Davies raised his telescope and saw *Sea Dog* bear away to take up station. The schooner was to be in the middle of the Straights, farthest south. *Harp* would be closest to Florida, just inside Cape Caniaberal, with *Avenger* closest to Great Bahama. An inverted triangle, *Sea Dog* the eyes of the fleet.

What would he have done if Fallon had not joined? Davies shuddered, for it didn't bear thinking about. As it was they faced long odds of accomplishing anything against a superior force, and in spite of his outward calm to the men, he was ravaged by doubt.

"Signal to *Harp*, Captain Kinis: *Proceed to take up station.*"

The signal was given and acknowledged. They were committed to a plan now, *his* plan. In another hour *Avenger* would tack and wear to await events. Kinis was already making preparations to shorten sail and had personally inspected the gun carriages and lashings, every one, out of nervousness. In the cockpit, bandages were laid out, saws and knives sharpened, and the bucket for amputated limbs pulled out from beneath a cot. The galley fires would remain lit until further notice.

All afternoon and evening they held station. No word from Beauty. Davies went back over Cortez's report in his mind, even going so far as to ask Cortez to repeat it, the part about the barman, for that was the part that gave him hope. When night fell, Davies took his fears to bed. He felt heavy, and alone, and truth be told, more than a little afraid.

FORTY-TWO

*T*HE RAIN *began on Sint Maarten in the late evening and, though the seas were moderate the next morning, the fisher-men refused to go out. Something told them to stay home, an instinct borne of thousands of mornings at sea in every condition imag-inable. It was the way the seas were making up, even without a great deal of wind, as if there was in fact a great deal of wind somewhere else pushing water toward the island. Yes, they would stay home today.*

In the village, the markets opened under tarps and umbrellas, bright patches of color against a gray day. Baskets and fruits and vegetables were put out on rickety wooden platforms for the few villagers braving the rain and muddy streets to become customers.

The fingertips of the storm were just to the island, and by afternoon the rain was falling in earnest, the wind gusting to 45 knots. Hardly a cause for concern; these islanders had seen storms before. But there was something about this one, they thought to themselves, and the markets closed early.

THE AFTERNOON had grown cloudy and the wind had fallen light. The approaching storm, still hundreds of miles away, sucked the wind out of the atmosphere to feed its insatiable appetite for power. All three British captains on their respective ships looked anxiously at the sky from time to time, wondering. Certainly Fallon had been in storms before, but there was something about this one . . .

Aja had joined Fallon on *Harp*'s quarterdeck and gazed at his captain, sensing a slight and unusual nervousness in the man. Aja had come to know Fallon's moods and feelings very well, indeed. Something felt off.

Colston, the master, was standing at the binnacle, a worried look on his face, his thumbnail tapping the Naire barometer. It was the newest design, thanks to Bishop's purse, with gimbal mounts housed in the ship's binnacle. Colston looked up as Fallon approached.

"Glass is dropping, sir. We're in for something." Colston looked around, over the side, and thought to himself, *this sea feels strange.* "And Captain, we're being set northwards by this damned current. Cape Caniaberal is well south of us now."

"Thank you, Mr. Colston," said Fallon. "I don't like it, and I'm sure the other captains feel the same. Keep an eye on the glass and tell me if it drops further, if you please."

In fact, the glass dropped slowly throughout the day as the three ships tried to hold their triangular positions in the Straights between Cape Caniaberal and Great Bahama Island.

The day grew darker and rain began falling and still no sign of the treasure ships. Fallon worried that perhaps they had cut it too fine. Perhaps the missed rendezvous hadn't happened at all. Perhaps. Perhaps.

Signal from the flag: *Hold station.*

Avenger's signal came just as Fallon was about to shorten sail to have greater control over *Harp*. The wind was getting up out of the east and as it crossed the northward current the seas were becoming confused. *A messy night ahead. And possibly dangerous.*

Fallon ordered Jones to begin a series of reefing maneuvers that would continue into the evening. All hands were called time and again to go aloft, their backs wet and hair streaming, fisting the sails into submission while clinging to spiraling spars drawing great circles in the low clouds. Jones supervised each maneuver, rain dripping from his hat, his light cloak tight against his throat, his sunburned face a grimace.

Each sail change sent a sodden crew below, where it wasn't much drier, the ship working in the seas and water dripping through the deck seams. The crew refused to complain, however, accepting the sailor's lot to be wet and miserable. It was better than soldiering.

At daybreak, *a cannon.*

Both Kinis and Fallon were on their respective decks, and both grabbed telescopes to look south. In the rain and haze they couldn't make out *Sea Dog*, which was probably why Beauty had fired a cannon instead of sending up a signal. Both captains ordered their lookouts to keep a sharp eye as events would now begin unfolding quickly.

Fallon was careful to parallel the coast of Florida, not wanting to inch to the middle of the Straights until he had a clearer picture of the situation but not wanting to get too close to Cape Caniaberal either. *Harp* was under deeply reefed sails in the building wind and seas; Fallon peered uneasily into the gloom.

"Mr. Jones, call all hands," he ordered.

The cry went out, the drummer tatted out the call, and all hands rushed to their stations, sand and shot coming up from below. Quids were spit overboard, lucky charms found and rubbed, the hands thinking of treasure. Fallon continued to scan the horizon for Beauty. Still, no sign. For that matter, no sign of *Avenger.*

Minutes dragged on as all hands stood at their stations in the slanting rain, the ship moving uneasily in the swells beneath their bare feet. Silence from the masthead, a particularly lonely and miserable spot in this storm.

Then, something *there.* Just off the larboard bow, emerging from the gray curtain of rain: *Sea Dog.*

"Deck there!" yelled the lookout. "Sail ahead!"

"What signal?" shouted Fallon as he raised his telescope to look forward.

"*Enemy in sight! Frigate!*"

That would mean the flotilla had a frigate in the van, ranging in front to be the first line of defense. Fallon felt the hair go up on his arms; he would engage the Spanish frigate first.

"Acknowledge signal," Fallon ordered the signal boy. "Make: *Well done.*"

Sea Dog was a clear picture now, and Fallon could see Beauty on the quarterdeck, hair plastered to her head, her fist raised in the air. She yelled something as their ships passed, but it was snatched away by the wind. For a moment Fallon looked fondly at his old command, *my God, she was beautiful.* Even reefed *Sea Dog* was a flyer, though he knew from experience she was a handful in these seas with this wind.

Fallon glanced quickly at Jones, and smiled to himself at the confidence in his First's face. A lot had happened in these past weeks of drill to put it there.

Now Colston was by his side. "Wind increasing, sir. And the glass is dropping, still. I think it's coming on to a gale of wind! Best mind your sea room."

Good advice. Fallon looked over his shoulder for *Sea Dog* but she had disappeared to find *Avenger*, visibility making signals at a distance impossible. Turning around he saw the Spanish frigate appear like an apparition from the impossibly gray gloom of the air.

"Oh!" left his lips before he could stop it. *That is a big fucking frigate!*

FORTY-THREE

FALLON'S MIND immediately went to strategy.

The Spaniard was less than a mile away, off the larboard bow, under reefed topgallants and indeed looked ready for a fight.

"Mr. Jones," Fallon said, "load the starboard battery but do not run out, if you please. And then lay aft."

Jones gave the order and the hands bent to the starboard guns. Fallon studied the oncoming frigate carefully through his telescope, holding course to pass *Harp* at two cables apart. The ship looked to him like a cut-down ship-of-the-line, a hybrid that Spanish shipwrights created to do battle with enemy frigates as well as heavier ships-of-the-line. Trading broadsides against so many guns, even poorly handled, would be suicide.

Jones joined Fallon and Colston at the helm. "Gentlemen, we haven't much time. Our job is to engage and hopefully disable that frigate until *Avenger* can come up." Jones nodded, rain pouring off his hat onto Colston, whose mouth hung open. "Here's what I want to do . . . " They listened carefully, absorbing the points of the plan, each knowing as well as Fallon that events could dictate otherwise. But, slowly, *Harp* began edging up toward the oncoming frigate.

Still no sign of Davies, or *Sea Dog*, for that matter. *Harp* was being pushed around by the surging waves; Fallon could only imagine how Beauty was handling the schooner. *Barely*, was his guess. He looked at *Harp*'s sails with a questioning eye. The last thing he wanted was to lose a spar in this wind and be crippled at the moment of battle. Jones caught Fallon's worried look and it only confirmed his own philosophy: *The time to reef is when you first think about it.* Jones ordered a third reef in the topgallants.

It was hellishly dangerous to go aloft in such a wind, but the rig was in danger of going over the side. Men trained to obey orders went up and up, clinging desperately to the ratlines as the ship's masts swayed through 60 degrees. It was slow going, toes and fingers clenching the ropes as one by one the men inched out onto the yards. One slip meant a man's death in ninety feet; his pigtail would be the last to know.

Half a mile now separated the ships. They converged on parallel paths set to pass less than a cable's length apart now, with *Sea Dog* still heading up to narrow the gap. Fallon stood on the quarterdeck, the wind tearing at his clothes, his hat long ago blown over the side. Aja was nearby, a small dirk in his belt courtesy of the lower deck, appearing braver than he felt. He looked at his captain, balancing easily on the heaving and plunging deck, and though Fallon could not see it—and would not have believed it if he *could*—the boy's eyes glowed with obvious pride in his captain.

The moment was at hand. Fallon had a word with Jones and the helmsman and *Harp* came up on the wind a bit more, ever so slowly inching over toward the Spanish frigate, not so much as to tip the hand, just so. A quarter mile, the ships closing at a combined rate of more than fifteen knots. Fallon clenched his jaw; Aja saw it and clenched his jaw, too.

"Now, helmsman, up you go," ordered Jones, and *Harp* moved to come hard on the wind and cut across the Spaniard's bows. "Run out the starboard battery, Mr. Jones!" yelled Fallon. "Give it to them, lads!"

The heel of the ship as *Harp* hardened up made the guns almost fly out of the ship.

"Fire!" came Fallon's order, and the full broadside roared and hurled their shot. Every shot told, tearing into the bow and larboard side of the frigate and sending splinters into the air.

"Reload and run out!" yelled a frantic Jones, and Fallon counted the seconds. They had to make this count; firing into the vulnerable and undefended bow or stern of a ship was a good idea until you inevitably showed your own stern to the enemy. *Then all hell.*

"*Fire!*" Fallon ordered again, and he guessed it was close to two minutes between broadsides. It gave him heart, as did the sight of the Spanish frigate's forestay parting when her jib boom exploded, her foresail torn from its hanks and sent flying over the waves.

"Good shooting, lads!" he yelled, cheering them on madly, but his words were lost in the scream of wind that seemed to increase with every second. It was backing solidly to the east-northeast, easily a gale of wind now, and it would make wearing ship dangerous, even untenable.

The Spanish *capitán* knew his business. The frigate came up into the wind, effectively drawing him closer to *Sea Dog* to prevent Fallon from loosening up and firing another broadside.

The Spaniard's starboard guns belched their deadly fire and shot, the wind tearing the smoke away, and *Harp's* fragile stern took several balls that destroyed the railings and bulwark, disintegrated the name board, and blew out all the windows on their way through the innards of the ship. Fallon shuddered at the loss of life below and wondered about damage to the hull, but he had to focus on the battle, for *Harp still steered!*

Estrella shot past—Fallon could read her name on the stern now—and he ordered the helmsman to fall off onto a broad reach, back on a course to intercept the main body of the flotilla.

Fallon heard another broadside—but behind him, by God!—as *Sea Dog* charged out of the gloom across *Estrella's* bow, just as *Harp* had done, all her shot aimed at the Spaniard's rigging. *Jesus!* The foremast was going over! *Good shooting, Cully!*

Now *Sea Dog's* stern would be exposed, just as *Harp's* had been. Fallon couldn't tear his eyes off the scene, fear gripping him as he waited for *Estrella's* response.

But then, *Avenger!* She plunged forward, loosened up and

shot down the larboard side of *Estrella*, 36 guns out and sending a monstrous broadside into sails and rigging, cutting ropes, and sending the ship's boats flying out of their lashings and taking men with them. *Estrella* ignored *Sea Dog's* stern and sent a broadside of her own into *Avenger*, effect unknown, for Fallon was jolted out of his focus on *Avenger* by Jones screaming into his ear that the flotilla was coming. Fallon's head snapped around and, by God, there it was, appearing like an apparition: five ships, one a ship-of-the-line, marching like soldiers hot-stepping it over the waves toward *Harp*.

Once more Colston yelled into Fallon's ear. "Glass dropping like a stone, sir! This wind is pushing us toward the coast and the current keeps setting us north. We must keep our sea room!"

Fallon only nodded, aware of the danger but determined to execute the plan Davies had set out. He picked up his telescope and found the ship-of-the-line easily, plowing water on the windward side of the flotilla, no doubt counting on the British penchant for choosing the weather gauge in battle. He motioned for Jones.

"We will pass on the larboard side of the ships, Jones. Load with chain shot and bar. And tell the gun captains rigging only." Davies had argued for disabling the Spanish ships rather than trying to sink them, hoping to capture at least some of the treasure. But in the face of the storm a disabled ship would very likely sink anyway. It was the best they could hope to accomplish.

The Spanish ship-of-the-line was effectively neutered, being on the far side of the flotilla, their starboard side, though if she were well-handled she could perhaps shoot the gap between her charges to engage *Harp*. Well, thought Fallon, *we'll soon see.*

Here was the first treasure ship, massive and dull, deeply reefed and riding low in the water. Fallon ordered the helmsman to pass her at less than a cable's length. Six gun ports flew open on the Spanish ship's larboard side; *Harp's* sixteen larboard side guns were run out, like black teeth in a snarl.

"Fire!" Again Fallon screamed into the wind, and *Harp* barked

and tore at the enemy's flesh, sending a hail of devastation across very few feet of water, balls joined by lengths of chain, balls joined by solid bar, cutting spars and rigging and shredding the delicate latticework structure that kept the sails aloft. The big ship's mizzenmast was completely cut in two and her standing rigging hung over the side like a sea anchor. She fired a ragged salvo, but these were not trained gunners on a fighting ship and, though some of the balls undoubtedly hit home, *Harp* did not shudder. Fallon looked over his shoulder as the ships passed—*Valiente* was on the treasure ship's stern.

Harp's guns were being reloaded, again with chain, as onward the next ship came. Fallon stole a quick look over his shoulder; the rain drove needles into his eyes but he could just make out *Avenger* coming down the other side—the starboard side—of the line of ships and preparing to engage *Valiente*.

Spanish signals were flying, stiff as boards in the wind, as the *capitán* of the Spanish ship-of-the-line sought to recover a situation that was rapidly deteriorating. *Avenger* was almost down to *Valiente*, her guns run out on starboard. Suddenly the Spanish ship-of-the-line made a move to cut between *Valiente* and the next ship, in effect to cross *Avenger*'s bows and *Harp*'s stern. Fallon saw the strategy with admiration, brilliant really, if the big ship could pull it off.

Avenger opened fire on *Valiente*'s starboard side, chain and langridge, trying to cripple her and finish the job *Harp* began. When the wind blew the smoke away there was virtually nothing left of *Valiente*'s rigging—mainmast and foremast were just stumps on deck, and her sails draped over the side as she sluiced around, helpless to make steerage way in the wind and seas.

The Spanish ship-of-the-line was now cutting across *Avenger*'s bows and loosed a terrific broadside of some 40 guns into her. *Avenger*'s bow was horribly savaged, forestay parted and all hands at the forward carronades cut down. *Avenger*'s warrior figurehead was obliterated and in its place a gaping hole right at the heads of the ship.

Captain Kinis called for the hands to quickly cut away the rigging, which acted as a powerful drag. And as the flagship passed the stern of the big Spanish ship-of-the-line—*Punta de la Concepción*—*Avenger* gave her answer. All guns bore on *Punta*'s stern, many double shotted, and ball after ball drove into that most fragile part of the ship, mauling wood and men alike. *Punta*'s mizzen rigging snapped with a sound like musket fire and the mizzenmast lurched forward, the force of the wind astern sending it crashing onto the quarterdeck.

Fallon feared an impending onslaught to his own stern and hardened up so as to present *Harp*'s quarter to *Punta*'s expected broadside. It came, and hell came with it. *Whump! Whump! Whump!* Almost two dozen times into *Harp*'s larboard quarter. The helmsman went down in bloody gore, and his splatter coated his mate in scarlet gobs. Men were blown backward, some blown overboard—there was no thought of turning around to rescue them, of course. They were simply *gone*. Splinters flew in the wind, striking men and jamming into the sides of the ship like giant darts.

Fallon reeled and fell from the concussive blasts, and Aja rushed to his side, his own legs bleeding from tiny splinters. "Aja, thank God," rasped Fallon. "Find Mr. Jones and ask him to have the carpenter sound the well. Quickly now."

But first Aja helped Fallon to his feet, and the full devastation was laid bare. Men were dead in heaps where they had stood gallantly at their stations. Huge furrows were cut into the deck, which looked like a freshly plowed field. The mizzenmast was gone, along with the mizzen sail, and Jones was busy ordering the men to cut the rigging away. A quick look at the mainmast showed damage, how serious Fallon couldn't tell. But damage.

"Fall off," Fallon yelled to the lone helmsman, and *Harp* bore away on a broad reach again, now on a parallel course to the next oncoming treasure ship. He ordered the topgallants taken in, the first reef in the topsails, and struck all the foresails except a small jib. The men obeyed without question and hurried aloft and forward. Now Fallon looked over his shoulder to see *Avenger*, sailing with a bone in her teeth, running out her starboard guns. The sight cheered him, if only for a moment. Then it was back to his own business.

"Mr. Jones! Mr. Jones!" he called, "Load and run out on larboard. Chain and bar only! Quickly!"

Jones appeared shaken and disoriented. Blood dripped off his hands from hidden wounds, but Fallon's order snapped his mind back to his duty, and he rallied the gun crews on the larboard side. Quickly they loaded the guns and ran out. "Elevate for the rigging, men!" Jones called. "Fire on the up roll at my command!" The ship was heeling to starboard, and it was doubly hard to run out the guns, but easy to aim high for the rigging as the *Harp* was leaning over dramatically.

Jones held his mouth open, steady now, steady, up the ship rose—"*Fire!*"

Chain and bar flew like whirling scythes, cutting apart anything in their way, rigging and sails and men and spars all sliced apart and blown asunder. A single bar cut a Spaniard in half where he stood and his upper body seemed to simply lift away into the wind and overboard.

"Load again, Jones!" yelled Fallon, relentlessly pushing the battle forward.

Here is where the training paid dividends, and the men bent to their jobs, each task completed mechanically as if timed to metronomes.

Here was Aja tugging at Fallon's sleeve. "Two feet in the well, sir. And rising. I told Mr. Jones," he said. Fallon knew the hull had taken some shots, but the report could have been much worse. "Hands are at the pumps," the boy continued. "But many men are dead at the guns."

"Thank you, Aja," said Fallon, fighting to get his dazed mind to think clearly. But there was no time. He quickly looked for *Punta* and saw her attempt to wear, to get onto the larboard tack so as to run down the far side of the ships on a course astern of *Harp*. It was a frightening decision, full of dire implications given the force of wind pushing her stern around. The timing had to be superb or . . . or, *My God*, thought Fallon as *Punta* wore around, her stern passing through the eye of the wind, her booms flying across the deck with tremendous power. Her booms snapped at the masts, rigging holding them over the side, the ship laying over so far Fallon could see her dirty copper, a massive hull struggling to right itself against wind and sea. Men would be overboard and forgotten already. Water poured in through her open gun ports on the starboard side.

Suddenly *Sea Dog* was back from oblivion, deeply reefed and heeled over as she bucked and plunged in the maelstrom. She disappeared completely in the heavy seas and then rose like a cork atop the next wave, Beauty at the helm, her peg leg stuck in a ring bolt, her face set hard. A signal broke out from her gaff: *Lost frigate*. Either *Estrella* had continued on for Spain or had foundered, Fallon thought. Either way, she was gone.

But here was the next treasure ship, *Río de Oro*—Fallon could barely read the name on her stern through his telescope—as she bore off westward toward *Punta*, breaking the line after seeing the wreckage that preceded her, sailing low toward the oncoming *Sea Dog*.

In the lull the air was rent by a single gun from *Avenger* to call attention to her signal: *Save your ship*.

Davies was calling off the action. *By God!* thought Fallon. Davies would not continue to force the fight in an untenable situation. Indeed, seas had grown truly mountainous. Spume filled the air, the foam painting the whole scene a streaked white. Fallon had been so engrossed in the tactics of fighting so many ships that he'd lost track of *Harp*'s position.

"Mr. Colston," he screamed to the man not two feet away at the binnacle, "where the hell are we now?"

Colston gathered his breath to scream back. "I believe we're off St. Augustine, sir. But I can't be sure." That meant they had been set farther north by the current than Fallon had thought. Great Bahama was now well south of them.

Fallon watched *Río de Oro*, still bearing off westward, presumably toward St. Augustine. And here was another treasure ship in the distance to consider, plunging northward carrying little more than canvas scraps for sails. Fallon wanted to keep fighting the ship, but *Sea Dog*'s situation was becoming untenable, and he knew it.

Quickly, he looked toward *Punta* drifting toward the shoals of the Cape; the ship had rolled back upright, low in the water either from bullion or flooding below decks, or both. Now *Sea Dog* was running out her starboard guns: *This small dog can bite!* remembered Fallon. Beauty had *Punta* at point-blank range, and all the schooner's guns sent their deadly charges into the Spanish ship-of-the-line's hull, low and deep into her bowels. There was no chance to salvage the treasure, so better to sink the ship. It was all mad, horribly, maniacally mad to fight such a battle on such a sea in such a wind.

Colston was saying something, but Fallon couldn't hear him in the rising wind. "Sir, another ship!" Fallon raised his telescope and looked to where Colston pointed off the larboard bow. There was a frigate, all right, less than a mile to the south. She must have been guarding the rear of the *flota*, thought Fallon.

But something about the ship sent a chill through him, though he was already soaked and shivering. The frigate seemed to fly toward the last treasure ship, which was even now bearing off away from it— *What the hell?* On the quarterdeck of the frigate was a giant of a man, black hair streaming around his face, the cutlass in his hand pointed directly toward Fallon's heart.

Clayton!

FORTY-FOUR

IT WAS NOW a hurricane with no upper limits in sight. The waves were deep valleys, momentarily blanketing *Harp* and much of the rigging from the wind, causing ropes and sails to go slack before the next wave lifted the ship up and the full force of the wind caught the sails again.

Fallon had just opened his mouth to call for yet another reef when a loud *crack!* shot through the air, and he knew instantly it was too little too late. The big courses had already ripped apart and fluttered like giant flapping shreds. The small jib was gone, as well, effectively reducing *Harp's* sail plan to . . . nothing.

Harp *was sailing under bare poles.*

"Mr. Jones, quickly, sir!" yelled Fallon to his First. "There's not a moment to lose. We are going in! Get some hands to lay aft with what's left of the fore sail. Hurry, man!"

Jones hesitated just a moment, casting a longing gaze toward the next treasure ship as it plunged toward them, but orders were orders and years of service said *obey*. There was still cannon fire around them but their first duty was to survive, and his captain had made a decision, a life or death decision, to take them into shore. No captain would willingly go to shore in a storm, but they had no choice. Having lost the ability to sail a course and facing scant sea room, they were going ashore *somewhere* whether they wanted to or not.

"Mr. Colston, steer a course for St. Augustine inlet as best you can tell!" yelled Fallon. "Helmsman, get the wind behind us!" There was no mistaking the calm urgency in Fallon's voice. Scared but weighing options, *in command.*

Slowly, *Harp* came off the wind and ran more or less before it toward an uncertain coast. Men came hurrying aft carrying the sail and Fallon gave instructions to tie it off the stern, a makeshift drogue, to slow their speed through the water and to provide some control to the helm. Fallon looked over his shoulder to see the next treasure ship sail northward past his wake—*Nuevo Año.* Well, there was nothing for it, he told himself.

"Sir, *Río de Oro!*" screamed a frantic Colston, and Fallon's attention was jerked back forward to see *Río* lurching for the inlet ahead of them, reefed down to nothing, on a broad reach, and making twice *Harp's* speed.

"Watch where she goes, Mr. Jones!" Fallon screamed over the wind. "Mr. Colston, be prepared to alter course if she strikes. Otherwise we'll follow her in!"

"Aja!" yelled Fallon, his orders coming rapidly as they closed the coast. "Run to the surgeon and tell him to get the wounded down on the deck. Hurry, lad!" He certainly didn't want wounded men thrown about if they struck. *No, when they struck.* And Ajani was off, lurching with the roll of the ship, as fast as his legs could work.

Fallon judged the distance to the inlet, which he could just see now, to be less than a mile. *Río de Oro* was perhaps half that distance ahead. *Harp's* speed had slowed to almost ten knots thanks to the makeshift sea anchor. But more had to be done, and quickly.

"Mr. Jones, tell the men to lay aft!" Fallon ordered. "Quickly, get them aft!

All of the surviving hands struggled aft, bringing with them a sense of dread, for they knew running aground usually brought death to the crew of any ship caught on a lee shore.

Harp was rapidly closing the coast, pushed forward by the howling hurricane wind and wall-sized waves and spume that obliterated land. Fallon steadied the helmsman, who was struggling with all his might to keep some semblance of a course. Colston stood beside

him for guidance. Jones had mustered the remaining men aft, and
Fallon yelled for them to lie down so they would not be thrown
about when the ship struck. And, too, when the spars came down,
and they would, the men would be aft of the tree-sized lumber and
attendant rigging falling forward.

It was all a wretched guess. *Harp* could sluice around in an instant, pushed by wind or wave or current or just fate, and they
would all meet at the bottom of the sea. Fallon shuddered, cold to
his core with fear, but his jaw jutted out in something like defiance.
He had to save his men. He could not spare a moment for anything
else, not for *Sea Dog* or *Avenger* or treasure ships or even Clayton.
Fucking Clayton!

Río de Oro was approaching the bar at the inlet entrance at
an angle; she would need to fall off quickly. Fallon could see the
breakers clearly now; there seemed to be an entrance of sorts more
northward but *Harp* had no chance to get there. The wind pressure
was coming more from the north as the outer bands of the hurricane's winds rotated counterclockwise. No, it was over the bar or
nothing, and even then bad odds. Fallon knew it, even if he did not
show it to the men.

There! *Río de Oro* was falling off! Fallon stared, mesmerized as
time suddenly seemed to speed up. The treasure ship struck the bar
and her masts snapped out of her, so abrupt was the collision, the
force of the wind still in the top hamper. She lurched forward as a
wave lifted her stern and drove her bow down. Fallon could see her
rudder grabbing air, but then she settled again, sluiced to one side,
was lifted by a gigantic mountain of a wave and was over the bar.
She hurtled into the inlet, yawing this way and that as her helmsman fought to regain control, but it was hopeless with so much top
hamper and rigging over the side.

"Steady," yelled Fallon to his own helmsman. "Straight in for the
inlet, a Sunday sail, eh?" The helmsman laughed through clenched
teeth, a bitter laugh but *something*.

And then it was upon them. *Harp* rose on the crest of a wave

breaking over the bar and then fell off abruptly, the wave passing under, the ship landing hard on her stern. Fallon could sense
the rudder snap, breaking free of its pintles, and a quick look to the
helmsman confirmed it. Now they were lifted again, even higher,
up and up and then, like falling off a cliff, they came down, an ava-
lanche of wood and cannon and human beings so violent that the
masts and all rigging crashed forward on impact, sparing the men
but rendering the ship helpless.

But *Harp* was over!

St. Augustine harbor was roiling, barely better conditions than
outside the bar, and *Río de Oro* was pushed stern-first toward land,
trailing her spars and rigging behind her off the bow. In a half mile
she would strike the far shore, which appeared to be deserted except for a small settlement of buildings barely hanging on against
the force of the hurricane.

On the two ships drove in a surreal parade, one leading the other,
both out of control. Fallon was back on his feet now after the crash
on the bar had thrown him down. Around him, other men struggled to stand. Most of *Harp*'s rigging was still aboard, unbelievably,
and she roared bow-first toward the far shore. *Harp*'s helmsman
still held the wheel, ironically, still moved it back and forth, accomplishing nothing but giving him a sense of duty.

As Fallon watched spellbound, *Río de Oro* backed onto the beach
at an angle; immediately sliding around to present her beam to the
onrushing seas. She went over on her side, lifted twice more and
lay over permanently, the seas breaking over her with great slabs of
water. In an instant Fallon saw how it would go and yelled to the
helmsman to get down. Then he threw himself on top of the startled man.

Harp rose and plunged forward, spearing *Río de Oro* with her
bowsprit, driving her bow into the upturned Spaniard's hull with
the momentum of three hundred tons momentarily free of gravity.
The impact was *cataclysmic*. *Harp* rode up over and through *Río*'s
hull at the waist, her men rolling over the deck. Aja slid by quickly

and Fallon just grabbed his ankle before the boy's head could strike the mast stump. Others weren't so lucky, with many knocked senseless against the railings or bulwark or sent tumbling into the sea.

"Up, you men, get off the ship!" Fallon yelled at the top of his lungs just as another wave lifted *Harp*'s stern farther. She would not last long before the seas dismantled her piece by piece.

Now Jones was on his feet, his face bloodied from a chance meeting with the binnacle. "Throw lines over the side," he shouted. "Quickly, men! Down you go! You men there, get below and get the wounded up. Hurry, there's not a moment to lose!"

Fallon wondered at Jones's composure and thanked God for it then and there. Indeed, there was not a moment to lose as *Harp* was shifting with each wave, her stern grinding into the shore, opening up seams and flooding the holds.

It was organized chaos aboard ship as the crew scrambled to save themselves. Down the men went over the side into waist deep but boiling surf, handling the wounded with special care, Crael—a *sober* Crael—directing all hands to be careful though many of the wounded were nearly dead already.

All of this Fallon noticed from the steeply angled quarterdeck where he leaned against the binnacle, all attention and care and *focus*. He alone saw the clustering Spanish seamen high on the beach, many armed, all looking weary but dangerous, many shaking their fists in anger. He could not see an officer, but assumed there was one organizing the rescue. Well, no one was in any condition to fight for anything but survival.

At last the wounded were handed down and all the able-bodied men evacuated. The ship was still largely intact and, as there was a semblance of a settlement nearby, Fallon did not think to attempt to off-load food or water.

For now, his men were as safe as he could make them on a hostile shore, controlled by the Spanish government, with many among them wounded, some mortally.

So, not so terribly safe.

FORTY-FIVE

THE HURRICANE lasted 24 hours. All through the night and the next morning it savaged the coast of Florida before it moved northward up the coast of the United States. Branches were stripped of their leaves. Skiffs were found hundreds of yards inshore. *In trees.* Sand was blown over two miles inland from the beach. Inlet channels were rearranged and sandbars erased and rebuilt. Beach shacks simply disappeared, often with their inhabitants.

The beach at St. Augustine continued to grind up the two ships. The men who belonged to those ships were divided into two camps: Spaniards and British. The camps were roughly fifty yards apart; men huddled against the wind and rain, happy to be alive but also miserable. There was no shelter or protection of any kind. Thirst was no problem—a man could open his mouth—but food was another issue.

Both *Río de Oro* and *Harp* were utterly destroyed, battered hulks resembling ships, too dangerous to go back into for stores, still heaving and breaking up. Crael had had the good sense to bring his supplies of laudanum and his instruments, such as they were. The wounded men moaned throughout the night, and Crael and his shipmates did their best to comfort them.

By mid-morning the next day the wind had lessened and, ironically, a blue sky appeared through the clouds. The sea was still up, however, and both ships ground into each other and the sand continuously with a sound like nothing the men had ever heard.

Fallon awoke from a deep sleep, stiff and worn and soaked from having lain on the open ground. His men were scattered about, many awake, some asleep, and others dead. He looked through the trees toward the Spanish sailors, who looked as bedraggled and wretched as his own men.

He rose and motioned for Mr. Jones. "Give me the butcher's bill," he said somberly.

"Sir, we lost 63 confirmed dead or missing," Jones replied. "Another 51 are wounded and dying. And we have 40 wounded that Crael believes with any luck will live. The rest are as fit as possible given everything they've been through." It was a horrible loss of life and Fallon dropped his head to his chest. "My God, Jones," he said softly. "My God."

Fallon shook himself out of his stupor at *Harp*'s losses, for there was still the Spanish crew to deal with, though their number was necessarily small owing to their ship carrying cargo, not men to fight a war. Still, the situation was volatile. He asked Jones to come with him down the beach to parlay, and Aja dutifully followed behind. The trees were denuded, stripped clean, and new sand and leaves littered the woodland floor. They walked uneasily toward the Spaniards, not sure what to expect, Fallon looking for an officer.

One appeared from the center of the group, his uniform proclaiming him a *capitán*, his mangled left leg dragging uselessly. Two of his men held him almost upright. Fallon could see he was deathly pale, obviously in pain and barely able to hold onto his aides.

"*Señor*, I am Captain Nicholas Fallon of HMS *Harp*," began Fallon. "To whom do I have the honor of addressing?" This in his best Spanish, which he hoped would be good enough and acceptable to a proud man.

Breathing deeply cost the Spanish *capitán* much, but he drew back his head to look Fallon in the eye. "I am Capitán Enrique Alvaron, at your service, Captain Fallon." He gave a slight bow; all he could muster given the circumstances.

And then he simply fainted.

Fallon and Jones quickly helped catch him before his aides dropped him, and Fallon asked for the Spanish surgeon but was told he was dead. Aja scampered to get Crael, who was fortunately awake and tending to several of the British sailors. Fallon looked at the Spanish faces gathered around him, fear and anger in their expressions. Alvaron was lowered to the ground gently and here was Crael, kit in hand, coming to his side while the Spanish sailors backed away, Crael seeming like *authority*.

Crael quickly examined Alvaron's upper body for serious wounds and, finding none, turned his attention to the leg. He tore the pants away and Fallon barely concealed a gasp of air as he looked at the mangled and bloody semblance of a leg before him.

"What do you think, Crael?" asked Fallon, but he was afraid he knew.

The Spaniards crowded around now, wanting to see the wound for themselves, fascinated and frightened for their *capitán* at the same time.

"There is nothing left to save, Captain," said Crael softly. "It is bad, very bad. He's lost a lot of blood. And if the leg doesn't come off he will die from infection. The leg will rot upwards into the body. The fever will be next, and he will likely live but a few days."

Crael stood to look at Fallon, then around to the circle of Spanish seamen, who knew from the surgeon's eyes that the wound was very grave, indeed.

Fallon looked for another officer, then asked in Spanish if there was anyone to authorize surgery on the unconscious *capitán*, but there was no one, all their officers were dead. The seamen all hung their heads.

"Do it, Crael," Fallon ordered, not easily, for if Alvaron survived he would always have Fallon to thank for being one-legged. Still, as his father used to say, *a man with no options has no problems.*

Crael sent Aja back to the British camp for bandages and ointments and the saw. In a moment he was back, and some canvas was spread on the ground onto which Crael placed the things he would need. Then Alvaron was lifted from where he had fallen and placed on the canvas, as well, next to the instruments needed for the amputation.

Two of Alvaron's men held the unconscious man down with little effort, for he was plainly delirious with shock and pain. Still, Crael dribbled a liberal dose of his precious laudanum into Alvaron's mouth.

Crael took one last look around, as if for a final permission, and then he began sawing.

SOMETIMES IN war humanity wins.

Fallon witnessed it that day, when the basic, human goodness that lives within most men, warriors or poets or warrior-poets, overcomes even their most evil and wretched instincts. That day on the beach of St. Augustine those instincts were held at bay as Spanish and British seamen alike gathered around the wounded *capitán* and watched an alcoholic Royal Navy surgeon try to save his enemy's life. And when the dead, useless leg was unceremoniously thrown into the harbor, the men all nodded in the universal language of approval.

Capitán Alvaron was carried gently back to his camp, with Crael in attendance, for there were several more Spaniards who needed urgent attention. Fallon sent Aja back to the British camp for two men to assist the surgeon, as the loblolly boys were all dead or missing.

In the early afternoon, as Fallon considered going into the settlement under a white flag in search of food, a ragged column of Spanish soldiers appeared and surrounded the British camp. The leader of the soldiers, a sergeant of militia, faced Fallon and ordered an immediate surrender. Fallon was in no position to refuse armed soldiers on the point, but several of the *Río's* seamen stepped forward to plead for mercy, as much to retain Crael's services for their *capitán* as anything. Though Alvaron was the senior

officer, he was clearly incapacitated and the sergeant, totally out
of his depth, became bewildered and then completely flummoxed
when the Spanish seamen told him what was in *Río de Oro's* hold.

Holy Madre de Dios!

The sergeant immediately placed guards around the ship and,
because there were not sufficient accommodations for so many
men in the barracks where his soldiers were billeted, gathered up
both Spanish and British seamen and marched all who could walk
toward Fort Mose, some two miles north of St. Augustine. Litters
were sent back for the wounded including, of course, Alvaron. By
the end of the day all the Spanish and British seamen were more or
less settled in their new quarters.

Fort Mose had been built in 1738 as a haven for kidnapped
Africans escaping the tyranny of slavery in the British colonies to
the north. Slaves largely built the fort and the surrounding settlement of small houses. All that Spain required in return for giving
the slaves their freedom was conversion to Catholicism, each slave
saying the magic words, "I want to be baptized in the One True
Faith." Then they would no longer be slaves, but freedmen.

But Fort Mose hadn't been in regular use since 1763 when
Spain traded Florida to the British. After that, most of the free
black inhabitants had migrated to Cuba with the evacuating
Spanish settlers. Now, of course, Florida was back in Spanish
hands—such is the way of war and negotiation. Years of neglect
had taken its toll on the fort, however, and much of it was overgrown and fallen down. Some of the settlement's houses were
without roofs, as well. The sergeant did his best to separate and accommodate the men, though the wounded were grouped together
in a common area to make it easier for Crael to tend to them. *Holy
Madre de Dios!* was all the sergeant could mutter as he posted
guards and sent a courier west on horseback to find an officer with
more rank to take charge of the situation, which was unlike anything he had ever seen or would ever see again.

In the event, it would be days before a *sergeant major* would appear, a fat man on a burdened mule, the gold in his uniform no doubt adding to the burden the mule felt. When he had the situation thoroughly explained to him by the sergeant, and when he had seen the ships and some of the bullion that had been carried ashore, he immediately left to find an officer of higher rank to take command. It was all too much.

Fallon himself had lost all interest in the treasure, concentrating instead on the health and well-being of his men who, on the whole, were marginally improving. Still, each day he led a burial detail into the woods carrying both British and Spanish dead, and each day they returned despondent. Fallon said the prayers, in both English and Spanish, which all the men seemed to appreciate but which, of course, brought little consolation to the dead sailors.

Alvaron, meanwhile, put all his feeble efforts into living. He was delirious with fever much of the time, with Crael by his side often, checking the ligatures that bound the arteries and smelling the stump for telltale signs of infection. During the worst days of Alvaron's fever, Fallon was often seen by the Spanish crewmen sitting with his counterpart, talking in low tones, even holding Alvaron's hand to give comfort. It was odd for them to see sworn enemies hold hands, men who had tried to kill each other and very nearly succeeded. They all agreed war was strange.

For Fallon, the daily conversation with Alvaron gradually grew into a small friendship of sorts. As Alvaron became more lucid, Fallon found a kindred spirit, a decent man who cared for his men more than he cared for glory.

Alvaron ordered the sergeant to retrieve a bag of coins from the treasure ship, which was accomplished at low tide when it was safest. The sergeant returned with the bag, a small portion of the treasure, yet more money than he had ever held in his hands before or ever would again. The sergeant handed it over to Alvaron with a curious look. His curiosity was quickly satisfied, however, for Alvaron gave him enough to purchase food and water from St. Augustine for both the British prisoners and his own men. Alvaron would continue to do this each day, for which the crews were grateful and as happy as shipwrecked sailors ashore could be.

The days were monotonous and long and filled with small walks, small talks, and much staring at the sky. The sun was relentless, and the noonday heat found everyone under shade of some kind, as if drugged or incapacitated.

One morning Fallon and Alvaron sat under a tree with naked branches overhead, the light breeze finding no leaves to tremble. The sky above was mercifully cloudy, and there was a hint of later rain in the air. They had just finished breakfast together, a little bread and blackberry jam and oranges. They spoke in both English and Spanish, moving back and forth between languages with ease.

"Tell me, Captain," Alvaron asked as he bushed a few crumbs from his shirt, "do you have a wife or family?"

"No, no wife or family save my father," replied Fallon. "And you, sir?"

"I have a wife, yes," said Alvaron, and then paused. "But I have not seen her in some time. Maybe it will be some time more before I do, no?" They both laughed at that, for they had no illusions about their predicament.

"I want to thank you for saving my life, Captain," Alvaron continued, getting to the point he wanted to make. Fallon moved to shrug it off, but Alvaron was not finished. "Another man would not have acted as you did. It was the surgeon's hands that operated, but it was your order that saved me."

Fallon looked at Alvaron, appreciating a growing level of intimacy between them. "It was an easy decision, *señor*. You would have done the same for me. And somehow I knew that."

"No," Alvaron corrected. "You would have done it anyway."

FALLON SPENT part of each day comforting the men and part wondering what the hell would become of them all. It was by no means clear, and he missed the pragmatism of Beauty more than ever for, try as he might to think of one, no strategy came to mind. On foot, guarded, unarmed, with abundant wounded in tow, and in a strange country with no maps or charts, there was no flyer to take.

Beauty—was she even alive? Fallon often dreamed of her at night, returning again and again to when they were caught in the harbor in a storm as kids, floating into shore on the swells, clinging to each other and singing. His confidence in Beauty was such that Fallon never doubted that she was alive after the hurricane. Or, more truthfully, he would not let himself doubt she was alive. But the reality of his own situation began to gnaw at his optimism for ever seeing Beauty again.

At least Alvaron and his men were Spanish, and Florida was under Spanish control. Yet for all intents and purposes, the Spanish seamen were prisoners at Fort Mose just as much as the British. Ships came infrequently from Spain; indeed, the sergeant told them the last one was eleven months ago, so there was no real expectation of another ship anytime soon. And though they had food and water thanks to Alvaron, Fallon felt the current situation was untenable and could not last.

In that, he was prescient.

FORTY-SIX

LIKE A message in a bottle, *Sea Dog* eventually washed ashore. Dismasted and helpless, the ship struck the reefs near St. Lucia and the bottom went out of her. *Not the life, the bottom.* In a miracle, fifty of the crew—Sea Dogs and former slaves—managed to fight the surf and make their way to shore; the rest drowned or were already dead. Beauty had jumped overboard, her peg in her hand, the last to leave. She rolled over on her back and kicked and sang until her bottom hit bottom. *An old lesson.*

The crew dragged themselves to shore with only the clothes on their backs. Kendricks had helped Theo to shore, and together they had dragged gasping men through the surf, many of whom were spitting up seawater and vomit. There was no thought of going back to the ship, not now, perhaps not ever. Already bits of wood and wreckage detritus were washing ashore. Most of the crew huddled together for warmth and support, stunned into silence and sobered by the sight of their ship, their home, their livelihood grinding itself to death on the coral. Some of the men were simply too drained to think.

Beauty sat off to herself, thinking very low thoughts. She had lost sight of Fallon after he had turned for St. Augustine, so busy was she with her own situation. And *Avenger*—who knew? *What a fucking storm,* she thought. *And we had the buggers!*

She had seen Clayton, for a brief moment, and wondered if Fallon had as well. Before she could ask herself *how in the hell?*

she thought of the waterfront bars of Nassau that Cortez had described. *Of course.* Clayton may even have been there *that night,* picking up information, making his plans. Well, to hell with him, too. He was probably wrecked somewhere himself or at the bottom, where he belonged. She had other things to worry about now. When the storm moderated she would send parties out to scout their situation and search for fresh water and, hopefully, something they could eat.

Maybe they weren't as fucked as she felt they were. *Maybe.*

IN FACT, the next morning a scouting party found a freshwater lake about a mile inland, which was excellent. Several buckets had washed ashore and were put to use carrying water to the camp. But as yet the scouting party had found nothing to eat; actually, nothing that even looked like it *could* be eaten. That made the men even hungrier, of course.

Beauty began work on a serious plan to stay alive. *Sea Dog* had broken up badly, was continuing to break up even though the surf had lessened, and a great many deck boards had washed ashore along with the remnants of life aboard—a few pots, some empty barrels, a slops chest with Theo's evening wear, and a shoe. More seemed to come in every wave, and Beauty set rotating details to gather up everything and pull it well up the beach, separated into two piles—building materials and *other.* Well, you never knew.

By afternoon they had enough material to make a rough lean-to. A sail had washed ashore to make the roof, and one of the freedmen had slipped off to the lake and returned an hour later with four fish he had speared using the whalebone stays in Theo's corset for spear tips. Of course, they had no fire, and the men refused to eat the fish raw. They were hungry, but not *starving.* Still, it was a useful exercise in sustainable living, and soon enough they would be hungry enough to eat anything.

Beauty vowed to make fire a priority, however. They had flint, but finding dry leaves or wood was impossible. She sent several details out again to forage for food—anything they could eat. Other details scrounged for anything dry that would burn, or would burn *one day* if left in the sun long enough.

The food detail returned by early evening with a variety of possibilities, some small nuts and berries, some strange-looking fruit and—coconuts, *by God!* Now that was encouraging, and all hands gathered around to supervise the cracking of the coconuts and the sharing out of the rest. It was hardly a feast, but all agreed it was better than nothing.

A fire detail also had encouraging results, having found a cave-like hole under an overhang of fallen trees that contained dried leaves and twigs. They gathered up all they could carry and retraced their path to the camp where the men with flint began sparking and blowing for all they were worth and, eventually, *voilà!* a flame was produced, whispered to, blown upon, prayed over, and fed baby bites of wood until it made up its mind to become a *fire*.

Theo busied herself dividing the food into meager portions and passing them out to the men. The men's spirits went up with food in their bellies and a general feeling of optimism took hold in the little camp.

They had shelter. They had food. They had a fire to cook the food. Now all they needed was a plan to get out of there.

FORTY-SEVEN

FALLON WANTED to write, but he hadn't paper or pen or ink, so he wrote in his head.

> *Look to the sky tonight and find the*
> *Brightest stars, for*
> *Those are my eyes.*
> *All night I will watch*
> *You until the sun*
> *Wakes you in the morning*
> *Next to me, all along.*

He swore to himself that he would say those words to Elinore one day, poor as they were. He thought of her often, going about her days, and wondered if she could imagine where he was at that very moment. No, he could barely imagine it, and he was living it.

Alvaron was improving daily, and his excellent spirits lifted his men's spirits, as well. Fallon encouraged the *capitán* to move himself and his men into the village of St. Augustine where he could be more comfortable, but he refused.

"No, *señor*," Alvaron said, "I want to be near your surgeon. We still have several wounded who are struggling. And I am enjoying your company, as well. My men are even learning to speak English! We are all in this together, my friend."

"As you wish, *señor*," replied Fallon, laughing with Alvaron because he knew his men were learning to speak Spanish as well.

What a strange lesson this is, he thought.

But it would not last. One week later a real officer arrived, a *coronel* sitting on a fine horse and bejeweled with the decoration of his profession and accompanied by several aides. He was heavyset, of very dark complexion, and quite sure of his own competence. He saluted Alvaron stiffly, compared commissions with the *capitán* and, as the *coronel* was senior, quickly assumed command of the situation.

He immediately directed that the Spanish seamen be billeted in the village, away from the British prisoners, drawing a definite distinction between the two groups. Alvaron made to object, citing the wounded and the need for Crael's attention. The *coronel* promised to find a doctor to look after the wounded Spanish seamen and the *capitán's* leg.

Next the *coronel* visited the ships and ordered the gold and silver to be off-loaded at low tide. All the treasure that could be reached was located and brought ashore, but it wasn't easy. The *coronel* had ordered a mule train to follow him to St. Augustine from his garrison to the west, and when it arrived the soldiers loaded the mules with the treasure and, under the command of the *coronel*, they left within two days for that same garrison, where an *even more important officer* would decide its fate. One thing seemed clear: The treasure would never get to France by going west.

The days dragged themselves into weeks at Fort Mose, and Fallon grew more restless and frustrated. The wounded men were almost healthy, but the rest were becoming indolent in spite of Jones's best efforts, lulled into a stupor by their captivity and the heat and a growing sense that they might die there. Fallon sensed their mood but, given their remote location, could think of no words to combat it.

"Colston," he said to the master one night as they sat contemplating a black sky awash in stars, "I want you to navigate us out of here. North to the United States. On foot. Can you do that?"

Colston paused. "I could do that if I had a map of the States and Spanish Florida, probably. But the best thing would be to just follow the coastline and *hope*. Assuming you could do that and get past the marshes and the thickets and the snakes and whatever else might kill you, and not starve, well, you would get there. Eventually."

Fallon considered. Much of Somers's salt trade was with the southern American ports, the closest being Savannah. And though hostilities with the United States had ceased years ago, he couldn't be sure of the reception there if 75 ragged British seamen suddenly showed up. Certainly there would be questions to answer, and memories of British control during the War for Independence might provoke latent animosity. Still, there were better odds of finding an English ship in Savannah going—*somewhere*—than if they stayed in Spanish Florida. He wondered if reaching the United States was even possible. Long odds, he reasoned, traveling along a strange coastline on foot with bays and wide-mouthed rivers to cross, constantly scrounging for food and fresh water.

First, of course, they would have to escape, and stay escaped; they couldn't exactly walk away. The sergeant and his men, a ragtag bunch though they might be, had a few horses and no doubt knew how to follow a trail. That was the problem on land versus sea, you left a trail.

FORTY-EIGHT

BEAUTY NEEDED to pace, and so sought out the hardest sand on the beach; anywhere else her peg leg sank to its length. She had divided up tasks for the crew, and everyone was doing something. She sent Theo out with a detail to scrounge for all the food they could find. Other crewmen untwisted massive ropes to get workable strands of fiber. Others measured boards and arranged them by size, and still another group wrestled with dead trees, dragging them by brute strength to the beach, using whatever they could fashion for tools to strip the branches. They needed the trunks.

Loyal to the last, dying slowly so they might live, *Sea Dog* had given them most of what they needed to build rafts. It would have been poetic to a more poetic person, but Beauty hadn't a poem in her body. It was strip the ship and get on with it. The men worked with the seaman's ingenuity, fashioning the rafts patiently, using what they had or could scrounge, accepting that they would be leaving the relative safety of land in the coming weeks for the vagaries of life on the sea again, this time with no ship. But it seemed like the only real option to a seaman: *Get to sea.*

Beauty had a rough idea where *Harp* had gotten to, and she remembered from the charts that St. Augustine had a harbor. She had no idea what was there, or even if Fallon was there, or if anyone aboard had even survived the bar, but *get to sea* her instincts told her.

"Kendricks," she said quietly to the master, "I have in mind to use the northwards current to float us toward St. Augustine. Can you get us there?"

They were sitting under a tree, the men scattered about in the noon heat, waiting for cooler temperatures to resume working. "Yes," Kendricks said. "And if Captain Fallon is not there I think we can get up the entire east coast of America, assuming we stay alive. Judging from what I know the current moves at about five knots." Kendricks did some calculations in his head. "I figure we're a good deal south, if I remember the chart. Figure several days to St. Augustine, with good weather and luck."

It was much as Beauty had suspected. Try as she might, she could see no other plan. To stay where they were, hoping for divine intervention, was a short-term solution to staying alive, at best. At least at sea there was always the chance of seeing a ship, even an enemy ship, and being rescued. It wouldn't be her preference to serve out the war in prison, but it couldn't be much worse than where they were.

She set a date to leave: two weeks.

FORTY-NINE

IT WAS A famous legend in Cuba, probably true, that years ago some thirty Spanish soldiers planned an attack on an aboriginal camp on the other side of the river from their port settlement. They hired local Cuban fishermen to row them across, but the fishermen betrayed them and purposefully overturned the boats midstream. The Spanish soldiers, burdened by their heavy armor, sank like stones. The port was thereafter called Matanzas, Spanish for *massacre*.

Time had burnished the legend, though Cubans in Matanzas still had a lingering resentment of Spain. Matanzas women cut their hair to signify their *independence* and opposition to Spanish rule, in an open rebuff to Spanish officials in Havana, and there were minor protests and demonstrations against tariffs imposed by the Mother Country. The revolt by the British Colonies against Great Britain was well known and served as a fresh example to Cuban loyalists that their dreams of an independent country could perhaps be realized one day.

One can only imagine the Matanzans' surprise when a British warship plunged into their harbor seeking shelter from a hurricane. Well, it had been a massive storm, to be sure. And the warship—*Avenger* was her name—had been badly knocked about and her sails all but shredded. She definitely needed aid and shelter, but the ship was *British*, which made her the nominal enemy of Spain, Cuba's governing country. So, of course, every short-haired Matanzas woman turned out to help, most dragging their men along.

Well, *every* woman didn't drag a man along. Paloma Campos was an ardent Cuban loyalist, brown skinned, brown eyed and, even by Cuban standards, strikingly beautiful. She had been among the first of the Matanzas women to cut her long hair, throwing her severed locks into the sea to float to Spain. *A message.*

Paloma was in the crowd of women and men who greeted Davies when he came ashore. It was she who stepped up boldly to welcome him to Cuba and to offer the help he so obviously needed. Davies, being a man with eyes in his head, immediately fixed them on the beautiful woman with the fire in her personality, the obvious leader on the beach, but her own eyes did not linger on him.

Davies had expected hostilities, but instead he was welcomed like royalty by the local people, and he was promised every able-bodied tradesman in the port. There was much to do to set *Avenger* right. The worst shot holes closest to the waterline had to be patched, along with the gaping hole at the bow. Spars had to be replaced and a new suit of sails bent on. And, of course, stores needed replenishing, at least enough for two months' duration, which is what Davies planned to spend trying to find *Harp* and *Sea Dog*. It was all on him, and in fact would likely bring severe disapproval or even court-martial from the Admiralty, but he would face that problem later. His problem now was finding his fellow captains and friends, either their ships, their bodies, or, God willing, their living, breathing selves.

Day after day tradesmen came down to the shore bearing the materials *Avenger* needed to be set right. Paloma was often with them, and in the way of things she and Davies became friends— her English was only as good as his Spanish, but it was enough. As Kinis was in charge of the shipboard work, Davies and Paloma could often be seen walking the streets of Matanzas, a dusty bazaar of a town with busy shops selling their wares and music coming from deep inside alleys that wound around the backs of the little homes and buildings.

Of course, like every Cuban town, Matanzas had Spanish informants. These informants had horses, and they rode them straight away to Havana to inform the authorities of the goings-on in Matanzas with a British warship, *Holy Madre de Dios!*

The authorities in Havana considered what to do, slept on the problem, ate dinner over the problem, and in the end decided to do—*nothing*. Their reasoning was simple: The British ship had more firepower than all the guns in Matanzas, there being no militia at the fort there, and as there was no Spanish warship in Havana to send, what could they do?

After four weeks of hard work, *Avenger* was nearly ready to sail. Davies had paid generously for all the work, of course, but he felt compelled to show his personal appreciation to the townspeople who had provided aid, so he and his officers met them at a small café near the beach for a celebration. The rum soon had everyone in excellent spirits, some even past excellent, and when the music began the Cuban culture went on full display as women pushed the wooden tables aside and led their men to the dance floor. Eyes flashed and skirts were whirled and lifted and the men—Cuban and English—did their best to follow along, some game enough to try to dance, while most stood still and watched the zephyrs move around them.

Toward the end of the evening, Paloma and Davies left the heat of the café and stepped outside for air. There was a light breeze from the east, the wind soft and suggestive. Certainly Davies *wanted* to suggest something, but he felt he lacked standing to do it. He and Paloma were friends, nothing more, and he wondered at it. Usually, in his experience, by this time things would have progressed along a bit further. Clearly this was a woman who did not want a brief dalliance, with a sailor no less, or perhaps it was just *him*. Still, being with her so much had caused something to happen to him, something he didn't really understand but which he liked.

"You're wondering about me, *señor*. I can feel it," she said as they stopped on the sand.

She was exquisite in the moonlight, and obviously perceptive, and Davies was quite at a loss as to what to say. He wanted to at least take her hand, but he didn't dare ruin this moment. Finally, he decided to say something stupid, but true.

"I have realized that I have no idea who you are. I know what you've done for me, for the ship, but each time we've been together I've revealed more of myself than you have of yourself. I don't know all that I want to know. And now I have to leave."

There, he'd said it, sounding like a schoolboy talking to his first girl. Oddly, that's how he felt. For a rear admiral with fifteen hundred men under his orders all over the Caribbean, it was disorienting and even humbling to be so obviously *not in command*. Something was stirring here, something new to him. A sailor, completely and utterly at sea.

Paloma stared out toward the harbor, taking longer than she perhaps should have to form a response. When she did, it surprised them both.

She stepped toward him, rose on her toes, and kissed him deeply, her tongue searching every part of his mouth, moving lightly across his teeth before plunging again and again into his soul, a kiss meant to burn his mouth forever.

"You must leave, Harry," she said as she withdrew. "But you can always come back."

FIFTY

A S A BOY on the farm in Africa, Ajani had been confined to the house by day, cleaning and doing menial chores for the family who owned his family. His father and mother worked the fields but, even though they were outside most of the time, they were never allowed off the farm and were never unsupervised. This instilled a natural curiosity in the boy for what lay beyond what he could see from the windows in the house. As a consequence, he began nocturnal explorations, slipping out of his room in the slave cabin where his family lived to explore the edges of the farm and beyond. He learned to be vigilant and silent, keeping his exploits to himself lest his family forbid them or, worse, he be caught and punished.

That natural curiosity to know the world around him, to escape confinement, led Ajani to nightly forays outside the walls of Fort Mose. It was easy enough to slip away on dark nights, and neither the guards nor crewmen nor even Fallon knew he was gone. He made his way into St. Augustine and found the barn where Capitán Alvaron and his men were billeted and also located the soldiers' barracks. He found fruit orchards and small gardens and shops and alleyways and a livery stable with mules and horses. St. Augustine wasn't so big and he could return to Fort Mose before daylight, having satisfied his curiosity. And anyway, what were they going to do if they caught him, put him in prison?

As it happened, one night he was indeed caught on a farm outside town, nabbed red-handed with eggs in every pocket and both hands as he stepped out of a henhouse. The rooster's crow had given the alarm that something was afoot, and when Aja stepped outside it was into a circle of men looking at him curiously, their dark faces showing more curiosity than anger.

Apparently, not all freedmen had gone to Cuba years ago when Florida became British. Some had stayed and raised families, and when Spain once again owned Florida the freedmen could once again own land and scratch out a living as farmers.

Aja stood sheepishly in the circle of three of these old, hard-working farmers and slowly handed over each egg, apologizing for each one, looking into the farmers' eyes as he did. In turn, they did something remarkable. They invited him inside their home.

It was a simple home with crude, handmade furniture and a rough kitchen table, which they sat around. One by one the three men introduced themselves as David, Ezekiel, and Samuel, three bachelor brothers. This was their farm, their whole life, and who was this boy who had come to steal their eggs from them, they wondered?

Aja sat before them humbled. They waited for an answer. Slowly, he told the brothers his life story, short as it was, about his childhood in Africa, his kidnapping and the slave ship, the slaughter onboard and how he had hidden below deck to escape being killed. Then the rescue by Fallon and the British crew, the battle with the pirate Clayton and the hurricane, ending with *Harp*'s wreck on the beach and the crew's captivity at Fort Mose.

The brothers listened, their eyes staring in wonder, and muttered to themselves at such a wild, frightening story from such a young man.

Aja told them the eggs were intended for the prisoners at Fort Mose, and he had stolen them on the spur of the moment to take to the men but, in truth, the men at the fort were fed enough. "I should not have stolen," Aja said meekly. "I . . . I have no excuse."

The brothers looked at him closely. It appeared to be a childish whim, not the practiced act of a thief. "If you had come to us honestly and asked for eggs, we would have given you some," said David, making Aja feel infinitely worse. "We have been kept in captivity ourselves."

Ezekiel and Samuel nodded their agreement, and David continued. "We were slaves in the north, in Georgia, on a cotton plantation. From the time we were little we went to the fields before the sun came up and came back after it went down. In the spring we planted the fields, many fields as far as we could see. Then in the summer we tilled the rows until the cotton was ready to be picked. Then all day we picked in the heat, our fingers bleeding from the cotton bolls. When winter came we cleared fields for more cotton, driving mules to pull stumps and haul logs to the mill."

Aja's eyes grew wide, and wider still. He thought of his own parents in the tobacco fields, and what it must have been like for them, leaving before sunrise, shuffling barefoot down the same path every morning, working in the heat every day, never bringing a complaint home at night.

"We had no shoes in the winter," Samuel continued, "so we wrapped our feet in rags and tied the rags with twine. The master was very bad to us and did not care if we froze. I lost the toes on my right foot. Ezekiel lost two fingers." With that, Ezekiel held up his left hand to show his remaining three fingers.

Samuel leaned forward in his chair, into the glow of the single candle on the table. "Tell me," he said, "how does your master treat you?"

Aja was a bit taken aback. He described Fallon like a father, not a master, though certainly he was a captain. He described a man who had taught him not to be afraid, but to be brave, a kind man whom the crew respected, perhaps even loved. A man who did not flinch under fire. And when he spoke of Fallon's desire to escape from Fort Mose, to lead his men to freedom, the brothers listened even harder, nodding their deep understanding of a dream to be free.

The freedmen rose from the table and went into another room.

Aja could hear them talking quietly but understood nothing of what they said. Finally, they returned to the kitchen table and sat down, looking at him kindly.

And then Ezekiel told him about the Slave Trail.

FIFTY-ONE

THE NEXT morning Fallon listened to Aja's remarkable tale, including his heartfelt apology for attempting to steal eggs. But when he described the freedmen and their escape years ago along the old Slave Trail from Savannah to Fort Mose, Fallon was stunned into silence. *Good God!* If the trail led one way it would certainly lead the other way! But there was more. The freedmen had promised Aja they would show him the trailhead, provide some food and supplies for the men, and then cover up the entrance to the trail, overgrown anyway and known to very few people outside themselves.

Fallon stared at Aja in wonder. *Really?* "Why would these men want to help British sailors escape?" he asked.

Aja looked at Fallon curiously before answering. "To be a slave is to be a prisoner," he said softly. "They remember."

Aja's eyes burned brightly. It was clear he remembered, as well. Fallon nodded his understanding and turned to look at his men in the fort's courtyard, idly sitting in the shade, pacing the walls and doing—nothing. They had to leave, simple as that.

Plans were made to escape on the next full moon, a week away by Colston's observations. Aja would communicate their intent to the freedmen, along with Fallon's grateful appreciation for their help. Jones picked men to neutralize the guards, which wouldn't prove hard as they usually slept off and on. After all, where were their prisoners going to escape to? Meanwhile, Fallon asked Aja to do one more important thing. He wanted to meet with Alvaron before they left.

The next night Aja slipped away from the fort and into the village after dark, moving stealthily along the alleys, and made his way to the barn where the Spanish crewmen were billeted. He tapped lightly on the barn door, and when a seaman opened it Aja asked to see the *capitán*. Alvaron grabbed his rough crutches and came to the door. Aja briefly explained that Fallon would like to see how his friend was doing. Alvaron nodded and smiled.

Aja suggested a spot on the edge of the town near the ruins of an old Franciscan abbey close by. Alvaron quickly agreed. Tomorrow night then. Goodnight.

FALLON WAITED at the abbey at the appointed time, not long, and Alvaron hobbled out of the shadows on his crutches. He appeared thin, perhaps that was to be expected, but somehow strong as well and genuinely glad to see his English friend. They sat on a bench in the glow of a rising moon.

"How is your leg, *señor?*" Fallon asked. "You seem to be adapting quite well."

"Oh, I am, Captain. I would rather have my old leg, of course. But I now have a new friend in you, and that is a better trade for me." He looked at Fallon and smiled warmly.

Fallon accepted the compliment, aware that it was a lie, but a lie from a gracious man who accepted the reality of war. Men died, men were maimed for life, men lost everything in war. At least something had been found.

"Are your wounded recovering?" continued Fallon, concerned since Crael was no longer caring for them.

"Well enough, I think," answered Alvaron. "Though the doctor in St. Augustine seems to have a hard time finding his way to us. He comes only irregularly. But all my men are able to walk and are gaining strength."

Here Alvaron paused, and looked at Fallon as one captain to another. "Truthfully, my men are becoming indolent, I'm afraid," he said in a low voice, almost a confession. "I try to cheer them and set them to menial tasks to keep their minds occupied, but we are in a situation with no end in sight. Even I cannot see a hopeful ending— we are not prisoners but there is no place to *go*."

Fallon looked at Alvaron closely and could see the frustration and worry in his face—and sense the feeling of impotence he felt as a leader losing control of his men.

"*Capitán*, I must tell you something in total confidence. Will you allow me?" asked Fallon.

"Of course, *señor*," replied Alvaron. "At this point we have no secrets between us."

"We have a plan to escape soon," said Fallon quietly. "To take an ancient trail to Savannah to the north. How we discovered it doesn't matter, but we believe it is an old trail that slaves used to escape from the British Colonies to Spanish Florida. Since there are no boats to be had here, as you well know, we must walk away from here if we want to be free."

Alvaron's eyes widened, not in shock but in admiration, and considered his friend's face in the moonlight. Honest. Open. Trusting. Telling him a secret that could end any hope for escape.

"I envy you, Captain Fallon," he said. "I fear I will rot here, and even if, by chance, we reach Spain again I have no future there. I will never have a command again after losing my ship and losing the treasure, never." Fallon stirred; Alvaron did not mention *losing his leg*. "No, do not say it is your fault, Captain. You do not blow the wind or make the waves, nor do I. We only make the war that our governments decree. Nothing more."

"Thank you, *señor*," said Fallon. "You are an honorable man, as well as brave. But I am wondering now, will you come with us? You and your men?"

Now Alvaron's eyes widened in astonishment. It was impossible, of course, it would be desertion or aiding the enemy or worse, whatever that could be. But . . . well, they were Spanish in a Spanish territory . . . surely they could move about freely, but to Savannah? He considered the only alternative, which was to rot in

St. Augustine waiting for a Spanish ship that might be years coming. His men were bored and dispirited and might welcome the
chance to reach an active port and find a way home to Spain. He
was already dishonored, they were not, and he could give them this
chance, but still . . . *all of them?*

"All of you, *señor*," Fallon answered the unspoken question.
And then, as if reading more of Alvaron's mind, he said "If we are
stopped by Spanish authorities we will act as your prisoners, *señor*.
That will be our story."

Alvaron's head was spinning at that, but perhaps it did seem
plausible. He had almost thirty men and they could perhaps pose
as guards. But how? When? Was this even possible? His mind
raced for answers.

And then Fallon told him the plan that Aja had arranged with
the freedmen and laid out how it could work for the Spaniards.
They would need to cache extra food and water, of course, and
Alvaron would need to purchase a horse for himself, as well as pack
mules to carry supplies.

Alvaron closed his eyes. He had more than enough money
from the treasure ship, so purchasing extra food and water casks
would be no problem, if done discreetly, away from the sergeant's
eyes. And he could buy mules and a horse for himself. That wasn't
the problem, either. It was the absurdity of the idea that was the
problem.

Then he thought briefly of Savannah, a port he knew nothing
about, other than it was *open*. Spanish and British ships alike were
welcome, and French ships for that matter, but he had no real idea
how far it was, or what the path would be like. Still, he knew what
it was like in St. Augustine, which was not good and getting worse
for the men.

Fallon watched Alvaron's thoughts play out on his face. No and
maybe. Maybe and yes. Definitely not. Finally, *yes*. What a strange
story to tell his children one day, no?

FIFTY-TWO

THE SALT trader *CASTILLE*, under the command of Captain Wallace, strained at her anchor in a southeast breeze that was anything but steady, having williwawed its way around Cockburn Harbor all afternoon, quite unable to make up its mind. Wallace squinted into the sunlight, anxious to see his cargo aboard, wondering at the delay. His bushy side-whiskers marked him as an old-fashioned, conservative man not given to fantasies, or vulgarities either, for that matter. He was devoutly religious, strict, and plainspoken. At society gatherings on the island, a dud.

When Wallace had returned to Bermuda from Charleston, Somers had talked to him at length, questioning him closely to get the full picture of the battle with the pirate Clayton. Wallace had expressed grudging admiration for Fallon, and some little remorse for sailing away in his hour of need. Well, how could he have known Bishop would turn out to be a coward?

Rather than send the ship to Grand Turk for another load of salt, Somers had another idea. He asked Wallace what he knew of Nassau, the capital of the Bahamas and the historic center of pirate enterprise throughout the Caribbean. Wallace knew the place well, having worked in a chandlery office there for several years outfitting ships for sea trade. Yes, he admitted, he'd also stocked the occasional pirate vessel, though he viewed it as a sin of the past now.

What Somers had in mind was to sail to Nassau for information. He reasoned that word of the Spanish flotilla's fate could be found there, and he hoped something of the British ships could be learned. Nassau was a busy port, a trader in salt and merchandise would arouse no suspicion, and every instinct in Somers's body told him Nassau was where he would find news. His great fear was that the news would be bad.

It was late afternoon when he and Elinore stepped into *Castille*'s boat and were rowed out to the ship. Their baggage had been sent out hours before, but there was no rush for them as the tide would not ebb until nearly sunset.

Wallace met them at the side and invited them to dinner, which they politely refused, preferring to dine together the first night and not wanting to include Wallace in their small, anxious circle at the beginning of this journey. Nassau was some fifteen hundred miles to the southwest, and that night they felt like very long miles indeed.

After dinner, as *Castille* slowly made her way out of the harbor on the ebb, father and daughter took a turn around the ship. The sun was low in the west as the ship found the wind and plowed along, not a great sailor by any means. As they paused by the larboard railing to watch the sun sink toward the horizon, Somers noticed that Elinore had grown quiet and was staring at the sea below. The look on her face seemed unbearably sad, and Somers knew dark thoughts had overtaken her and she was losing her confidence that Fallon would be found alive.

In an awkward effort to engage her and hopefully change her mood, he said quietly, "Elinore, have you ever heard of the green flash at sunset?"

"No," said Elinore, her voice flat and uninterested.

Somers pressed on. "Well, just at the moment when the sun dips beneath the horizon at sea, the sailors say look for a green flash. If you see it, it's good luck," he said as brightly as he could. He was hoping Elinore would at least look up, but she didn't.

The sun was sinking fast now. "Nico told me he's seen it many times, and you know how lucky he is," said Somers. Elinore raised her eyes and they both stared at the sun now, just touching the horizon, its golden glow washing over the ship and themselves.

Suddenly, Elinore turned and buried her face in her father's chest. "I don't want to look," she sobbed, her body racked in convulsions. "I . . . am . . . praying . . . so . . . hard . . . " she cried, her breath coming in gasps between each word, and Somers held her tightly to his chest. He knew all the emotions she'd held inside were finding release, all pretense at stoicism going out to sea. The brave face she'd been wearing like a mask was off.

Somers closed his eyes, for in that moment he felt like the father he had desperately wanted to be for so long. He held his daughter's shaking body, her hair blowing wildly about his face. And when at last he opened his eyes it was just as the sun left their side of the world, a bright tip of yellow, followed by a green flash.

FIFTY-THREE

THE ROYAL Navy of St. Lucia was nearly ready to sail. The rafts were quite large; each could hold more than twenty men plus stores. The seamen had rigged an ingenious scull to propel as well as guide them: a single long oar roughly hinged at the stern of each raft. The idea was that when the sculler pushed the scull back and forth in a thwartwise motion, the raft would move forward. There was also something of a mast with a small square sail set on each raft, which would help the raft sail faster than the speed of the current so the sculler could have steerage. The hope was to reach the current as quickly as possible and ride it northward.

For the past weeks, Kendricks had paid particular attention to the clouds, studying formations and noting the weather patterns around each. He'd always studied clouds, of course; it's what navigators did when captains thought they were just idly looking off. But this study took on a particular urgency, for it would not do to be caught in a strong current with an opposing wind in a raft with only a foot of freeboard. No, it would not do at all. It was to be his call when they left, and he felt the responsibility keenly.

Beauty was in full command mode now, ordering the men to quickly complete the rafts and to gather what they would need for the journey north. Food parties were sent out, returning with coconuts and berries and fruit, and were then sent out again. Fishing parties returned with their catch, and the fish were either smoked or dried in the sun and wind and stored away. Water would be precious, and the few buckets they had would have to last them, which they should, of course, but nothing was certain at sea.

The men went about their preparations with eagerness and anticipation. Beauty knew they were relieved to have a plan, especially as it meant getting to sea where they were most comfortable. Those men building the rafts did a remarkably good job considering the lack of tools and the materials at hand. Luckily, *Sea Dog* continued to do her part to help, sending planks and ropes and bits of furniture to shore as the ship continued to break up.

Sometimes Beauty would pause on shore and stare out at her old command, and a great feeling of sadness would engulf her. She had known every inch of that ship, every quirk and nuance and smell and sound and vibration. She had stood at the helm and seen sunrise after sunrise and also bid days good night without number. *My God*, she thought, *it is a lot to let go.*

At last, enough food was gathered, the water buckets were full, and the rafts were complete. It would take all hands to get each of the three rafts to the surf, even with rollers under them, for they were that heavy. Each raft had a rough box in the middle for food and water, with a sail cover tied down over it in case of rough weather. They were as prepared as they were going to be.

And finally Kendricks looked at the sky and said: *Today.*

The crew grunted and strained to move the rafts over the soft sand; it was heavy going, and without the aid of some imaginative and motivating curses it might not have happened. But at last the fleet floated and three scullers began their slow back and forth to take the rafts out to sea, with some small help from the sails.

It was a very sad and reflective moment as they approached *Sea Dog*, or what was left of her, balanced on the coral reef, her guts torn out. All hands were silent as they eased by their old ship; it was not easy to tear their eyes away and look forward. Beauty steeled herself to give *Sea Dog* one last farewell look, then called to the men to give a cheer. They did, and it seemed to lift their spirits immensely. And hers.

Kendricks estimated the current to be ten to fifteen miles to the east, but it was only a guess from his memory of the charts. He hoped they would notice the water temperature change; the current was noticeably warmer than the surrounding sea. It was slow work, the rafts being awkward craft, and the scullers and the little sails did their best to keep the rafts moving. With every hard-won yard of progress, Beauty adjusted their estimated arrival at St. Augustine backward.

Soon they were strung out over a half a mile, a ragged line to be sure, but all making small gains with every stroke of the scull. Beauty looked back over her fleet, which is to say she looked back over her *decision,* and she still felt that leaving the coast was the only option. The men were behind her, as well. It was a simple black-and-white world for most seamen. No one wanted to eat coconuts the rest of their lives.

FIFTY-FOUR

SOMETIME AFTER 3:00 AM, Fallon ordered the first guard to be knocked on the head, his rifle and powder taken, his arms and legs tied up. The other guards put up more of a fight, but all five were rushed by sailors simultaneously so when they yelled for help it did no good.

Jones pulled the men together and they marched single file out of the fort with Aja in the lead, the only one who had seen the world outside the walls. It was a darkish night, the moon obscured by low clouds, but Aja was sure-footed and in short order he raised his hand and the group stopped at the edge of the village. He went forward alone, picking his way through the streets until he reached the barn where the Spanish sailors were billeted. He gave a low whistle. A horse whinnied, as if in reply, and Capitán Alvaron stoically rode his horse out from the shadow of the barn, followed by all of his men and several mules. They moved silently, the men calming the animals, and there were no shouts of alarm from the soldiers' barracks as they moved away.

Soon enough the two groups were reunited, Spanish and British, and Fallon and Alvaron clasped hands, showing tight smiles. It was all madness, and both men knew it. Fallon turned over the guards' rifles to Alvaron so the Spanish could appear to guard the British sailors if they were stopped. "Aja," Fallon said quietly, "lead the way, if you please."

Slowly Aja led them around the town to where the outlying farms were, farms he once scouted on his nightly forays. After some time, perhaps most of an hour, they came to the freedmen's homestead and, true to their word, three black faces appeared in a window of the barn, looked at the unexpectedly large assembly in amazement, and smiled broadly.

The freedmen introduced themselves through the window, and then invited the sailors to bring water casks out of the barn along with many sacks of food, including smoked hams and pickled vegetables and dried meats, and also machetes and axes; the seamen would need the latter to clear the path from overgrowth, certainly, as the Slave Trail had not been traveled for many years.

"Look for the old machete marks on the trees," said David. "I put some of them there myself to help mark the trail," he added proudly.

Since Alvaron was the only one with money, he and Fallon had agreed that he would pay the freedmen for their help and supplies. Now he produced a purse that jingled with coins and held it out to them.

"No, no payment is necessary," said Samuel, as he and his brothers physically backed away from the money. But Fallon and Alvaron put on a united front and Alvaron pressed the purse into Ezekiel's hand, his three fingers grasping it, his face showing surprise and appreciation for something never expected. It was more money than the freedman would normally see in a year.

To this point, Fallon and Alvaron had been spectators behind Aja's leadership, and now the freedmen took the lead for the final leg to the edge of the woods, nearly a mile distant. No one talked on the way as Alvaron rode his horse and the mules carried all the food and water.

At last the group approached the edge of the pine forest, and the freedmen began to move in and out of the tree line, talking in low tones among themselves, probing for the overgrown entrance to the Slave Trail. It was here *somewhere*.

With something like a muffled *Eureka!* they converged on a spot between two tall pine trees and began cutting the small vines and saplings in between them. Gradually a hole in the forest was revealed, like an overgrown tunnel made by overhanging branches. It was nearly impossible to see, even in the moonlight, it being much darker in the woods, but soon enough the path opened up to a clearing of sorts and the men could gather and rest. It would be daylight soon, and then they could see what lay before them.

The freedmen stood silently as the men hobbled the animals and began to settle down. Fallon and Alvaron approached the brothers with gratitude on their faces, an unspeakable gratitude for the risk they were taking to help them escape. The freedmen extended their hands in friendship. That was enough.

"Every man should be free," David said simply. As Fallon looked into his dark face he felt the man's strength enter his own body, and his own fears for the journey leave, for David had taken the trail to freedom that Fallon would now take in reverse.

For Aja, the freedmen reserved a special affection, gathering around him to shake his hand and pat his shoulders. Fallon watched these former slaves all, and knew there were some things, some emotions, some bonds he would never feel.

Finally, the freedmen did their best to explain to Fallon and Alvaron what lay before them on the trail, the vines as big as a man's leg, thorny underbrush that could slice open flesh like a knife, and rivers and marshes teeming with danger—what they could remember from their own journey years ago.

Then they produced three drawings of animals—*monsters*, by the exaggerated drawings—that they had seen on the trail with warnings to avoid them specifically. The first was a long brown snake with a head like a triangle, rough in the drawing, but plenty evil looking. This snake could swim fast in the water and if it bit a man, he died. The second drawing looked like a log—*with eyes*—a log with a long snout full of teeth and a long tail like a lizard. This

animal could swim very fast and could also run on land. It was
so large it could grab a man in its teeth and pull him into the water. Aja, who was standing close by, looked at Fallon and Alvaron,
imagining what the monster lizard could do to a *boy*. The last
crude drawing looked like a rock sitting in water, a large rock with
a smaller rock for a head, only the smaller rock had its jaws open
wide. The freedmen explained it was a giant turtle that waited
quietly in the water for prey to come along, perhaps a frog or another turtle, and it had a little tongue that it could wiggle, like a
worm, and when the prey came by to eat the worm—*snap!*—the
jaws would close with a sound like a tree cracking. The message: *Do
not sit on the rock.*

And then, with handshakes all around again and good luck
wishes, the brothers were gone. At the edge of the woods they piled
the bushes and saplings back between the two trees to cover the entrance to the trail. Then they began sweeping, using long branches
to smooth out the animal hoof prints and the human foot prints
until they reached the edge of their farm. It took them until dawn
to sweep the full mile, all the way back to their home.

At first light Fallon roused the men and they began hacking
their way through the forest, following the old machete marks.
Aja went ahead, wriggling under vines and calling back when he
reached a marked tree so the men knew in which direction to follow.
The Slave Trail was greatly overgrown in spots, still remarkably
open in other stretches, and the journey thus had fits and starts and
stops while branches were cut and tossed aside. Alvaron was forced
to duck low in some parts to avoid being swept off his mount. But
they made progress and put first one mile and then another behind
them, and finally Fallon began to breathe normally.

The sergeant at Fort Mose, however, could barely breathe at all.
He had walked idly to the fort this morning, thinking idle thoughts,
but this! *What happened?* Everyone was gone, *Holy Madre!* His
guards were tied up and knew nothing. Quickly he returned to the

garrison to rouse his other soldiers and report to Alvaron. *Aye aye aye!*

It was all too horrible, it would be the end of him, but then it got *worse!* The Spanish sailors were gone, too! *Holy Madre de Dios!* It was a terrible dream—more than one hundred men had disappeared into thin air. And he had no idea where to look.

FIFTY-FIVE

REAR ADMIRAL Harry Davies walked the deck at dawn and was still walking some hours later. He was of two minds or, better said, two hearts that morning. He was on fire for Paloma, with a longing whose intensity surprised him and overtook his thoughts when they should have been elsewhere. The *elsewhere* was the search for a needle in a haystack, for above all his focus had to be on finding Fallon and Beauty. *God*, he thought, *get to the job!*

The Florida coast was very long, with several natural harbors, but charts were poor on the matter of soundings and Davies dared not attempt to take his ship inside. The alternative meant heaving-to off the coast and sending in the pinnace to nose around and look for wreckage or signs of life, *English* life. But this was hostile country, and at any moment a Spanish warship might appear, and thus Captain Kinis paced the deck incessantly until the pinnace returned from its forays and they were under way again.

They had begun the search among the small islands and keys off the southern tip of Florida, reasoning that the storm may have pushed Beauty that far. The idea that *Sea Dog* might simply have sunk never occurred to Davies; no, Beauty was too good a sailor for that, hurricane be damned.

It was hot work in the late summer so far south, sailing and heaving-to, lowering the pinnace, waiting, raising the boat, repeat. Telescopes were trained on the coast, and the masthead lookout scanned the horizon for enemy ships, but nothing and nothing.

With each empty harbor or bay, Davies felt his optimism sink a bit, but St. Augustine still lay ahead and Davies had seen Fallon make for that harbor, though he did not see him succeed. *Avenger's* view had been blotted out by *Nuevo Año* bearing down upon them, and the need to loose a broadside of bar shot and langridge on the up roll had taken precedence. It had been a glorious sight, seeing rigging part and sails shot through with holes; *Nuevo Año* had sailed past but how far she'd managed to go he didn't know. His own *Avenger* had been forced to reduce sail once again and flee south before the storm to survive. His last glimpse before sunset was a strange sail to the east, though in the dimming light and spume and rain he could not be sure.

"Nothing, I'm afraid, sir," said Kinis as the pinnace was hoisted yet again to the deck. Davies looked at his captain's face, but Kinis betrayed no frustration or impatience, though he might well have been feeling some.

"Very well, Captain Kinis," replied Davies. "Secure the pinnace and pipe the hands to dinner. We'll continue the search tomorrow." He could have added: *And every tomorrow after that.*

Over the next several days *Avenger* looked in on Cayo Largo, Los Tetas, and then Cayo Biscayne without sighting anything that resembled a ship or a shipwreck. The pinnace reported signs of the hurricane and devastation of settlements, but no ships or evidence of survivors. By week's end they had looked in at Boca de Ratones, still farther north, with nothing sighted, and spirits on *Avenger* were low. Even Captain Kinis let some emotion creep into his face and seemed increasingly dispirited at their lack of success. He gave the repetitive orders to heave-to in a more desultory tone than usual.

IT WAS LATE in the afternoon, a sultry afternoon with a middling wind, when the hail from *Avenger's* masthead brought all telescopes to bear on a tiny indentation in the coastline, not really a harbor. On the chart it was Río St. Lucia, and the image in Davies' telescope revealed part of a ship aground on a reef about a quarter of a mile from shore. Quickly the pinnace was lowered, along with several of the ship's boats, and Davies himself elected to join the search party. Kinis remained behind and paced *Avenger's* quarterdeck, deep in hope.

As the boats moved in closer, the crews could see the wreck more clearly, and Davies knew immediately they were approaching what was left of *Sea Dog*. Small breakers ran under her uplifted stern, part of her name board plainly visible now, but it was not until they approached even closer that they could see her hull was mostly gone; in some places they could see clear through the ship. Davies' heart sank, but he led the boats down the reef line until they found a small opening through, and they made for the beach in flat water. He looked over his shoulder at the gaping hole where *Sea Dog's* bow had been; it looked empty and dark inside.

As they approached the beach it became clear that much of the ship had broken up and drifted to shore. Even from a distance they could see deck boards and ropes and all manner of shipboard items. A barrel floated in the surf, rolling up and back on the beach.

But something else. The black outlines of a fire, *by God!* And cracked coconut shells and the remnants of a lean-to stood out as they drew closer, and all hearts leaped. The men beached the boats and pulled them easily up onto the sand. It was completely, utterly quiet. Davies yelled, they all yelled, but no sound came back, not even an echo. They fanned out, yelling and searching for any sign of the Sea Dogs.

Davies studied the beach carefully. It looked like the crew had been chipping wood and dragging trees from the forest. The furrows were clear enough. He thought of rafts right away, and indeed all the evidence seemed to suggest it. How many were still alive he could not guess. But at least some were, and they were desperate enough to take to sea.

One thing more Davies noticed. There were deep holes in the soft sand, the kind a small-diameter pole would make. Or a peg leg.

AT THAT very moment, that peg leg was stretched out in front of its owner in the lead raft, riding a fast-moving current northward, feeling pretty good about the Sea Dogs' chances.

The rafts had found the current about ten miles offshore as first one and then the other began to move northward with real purpose. They had steered by the stars all night, and morning had found them off Cape Caniaberal, pushing off to the east enough to round it with room to spare, then edging back to the west as the current swept them along by some peculiar force of nature. Kendricks had been right to wait; the weather was cooperating wonderfully. The men were in good spirits, the sculling having ceased and the small sails drawing just enough to allow steerage. Water shipped aboard only randomly, the northeast wind being mostly light and their path being on the far western edge of the current.

On board the rafts, the Sea Dogs looked to the east for any sign of a ship, but the horizon revealed nothing. The men were comfortable enough, stretched out around the ration box, tending to the sail or taking turns steering with the scull. Many chatted about home and what they would do when they returned. Being back at sea had made them somehow optimistic in spite of the fact that they had no idea what lay before them, no weapons, and were sailing so close to a hostile shore.

Beauty had been working out the logistics of getting into St. Augustine, for they would have to depart the current early to avoid being swept right by. If that happened, there would be no turning back on the awkward rafts.

During late afternoon Beauty made the decision to leave the current and begin sculling and sailing in a northwest direction under their own power. This shift slowed them down enormously, but there was nothing for it. Running past St. Augustine wouldn't do.

As dusk approached she ordered the rafts to shore, and they nestled in a small mangrove swamp and tied off for the night. They were safe, and tomorrow should see them in St. Augustine. What they would find there was anybody's guess.

But probably not what they were expecting.

FIFTY-SIX

FALLON AND Alvaron kept the men hacking at the Slave Trail, resting often in the hottest part of the day but moving until it was too dark to travel. They had no idea how far they'd come or how far they still had to go. The trail had its twists and turns around swamps and thickets, so estimating distances was impossible. They just kept at it, one slash mark to the next.

Often they came to streams or shallow rivers that had to be crossed, and this could take the best part of a day. Scouts had to go east and west looking for the best places to cross and, once across, they had to pick up the trail on the other side. Colston's unerring sense of direction was critical.

The biting flies were the biggest irritant, and humans and animals alike felt their stings. The men cursed, but the animals bore their irritation stoically. There were minor cuts and abrasions for Crael to tend to as well.

Jones rationed the food so each man ate just enough to keep strength. They saw little in the way of wildlife, just the occasional bird or squirrel. Then one afternoon Aja came bounding back from ahead with news that a giant lizard with a long snout was in the water. A *monster!* Fallon halted the group's progress and proceeded cautiously ahead with several British and Spanish sailors armed with machetes and rifles. They walked slowly, flies buzzing about their heads, measuring every step carefully until the ground grew soft from water and they knew they were coming to a swamp. They stopped and listened, but heard nothing except the sounds of the forest, a distant bird's call, and buzzing insects.

Fallon moved to his left and motioned for the men to fan out. Slowly, they came to the edge of swampy water, shallow and brown. They would have to cross this water or find a way around it. He looked carefully at the surface, at the downed trees and branches, *looking for eyes.*

Suddenly a scream from his right, a horrible scream with fear and pain in it, and immediately Fallon moved toward it, his machete held out in front of him like a sword. One of the Spaniards was being pulled into the swamp by a large reptile, its giant jaws clamped around the man's leg. Two British sailors had jumped into the water, ignoring their own safety, and were hacking at the reptile furiously. The reptile's hide seemed almost impervious to the blows. Two Spaniards fired their rifles into the reptile's body to no effect. Quickly, Fallon leapt into the water, stepped past the screaming man, and with all his might brought his machete down on the reptile's snout. Again and again he swung at the snout, summoning all his strength until he cut through the nose with a last, desperate blow and the reptile released its grip. Slowly it made to swim away when, finally, a last rifle shot to the eye seemed to kill it. Quickly the men gathered the flailing, wounded man and carried him to shore.

"One of you men get Crael," Fallon called, clearly exhausted as he staggered to shore himself. He half crawled to where the wounded man lay writhing in pain, the blood running down his left calf in rivulets. "Easy, *señor*," Fallon said softly, speaking in Spanish to give the man any comfort he could. "The surgeon is on the way now. You're going to be all right."

Crael arrived quickly and the wounded man seemed to relax. A quick examination told Crael the leg was not broken and the man had suffered only puncture wounds—*many* puncture wounds— and barring infection should make a full recovery. Still, a little laudanum wouldn't hurt and Crael dribbled a few drops into the poor man's mouth.

It was growing late in the afternoon so Fallon and Alvaron decided it was best to make camp for the evening. The men were
rattled by the giant lizard's attack, but in truth it could have been
much worse.

The next day the wounded man was hoisted onto the back of a
mule whose load of provisions was distributed to several of the men
to carry. Once again, the sailors began hacking their way through
the forest, now with extra vigilance. Aja ranged ahead, alert for
anything that moved.

Fallon walked deep in thought. It took little enough to imagine slaves making their way along this trail, facing the dangers the
freedmen described, mothers holding babies, children dragged
along, the men cutting and hacking their way toward—*what?* A
dream place where they could be free, raise their families, work for
wages, and maybe own land; all the unknowns waited for them at
the end of the trail. Fallon thought of them stepping out from the
Florida forest into the sunshine, blinking at their new home, holding their fears and hopes in their chests.

Each day they made progress, and each night the men collapsed,
exhausted. One night, after most of the men were asleep, Alvaron
and Fallon talked quietly about all the minor and major events
that led them to the X upon the ocean where they met. Fallon
mentioned the intelligence Davies had received that the Spanish
treasure was meant for France, and Alvaron stiffened.

"Captain Fallon, are you sure of this intelligence?" Alvaron asked,
disbelieving that the treasure he had almost given his life for, and
in fact had given his leg for, was meant for France. It seemed inconceivable that Spain would pay so much to be safe from French
predations; a treaty was one thing, but to pay France a treasure, especially when Spain's own people were poor and starving in every
town after years of war, was just . . . he was speechless.

"Yes, *señor*," said Fallon. "I believe the intelligence is correct. The
French need money to press the war in Europe. Our mission was
to prevent your treasure from getting to them. I thought you knew."

"No, nothing!" said Alvaron. "None of the Spanish *capitánes* were told the treasure was meant for France when we received orders for Portobelo. It is a disgrace."

Alvaron was clearly distressed and became quiet. He had envisioned finding a Spanish ship in Savannah aboard which he and his men could sail to Spain, for at the end of the day he was not a coward, and the honorable thing was to go home. Better to face disgrace than live silently with it. Now he felt not only disgraced but betrayed by his own country.

Fallon moved away silently to leave Alvaron to his troubled thoughts. For his part, Fallon had no scheme in mind once they reached Savannah. Instinct told him to go slow and scout the situation carefully. Perhaps they would be lucky and find a British ship, but perhaps not. Then the situation would dictate a plan.

Throughout their journey they had seen clear evidence of the hurricane in the stripped and overturned trees. Apparently the storm had come ashore with a vengeance, and Fallon wondered how far it had penetrated before it eventually weakened or went back to sea. But the forest was dramatically thinned, and the men could finally walk among the pines without using their machetes, only low ferns brushing their legs.

Then one day there were fewer trees still. Aja ran forward, sensing an opportunity to see farther ahead, and was quickly out of sight. As the men sat in a clearing eating their meager lunch, he came running back breathlessly.

Savannah.

FIFTY-SEVEN

As the wine goblet was about to touch his lips, word came to the sergeant at St. Augustine that three rafts full of people had entered the harbor. *Not again!*

It was true. And as he led his ragged line of soldiers to the beach once again he found rafts full of men—and two women—drifting to the shore. He ordered his men to form a semicircle, muskets raised.

Sea Dog's crew noticed the soldiers ashore, of course, but they could not take their eyes off the two ships on top of each other on the beach, especially as one was *Harp*. This was something none had ever seen before; indeed, a sight so incomprehensible as to be a mirage. But it was real enough. The rafts drifted toward the beach, each of the crewmen staring silently at the destroyed ships and the soldiers waiting patiently high on the sand. Beauty stared, as well, but she forced her attention to the sergeant, now walking down the beach toward the water, a mixture of bewilderment and curiosity on his face. His life was getting stranger and stranger.

Soon enough all the rafts touched and the crew disembarked. The sergeant stepped forward on the sand with one of the soldiers who spoke uneven English. At the sergeant's direction the soldier asked, "Who are you and where do you come from, please?"

Beauty looked at him a moment, then shifted her gaze to *Harp*, which even then seemed to be pushing deeper into the other ship as each small wave lifted her stern. "What happened here to those ships?" she asked.

The sergeant blinked at her in the strong sunshine, frustration in his expression. Then he conferred with the interpreter, who said, "Those ships are not your concern. You are our prisoners. Get your men onto the beach now, please."

Beauty fought to keep her anxiety down but it wasn't easy. To have found *Harp* was a miracle after all they'd endured, but seeing the catastrophe of the shipwreck—to *hear* the ships grinding away on the beach—filled her with dread that Fallon had been lost. "Where are the British sailors?" she asked anxiously.

Again the sergeant hesitated, aware that he was getting nowhere with this woman, even though armed soldiers pointed their rifles at her. But of course he couldn't answer her questions, especially the *last* question, for he had no idea where the British sailors were. Or where the Spanish sailors were, for that matter.

The sergeant had had enough, though, and needed to get back in charge of the situation. He ordered his men to cock their rifles. This got the sailors' attention, and Beauty's, and she immediately motioned for the ragtag raft crews to move up farther onto the beach. The interpreter barked orders to form a line, which the sailors reluctantly did. With a last look over their shoulders toward *Harp*, they marched in the direction of Fort Mose along the same path Fallon's crew had taken.

This déjà vu was not lost on the soldiers, and certainly not on the sergeant, who walked at the head of the column shaking his head. After some time, they reached the fort and the prisoners looked over their new quarters. It was immediately clear there had been other, more recent prisoners, for there was a fire pit, food scraps, and articles of discarded clothing scattered about—ship's slops. Beauty's hopes rose as the crew tried to settle in, and she turned on the sergeant.

"Sir, who was here before us?" she demanded, looking at the sergeant and then to the interpreter with a look that refused to be denied an answer.

The sergeant relented, if only partially, and instructed the interpreter to reveal that yes, the crew of *Harp* and *Río* had been quartered here, but they were gone. Where they were now the sergeant would not say. The sergeant stationed *ten guards* around the fort and left for the village to get food and water for the prisoners. He considered sending west for an officer of higher rank, but he couldn't keep doing that forever. He was beginning to look like a fool.

Beauty settled the men, encouraging them to be patient and to be ready, for the very fact that Fallon was not there almost made her smile.

AT THAT very moment Fallon's face was filled with curiosity as he and Alvaron peered from the woods at the strangeness of flooded fields of rice, a practice recently introduced to America as a potential cash crop. It was an odd sight, out of their experience, and they considered how to navigate the fields to get to the harbor, which they presumed would reveal itself on the other side. Colston was clear on the point that Savannah lay on the Savannah River, almost twenty miles from the ocean, but that made it no less of a port city for much trading in the southern part of the country took place there. The river was easily navigable with a deep-water entrance from the ocean and only a few scattered islands to negotiate. All this they considered as they rested just within the woods, at the spot where desperate slaves departed the known for the unknown, likely not looking back.

Fallon and Alvaron conferred, and it was decided that Fallon would find a way across the rice fields and attempt to scout the harbor, taking note of shipping and attempting to gain what information he could. The food and water supply was still adequate for a few days longer, if need be, and too many fresh faces in the town might arouse unwanted attention, neutral port or not.

Off he went, a traveler on foot, not unusual in any way except his clothing was tattered. Soon enough he found a dividing dam between rice fields and crossed into the outskirts of the town, taking his time and missing nothing.

The town of Savannah was laid out in a grid fashion, seemingly very orderly and organized. Many of the homes were lavish, large, and ornate. And the commercial buildings were several stories high. But apparently the city had been ravaged by fire recently, for it looked to Fallon as if half the city had been reduced to charred rubble. Though he could see rebuilding in progress, it might be years before Savannah would be whole again.

He walked on past shops and homes, passing buggies with footmen, deliverymen, and ordinary townspeople going about their business. He had no trouble finding the waterfront and was soon greeted by the sight of dismasted, damaged, and partially wrecked and submerged ships. The hurricane had done its work on Savannah's harbor. The sound of mauls and *belay this* or *avast there* rang out as spars were shaped or sent up on several vessels. Around less-fortunate ships, men pulled at their beards and scratched their heads and conferred in deep tones, *what to do, what to do?*

A freshly coppered ship whose cargo had apparently been lumber lay over on its side in the middle of the harbor. Odd boards floated around it and bumped up against pilings and bulkheads, having somehow resisted the pull of the tides toward the sea. Or perhaps the sinking ship was simply giving up her cargo little by little; her lumber might be the only thing keeping her afloat.

Several smaller vessels had run up on the shore here and there, as well, and there were small boats going back and forth near Hutchinson Island in the middle of the harbor. There a large cargo ship was hard aground, her masts missing and her rigging hanging over the side.

Up ahead, in the middle of the long wharf, Fallon noticed a small French trader, wormy and ill-used and made worse by the storm. On the dock beside her an old *capitaine*, a white-haired Frenchman, sat leaning against a piling and barking orders to the crew doing the work. Bales of deer hides were stacked haphazardly near the ship, apparently part of the cargo, for deer hides were a major export out of Savannah for Europe.

"*Capitaine*," Fallon greeted the old Frenchman, "I see the hurricane was very bad for you, no?"

"*Sacré bleu!*" the Frenchman spit out. "It was the worst thing I have ever seen." So preoccupied was he with supervising the work aboard his ship, *Étoile*, that he didn't look at Fallon, perhaps afraid his men would malinger if he took his eyes off them.

"Where are you bound, *Capitaine?*" Fallon asked, trying to get a conversation going that might be helpful later.

"I sail between Savannah and Northern European ports, *monsieur,*" the Frenchman answered, still looking at his crew. "I have not stepped foot on French soil in two years."

Fallon lingered a while watching the work but gradually drifted away lest he be questioned in return, although the French *capitaine* had no real interest in anything except his ship.

Fallon could see no British ships in the harbor, which was hugely disappointing, but they may have moved on upriver or even been sunk. Bits and pieces of wood, tree trunks, and crates continually floated out with the tide. Fallon took his time as he strolled along the waterfront, past innumerable bars and chandleries undergoing their own repairs. Several times he was eyed curiously, and once he was asked if he wanted work. Well, from his appearance it certainly looked like he could use some money.

Up ahead, at the end of the wharf, near what appeared to be the port office or customs, was a large schooner—*Élan*, of 18 guns— obviously American built but flying a tattered French flag. She was quite dashing, with a pronounced bow and raked masts. The Americans had used these fast schooners successfully in their War of Independence against Great Britain, heavily arming them to take on enemy brigs and, in at least one instance, a British frigate. After the war, England had bought several of the type from American yards, as had France, for they were formidable weapons of a design not yet built in their own countries. From the lack of uniformed crew, Fallon concluded *Élan* was most likely a privateer, perhaps taken in battle. The big schooner's new sails were being fitted, as the old suit must have been blown out by the storm, and crews seemed to be busy all over the ship; her new rigging was being blackened, new railings painted, and a new binnacle fitted as well.

As Fallon nonchalantly drew closer he could hear the schooner's crew jabbering in French; well, mostly French, though at least some were perhaps Portuguese and one, a big fellow with a bushy black beard, was cursing like an American. The crew was large, as befitted a privateer that would need to man prizes, and thus Fallon tried to put any thought of taking the ship out of his head.

Fallon looked at the schooner longingly, for though she was bigger than *Sea Dog* she reminded him of his old command. He wondered, yet again, what had become of the ship and Beauty and all the rest of his old crew. Beauty was an excellent sailor, and if anyone could bring the ship to safety it was her, but the hurricane was beyond the pale of anything either of them had ever experienced at sea. Still, he had not begun grieving for Beauty; in fact, he had never considered she could be dead. Just . . . *missing*.

Satisfied that he had all the information Savannah was going to give him for the moment, Fallon cut through town and found his way back over the dams to the edge of the woods again.

The British and Spanish crews gathered around to hear his report, which did not do much to cheer the men, there being no Spanish or British ships in port that Fallon could see. The men could imagine no way home, at least anytime soon. And they could tell by listening to Fallon that he had formed no other plan else he would have revealed it.

Alvaron had been listening intently to Fallon as well and had caught the spirit of disappointment the men felt. As it was late by this time, the crews ate their small rations and wandered off to find a soft bed of leaves for the night. Alvaron motioned to Fallon to join him a little ways off to talk. They sat alone at the edge of the woods, their backs against a massive, mottled sycamore tree, staring at the emerging night sky.

"What are you thinking, *señor?*" asked Alvaron. "No, let me guess. You are wondering how we will bring over one hundred men into town, find them work, a place to stay, and keep them together somehow *under command.* Correct?"

Fallon smiled ruefully. "How did you know?" he wondered aloud.

"Because I have been worrying about these things as well," said Alvaron. "It is a neutral port, of course, so we can just walk into town. We are shipwrecked sailors who need help, no? But then what? I do not like splitting my men up, letting them fend for themselves wherever they find work, or *if* they find work."

"What can we do?" Fallon asked. He knew that Alvaron, like himself, had been reared in the discipline of command and felt responsible for his men. They both knew that, should their crews be absorbed into the town, their command would disappear. And with it, their ability to protect their men. But here was reality: When the food and water were gone, they would all have no choice but to go into Savannah and find work; it would not do to be caught stealing.

"Perhaps, Captain Fallon," said Alvaron, "it would be better if we split our crews at this point. I believe it would be easier to consider options."

"Yes," replied Fallon, "perhaps you are right. But first, would you consider coming into town with me tomorrow morning? I would like you to see Savannah, *señor,* and perhaps you can see another opportunity I could not. I believe if we transfer you to a mule he will be more sure-footed than a horse and should have no difficulty with the rice dams."

"Gladly, sir. I have always wanted to see Savannah from atop a mule with a British captain as a guide. What could be more natural, no?"

FIFTY-EIGHT

THE NEXT morning, they set off, Fallon carrying Alvaron's crutches and the mule carrying Alvaron, who had dressed in ship's slops for the trip. It was a bright morning, with a light breeze from the southwest, and the surface of the rice fields rippled in tiny wavelets. The sky was perfectly, brilliantly blue.

They made it into town with the help of the sure-footed beast, and Fallon tied him off to a post at the end of a street that led to the wharf. The town was not really awake yet, but there was some work beginning along the waterfront and, by the time Fallon and Alvaron made their way to the western end, most of the crews were starting their day in earnest. Alvaron moved fairly well on his crutches, stopping only occasionally to rest, his leg healed for the most part. He saw much of what Fallon had reported, the aftermath of the storm written on every building and street. Once at the waterfront he saw clearly that docks were in need of repair, of course, along with ships. No doubt the chandleries had all but exhausted their supplies of nails and cordage and tar and other items necessary to float men on the sea.

"The hurricane reached far inland, sir," Fallon said. "I wonder how far north it . . . "

But Alvaron was not listening. His expression was immobile, his eyes focused across the harbor toward Hutchinson Island. Fallon followed his gaze, but there was nothing to see that he hadn't seen before—the boats going to and fro, the big ship aground and listing, the rigging still over the side.

"Captain Fallon," Alvaron said quietly. "I must tell you something and trust you not to act on it. May I have your word?"

"Yes, of course, *Capitán*," Fallon wondering what on earth had brought his friend up short.

"Look there," Alvaron motioned with his head. "That ship is Spanish."

"Excellent, my friend!" said Fallon enthusiastically. "I did not look closely before." A ship without masts could hardly fly a flag, and Fallon had not paid enough attention to her lines. Alvaron kept his eyes on the ship, taking in every detail, watching the men rowing around in boats.

"I know that ship," Alvaron said, "because she was carrying treasure in our fleet. She's the *Nuevo Año*, sitting across the harbor with part of France's tribute in her hold." Alvaron fairly spat the word *tribute* from his mouth.

"*Good God!* Are you sure, sir?" Fallon blurted out. "Well, of course you are, by God. How . . . I mean, she made it all the way here and up the river! It's . . . it's . . . do you think the treasure is still in her?"

"I assume so, *señor*," said Alvaron. "I doubt anyone in Savannah knows what is sitting there. They are all too busy attending to their own problems from the storm. But look, see how the men row guard around the ship? They don't want to take chances."

They kept their voices low, and Fallon tried not to stare but it was difficult. What a feat of seamanship to get that ship into the river in the first place, and then to navigate up the river in a hurricane! It defied imagination, but there she sat, treasure and all.

"We must get across the harbor, Captain," implored Alvaron. "I must get closer and see for myself. Can you arrange it?"

Fallon quickly found a boat with oars and, as he could see no one to ask, helped Alvaron in and shoved off. They made it easily across the harbor, Fallon feeling muscles he hadn't used in some time, until finally a hail from one of the guard boats brought the boat to a slow drift.

Alvaron returned the hail in Spanish, identifying himself, and the guard momentarily froze in surprise before a huge smile of relief painted his face. Fallon resumed rowing around the stern, which they could now clearly see, reading *Nuevo Año* as they passed—*New Year*. Fallon brought the boat to the starboard side as curious seamen in their red caps—*barrettinas*—gathered at the railings. With a curt order from Alvaron, the seamen lowered a bosun's chair by hand over the side for him. Fallon clapped onto the mainchains and climbed up and over the channel, his feet hitting the deck just as Alvaron was pulled up the side. He was helped over the railing, stood upright on his crutches, and was greeted by someone in a slightly tattered officer's uniform.

Fallon heard the officer introduce himself as Teniente Garin. "I served under Capitán Tornell until he was killed by a falling block," Garin explained, "then I assumed command. Many of the crew were dead from the fighting, and we had much to repair quickly. The storm was . . . well, you know of the storm, of course, sir."

Here Fallon looked hard at the deck, not in shame but in helplessness. War demanded that men die, of course, all soldiers and sailors knew this. But it was not easy to hear Garin's account of death and destruction for which Fallon felt at least partly responsible.

But Alvaron was completely absorbed by Garin's story. "How did you get the ship so far up the river, Teniente?" he asked. "It is astonishing to find you here."

"The current drove us very far north while we tried to get the ship under control," said Garin evenly. "We were pushed away from the British but our sails were blown out, and we had to cut the rigging away to steer. We saw the river's entrance and by the Grace made it inside. The wind pushed us up the river, and when we reached the town we beached the ship on this island. Unfortunately, we lost our masts."

Garin had related the events without emotion and, it seemed to Fallon, without taking credit for a truly heroic effort. But it was not

Fallon's place to comment or praise. He waited to see how Alvaron would respond.

Alvaron responded by heartily shaking Garin's hand and congratulating him on an exceptional feat of seamanship. "Amazing, Teniente Garin, wonderfully amazing," Alvaron said, and his beaming face told Garin he meant it. "What seamanship!"

Garin exhaled in relief, happy that this one-legged *capitán* had been pleased with his actions. No doubt he was also relieved that he was no longer the ranking officer aboard, for he admitted he had done nothing since his ship had run aground because he couldn't think of anything that would not risk disclosing their cargo. So, he'd posted guards and prayed for divine intervention. *Madre de Dios!* it had come in the form of a new *capitán!*

Well, it was a pretty pickle. The best chance to float the ship was to lighten it, but to lighten it would put a fortune in gold and silver on the shore. How that could stay a secret for long was a good question. Fallon could see the problem working on Alvaron, for clearly he was back in command.

Alvaron introduced Fallon without explanation, and Garin bowed with good manners, revealing nothing of his feelings at meeting an enemy captain on his deck. Alvaron did not say *which* enemy captain he was, thank God, as in: *one of the British who attacked the treasure fleet.* They then took a slow turn around the deck, a sight Fallon was familiar with, and ended up in Capitán Tornell's cabin to sit comfortably with a glass of wine and discuss the situation.

Alvaron asked to see Tornell's locker and withdrew the dress uniform, holding it up to his chest. It was a decent fit, if a little full, and he asked Tornell's steward for help putting it on. Garin sent for the carpenter to cut off the useless pant leg and pin it up, and when that was done—by the second glass—Alvaron slipped on the embroidered jacket and he was *El Capitán.*

"I may need this to impress the dockyard," Alvaron said with a smile. He certainly knew how authority worked around the world.

"I will also ask the carpenter to make me a wooden leg. Perhaps Señor Crael will help fit it."

Fallon nodded, of course. He was quite struck by the change in demeanor in Alvaron now that he was on a ship again, even a ship hard aground.

"Now, gentlemen," Alvaron continued, "here is how I see it. We have a fortune in treasure and specie aboard, there is a willing dockyard just across the way from which I know we can buy what we need, we have thirty more men to help unload the ship and form a human wall around the treasure, if need be, to keep it from prying eyes on shore, and *we will float this ship again.*"

"Correction, Capitán Alvaron," Fallon said quickly. "We have over one hundred more men. Count us with you and the unloading will go three times as fast."

Fallon had offered before even thinking about it, as Alvaron's friend now, not his enemy. They were long past being enemies, and Fallon had no interest in the treasure aboard *Nuevo Año* anymore. Even if it eventually reached France it would do her little good as Fallon was convinced most of the *flota* had been sunk or destroyed. Besides, helping Alvaron would give his men a *mission* and postpone having to be split up in Savannah, at least for a few days.

Alvaron smiled and nodded to Garin—*see?* he seemed to say. "Captain Fallon, once again I am very grateful to you. Will you be so good as to get *our* men to a secluded place on shore to be picked up, for I fear the dock will provide too broad an audience, no? You may borrow my mule to go back—*ha ha ha*—I would be very grateful. We will use the ship's boats to ferry the men to the ship this evening after dark. Tonight we will all be aboard and tomorrow we begin. I would welcome any input, sir. For I know your mind is turning."

And Fallon's mind *was* turning, very fast, but it would not land anywhere.

FIFTY-NINE

REAR ADMIRAL Davies was taking no chances, and he sent *Avenger*'s pinnace in to sound the channel into St. Augustine and to be sure of any ships inside. The pinnace returned with a report that the channel was awkward but navigable by *Avenger* with care, and there was massive wreckage on shore.

"Captain Kinis," Davies ordered, trying to keep his voice under control and appear calm, "please have all *Avenger*'s guns run out." He was apprehensive about what the wreckage meant and what resistance he would find. He intended an intimidating show of force demonstrating the long arm of the British Royal Navy reaching into a Spanish port.

Avenger sailed in thus, ready for a fight, and anchored fore and aft with a spring line turning her starboard guns seaward toward the channel. Her larboard guns were turned on St. Augustine. That done, Davies left Kinis in charge and took Cortez as a translator with him in the gig to shore, dreading what he would find in the wreckage.

As the crew rowed closer to the beach, the two wrecked ships and three rafts were plainly visible, and Davies fought to keep down his apprehension. Much could have happened here, he told himself, so expect anything.

What he did not expect was the Spanish sergeant, who by this time would not have been surprised to see the second coming of Christ, arrive on foot leading a small column of soldiers who stopped, then pointed all rifles toward the gig as it reached the shore. The sergeant demanded the British immediately surrender in the name of His Majesty Charles IV, King of Spain. Davies could not be sure of the words but understood the intent well enough.

Cortez translated, yet Davies did not move in the boat, except to smile. "Tell the sergeant, Cortez, that if he doesn't put down those silly rifles and welcome us to his beautiful beach in a civil manner his Britannic Majesty will be offended. We come as friends, but unless he welcomes us as such I will order the great guns to annihilate the village while he stands there."

Cortez translated, earnestly. And all pretense at a show of bravado on the beach dissolved. The rifles came down, and Davies and Cortez stepped ashore to a deflated sergeant. It was quickly apparent after some back and forth that, yes, the crew of the rafts were prisoners at the fort where the other crew of the British ship had been prisoners before they disappeared into thin air—*Madre de Dios!*—and maybe took the crew of the Spanish ship into thin air with them for they cannot be found, *señores!*

Davies smiled to himself: *That damned Fallon!* Then he demanded to be led to the fort, whistling to himself as he walked, for this was turning out to be a wonderful day.

While the gig's crew waited at the beach, the sergeant led Davies and Cortez along the same path he had recently followed with all the British and Spanish crewmembers. They wound around the village of St. Augustine and moved north, through scrub and pines, until they at last reached Fort Mose.

The reunion at Fort Mose was jubilation itself. Great back-slapping and handshaking and elation enough for a victory in Parliament. Beauty even hugged Davies, which was made more awkward by Beauty's peg sinking in the soft sand and very nearly toppling her over, taking the Rear Admiral with her. To Davies she looked worn and quite a bit thinner, her ship's slops hanging rather loosely off her frame. But there was no mistaking the joy in her eyes.

The sergeant and his men stood in the background, perplexed by this latest turn of events, to say the least. It was all a mystery, the whole of it, and the sergeant reasoned some things were just beyond the abilities of a simple man to understand.

In very little time Beauty and her crew were back at the beach, back near the wrecked ships settling deeper into the sand, and to the rafts that had brought them so far. After a last look, the gig took Beauty, Davies, and the first load of prisoners out to *Avenger* to general acclaim by the ship's crew, for the rescue of shipwrecked sailors was seen as the highest form of good luck for the ship, not just the survivors.

Kinis wasted no time getting other boats to shore to bring the rest of the prisoners out to the ship. That done, he ordered the spring line taken in and sent men to the capstan to hoist the anchor, being very anxious to get away from an enemy harbor, even one undefended. In fact, he kept his guns run out until they cleared the channel and were at sea.

Davies ordered Kinis to continue up the coast to look for Fallon, for his instincts told him a seaman would go to the sea, not inland. Meanwhile, Davies and Beauty went below to the great cabin, for he wanted her full accounting of events since he'd lost track of *Sea Dog* in the storm.

What a story! Davies' mouth came open at every turn of events, and his estimation of this remarkable woman soared. Where were captains like this in the Royal Navy? She talked until she was talked out, covering every detail and commending the men at every turn, and then retired to the cabin Kinis had given up for her.

Avenger hove-to for the night off the entrance to Río de San Juan, a large river near the border of Spanish Florida and Georgia. They would explore this river tomorrow, and then if necessary continue up the coast to investigate several small islands: Talbot Island, Amelia Island, and Jekyll Island. No one was discouraged; in fact, with Beauty aboard Davies felt like luck was on his side.

SIXTY

THE SALT packet *Castille* with Captain Wallace in command anchored at the far end of Nassau harbor in the early morning after heaving-to off Exuma the night before to await good light to navigate the shallow waters. Even from the deck Elinore could see the markets were already beginning to fill with people and the waterfront was coming alive.

Wallace had told her that fifty years ago Nassau had been called the *Republic of Pirates*—a stronghold for pirates and privateers with their own laws and customs—with Edward Teach, or Blackbeard as he was famously called, as its magistrate. The Governor of Bermuda had estimated there were more than one thousand pirates in Nassau then, vastly outnumbering the permanent inhabitants by 10-1. Though those days had passed, the vestiges of that time remained, and no other town in the Bahamas was so populated by scoundrels.

Castille was anchored between Nassau, on the northern end of the island of New Providence, and Hog Island, a smallish island that buffered Nassau from the sea. Hog Island had once sheltered the likes of Anne Bonny and Calico Jack and other lesser and greater pirates. The Republic came to an end when Great Britain sent Governor Woodes Rogers to Nassau, armed with three warships and a motto: *Expulsis Piratis—Restituta Commercia*, or Pirates Expelled—Commerce Restored.

The pirates were expelled, slowly. The Bahamas were a British colony and generally followed British laws and customs, having received and settled many Loyalists during the American War for Independence. But old customs die hard, and privateering and pirates were quietly tolerated, if not exactly encouraged, for they were a boon to the local economy, particularly the personal economies of local officials who looked the other way.

Elinore stood watching the shipping in Nassau Harbor. There was quite a bit of activity about, with boats of all sizes and types, small coastal traders to larger ships from several nations, at least those countries not currently at war with Great Britain. She and Somers were next to Wallace at the starboard railing, and the Captain had his telescope to his eye, sweeping the scene. Elinore saw him suddenly stiffen.

Wallace was staring at *Renegade* through his telescope. The ship was anchored at the far end of Hog Island, some half mile away. She appeared to have been battered about by the hurricane and was undergoing general repairs, riding below her waterline—no doubt the pumps were at work—having new yards sent up and, as he watched, a new crow's nest was just being fitted.

"That's the blackguard pirate that did for Captain Fallon in Caicos Straights," he said through clenched teeth.

"What do you say, Wallace?" asked Somers incredulously. "That's Wicked Jak Clayton?"

"The same," replied Wallace. "Looks like he's in for repairs after the storm. The bastard should have sunk."

Somers and Elinore were momentarily speechless. There across the water was the source of all their troubles, of death and intrigue and loss, close enough to hit with a cannon. It was incredible, watching the ship at work as if nothing in the world could be more normal. In reality it was an odious and evil thing getting ready for sea again.

"What can we do, Wallace?" asked Somers, growing agitated. "We can't let that son of a bitch just sit there!"

"We can't attack a frigate, sir," responded Wallace coolly.

"Perhaps we can follow her when she leaves, but if she turns to attack us we're finished. I don't know what else to tell you."

Somers paced the deck in small circles, growing more upset by the minute. Elinore saw that her father desperately wanted to take action, but she didn't know what they were in a position to do. They were on a virtually unarmed ship in a strange harbor, though a harbor under nominal British authority. Surely Clayton was known to Bahamian officials and even the governor himself for what he was.

The color had risen in Elinore's cheeks, a sure sign that usually precipitated anger, at the least. At the most it was every man for himself and hide the bullets.

"Let's go, Elinore!" Somers suddenly announced. "By God, we'll see the governor!"

Somers called for Wallace's gig to row them to shore. It was an idea born of desperation to do *something*, and even if it produced nothing substantive it would at least make them feel better. They tied off at the town dock easily enough and began the long walk to Government House, Somers's gout held at bay, no doubt by his anger. Most of the homes were opening their shutters and delicious scents were drifting out to the streets, reminding Somers that, in their haste to come to shore, they had quite forgotten breakfast. Small children stood in doorways rubbing their eyes, putting sleep away. Women carrying baskets full of fruit on their heads swayed past in bright dresses and clucked to each other as they passed.

At Government House a servant swept the steps and the giant doors were open to reveal a cool stone entryway inside, a clerk at the ready dressed in white from head to toe. *No, the governor was not in, well not exactly in, there is no current governor but an acting . . .*

Somers wasn't having it. He took Elinore by the hand and brushed past the clerk like he was white mist and marched down the hall to the large wooden doors at the end, bursting through them without knocking and startling the governor's secretary and an aide into spitting up their coffee through their noses.

"Where is the Governor of the Bahamas this morning?" Somers

asked in a voice that would not be denied an answer. "We've come from Bermuda to see him!"

"Sir, sir," replied the secretary, attempting to dab the coffee from his frock coat with a handkerchief. "This is really a bad start to the day, I must say. Very rude of you to come barging in like this without an appointment or so much as a knock. Who are you and whatever are you thinking?"

"I'm Ezra Somers and this is my daughter, Elinore, sir. We own the Somers Salt Company on Grand Turk Island, and I'm thinking if you don't tell us the governor's whereabouts this instant you will never see another teaspoon of salt on this island!" Somers's face was now as red as a radish.

"*Good God!* We don't have a governor at this moment, Mr. Somers," said the secretary. "Well, not technically. Lord Dunmore left office, and we have an acting governor for the moment; Robert Hunt was appointed just weeks ago. But he isn't here either."

"Then where the hell is he?" demanded Somers.

"He is touring our fortifications at the moment. He's at Fort Charlotte. I'd be happy to—"

But Somers and Elinore had turned on their heels and left. Fort Charlotte was clearly visible from the harbor and it should be no trouble getting there; they were in comfortable walking clothes and the sun was not too unbearably hot as yet. Fort Charlotte was a new fort, having been built by Lord Dunmore in 1789 and named for the wife of King George III. Thus far it had never fired a shot in battle, but perhaps Somers would have something to say about that, too.

Within thirty minutes they'd crossed the waterless moat surrounding the limestone fort and gained entrance through the massive doors that were guarded by no less than five sentries. Robert Hunt's entourage could easily be seen on the upper rampart with its commanding view of Nassau Harbor. Somers limped up the steps gamely, Elinore not far behind, and he broached the small group surrounding Hunt more or less the way he'd entered

Government House, that is, in a *burst*.

"Governor Hunt, sir, may I have a word?" Somers was calmer when out of breath, and Hunt turned to him with a curious look on his face, less appalled than his secretary had been.

"Yes? How can I be of service, sir?" Hunt replied. "You are quite out of breath, I see. Pray compose yourself."

The entourage moved outward slightly, allowing Elinore to enter the circle. "Sir," she began evenly, looking Hunt squarely in the eye. "My father and I have come to call your attention to a pirate, an infamous and dangerous pirate, in your harbor just below who has raided and plundered the Somers Salt Company of Grand Turk Island and killed many of our sailors and those of the Royal Navy." This might have been a stretch but Bishop *might* have lost men in Caicos Straights.

"But Miss . . . ?"

"Elinore Somers, and this is my father."

"Miss Somers, what you say may well be true, but we would need rather more substantive proof of this pirate's activities. Who is he? What ship is he on? Are there witnesses who will come forth? What would you have me do?"

Now Somers was recovered, color rising on his throat. "You're leaning against a Goddamned cannon, sir! And Jak Clayton is down below, a murderer and thief! He's in that big frigate in the harbor just there . . . *shit!*"

And they all turned to follow his gaze, his bulging, disbelieving eyes as *Renegade* was just making sail, the land breeze taking her out of Nassau Harbor. Silence in the group.

"I'm sorry I can be of no help to you," the acting governor said kindly. And they chose to believe he meant it.

SIXTY-ONE

IT WAS a clear night, and Fallon briefly thought of Elinore, wondering if she could see the same stars as he, wondering what she was thinking. He would have liked to have thought of her longer, much longer, but there was work to do.

Fallon had led the British and the Spanish crews out from the woods in single file, skirting the rice fields and opening a gate to a pasture along the way, letting the horse and mules inside. He had them at the appointed place—about half a mile upriver from Hutchinson Island—at the appointed time and found *Nuevo Año's* boats waiting to ferry the men to Hutchinson Island.

After more than an hour of back and forth, aided by slack tide, Jones had all the men aboard the beached ship. Alvaron greeted them warmly, British as well as Spanish sailors. Much of the bullion had already been brought up on deck, though by no means all, and the men fell to work immediately off-loading it onto the beach. *Nuevo Año's* crew initially stiffened at the sight of the British crewmen, but Alvaron's men spread the word of their goodwill, particularly toward their *capitán*, and gradual acceptance took hold. Since the ship's larboard side faced the wharf across the harbor, the combined crews were unloading off the starboard side, so there was little chance of the treasure being discovered. Still, Alvaron had a sail ready to cover the growing pile of bullion come morning.

They worked that night in shifts, bringing the bars up from the lowest depths of the hold to the deck, then throwing them off the side to land in the soft sand. Other crewmen then picked up the bars and stacked them high up the bank above the tide line. Occasionally, the British seamen stopped to stare at what was in their hands. Any single bar was worth more than any man would see in his lifetime. And while it might have been tempting to steal, such was their loyalty to Fallon that they resisted.

Fallon had asked Jones to mark the waterline before they'd begun shifting the bullion, and watched with satisfaction as it gradually, minutely, rose higher. The next high tide would be mid-morning, some six or seven feet, and so they worked diligently throughout the night to be ready.

By dawn they were nearly finished, the men exhausted, the treasure moved up the beach and covered by a sail. The men slept about the deck, some on the beach itself, oblivious to the light of day. Fallon dozed against the binnacle, having worked alongside his crew throughout the night. His last thought before sleep was that there were *six ships* loaded like this one, and he wondered that there was that much gold and silver in the world.

Fallon awoke to Alvaron nudging him gently with his crutch. "Captain Fallon, do you feel that?"

Fallon did not want to wake up, wanted to sleep forever in fact, and was about to resent the nudge when he felt the ship move, just a bit, but *move*. Instantly he was awake, for by now it was mid-morning and *Nuevo Año* was—again that barely perceptible rocking—she was going to float, by God!

And indeed, within three hours *Nuevo Año* was anchored close off Hutchinson Island, floating as proudly as an empty, mastless hulk of a ship could float. The tide was still making, and the ship had pulled around with her bow pointed downriver toward the sea, revealing her cargo piled high under a sail on the shore. Alvaron wisely had posted just one guard, and he without a musket, so as not to call undue attention to the value of what lay beneath the sail.

Bleary-eyed men, aching and sore from using muscles not used in some time, ate their breakfast and rested until mid-afternoon, when the tide had turned and the ship swung around again, bow upriver to the west now, her bulk hiding the boats going back and forth removing the treasure from the beach. This required a new plan, and a different set of muscles, as there was no boom and tackle to lift the bars; so the bars were stacked in threes or at most fours and hoisted up to the deck by hand in canvas bags. Groups of men lined the entire starboard side of the ship, leaning over with their bags, awaiting their loads. They worked all afternoon until evening, loading and hoisting and lowering the bullion down into the hold of the ship until the tide turned again, and they could at last rest. Only half the bars had found their way into the hold; the rest would have to wait until tomorrow.

Fallon joined Alvaron for dinner in the great cabin while Garin set the watches and changed the single onshore guard to several guards for the night. Fallon could see that Alvaron was very tired, the strain showing on his face and in his sagging shoulders. But there seemed more to it than that.

"Captain Fallon, I must come to a decision about the treasure," Alvaron confided. "That is, if we get out of here with it, whenever that will be."

Fallon had just finished pouring a fresh glass of wine for them both, and looked up, curious that his friend had been wrestling with a problem to which he was oblivious.

"When we first saw this ship you gave me your word you would not act against Spain's treasure," Alvaron continued. "And you are an honorable man. But I find myself in the curious position of considering an act against Spain myself. You see, Captain, I have no wish to see France get this bullion. Not when Spain herself needs it so badly. Besides, I have fought the French for many years. I don't see France as an ally we can trust."

It was indeed a difficult position for Alvaron, and Fallon could see the problem: How to get the treasure to Spain, but keep it out of French hands, when the government had specifically sent him to Portobelo to get it for France? If Alvaron did not deliver the treasure, now that he had at least part of it, he could be hanged for treason. And yet, fate, in the form of *Nuevo Año*, may have handed him an opportunity to recover his honor by doing his duty.

"Are there loyalists like yourself, Capitán Alvaron, who would see Godoy's actions as betraying Spain?" Fallon asked.

"Yes, Spain is so political there is always opposition to anything." Alvaron laughed, breaking the tension of the moment. "Perhaps we deserve our history, no? Always so much intrigue. But to your question, there are those like myself who see Charles IV as a puppet controlled by France. He can usually be found hunting somewhere on the continent, leaving Godoy in charge of the government. Spain is no longer one of the great powers of the world, *señor*."

They sat at dinner, then, mostly in silence, each with his own thoughts leading in different directions. Each silently concluding that unless the treasure was taken to Spain it would be treason. For his part, Fallon would honor his word not to attempt to re-take the treasure and hope that Alvaron would find a way, any way, to keep the bullion from reaching France, though he couldn't imagine what it would be.

SIXTY-TWO

A T FIRST light Davies sent the pinnace to explore the Río de San Juan. The river had a wide entrance, which would have made for an easy escape from the storm, and then it rather dramatically narrowed and swung south, back toward St. Augustine.

Davies had high hopes of finding some trace of Fallon and his crew there, but after spending most of the day exploring the river they found nothing to suggest Fallon had come that way. The pinnace came back aboard, having taken soundings of the river, and *Avenger* made her way inside the entrance and anchored for the night.

That evening and the next day brought storms, raging late summer storms that, although certainly not of hurricane strength, nonetheless brought strong east winds that effectively kept *Avenger* bottled up in the Río de San Juan.

Davies spent the day looking deep within himself. He was not normally so introspective, but something had happened to him that night in Matanzas that had destabilized him emotionally, and he was heeling in the stiff breeze of confusion. If the truth be told, he had never been in love before, only deep lust. And so this feeling for Paloma was entirely new, both welcome and not, and he paced his cabin most of the day trying to come to grips with it.

Beauty spent the day studying the charts of the east coast of America, for this was new country to her. Kinis had very kindly told her all he knew, genuine respect in his voice, pointing out the entrances to Savannah and Charleston as being particularly easy to navigate according to the sailing master.

Damn this storm, she thought to herself, wondering if Fallon was even alive and, if he was, what the hell he was doing. And, as she looked at the charts, *where was he doing it?*

THE FIERCENESS of the wind and pelting rain did not keep the British or Spanish seamen from their work of moving the treasure aboard *Nuevo Año,* and thankfully the storms meant there were few men on the wharf today to observe them.

At some point in the early forenoon, Alvaron asked Fallon to take over supervision while he went below with Crael to fit his new peg with a leather bucket to hold his leg. Crael had rather remarkably adjusted to life without liquor, albeit much of his abstinence had been forced upon him by the shipwreck. He adjusted a strap on the bucket and wiggled the peg, then adjusted another strap, for it was critical that the peg be an extension of the leg—and stable.

The peg was a fine piece of work, but thumping around the cabin Alvaron could see it would take time to master. Turning quickly was a particular problem, and several times he fell into the furniture as he practiced. Crael left him to his efforts and went back on deck to report success to Fallon, with the caveat that Capitán Alvaron would need some time to adjust to walking.

"Thank you, Crael," said Fallon to his surgeon. "You have been indispensible to the Service these last weeks. Many men would be dead without you. Capitán Alvaron among them."

Crael looked at Fallon, the author of his abstinence, but also perhaps his savior. "Thank you, Captain," he said simply, but there was deep gratitude behind those words.

By the forenoon all the treasure was at last aboard, and the wet and bedraggled crew went below to attempt to dry off. Fallon stayed on deck, looking at the wharf, specifically toward the far end of the wharf where the French privateer nestled against the dock.

An hour later he still stood, the rain running unnoticed off his face, until the wet hair on his arms managed to stand up. My God, he thought, perhaps there was a chance to get home and strike a blow for Great Britain at the same time! The idea was madness, of course. But it had the virtue of being the only idea he had to get out of Savannah.

Below decks at last, Fallon called for Aja to bring towels and fresh slops. "Thank you," Fallon said gratefully. "How are you coming along, Aja? We've barely spoken since we reached Savannah."

"Well enough, Captain, sir," said Aja. "Have no worries for me. I am very happy to be off that trail." Fallon could understand, and he knew it was true for all the men. It was good to be on the water again, if only temporarily.

"Aja, I can only imagine how you must feel having experienced so much in these past few weeks," Fallon said sympathetically. "Your head must be spinning with all that's happened. Are you sure you're all right?"

Suddenly tears began filling the boy's eyes and ran rivulets down his dark face to drip noiselessly on the deck, mixing with the raindrops falling off Fallon's clothes. On instinct, Fallon opened his arms and Aja stepped inside their circle; the strength of Fallon's embrace seemed to relieve him of the need to be strong or brave or a *man*. His body heaved with sobs for a moment, then quieted.

Slowly, Aja stepped back and dried his eyes with his sleeve, then straightened his back. "I don't know why I did that," he said sheepishly.

"You don't have to know," said Fallon gently. "You just have to know that everything is going to be all right now. No matter what happened in the past. Do you believe me?"

Aja looked at Fallon with hope and concern on his face. "Yes, Captain, sir. Everything is going to be all right now," he repeated.

Fallon squeezed the boy's shoulders. "Good," he said in an upbeat voice. "Now off you go. I have to dry off, and you do, too! Between the two of us we've gotten you very wet!"

Aja smiled weakly and almost laughed a little as he left. Fallon watched him go and in that moment felt an emotion he'd never felt before. It caught him unawares and flooded over him. He felt . . . like a *father*. It both took him aback and pleased him. And, truth be told, it frightened him a little because it felt like a different kind of responsibility than all the other responsibilities he had on his shoulders.

Fallon shivered, for he was still soaked through, and it quickly brought his mind back to the situation at hand. He took off his wet slops, then dried and dressed and went aft to see Alvaron. He found him in the great cabin, pacing and turning and, occasionally, staggering, determined to master his new leg.

"I see you are doing wonderfully, sir. Your new leg suits you admirably," Fallon said in greeting.

"It's almost mine to command, Captain Fallon. But I must thank you for loading the rest of the bullion today; in fact, I must humbly thank you and your men for all that you have done. I doubt in the annals of war there has ever been such cooperation between allies, much less enemies."

They both laughed, and when they were almost finished, laughed some more. They certainly were an incongruous pair of friends.

"Tomorrow I will put on Capitán Tornell's best uniform and pay a visit to the dockyard to negotiate for spars and rigging," said Alvaron, sitting down on a chair to rest. "It could never have happened without your help. I am quite at a loss to repay you."

Fallon hesitated to ask what he had in mind to ask, for it was not a quid pro quo, just a favor. An enormous favor.

"Capitán Alvaron, if there were an attempt on the French privateer at the end of the dock tomorrow night by a desperate group of Englishmen, is there a chance you could, well, be asleep?"

Alvaron smiled, not even needing to consider his answer after all Fallon and his men had done for him. "The French privateer means nothing to me," Alvaron said, "especially after learning that France is to receive my country's treasure. I wondered when you would decide on a plan, sir. And I can do more than be asleep tomorrow night. I can stay awake to help you."

"I was hoping you'd say that, my good friend," said Fallon with relief in his voice. "Allow me to tell you what I am thinking."

SIXTY-THREE

THE NEXT day dawned a hazy yellow, and after the hands had had their breakfast and the tide had slacked, Alvaron had the ship warped across the harbor toward the dockyard. Jones had hidden the British seamen below decks with orders to remain quiet.

As the boats pulled the ship to the shore, Alvaron stood alone on the quarterdeck, resplendent in his uniform of gold lace, looking very important indeed. Garin assembled the Spanish crew and went over the plan Fallon had proposed to Alvaron, which, after all the British sailors had done to help them, they greeted warmly. Sailors from all countries loved a good fight.

The negotiations with the dockyard took most of the day, there being the usual back and forth over the available spars and rope and the timeline for completion, given as several weeks, for Garin's crew would do most of the work, day and night.

It was not unusual for the crews of ships calling at Savannah to be allowed to go ashore at night, and tonight was no exception. Garin turned his men loose after dark with orders to wait for Fallon's signal, but otherwise to enjoy themselves and their rum. The tide should turn around midnight and begin the slow ebb out to the sea. They were to look for the signal then.

Well after dark, Fallon found Alvaron at the taffrail, staring to the east toward—*Spain?* He wondered if Alvaron would ever get there, and what he would do in consequence about the treasure.

Fallon was glad it was not his decision to make.

"*Señor*," said Fallon softly, "I fear it is almost time to say good-bye. Somehow fate brought us together and now fate must drive us apart. I can say many things, but I most want to say I am the better man for knowing you. And, God willing, we will meet again. When our countries decide we need not be enemies, we will already be friends."

Alvaron turned toward Fallon, his eyes moist but his voice under control. "Captain Fallon, never have I met a more daring man, a more courageous leader of men. Yours is an indomitable spirit, and you have inspired not only me, but my men."

Fallon made to demur, but Alvaron wasn't finished.

"I will miss your guidance, *señor.* Your wisdom. But most of all, I will miss my friend."

They embraced, held a moment, and then stood apart. Finally they clasped hands one last time, and then Fallon climbed down to the dock.

MIDNIGHT.

Garin walked along the wharf and eyed several of his men, most of whom were fairly drunk, but no drunker than any of the other sailors. It was a warm night, the sickle moon lighting very little of the dock and virtually none of the harbor. This was just as well, as the first of the British sailors were even then easing themselves down into *Nuevo Año's* boats, only to sit anxiously, awaiting events. They were not long in coming.

At the Eagle's Nest, a bar that was more a hole in the wall than a nest, or a building for that matter, Fallon spent some time nursing his ale and studying the American sailor off the privateer. He was a loudmouth, brutish and profane; he'd had enough to drink for two men and was loud enough for four. Nearby, a small clot of American sailors kept to themselves, eyeing their erstwhile countryman with disdain. Fallon sensed the time was now or never and, with a scowl painted on his face, he approached the big American and squared off in front of him.

"You're on the French privateer, aren't you, mate?" he fairly yelled to the man. "Seems like bullshit to me!"

The American's eyes widened in disbelief. "What the hell is it to you, you cockeyed fucker? I'll sail with whom I please and anybody who don't like it can kiss my ass!"

"Seems like an American sailing for the French is like treason or something. They're still attacking your shipping, for Christ's sake! Why would they want *you*? That's what I'm wondering. Maybe you're a spy or some shit like that! Or maybe you just like raiding *American* ships!"

And with that the small group of Americans seemed to grow and move closer, sensing the fight coming, provoked by their own sense of patriotism and wondering at their countryman's motivations. The big American reacted predictably, but as he drew back his hand in a fist, Fallon moved inside, rocked his head back, and brought it forward with huge force, his forehead landing on the bridge of the big man's nose and splitting it open like a tomato.

The Eagle's Nest erupted. The Americans piled on their rogue countryman, and Fallon backed slowly away. Now some of the French crew jumped in, along with a few Portuguese, and the call went out for reinforcements. Quickly the crew from *Élan* who were still aboard disembarked and came running, perhaps twenty men. Garin gave the signal for his own crew and suddenly there was a full-scale war on the docks, with tables being thrown aside and chairs breaking over backs. Men from up and down the wharf dove into the melee to hit somebody, anybody they did not know, and the fight grew until it had engulfed the waterfront.

Meanwhile, Alvaron's men silently rowed Fallon's crew the short way down the river to the far side of *Élan*. Quickly and quietly the first wave of British sailors subdued the few Frenchmen still on deck and hurried below to find the *capitaine*, who was actually in the heads at the moment, and barricaded him inside.

In a flash the ship was theirs!

The rest of Fallon's crew were quickly ferried down to the privateer while the battle on the waterfront raged. It was doubtful the fighting would end anytime soon. No one was really winning; in fact, few even knew why they were fighting.

Fallon made his way to the schooner, dodging a few fists along the way, and with help from Aja untied the lines holding the ship to the dock. Fallon ordered the jib and staysail set and the helmsman edged *Élan* out into the ebbing tide and the dark night. In a quarter mile the French crew, including the *capitaine* still inexplicably clutching his trousers, were put into a ship's boat and cast off into the darkness. Colston stood in the bows of the schooner, a purloined chart in his hand and, by the light of a dim lantern, navigated as best he could, for it would be a catastrophe indeed to run aground after having executed such a glorious, ridiculously glorious, blow against France.

SIXTY-FOUR

FIRST LIGHT saw *Avenger* catch the land breeze and edge out the Río de San Juan to leave the anchorage in her wake. Davies was on the quarterdeck taking his morning exercise along the larboard rail, while Kinis stood by the helmsman as the sails were let fall and the ship gathered speed.

It was almost slack tide at the mouth of the river. The sea before the ship was as placid as a lake, there being some miles before the edge of the northward current. Once clear of the river's mouth, Kinis set the course northward toward a line of low islands just off the coast that bore exploring; if no trace of Fallon was found they would continue on up the coast, checking each port and river as far as Charleston. If still nothing was found by Charleston, well, there was no plan beyond that.

Davies stopped his pacing and leaned on the rail to consider the coastline. It was beautiful from aboard ship. The tidal marshes and lowlands were a vibrant green against the wooded backdrop of America. It was along these same shores that Great Britain had fought and lost to the rebellious Colonists who barely had a navy. Incredible to think about really, and Davies saw it as a testament to the power of American determination and courage versus British hubris.

Beauty appeared on the quarterdeck in fresh slops, looking rested, two cups of coffee in her hands, one of which she passed to

Davies at the rail. "Nico would say this was a day when anything was possible," she said amiably. "Fine morning, good breeze building, so let's find that fucker."

Davies smiled, envying Fallon his friendship with this able woman and appreciative that his own relationship with her was growing closer. She'd even insisted he call her Beauty, as Fallon did. They sipped their coffee and chatted about small things, the ship and this and that, the building of the rafts, the value of Kendricks, and how a steady diet of coconuts could work on your insides.

For some reason Davies wanted to tell her about Paloma; well, he felt the need to tell *someone*. But what? That he'd met a woman who had kissed him and then said good-bye? That wasn't a story. That was a moment in time.

"Deck there, sail off the starboard bow!" called the lookout as Davies was finishing his coffee. "One of those American schooners, I make!"

The day was growing increasingly clear, and from the masthead it was possible to see for some fifteen miles. Davies and Beauty both moved to the starboard railing and trained telescopes on the schooner, still a small image to them. If she turned and ran there would be no catching her; besides, the war with America was over. Still, another ship was always intriguing.

Kinis ordered the British ensign sent up but did not alter course, for Talbot Island was off their larboard bow and would need exploring. In fact, within minutes it would be time to lower the pinnace. Those minutes went by, but Kinis held off bringing *Avenger* into the wind to heave-to. He wanted confirmation of the schooner's intent first.

Now signals were breaking out from the schooner's gaff, but the wind had come northerly and blew the flags toward *Avenger*, making them difficult to read.

"Deck there, schooner is flying a British ensign. And she's

signaling," came the call from the lookout. "Trying to make out the flags . . . *Have Admiral Fallon aboard.*"

THE CREW aboard *Élan* had recognized *Avenger* immediately, and soon the cheering began. More than seventy men with one voice, one joyous voice, climbed the ratlines and crowded the bows of the schooner as the two ships converged. Fallon smiled broadly at Aja, whose idea it had been to promote him, and found himself totally, wonderfully giddy. After weeks under the constant strain of command, holding his breath at every twist and turn, he could finally exhale.

Now he could see Davies clearly, and Kinis, and someone next to . . . *by God it was Beauty! It was Beauty!* Now all hell broke loose on board *Élan*, and Fallon and Aja found themselves jumping and waving with the rest, for seeing Beauty safe—and there was Cully! In spite of himself Fallon began crying; he tried to hide it but couldn't, and he was still biting his lip and trying to stop when *Élan* rounded up into the wind and hove-to on the starboard tack, half a cable's distance from *Avenger,* who had also rounded up to heave-to.

A signal broke out from the big ship's gaff: *Admiral report on board.*

That dried Fallon's tears, and he was still laughing at the joke when he and Aja climbed down into *Élan's* gig and were rowed to *Avenger's* side, there to be greeted by the entire crew, Davies and Beauty at the front, followed by Kinis and the rest, all sense of decorum and naval etiquette out the window. Now there were wet eyes all around, in spite of themselves. Beauty hugged Fallon so hard it almost cracked his ribs; she was thinner but had lost none of her strength.

They looked at each other a long moment. "Welcome back, you fucker," she said, a broad smile on her face.

"Welcome back yourself," he said. "I never doubted it."

But now the backslapping and questions began in earnest, and it was some time before Fallon realized he had left poor Mr. Jones aboard *Élan* without orders and, besides, the crews would want to be together. At last, Davies suggested they anchor back in the Río de San Juan for the remainder of the day and night, as he really did want to hear Fallon's report, though he could already foresee the parting to come.

IN THE early evening *Sea Dog's* old crew transferred to *Élan* and *Harp's* old crew transferred to *Avenger*, bringing things more or less full circle. Fallon shook Jones's hand warmly, for here was a First among Firsts by his lights. And here was Crael, looking thin but clear-eyed and fit, and Fallon clapped him on the back to congratulate him on his particular journey from captivity.

That night Fallon, Beauty, Davies, and Kinis dined in the great cabin on board *Avenger*, and within four bottles of claret all things were known that would ever be known. Davies listened to Beauty tell her story again for the benefit of Fallon, and heard Fallon tell his for the first time, and Davies recounted the story of Matanzas and the short-haired women, leaving out a *particular* short-haired woman. When it was all told they were fairly well drunk and more than a little glad to be alive together. They counted two treasure ships definitely wrecked or sunk, *Punta* and *Rio*, with *Estrella* and *Valiente* doubtful to make it to Spain or even to have survived. Davies had loosed a full broadside into *Nuevo Año* before he broke off action and took his own orders to heart: *Save your ship.* Of the last treasure ship's fate there was no telling. Perhaps she had fallen to Clayton, or perhaps she had survived, or more likely she'd sunk.

Even under the effects of the wine, Fallon omitted the existence of *Nuevo Año* in Savannah per se, only suggesting that Alvaron had spotted a Spanish ship in the harbor and intended to sail on her to Spain. Davies could not be expected to give his word not to attack a treasure ship when those were his explicit orders. For Fallon there was no moral dilemma. His commission as Acting Commander in the Royal Navy was effectively over. He was only a privateer again. And besides, he had given his word to Alvaron.

At last Fallon and Beauty were rowed back to *Élan*, doing their best to sing together but hopeless at it. Still, it was a spectacular night under a cloudless, impossibly starry sky, and they were all free. A little bit very drunk, but free.

SIXTY-FIVE

THE NEXT morning crept in under low cloud, a somewhat dispirited beginning full of humidity and headaches enough to go around. It was well after what passed for sunrise when Fallon was rowed over to *Avenger* with a throbbing head and a lump in his throat. Both he and Davies knew without knowing that the wind was about to blow them in different directions.

Over coffee in the great cabin, a heavy silence was punctuated by attempts at starting sentences. All around them the sounds of a ship preparing for sea.

Finally, Davies. "I must say, Captain Fallon, I'm not sure I can adequately do justice to your service to the Crown, or to me personally, in my dispatches. You volunteered to put yourself and your ship and crew into grave danger, made more horrifically dangerous by the hurricane. And look what you've accomplished! Really, I'm afraid words will fail when I write my report for their Lordships."

"Sir, it was an honor to serve you," Fallon replied. "My regret is that you don't have a fortune in Spanish treasure aboard after all you went through."

"Well, it was never about getting the treasure for either one of us. It was about keeping France from getting it. And by God we did that."

Fallon swallowed hard. He hoped it was true, and would stay true.

They sat a bit longer, looking out the stern windows, and then it was time to leave. "Where are you off to now, Captain? Home to Bermuda?" Davies asked.

"Bermuda by way of Nassau, sir," Fallon answered. "Not a direct route, but I am hoping to learn something of Clayton—alive or dead—and that is where there will be something to learn. I want some resolution for all of us."

"Then Godspeed, sir. It has been a remarkable voyage with you. If ever I can repay the debt, on behalf of England or myself, you have only to ask."

They shook hands briefly, and then Fallon was over the side to be rowed back to *Élan*. Before he was aboard and the boat hoisted, Kinis had *Avenger's* anchor up and was setting sail for English Harbor. Davies stood at the stern, his ship gathering way, and as Fallon glanced at his friend one last time, he saw him salute.

For Davies, it was back to English Harbor and all the problems he'd left behind. There were troubles aplenty in the Caribbean and not enough ships or men or time to deal with them all. Part of him stayed behind with Fallon, a good friend now. Part of him was still in Matanzas, on a beach in the starlight, falling in love with a woman he barely knew. He wondered, now, as he watched *Élan* sink below the horizon, which part of him exactly was going home.

"WELL, ADMIRAL," Beauty said to Fallon with more than a hint of sarcasm, "we're ready to get underway. I would suggest some gunnery practice along the way, if I might. I've asked Cully to try the great guns and allot men to their positions."

"Yes, by all means, Beauty," replied Fallon, easily letting the sarcasm roll off his back. "Let's be off to the south. We'll drop some barrels in a few miles and give Cully his head." Fallon was in an apprehensive mood, not knowing what he would find in Nassau, or if he would ever find Clayton and have to return to Bermuda with unfinished business in his wake.

They sailed southeast for most of the day, Cully getting in his gunnery practice and pronouncing himself satisfied, and the crew getting adjusted to the sailing qualities of the big schooner. She was fast, even in a light breeze, and after handling the wheel for the better part of two hours, Beauty was satisfied she knew the ship.

That night they anchored in a small cove inside a reef off Great Bahama Island. They were in the lee of the island, thus the breeze was light and they needed to set only one anchor. It was warm, and Fallon went for a quick plunge before dinner, swimming around his new ship and admiring her lines. He hadn't learned much after rifling the *capitaine's* cabin, further proof that she was a privateer. As he swam down the side, the glow of the sunset radiantly lit the stern and as he rounded he noticed that *Élan* had been painted over a previous name. Apparently she'd been renamed after her capture, but the French had not made much of a job of the painting. The light was fading quickly, but Fallon could just make out her original name underneath: *Rascal.*

Now that's more like it, he thought to himself. Besides, it was always bad luck to change a ship's name. As proof, look what happened to the last owners! He decided to change the name back at the first opportunity, not knowing when that might be.

That night Fallon invited Beauty to dinner to discuss plans for Nassau. It was a fine dinner, the French *capitaine* having stocked the hold with fall vegetables and a suckling pig, and there were enough stories that hadn't been told before and were only just remembered to keep the evening going. Still, Fallon was reflective. When at last it was time for the evening's business, Fallon asked Beauty for her thoughts on gathering information in Nassau, now that Cortez had sailed away with *Avenger.* It required someone who could go ashore and fit in easily without attracting undue attention, someone who could handle themselves if things got dicey.

"I think I have just the person, Nico," Beauty said smiling. "But it's someone you likely haven't noticed before now. It's a little surprise."

And then Beauty looked toward the cabin door and called for Aja. When he appeared she winked at him and said, "Would you please fetch Theo?"

SIXTY-SIX

AT THE very moment Fallon dove into the water off Great Bahama, Ezra Somers was diving into the wine aboard *Castille* in Nassau Harbor. To say he was both livid and flummoxed understated his condition, but it was close. He had grown increasingly despondent as he and Elinore had made their way back to Nassau from Fort Charlotte and were then rowed out to the ship. Elinore knew her father was a man of action, decisive in a pinch, and yet he could think of no action to take.

She and her father had said little that evening; she was in her own mood, as well, complicated by her worry for Fallon. They still needed news, for the only information they had at the moment was that Jak Clayton was not in Nassau Harbor at present. That didn't help the search for her captain.

Just before turning in for the night, she stepped up the companionway to take a turn on the deck. The sky had prepared a rich show of stars, a show for lovers, and she looked at the constellations with a worried heart. She made her silent wishes, the music of Nassau's waterfront drifting over the water as a counterpoint to her low spirits.

MORNING BROUGHT a massive hangover to Ezra Somers, and the bright sunlight did nothing to make him feel better; in fact, it made his head hurt worse. He had wisely skipped breakfast and gone straight for coffee on the deck with Elinore, and they watched

Nassau's day begin together from the bow. Ships were moving about the harbor, some weighing anchor to get underway for points unknown.

"I am going ashore this afternoon, Father," Elinore announced abruptly. "And I am not coming back until I have talked to every person on that damned island to see what they know." Elinore had her chin out and her head up, meaning business.

Somers took his daughter's hand in his own and held it tightly. "I'm going, too, Elinore. Two will be better than one; we can cover more ground. By God, we'll find someone who knows something."

He said this, and he mostly believed it, but his normal determination was under siege at the moment and the ridiculousness of an old man and his daughter traipsing around an island talking to people they didn't know about hurricanes and lost British captains hung like a cloud over his thoughts.

As they squinted into the bright sun a lovely schooner rounded Hog Island under all plain sail. Her oiled hull cut a fine figure dancing into the harbor to pass by their stern. They watched the ship, transfixed for a moment, Elinore staring intently at the man standing near the helm, his dark hair blowing straight back off a fine, lean face.

Then she screamed, and everyone on Nassau who wasn't already awake sat straight up in bed. "Nico!"

"My God!" yelled Somers. "My God! My God!"

BEAUTY BROUGHT the schooner into the wind and the sails were taken in as the anchor dropped toward the seabed some twenty fathoms below. Fallon had spotted Castille's stern immediately upon rounding Hog Island but so intent was he on absorbing Wallace's presence in Nassau that he had not seen Elinore nor her father in the bows of the ship until she'd screamed. Now a huge grin plastered his face as he rushed to the railing, ordering the ship's boat lowered almost before the anchor had set.

Quickly he and Aja scrambled over the side, Beauty watching

them go as she waved to Somers and Elinore not half a cable's length away. She had no idea why they were here, or what they'd hoped to gain by coming, but already something significant had been accomplished: Nico Fallon was laughing like a madman.

Fallon and Aja hurried up the side of *Castille* into waiting arms and enough tears to start the pumps, with the hands standing quietly to the side, Wallace himself a little watery. Well, it *was* a moment. Every time Fallon made to speak he had the wind hugged out of his lungs, or his back slapped, or Elinore's hands searching his face to make sure he was, in fact, real.

At last it seemed he was, and Fallon waved to Beauty to join them and, as soon as the ship was squared away, she left Cully in charge while one of the hands rowed her over. After the bosun's chair brought her over the side, grinning broadly, and after *that* re-union was celebrated, they all repaired below to the great cabin.

There was just room enough for all of them, Wallace included, as there was no cannon in the cabin. *Castille*'s cook produced cheese and toast, a steward poured wine, and they ate like they'd never seen food before as the tale of *Harp*'s battle and wreckage unfolded, followed in turn by Aja's nightly forays and their escape via the Slave Trail to Savannah. Fallon's voice unconsciously lowered when he mentioned *Nuevo Año* and the treasure, but he was back at full volume recounting their escape downriver and the joy of finding Davies and *Avenger* with Beauty and the rest of *Sea Dog*'s surviving crew aboard.

Somers and Elinore listened raptly, as if a great mystery was un-folding before their eyes, now coming to be understood but no less astonishing. Now it was their turn to describe finding Wicked Jak in Nassau's harbor, the governor gone, and the acting governor no help. Fallon could feel the anger in Somers's voice as he described *Renegade* sailing away. He was becoming angry himself.

"We are not through here," Fallon said evenly. "In fact, we haven't even begun." And then he told them about the plan to place Theo ashore that very night, ostensibly in her old profession, to learn what could be learned about Clayton's whereabouts.

"Elinore," Beauty having a thought now, "this is a Godsend because Theo has nothing to wear tonight except ship's slops and, if you take my meaning, she's used to dressing up a bit ashore. Do you think you'd have something that might serve? You're about her size, but I warn you not to expect it back, at least not the way you remember it."

"I think I may have just the thing, Beauty," replied Elinore enthusiastically. "Bring Theo aboard late this afternoon and let me have two hours with her. I think she'll turn a few heads when we're finished!"

SIXTY-SEVEN

FALLON AND Elinore had spent most of the day on *Castille's* deck, holding onto each other tightly, decorum thrown to the wind. Everything he'd prayed to the stars for was in his arms and he was not about to let her go until Theo came aboard. By then they'd talked their way into low voices and very soft words and it was probably a good thing to be interrupted.

Theo climbed eagerly over *Castille's* side, anxious to repay the debt she felt she owed Beauty and Fallon, though not without a little trepidation at returning to her old haunts ashore. They'd given her a plausible story for her absence, however: Being kidnapped by a scoundrel and held against her will at the far end of the island, a virtual prisoner is what she was, until at last she'd hit the bugger with the biggest stick she could lift and run off. The message clear: *Don't fuck with me.*

She went below with Elinore immediately, the two of them instantly comfortable with each other, to begin Theo's transformation from deckhand back to hussy. Dresses were tried on, accessorized, and discarded. Makeup was applied, heavy on the rouge. Jewelry was tried on, taken off, and put back on again. At last a dress was found that seemed to fit the occasion, though Elinore cut the bottom off to make it a bit shorter than she'd ever worn it. A scarf around the waist seemed just the thing to bring the ensemble together. Theo looked in the mirror and smiled nervously, certainly liking what she saw, but aware that what lay ahead would be dangerous. She was determined to see the thing through.

Meanwhile, Fallon and Beauty fretted about the plan and what could go wrong, which was quite a lot, weighing the risks against the possibility of valuable information, the time growing closer at hand. This was their best chance and they knew it.

Evening came and the waterfront buildings began to light up slowly, first this one and then that one, the darkness between them still an incubator for mischief. At last Elinore appeared on deck with her wonderfully tarted-up new friend, one *Theodora of the Night*, looking you would have to say spectacular. A few last-minute words to settle her nerves, details of the plan reviewed, and she was over the side with a brave smile. Cully rowed her to shore, choosing a spot on the beach close but not too close to the now noisy waterfront. He would not leave until he had her back aboard.

Cully looked around the beach and, seeing nothing out of the ordinary, lay down in the bottom of the boat to look at the sky and stay invisible. It was a warm night, and he could have been drowsy if every nerve in his body wasn't jumping with excitement. Fallon had entrusted him with this duty of bringing Theo safely back to the ship even if he had to go into town to find her.

The night dragged on and the music picked up, and Cully could hear the laughter growing louder, spilling out of the shutterless bar windows and doors onto the beach. He was only reasonably comfortable stretched out over the length of the boat. He amused himself by counting stars, then trying in vain to remember the name of every sweetheart he'd ever had, without success.

It was sometime later that he heard Theo, in a loud voice he thought was meant for him to hear, arguing with a man, pleading with him to let her go. He raised his head up over the gunnels of the boat and saw Theo wrestling with a drunken oaf of a sailor, half running away, only to be caught and pulled back again. As they drew closer, Theo maneuvered herself so as to leave the man's backside to the water, and Cully slowly rose up, lifting an oar with him, intent on his duty to bring Theo back.

The oar's blade landed with a satisfactory thump on the back of the sailor's head, the blood coating the back of his shirt even before he hit the beach. Cully smiled at Theo, and she smiled back coyly, still in character, before stepping into the boat to be rowed back to the waiting ship, *Theo of the Night*.

Fallon, Beauty, and Wallace huddled in the great cabin to hear Theo's report, which she was able to give without slurring or giggling, for she'd nursed one rum the entire night.

"I knew where to go first, my old favorite place, but there was no one there who knew anything," she began. "But at the next place I went I heard that Clayton had attacked a flotilla of Spanish treasure ships off Great Bahama Island in the hurricane. No one seemed to know for sure what had happened, or if he'd gotten any treasure, so I kept moving."

Beauty looked at Fallon, who was totally engrossed in Theo's story.

"Then I heard from a grizzled old sailor that British ships had attacked the flotilla in the hurricane, as well. But they wrecked on the coast of Spanish Florida. And then," she paused for effect, "I heard what happened to Clayton. He fired a broadside at the last treasure ship in the flotilla and a lucky shot took her mainmast down. The Spaniard was driven onto a reef off Great Bahama Island and broken up. Clayton ran into a secret cove where he used to hide and waited out the hurricane. When it was over he went back to the Spanish ship and sent his boats in to get as much of the treasure as he could. It took over a week, and he made what was left of the Spanish crew help him until they'd finished; then he fired the ship and murdered them all. He got all that he could."

Here Wallace's eyebrows went up, perhaps remembering *Renegade* in the harbor, low in the water, which he'd thought was caused by the storm.

"My God, young lady," he blurted out, "you'd have thought you were talking to Clayton himself!"

"It was just as good, sir," Theo answered coolly. "It was his woman."

The end of her story was even more interesting. Clayton had

made for Nassau Harbor to effect repairs to his ship, it being the closest harbor to get spars and cordage, for he had no spares aboard. After three days in harbor, he had put most of his crew ashore, including his woman, and sailed away to hide the treasure, trusting as few of his crew as possible with the exact location.

But he was coming back for them. He promised. In one week.

Fallon looked at Theo with a mixture of admiration and astonishment. Really, women talked, *but this?* This was incredible, and had the ring of truth in it, and he believed every word. Now the question was how to use the information?

Wallace was the first to get his brain into action. "We should try to find his Goddamned hiding place!" he exclaimed, temporarily forgetting his religion in the hope of riches. "We could poke into every harbor and cove in the islands until we found it!"

They all absorbed this idea until Fallon finally responded with some sense. "There are roughly one thousand islands, Wallace. It could conceivably take us the rest of our lives. Besides, it's not like he left signs about."

Wallace's face fell, struck by the absurdity of his own idea. "But tell me, sir, just as a point of information," said Fallon soothingly, "do you think Clayton saw you in the harbor? How far away were you?"

"I doubt very much he saw us, Captain. We were a good ways off and there were many boats anchored between us. Besides, his ship was very busy and likely occupied all of his attention."

"Why do you ask, Nico?" Beauty curious now, hearing the old Fallon plotting and scheming something.

"Oh, nothing," replied Fallon with a far-off look in his eyes. Which meant, in effect, *something.*

"One more question for you, Mr. Somers," said Fallon. "Or Elinore. You say you saw Clayton sail out of the harbor. Could you tell which way he was headed?"

A moment's pause, then Somers responded, "North. He sailed north." He was sure, and Elinore agreed.

◆ ◆ ◆

In the beginning, Fallon had only wanted to stop Clayton's predations on the salt ships, but it was more now. He wanted the treasure
for his men, and for the men's families who had died. And, truth
be told, he wanted revenge for the misery and the murders Clayton
had caused on his hell-hole of an island hideout. And he wanted
Clayton dead.

That night Fallon sat with Wallace's chart of the Bahamas and
studied it carefully. *Where could Clayton have gone?*

If he stayed north, the most logical choice would be a small
group of islands to the west of Abaco, the Berry Islands, which
were uninhabited as far as Fallon knew, with reefs and coves only a
local would know, particularly a local pirate. Still, *Renegade's* draft
would mean not every cove would suit, unless they stood off and
ferried the treasure to shore, which would be impractical and take
longer than a week to accomplish.

Here the soundings were incomplete or inaccurate at best, being
only approximations of depth on the chart. Fallon did his best to
think like a pirate, *what would I do?* He decided he would look for
a cove not easily seen from Providence Channel, of sufficient draft
that he could beach the ship and off-load the treasure directly to
the shore, like Alvaron had done on Hutchinson Island. But the island had to be easily defended in case of attack, with a quick exit to
the channel.

His finger went to Misery Island. A small island with a tiny indentation on its north side, it appeared to be a cove, located about
ten miles north of Providence Channel. Misery Island was part of
the Berry Islands and was named for the bones of shipwrecked sailors found there in the late 1600s who had perished from starvation
and thirst. It was inhospitable to say the least. So, a good guess.

Suppose he was wrong?

Well, Providence Channel was the east–west passage through
the upper islands of the Bahamas, as was clear from the chart. If
Clayton had indeed sailed northward, he would need to cross the

channel to return for his woman and crew at Nassau. It was a *pig in a poke*, as Fallon's father would say, but the only idea he had.

Even though Clayton's ship was undermanned because he wanted as few people as possible to know the exact whereabouts of the buried treasure, *Renegade* was still a formidable enemy. Fallon had no thought to come under her guns—he'd done that once, and once was enough.

He stood at the stern windows of the great cabin, staring at the moon's dance upon the water, presumably everyone in the ship except the watch asleep. He had seen Elinore to bed and had wanted to stay, but a long and very suggestive kiss was all she would allow. After all, her father was literally behind the screen next to her cabin, there being no privacy in a ship.

And so he gazed astern, feeling the weight of responsibility on his shoulders, wondering what if anything was possible to deal with Clayton. He thought about the man, that high-pitched laugh, the merciless killing of the Swede, the debauched mind, and the insatiable need to raid and plunder. *Renegade* probably carried almost three hundred crew, which was a lot of mouths to feed and water three times a day, with a prodigious amount of rum required, as well. The pirate credo was equal shares for everyone, and a vote could be held at any time by the crew to remove the captain. Perhaps that was one reason Clayton was so fierce—it was his insurance policy against insurrection. But a pirate captain, even one as wicked as Wicked Jak, had to be successful to stay in office. So greed was the driving force in every decision.

Greed. The word stopped Fallon's mind from spinning in a hundred directions and settled it on one. And as it did, the old familiar feeling came to him, and the hair on his arms stood at attention.

He called for Aja to rouse Beauty, Somers, and Elinore from their sleep, and to fetch Wallace, who was on deck. He was burning with the idea now, mad with excitement and fear in equal portions, fully committed to risk everything for the main chance.

The sleepy group assembled around the chart table, waking up quickly when they saw Fallon's eyes on fire; now they were pre-pared for anything. He outlined his thinking on the probable route Clayton might have taken, and his best guess where the treasure was to be buried.

"Strictly from a timing standpoint," Fallon said by way of ex-planation, "the burial place has to be where the bullion could be off-loaded easily from the ship. I can't imagine that taking less than several days under the best of circumstances. Then they have to bury it. My guess is here, somewhere in the Berry Islands." Fallon pointed to a spot on the chart, a cluster of small islands north of Providence Channel. The little group leaned in to study the chart. "From here," Fallon continued as if to himself, "he's got time to sail back to Nassau to pick up his woman and crew within seven days."

They all looked at him, blinking skeptically, but as they had no other ideas to offer they had to admit it sounded *plausible*. And then he told them about the monsters of the south, and the giant snapping turtle, and the crazy idea he had to wiggle his tongue at Clayton.

SIXTY-EIGHT

THERE WAS not a moment to lose.

At high tide the next morning and with the help of *Castille*'s boats, they brought the big ship closer to Hog Island, so close that she would beach herself when the tide withdrew. That's when the work would begin, for it was Fallon's idea to spend three days loading *Castille* with all the sand they could load, which should be a prodigious amount with two crews to do the work. It was not the best way to load a ship, but there was no hoy to bring alongside so it seemed like the only way. Cully and some of the hands rowed to shore to procure shovels and canvas for bags, which brought to Fallon's mind the loading of *Nuevo Año* with bullion—a little different in this instance—and he wondered briefly where Alvaron was just then. Likely still refitting if the American yards were anything like the British.

The loading began as soon as the tide went out, with many sand bags already full and ready to hoist aboard. It was backbreaking work, as Fallon well knew, but some part of the success of the plan depended on the ship being low in the water. They worked literally day and night, in shifts, all hands all in. As *Castille* grew heavier, they backed her out with the flood, just a little, so that at the last she would float off the island. It would not do to have done so much work only to be stuck.

Even Somers and Elinore worked alongside the crews, which

earned them undying respect and sore arms and backs. And gradually the big ship dropped lower into the water, and then lower still—the effect of several tons of sand showing—until by the third day she was quite low and barely made it off at high tide. *Castille* was built for a load, however, and floated rather proudly with her new cargo aboard.

On the fourth day most of the crew from *Élan* transferred to *Castille*, bringing the packet's complement to well over one hundred men and bringing pistols and cutlasses and shot and powder enough for a small war, which is what they anticipated. Fallon elected to leave three older men on board *Élan* to guard the ship, along with Elinore and Somers, against strongly worded objections by all, but he would not hear it. It was a harebrained idea as it was, he could not in good conscience endanger the older, slower hands on board, plus taking an even older man and his daughter would make success even more inconceivable.

At the last, Somers pulled Fallon aside. "Listen to me carefully, Nico," he said quietly, as quietly as Fallon had ever heard him speak. "We can do this two ways. Since you work for me now that you're out of the Royal Navy, I can order you to take Elinore and myself with you." Fallon's face must have registered the surprise he felt, for Somers nodded *yes that's what I said.* "Or you can just listen to reason. Elinore and I can't take more worrying about you. We want to be with you and be part of this. You're family, son. And anyway, we've come this far on our own and done a pretty good job of it. We even helped a little. Look, Nico, I can shoot the eyes out of a turkey at a hundred yards. And Elinore can help Theo down below with the wounded, because we both know there *will* be wounded, and you don't have a surgeon on board anymore. I don't want to order you. Hell, I won't order you, I guess. But consider this a very strong ask." And then he added, "If you think you can say no to Elinore, don't waste your breath. She's already made up her mind." Then he smiled a very knowing smile.

With that, Fallon knew he was beaten. There would be no argument worth making. Somers and Elinore remained aboard *Castille* and the heavily laden ship weighed just before sunset. And as they left the harbor sailing northward, every man and woman aboard wondered if they would ever return.

SIXTY-NINE

B
Y MID-MORNING on the fifth day they were hove-to in
Providence Channel, about in the center of the triangle
formed by the Berry Islands to the northwest, Spanish
Wells to the northeast, and Nassau to the south. As the crow flies,
they were about twenty miles from each.

Fallon asked Wallace to have an old suit of sails brought on deck,
which the crew set to work ripping to pieces. They had all furled
torn and ripped sails aplenty and knew the look well enough. It was
the work of an afternoon to finish tattering the sails and get them
bent on. The topmasts were struck below, the yards hung cockeyed,
and only a lowly foresail drew at all, just enough to provide steerage.
Fallon had himself rowed around the ship; *Castille* was now riding
very low in the water and virtually a wreck to all eyes—almost a
ghost ship, something back from the dead.

Rowing under the stern he had a final thought, and as soon as
he was back on board and the ship's boat was hoisted into place, he
detailed two men in harnesses to be lowered off the back of the ship
with paint and brushes. He gave them a rough sketch of what he
wanted, which they nailed to the stern above *Castille*'s name board
as reference before they started work. It took several hours to complete the job, but by nightfall *Castille* had ceased to exist. *Nuevo
Año* floated in her place.

Perhaps Clayton had seen *Nuevo Año* during the hurricane, perhaps not. If he had, the sight of her—if he believed his

eyes—floating helplessly and deeply laden should make him rabid. If he hadn't, he should at least be interested enough to investigate a Spanish ship that appeared unable to defend itself. Fallon was counting on greed to make Clayton believe that what he saw was true.

Finally, the Spanish flag that Aja had found aboard *Élan* was brought on deck to be shredded and virtually destroyed, and then hoisted to a dangling gaff. The illusion was complete. Here was the *Nuevo Año*, a Spanish ship carrying a fortune in bullion and specie that had apparently been drifting helplessly since the hurricane weeks ago, which had now drifted into Providence Channel to an X upon the water just off the Berry Islands. *What other explanation could there be?*

Fallon smiled at the idea, a deceptive little ruse that a turtle had had first. Yes, the image of the freshly named *Nuevo Año* as a snapping turtle lying motionless in the water with its jaws open was exactly right. Fallon squinted, seeing it all through the turtle's eyes. Now if the prey would just happen to swim by . . .

On the sixth day, it did not. They drifted within the triangle all day, ripped sails hanging loosely, running rigging hanging over the sides, a disaster afloat. For the deck, Fallon had selected five crewmen with dark hair and skin to appear to be all that was left of the Spanish crew. Elinore and Theo had sewn canvas caps for the men and covered them in red dress material to imitate the *barretina* caps worn by Alvaron's men. Convinced they looked the part, Fallon joined Beauty and the others below decks. *Renegade* would have more men than *Castille*, but not terribly more, as Theo had reported that more than half of Clayton's crew had been put ashore in Nassau. Still, not good odds in a straight-up battle. Everything depended on looking so helpless as to be unable to fight the ship. If they could manage that, Clayton might decide to board, without even a shot, Fallon hoped.

Below decks, cutlasses were sharpened and pistols primed. Aja shifted his dirk from hand to hand, trying hard not to show his nervousness and not succeeding. Beauty had a pike, her weapon of choice, which she meticulously sharpened and then re-sharpened to a fine edge, the blood of a Scottish warrior in her veins. Somers was off to himself, having gathered fifteen pistols to load, and as he did so he placed them gently in an empty sand bag.

That night Fallon sat in the stern window seat and dozed fitfully, wondering if Clayton had held his course north out of Nassau, perhaps for Misery Island, perhaps with treasure to bury. Jesus, it was all thin.

Well, he decided after stretching out on the seat to stare at the stars, regardless of where Clayton went it might all simply depend on whether he kept a date with his woman in Nassau. Tomorrow would tell the tale, and if Clayton did not appear, Fallon had no plan for the next day.

SEVENTY

IT WASN'T easy for the five men on deck to act like they were on a derelict ship, likely malnourished and weak, and still keep watch for a pirate coming over the horizon. It's not like anyone was at the masthead with a telescope. No, for the ruse to work it had to appear that they were lost and hopeless and *leaderless.*

All morning they lolled around the rolling ship, the pitiful slip of a foresail doing just enough to keep her off the islands, doubling back on their track to keep the ship within the triangle and easily within view of Clayton should he be coming from anywhere northerly across the channel heading for Nassau. Below decks it was already growing warm, warm and tense as this was the second day in that dark, unventilated space. So many bodies, packed together and sweating with heat and nerves, made for an aromatic nightmare.

Fallon did his best to make the rounds of the men but it was next to impossible. It was dark and men were bunched together, some sitting on barrels, others sprawled across the narrow passageway. He was as nervous as they were, maybe doubly nervous. First, worried that Clayton wouldn't show up, and second, worried that if he did show up he wouldn't take the bait. As close as it was, they didn't dare open a hatch to daylight for fear something would look amiss to *Renegade*'s lookout, something would throw Clayton off and put doubt in his mind.

Noon, the heat of the day. As time crept by, Fallon's mind, as always, went to doubt and inevitable failure. With every minute it felt like his hubris had gotten the best of him, his deep self-belief in his own cleverness had deceived him into thinking he could read the future, even control the future, and pre-ordain events. He was on the point of throwing open the hatches and declaring it all a mistake when Elinore slipped up behind him and, unnoticed in the dark, put her hand under his shirt and moved her fingers lightly around his waist to his belly, and then *down*. He stood stock-still, smiling and almost giggling at the release of tension, as she deftly undid the first button on his pants. Things were about to get interesting below decks.

Suddenly two raps on the hatch!

A deckhand had given the signal that a ship had been sighted. Everyone froze, including Fallon and Elinore, all thoughts of foreplay gone, every nerve tense again. The mystery ship could be a trader or a French sloop or anything else, and they waited, holding their breath for a single tap more that would identify the ship as Clayton's.

Seconds. A minute. Two minutes. Five minutes more. Then . . . a *tap!*

The game was on! Now the men on deck had their role to play, the coup de grâce to kill any doubt in Clayton's mind that he was looking at a foundering ship. First, the helmsman let *Nuevo Año* fall off slightly, ever so little, so as to show the stern of the ship to Clayton. *The wiggly little worm.* Now *Renegade* shortened sail, her gun ports still closed, her men lining the railings in curiosity mixed with excitement. The distance closed, a quarter mile, then less and less, and finally close enough to prepare the grappling hooks. Seeing her so close and appearing to recognize her for a pirate, all five men on *Nuevo Año's* deck suddenly threw up their hands, screaming loudly, loud enough for the crew below decks to hear, and they backed against the far railing in fear.

The sails were clewed up on *Renegade* to take off way and then *bump!* The ships came together. *Bump!* Quickly, grappling hooks secured the two ships as one. Over the side leapt dozens of pirates, landing with a yell on *Nuevo Año*'s deck and then oddly becoming silent since there was no opposition, the sailors in their red caps cowered in fear. The pirate crew seemed wary at first and then relaxed their muscles. Some even started to laugh at how easy it was, perhaps a fortune under their feet and no one to fight. *Could this be?*

Not for long. Suddenly the hatches flew open! Up came tens upon tens of screaming sailors, bloodthirsty and wild-eyed sailors who had sworn to give no quarter because defeat at the hands of Wicked Jak Clayton was unthinkable. Up they swarmed from the companionway, out of the hatches in an unending outpouring of rage and violence, and fell upon the startled pirates with a vengeance borne of desperation and fear. Clayton screamed his high-pitched yell, last heard on the beach when he had been tricked then, too. As Fallon reached the deck and heard Clayton's scream, it sent shivers through him because he knew it would be a fight to the death now—no mercy given, none expected—until one of them was dead.

The pirates remaining on *Renegade* jumped aboard *Nuevo Año*, cutlasses slashing at the flesh that stood between them and their prize, still believing a fortune was beneath their feet. The fighting moved like a wave across the ship, ebbing and flowing, and Fallon and Aja stood together, parrying and thrusting and stabbing at any face they did not know. Fallon slashed the belly of a brute of a man, who dropped his sword and looked down to see his guts protruding from the wound. As the man looked down, Aja stabbed him in the heart with his dirk and the man went down. A shot rang out, *Crack!*, then another, Ezra Somers taking target practice from the quarterdeck, shooting the eyes out of pirates instead of turkeys. And here was Cully, a cutlass in both hands, swinging his arms like a lethal windmill, cutting down two pirates at a time and screaming at the top of his lungs: *"Come on, you fuckers!"*

Men were dying in heaps, bloodied beyond recognition, sometimes with a limb cut off and missing. And the fighting was not letting up. A fury had taken hold that possessed each man's soul, and every man knew it was fight or die. Beauty swung her pike like a staff, backing first one man and then another away before flipping the shaft and stabbing them through the chest. She was merciless and efficient, her peg leg anchored to a ringbolt, letting the fighting come to her. *Crack!* Another shot, and a pirate dropped dead, his head blown open by Somers just as he'd raised his sword over Beauty's head from behind. *No time for thanks now,* she thought, *but that was a hell of a good shot!*

The decks were pooling red, the sticky red of men bleeding out their lives, never intending to die this way, in the hot Caribbean sun, a scream in their throats that no one could hear.

Now a fresh charge, the pirates making a last push for control. They were rallied by Clayton himself who had jumped down onto the deck, his eyes blazing with hatred at seeing Fallon near the mainmast, furiously slashing at his men. Fallon, who had made a fool out of him once, then twice; Fallon who must now die without pity. Clayton was wild, with his black beard and scarlet ribbon and maniacal laugh, and he hacked his way through the throng, stabbing first one man and then another, seemingly impervious to injury. The sea of death seemed to part for him and at last there was no one save a black boy between him and Fallon. With a flick of his wrist, Clayton slashed at Aja's back and sent him down, his white shirt slit open like an envelope, a bloody message inside. He lay as still as the dead man he fell next to.

"Aja!" yelled Fallon, a gasping rage in his voice, but there was no time to kneel, no time to take his young friend's hand and lift him up. Clayton's sword was on the way down toward Fallon's head and he just had time to meet it with his sword, though Clayton had the strength to very nearly decapitate him.

Swords locked, Fallon brought his knee up into Clayton's groin and saw the effect on his face, wide eyes and a gaping mouth that might vomit. Quickly Fallon moved around, putting Clayton against the mast now, and drove his sword into the pirate's fleshy thigh, just missing the muscle. But the wound only filled Clayton with new rage and, his back protected by the mast, he swung his cutlass in an arc that slashed Fallon's shoulder open. Instantly, Fallon dropped his cutlass, and as he stooped to get it with his other hand he knew that he was finished, that everything was lost and he would die. Trying to stand quickly he slipped in blood and fell to the deck on his knees. Now there was Clayton's scream, that high-pitched, terrifying scream that had—not victory—but bewilderment and surprise in its upper notes as Beauty whirled around the mast, her wooden leg anchored in the ring bolt, her pike level with her waist, and drove the tip of that medieval spear into Clayton's bowels with a force that pinned him to the mast like a collector's specimen, wiggling and screaming and coughing up his life in red bursts of blood.

Fallon rolled over on his back and stared up at Clayton's eyes looking down at him, uncomprehending at the last, full of fury and tears. For a moment Fallon couldn't be sure if Clayton was really dead, and then *Crack!* Clayton doubled over like a rag doll, still pinned to the mast, his face landing inches from Fallon's own, a small hole between his eyes dripping blood onto the deck to mix with Fallon's own.

Fallon tried to roll away and rise, but then the deck seemed to pull him back, back to the warmth of blood and sunshine and the quiet, unconscious world of the violet hour before death. His last thought was that, before they buried him at sea, he would like to button his pants.

SEVENTY-ONE

IT WAS late afternoon, *Nuevo Año* and *Renegade* still drifted together, the fighting over but not the dying. The field of battle
revealed its horrible tale, a massacre of humanity on a scale
none of the survivors had ever witnessed.

Every pirate was dead, or would soon be, for indeed there had
been no mercy that day, no answer to pleas for help except a quick
death. Fallon's remaining crew simply collapsed in place, spent and
exhausted, unable to move or think. Wallace lay near the binnacle,
his eyes open and looking skyward, gone to meet his God. Cully sat
beside him, alive but sightless in one eye, blood running down his
cheek and soaking his pants, insensibly staring at an eyeball on the
deck that would never sight another gun.

Aja had been carried below, still alive but perhaps with too little
blood left in his body to survive the night. The gash on his back was
over a foot long, and Theo cooed to him softly as she wrapped him
in gauze. She would spend the entire evening holding his hand.

And Fallon would live, though with less movement in his right
shoulder than he would like; unable, for instance, to ever again
raise his arm to wave good-bye to Elinore. Still, he recovered consciousness and was on his feet, his shoulder tightly bandaged by
Elinore and his arm in a sling.

Ezra Somers was in fine health, fifteen kills to his name, good
as his word. The last shot had been the easiest, but probably

unnecessary, as Clayton was dying anyway. *But hell*, he thought, *I had a dog in the fight, too.*

Beauty's leg had been cut off. She couldn't remember how it happened, maybe it had snapped off when she pirouetted in the ringbolt, but she limped around on a shortened, splintered peg, trying to get the remaining seamen on their feet. It was late afternoon, and as Fallon was below decks being treated for his wound, Beauty decided to get the ships to the lee of Eleuthera Island to anchor for the night.

She assigned a crew to *Renegade* and, as they let the sails fall, she released the grappling hooks to free the ship from *Nuevo Año*'s side. Then she ordered her weary men to set a decent foresail and mainsail on *Nuevo Año* so they could make their way across the channel, as well. Both ships anchored in thirty fathoms of clear water, protected and safe, with utterly exhausted men having to climb aloft to furl the sails and snug the ships down for the night.

Elinore and Fallon appeared on *Nuevo Año*'s deck, she holding him more or less upright, just as Beauty returned from the bows of the ship.

"How are you feeling, Nico?" Beauty asked, although she was arguably covered in more blood than Fallon. At least she could stand on her own two legs, even if she did lean a bit to one side.

"Well enough, Beauty. Well enough," answered Fallon, with a pained expression on his face as he looked about *Nuevo Año*'s deck. Men lay where death had befallen them, splayed and crumbled bodies already stiffening, sightless eyes staring wildly into the sky.

"It worked, Nico. Remember that the wiggly tongue worked and Clayton is dead," said Beauty. "The price was high, too high, but that fucker will never kill another person. None of those pirate fuckers will. So just hang onto that."

Fallon looked at her and knew she was right. They'd done what they had to do, had sworn to do, and there could be no second-guessing the price.

The dead pirates were thrown into the sea without ceremony. Then the Sea Dogs were lowered overboard, each body sewn in canvas weighted with round shot so it would sink quietly to the ocean floor and not wash ashore. Fallon said the prayers for the dead in a barely audible voice, and the living hung their heads in silence. After that, it was agreed that Fallon, Somers, and Elinore would transfer to *Renegade* for the night, it being more commodious, while Beauty would remain to manage the rehabilitation of *Nuevo Año* from a killing field into a sailing ship again. The blood on the decks would have to wait until the morning.

Fallon stood uneasily with Elinore and her father on the quarterdeck of *Renegade*, that hated ship that had caused such death and misery for so many. To his surprise he found he could admire her lines and armament in spite of himself. Somers suggested they take a look below, while there was still light, and they slowly made their way down the companionway steps.

They expected a slovenly mess, and they were not disappointed. It was a pigsty—but now that the pigs were all dead it could be cleaned and washed and made as habitable as it had ever been. While Fallon and Elinore moved to see the great cabin, Somers went to explore the hold for food and water, for they had more than thirteen hundred miles to sail to Bermuda.

Fallon opened the door to Clayton's cabin and was struck by the reek of old food and spilled wine. He quickly opened the stern windows for some air.

"It looks like Clayton wasn't much for housekeeping," said Elinore. "Neither was his woman."

Fallon looked in the desk drawers for papers and a ship's log, but found nothing. Well, he mused, it wasn't like pirates had orders or kept a log.

Elinore held up a scarf, a *familiar* scarf, and Fallon gave a low whistle.

"I think I'll just take this and wash it," Elinore said, folding it up. "I may wash it twice, in fact."

The scarf had been Fallon's once, given to him by his father years ago for Christmas, and Elinore had seen him wear it many times. He always carried it aboard *Sea Dog* every voyage for good luck. It had turned out to be bad luck for Clayton.

They were just going through Clayton's few clothes out of morbid curiosity when Somers appeared, a massive grin on his craggy face, and in his outstretched hand he held gold coins.

"Bags and bags of them, Nico," he exclaimed. "And silver bars. Enough to buy a country! It's all in the hold stacked up as pretty as you please!"

Apparently, Clayton had not buried all the treasure on Misery Island, or wherever he'd buried it, for no doubt he needed working capital to keep the ship running and to pay the men at least some of the split. What Somers described was a fortune below, and every man jack and woman aboard their two ships was now rich beyond imagining.

Correction: Their three ships, for Fallon had nearly forgotten *Élan*, so utterly exhausted was he. Tomorrow they would rig a ship's boat with sail and send it to Nassau with the good news, and hopefully by noon the schooner could join them. He would need to confer with Beauty about dividing the small crew among three ships, for there were not many hands to go around, but somehow they would get the little fleet to Bermuda. *My God*, he thought as he struggled into the cot in his new cabin that night, *Bermuda*. It seemed impossible and absurd to believe they were going home.

SEVENTY-TWO

IN THE twilight the three ships entered St. George's Harbor and dropped their anchors—home. There was still daylight enough to see that nothing had changed. The buildings still glowed at sunset, the windows a shimmering gold, the shrubs and trees and beach around the harbor all the same. Fallon stood at *Renegade*'s railing with Somers as the ship glided into the harbor, the two men quietly discussing their possible partnership, with Fallon agreeing that maybe it was time to settle down a bit and look to the future.

"One thing," Fallon said, unsure if this was the time to bring up a potentially divisive subject, but he pressed on, "I'd like to talk about the slaves."

Somers looked at him quizzically. "If you mean the slaves on-board who are still alive, they are free men thanks to you and will share in the fortune aboard. By God they will!" said Somers with conviction.

Fallon took a deep breath. "Actually, I mean the slaves who work for the company on Grand Turk," he said firmly, sticking his nose squarely into Somers's business. "Raking the salt pans is a truly miserable living, as you must know, and dangerous, for no wages, and under the thumb of an overseer. I can't imagine it for myself or any man or woman."

This took Somers aback, and he grew pensive and dark. "Where is this leading, Nico?" he asked.

Fallon realized he was breaking the spell of a victorious home-coming, and he was certainly aware of Somers's volatile temper, but the question of Somers's slaves had nagged at him since Grand Turk and now seemed as good a time as any to bring it up.

"Can you imagine Aja a slave on the salt pans?" he said softly. "Half-blind from the sun with boils on his feet? Raking salt every day for the rest of his life?"

Somers stared at Fallon a moment, then looked out across the harbor toward his home. A home he'd built and paid for with salt. He took a deep breath and put his shoulders back.

"Nico, be reasonable," he said. "You have to take emotion out of it. This whole business of salt is based on labor, slave labor. It's like tobacco or sugarcane or cotton. If you don't have slaves, you don't have salt."

All three ships were swinging at anchor now, the men preparing to go ashore. There would be no need for an anchor watch except on *Renegade*, a wise precaution with a fortune in her holds.

Somers looked at Fallon seriously, aware that the fate of their potential partnership hung in the balance. Perhaps their friendship, as well.

"I'm waiting for your answer about Aja, sir," said Fallon respectfully, but digging in now, giving no quarter. "He's a strong boy, so I'm assuming you'd want him on the *salinas* raking salt. No emotion now, as you said, just a simple question about a slave."

Somers's shoulders dropped. "No," he said in resignation. "In answer to that specific question about that specific person I . . . I can't imagine that, I guess." And then Somers grew very quiet, almost whispering, "I can't imagine that boy as a slave, much less *my* slave, putting him to work raking salt."

Fallon stood looking at the shoreline, grateful Somers didn't blow up in anger at the conversation. "I know it changes everything," said Fallon at last. "But sooner or later everything has to change."

Somers turned to look directly into Fallon's face. They were now at a *place*, and he knew it. It could be confrontation or cooperation. "What is it you suggest we do, Nico?" he asked, deliberately using the plural, *we*.

Fallon relaxed his grip on the railing, unaware that he had been clenching it tightly. *Well*, he thought, *it was in for a penny, in for a pound*.

"We could pay fair wages to free men, sir. And give them boots and big hats. And not ask them to rake in the heat of the day. I mean, the company practically has a monopoly on salt in the Caribbean. Can't we adjust our prices to fit new expenses?"

Fallon was trying to think like a businessman now, trying to make it make sense *rationally*. He knew Somers was fighting change, giving into it, backing away from it, an old man being asked to adapt his thinking, no doubt his mind busy working on the financial implications to the company of wages and boots and big hats.

Elinore came up from below at that moment, lovely in the soft light, to give both her father and Fallon a hug, glad to be home. Then she stood back, aware that she had interrupted something important but not knowing what. The two men looked at each other a long moment, Somers seeing a captain who had proved to be as fearless in conversation as he was in battle. And the dark shadow seemed to leave the old man's face and his mood appeared to lift.

"Do you know Heraclitus, Nico?" Somers said with a wink. "He said, 'Nothing endures but change.'"

"I don't know him," said Fallon smiling back. "But he should be in the salt business! He's the partner you want."

Somers moved to put his hand on Fallon's shoulder. "No, son," he said firmly. "I know the partner I want."

The ship's boats were dropped overboard and Somers shook Fallon's hand, kissed Elinore lightly on the cheek, and went over the side to be rowed to shore by Aja, chatting with the young man the whole way about the battle aboard *Renegade*. Somers was enormously satisfied that he'd played a part in sending *Wicked Fucking*

Jak Clayton to hell. Old though he might be, he could still fight.

The Sea Dogs headed to the White Horse, which they never planned to leave until the senior Fallon ran out of drink. They had a deep thirst and enough stories for a lifetime of telling. And, just as important, their credit was now good.

Beauty was the last to leave *Élan*, helping first to see the wounded into the ship's boats to be delivered ashore into the care of a local doctor who took them into his home. One of the men had made a splint for her peg so she could walk without limping, and she pushed off the side of the ship for the short row down the harbor to be closer to the walk to Suffering Lane, where she was raised and where she lived, and where there might be a light in a window that had burned for months just for her.

And finally, Fallon and Elinore rowed to shore from *Renegade*, the moon lighting the way to the dock and then, once they'd tied up, they walked and half-ran up the dock and then down the familiar path to the old fisherman's shack, Elinore running ahead to open the door with the key Fallon had produced from his pants pocket. She went inside and lit a candle while he stood for a moment and looked at the stars just coming out.

Elinore called softly from the bed inside, her voice low and husky, suggesting the promise of the night. He smiled and stepped over the threshold and shut the door.

Indeed, Fallon thought, *it was a night when anything was possible.*

green press
INITIATIVE